The three creatures seemed to ex.
ing man with eyes that looked l
glued to colored spring metal. The
the wind on a warm Kansas afternoon. They clicked their powerful claws rapidly, as if communicating to each other in Morse code. Jeremiah stood in numbed shock for a moment, watching them. The clicking sound sent another volley of shrieks to issue from his throat. He started fumbling with his left arm again in another attempt at freeing himself from the wire line.

The creatures moved spider-like into the boat and raised their stingered-tails menacingly over their backs. They advanced on him.

Jeremiah looked around for a weapon, anything to fight off those things. His wounded arm had started to pulsate from the toxic fluid that had been injected into his system. Nausea hit him like a sledgehammer. He doubled over and tried to fight back the sickness rising in his stomach. *Jesus Christ, what's happening to me?* His fingers swelled like fat sausages inside his gloves. His whole arm was numb, just like the time he'd caught his finger between a boat hull and a steel support. The doctor at the emergency ward had injected his hand with Novocain and he was numb for days.

There had been so much blood. Just like now.

He shook himself back to reality as the first creature crawled onto his leg. The grip of the thing's claws was incredible, like being caught in a bear trap.

CLICKERS

J. F. Gonzales

Acknowledgments

Clickers took about six months to write, spread out over a period of three years between our various other writing and film projects. Our intention from the beginning stages of this novel was to create a tale that will entertain—this was a book born of our love for 1950s horror/science fiction 'B' movies and the early novels of James Herbert, Richard Laymon and (in Mark's case) Guy N. Smith. In short: pull up a chair, make yourself some buttered popcorn, pour yourself a tall glass of soda, turn off all the lights in the house (except for the one by which you are going to read), and pretend you're curling up on the sofa watching a late-night Creature Feature on a dark and stormy night.

Thanks and acknowledgment must be given to Craig Spector, Matthew J. Pallamary, Cathy J. Gonzalez and the late Mike Baker for their encouragement and keen feedback on the first draft of this novel. Thanks are also due to Pat LoBrutto for his initial enthusiasm and suggestions; to Mary Z. Wolf at Hard Shell Word Factory for giving *Clickers* its first home as an e-book; to Bob Strauss for helping me with proofing; and to David Nordhaus, Butch Miller, and Keith 'Doc' Herber at DarkTales Publications for giving *Clickers* the home it always deserved in paperback.

More thanks: Ray Greer for information on deep sea fishing; Buddy and Holly Martinez; Debbie Smith; all the writers who appeared in Phantasm Magazine; Cathy J. Gonzalez (for being the best wife a writer could ask for); the much-missed Afraid Magazine; Kurt and Amy Wimberger; Brian Hodge; the Friday Night Guys Without Dates Club—Tim Murphy, Brian Benison (I can't wait to quit!) and Ted Newsom (especially to Ted for all his work in the aftermath and helping to clear rights); Brian "Skippy" Moore; Rikki Rockett and the Poison guys; Alice Cooper and Brian 'Renfield' Nelson for giving Mark work; The Shroud; Rikki (again), Malina Shirley, Riki Valentine, Shon Kornfeld and anybody on the No Mercy Comics Staff I may have missed; Dave DeCoteau; Charles Band and Full Moon Productions; Dave Schow; Pete Atkins; Doug Clegg and Raul Silva; Gary Zimmerman; Del & Sue Howison & Dark Delicacies Bookstore for providing a second home; Art Cover and Lydia Morano & Dangerous Visions Bookstore; John Skipp; Ramona Pearce for being way too cool; Trish and Tim Chervenak; Jesus and Glenda Gonzalez; Ivan Graves; and last but not least, anybody who paid Mark to write scripts and make cool monsters for movies. Well … almost everybody!

JFG,
28 Jan, 2000
Pasadena, CA

Foreword
to the 2011 Edition

This is the sixth edition of *Clickers* to see print (seventh if you count the recent, and brief, eBook appearance from Mundania Press ... more on that in a moment). It is my first published novel, and has been in print consistently since its original publication as an eBook in 1999.

Editions prior to the Delirium reissues in 2006-2008 were riddled with varying degrees of typos and bad copy-editing. Some of the fault is mine. I was still green, more concerned with being published and making sure the story was king than with proper grammar and punctuation. Don't get me wrong—grammar and punctuation was important to me, and I took it seriously. But back then, my method of correcting and proofing my own work was radically different than it is today. Back then I had no copyeditors, proofreaders, or pre-readers. It was all me. I would write it, revise, edit, do the best I could with proofing, then send my work out with fingers crossed. Most of the time it was rejected, but sometimes I was able to place my work.

The original eBook edition by Hard Shell Word Factory wasn't proofed or copy-edited very well. My editor there made some good suggestions for revisions to the story (including the ending ... the original ending Mark and I wrote was included in the limited-edition Delirium published). But when it came to a detailed line-edit, the ball was dropped. I did my best on my end when I received the galleys, but I had read the book so many times that I was not the best judge. My old friend Richard Laymon helped me through the first third, but there were a lot of errors. I corrected as many as I could find and sent them off.

About half of those errors were corrected in the final version. When Hard Shell issued the book as a trade paperback six years later, I sent along a more polished copy but they never used it. Instead, they relied on that original error-ridden file.

The first trade paperback edition (from now defunct but much-missed DarkTales publications) was much cleaner. My editor there, Butch Miller, prided himself on being a grammar-Nazi and we were able to clean up much of the text. Still, a few things were missed, but for the most part, the DarkTales edition was pretty clean and typo free.

Ditto the Delirium editions. Enough time had passed by this time that I was a stronger copy-editor of my own stuff. Plus, I had a network of pre-readers and proofreaders to fall back on. Shane Ryan Staley had a great copy-editor too, so between all of us we got the job done right, for once. The Delirium trade paperback (and the preceding limited-edition hardcover) consisted of what I felt to be the corrected and preferred text of *Clickers*. I wish those few readers who had the misfortune to pick up the Hard Shell trade paperback had gone for this one instead.

The Mundania Press eBook is the more recent edition, and it was this edition that was the primary cause for rushing these new editions to print. Long story short—Mundania Press bought Hard Shell Word Factory and an employee at MobiPocket—a company that basically pushes out the various eBook formats to all the distributors and vendors—inadvertently put the entire Hard Shell catalog back into print, including titles in which the rights had reverted to the authors (of which *Clickers* was one).

Oops. You can imagine all the angry letters and emails the folks at Mundania got from authors angry that their work was available (in clear violation of copyright). I was one of them.

Because *Clickers* had enjoyed such a long and fruitful life and readers were still being introduced to it for the first time, many people downloaded the Kindle edition when they discovered it available. Unfortunately for them, when MobiPocket transferred the files, they used the old error-ridden version from Hard Shell Word Factory. To make matters worse, somehow the text got even further mangled (probably during file transfers to create the Kindle file). The result was the first time I received feedback from fans telling me "I bought the eBook edition of *Clickers* but I couldn't understand it." The first such email sent me on an Internet search and that's when I learned of the mishap. As a result, the Mundania Press eBook editions were recalled. If you are among those that bought a copy of this edition, my apologies.

If the Delirium edition was the unofficial corrected and preferred edition, this edition makes it official. Accept no substitutions. Typos be damned! Cheap and pulpy narrative ... well, that stays. After all, first and foremost, *Clickers* is a pulp horror novel. It was not written with the intent to be considered great art or literature. It was written by two huge fans of pulp horror and 1950s SF/Horror B movies. It is an homage. Nothing more, nothing less. So grab the beverage of your choice, rustle up some buttered popcorn, turn on the light, and let's travel to Phillipsport, Maine, where people are about to meet something rather nasty from the depths of the ocean.

J. F. Gonzalez
July 27, 2010
Altoona, PA

Prologue

North Atlantic Sea
October 20th

It was unusually cold that day.

The chilling wind licked at the surface of the water, causing frigid whitecaps on the churning waves. This section of the Atlantic, roughly fifty miles off the coast of Nova Scotia, was always cold, but never like this. Captain Kim Isaac had never seen the ocean behave this way in all his twenty years of experience at sea. It was just too weird.

Kim stood on the upper deck of the Lucky Mariner—a weathered fifty-six-foot Seine Boat that he'd bought ten years ago—as it crested a rising swell. A spray of foam splashed over the railing. The burst of cursing that rose from below told him that a good portion of his crew was drenched with the icy brine.

Kim gripped the metal railing and gazed out at the ocean. He took a long pull off his old walnut pipe, letting the scented smoke warm his lungs. His mood was pensive. This excursion had been plagued with unnatural occurrences from day one. After three days at sea, his crew of seven had hauled in less than seven hundred pounds of fish. Cod and herring were usually plentiful in these waters at this time of year. He had brought in nearly two tons of Cod on one trip alone last season, but now there was almost nothing. The ship's cook, Danny Walters, told him that it could all be blamed on the overfishing. That was the *rational* explanation for it.

Directly above the main cabin, Kim heard his first mate, Dave Johnson, curse as he swung the wheel to avoid another swell that was rapidly approaching. The waves had been rising steadily during the past hour and the wind whipped from the north, blowing freezing cold air across the bow. The black mass of clouds from the east indicated that Mother Nature was going to bless them with a mighty storm. There had been nothing about it in the latest weather forecast. Kim shook his head in dismay. *Great, just fucking great!*

One of the crew sat in a skiff fifty yards out, maneuvering the far end of the gill nets. They had been dragging the nets for the past four hours and had come up with nothing—another oddity. Gill netting was constructed with a lighter gauge weave. It floated in the water, creating a purse-like shape that trapped fish in currents like the scoop of a shovel. The fishes' gills got hooked in the netting and they couldn't wiggle free because the rest of them would pile in behind, trapping the whole school. When you thought about it, it was pure torture.

But for some reason the fish were getting out this time. They were tearing themselves from the nets, leaving bloody strips of flesh and scales tangled in the weave. They were swimming madly, as if propelled by some unseen force. It had happened the day before as well. It was the first indication that this trip was in no way normal.

The second indication was when the bottom-dwellers had come up in the nets earlier that morning. Flounder, lamprey and others of their ilk were rarely seen by surface fishers. They preferred to stay on the ocean floor and suck up anything that happened to settle there. Usually they stayed far below the bottom edge of the nets.

Kim had stood on the deck and watched the men haul them up in disgust. Most of the bottom-dwellers were worthless on the open market except for the flounder and a few specialty fish. The creatures just seemed to spew up from the depths in an unending hoard, as if they were being driven up by … something.

Forty minutes after the first wave of bottom dwellers, one of the crew yelled that they'd caught a large lobster in the nets. They tried hauling it up but before they could bring it to the surface, the net was torn apart and the creature scurried away into the deep. A moment later, another was captured. And then another. And another.

Kim had hopped down to the lower deck to catch a glimpse and couldn't believe what he saw; it was some type of crustacean, roughly three feet long. Its shell was deep red, darkening to black around the edges; its claws were a good foot long and serrated, making sharp little clicking sounds as it snapped at the net. Round, black marble eyes glared from long, wavering stalks. Its tail was segmented, tapering down to a needle protrusion that whispered stinging pain. In all, it resembled a cross between a mutant crab and a giant scorpion.

Kim saw the creature as the net came up in a spray of foam. The men beside him yelped in surprise as the thing clipped and wriggled through the net with a snap of its claws and slipped beneath the ocean's surface. The cut section of net floated limply in the water.

Some of the crew helped Kim bring the net up and he held it in his weathered hands. The thing had snipped through it as neatly as scissors through string. Quite a feat, considering that this was a wire-based net built to withstand the power of thousands of pounds of thrashing fish. Kim watched the creatures periodically get caught, only to escape before the crew could drag them aboard. He tried getting Ralph Hodgson, the lead crew man, to shoot them with the high-powered rifle kept on board to fend off sharks and barracudas, but all his shots went wild or missed altogether due to the awful thrashing the boat was taking from the stormy sea.

His heart raced furiously. He looked out into the rough sea, turning his head to watch as a couple of his crewmen brought up another of the creatures amid excited yells. It snipped through the weave and scurried away with a splash as Ralph popped off a few more useless shots.

He turned to Dave who was at the helm, fighting the wheel. "What the fuck are these things?" Kim yelled.

"I don't know," Dave said through gritted teeth. He gestured out to the water. "It looks like a big school of them heading southwest. Must be what's driving the fish crazy!"

Dave shrugged and scratched his bushy head. The wind

whipped at his heavy coat, rippling it like the waves of the sea. "They must be following this current. Never seen anything like it."

Kim looked out into the gray ocean. The seagulls were circling in wide, erratic circles, cawing frantically. Kim jerked a thumb toward the excited gulls. "Birds are acting real strange."

"Everything is!" Dave said. He had both hands on the wheel, his knuckles growing white as he struggled to keep the ship on course. "Everything in this part of the sea seems to be trying to get away from something."

Kim felt the boat lurch violently. He nearly lost his balance as he grabbed at the wooden railing. He righted himself, his heart still lodged in his throat. *Jesus, this storm is getting worse.*

Another length of net was brought up with three of the creatures hanging on by their insect-like legs. He studied the animals intently as he gripped the railing. He had never heard or read of any crab or lobster reaching the size of the things in the nets. Logic dictated that they probably dwelled on the bottom of the ocean and rarely came to the surface. If that was so, why were they coming up now?

He shook his head as the cawing of the gulls gnawed at the base of his skull. The sky was darkening rapidly. The wind was blowing stronger, the swells rising higher. The mass of dark storm clouds had grown larger and more sinister, painting the sky a dark black. The Lucky Mariner bounced off a swell, nearly knocking Kim off his feet. Some of the crew members weren't so lucky; a few of the men were thrown to the deck. Heart racing, Kim gripped the railing and made his way carefully to the ladder that led to the lower deck. He climbed down carefully and joined Ralph Hodgson.

He nudged Ralph's shoulder. "Get Jeff out of that skiff and get those nets up!"

"We pulling in?" Ralph asked sharply. He had nearly ten years of crew experience on commercial fishing vessels and the motions of the sea were disturbing him too.

"You bet your mother's ass we are." Kim leaned over and yelled to the upper deck where Dave was fighting the wheel with all his strength. *"Hey, Dave! We're bringing up the nets and headin' in!"*

Dave acknowledged the order with a wave and steered the boat into the swell to aid in retrieving the large nets. Kim barked the order to those on deck and then turned to steal another glance at the storm before all hell broke loose.

A commotion off toward the skiff caught his attention. The man they'd sent out to drag the net—an experienced seaman named Jeff Bowers—was yelling and slapping at the water with his oars. His screams washed toward them, high pitched, loud and clear.

"What the fuck?" Kim hissed, stepping toward the railing. He took the pipe out of his mouth and put it in his jacket pocket. His heart beat wildly. He could barely make out roiling, undulating movement below the tiny skiff as Jeff beat at the water with the oars.

The tiny skiff was listing to one side pretty badly as the net grew taut. One good wave and the small boat would capsize. Jeff was trying to cut loose the net, but the rough sea made it impossible. The rough thrashing of the boat made it appear that the net was being pulled out of Jeff's hands.

Suddenly the net attached to the skiff was yanked below and the tiny boat flipped over, spilling Jeff Bowers into the freezing ocean.

The skiff floated in the water half submerged, and finally sunk. Jeff was nowhere in sight.

It all went down so fast that Kim couldn't believe what he saw. The crew watched in stunned terror, finally gasping exclamations of shock. Kim felt the tension among his crew as Jeff's dark form broke the surface briefly.

Ralph pointed and yelled. *"Man overboard!"*

The heavy dark clouds finally split open and spilled their contents on the hapless crew. The rain added to the mounting confusion as the men clamored to save their lost mate.

Jeff Bowers treaded water and gasped for air as he bobbed in the ocean. A moment later he was yanked under. For good.

As the crew scrambled to save Jeff, Ralph looked at Kim. His eyes were wide and scared. It looked like he was about to scream when a heavy shock hit the bottom of the boat.

It threw Kim against the wall of the cabin. The shock tossed most of the men to the deck. They scrambled to their feet, resuming rescue duties. Kim's heart raced frantically. It was as if they'd hit bottom, but Kim knew that was impossible … not this far out!

Something had taken Jeff Bowers down and the ocean was becoming increasingly dangerous, more alien than he had ever seen it. He pushed the thoughts from his mind. If he didn't act quickly, his men were going to die out here.

"Let's get the fuck out of here!" Kim screamed. There was no sense in trying to rescue Jeff Bowers now. He was as good as dead. Kim moved across the deck and the shock wave hit again, louder and stronger, shaking the vessel. Kim stumbled, but managed to remain on his feet. It felt like the bottom of the boat was being torn apart.

Kim grabbed Ralph by the shoulders and spun him around. *"You! Come with me!"*

They turned and were about to climb up to the wheel when Danny appeared from below deck. His expression was grave. "Somethin's ripping the hell out of the hull."

Kim felt his stomach drop into his bowels. "Something … ?"

"I don't know what," Danny said. His voice trembled. His eyes looked like white marbles set on his black face. The intensity of Danny's fear sparked a new tremor of terror in Kim. He had never seen Danny scared of anything before. Seeing him genuinely frightened provided the reality check he needed.

"What's going on down there?" Kim shouted over the loud thunderclap. Danny motioned for Kim to follow and turned back toward the door.

Suddenly the boat lurched from some unseen impact.

The crewmen fell to the deck, trying to hold on for dear life. Kim fell and hit his face on the deck. The sharp pain of his nose breaking exploded in his mind, fueling his adrenaline. He scrambled to his feet quickly and saw that most of his crew was suffering the same fate; one man had smacked his head against the deck, while another lost his grip on the ladder and fell to the lower deck. Another man had tumbled through a window to the sound of shattering glass and garbled screams of pain. Kim almost laughed at the sight but stopped himself before he launched into a volley of giggles—the scene looked almost too comical, like out of a cartoon.

The sounds of snapping wood amid the yells of his men brought him back to reality yet again. Something was tearing the boat out from under them. He looked through the open cabin doorway and fear gripped his heart like a vice. An entire plank was missing from the side of the ship and the sea was invading the warm interior, flooding the lower deck. *Holy Jesus, fucking Christ!*

Kim moved forward and another lurch toppled him back onto the deck. His head thunked the wall. Stars blossomed in his field of vision. The deck listed at a forty-five-degree angle. Behind him Danny and Ralph were cursing and scrambling to their feet.

Danny's scalp had been laid open during one of his falls, bathing his face and the front of his shirt with dark blood. Ralph was heaving with exertion; he hadn't suffered any physical wounds yet. Kim struggled to his feet and gripped the railing, barely feeling the blood from his broken nose. Ralph hoisted himself up and fell on his face. Danny rose on wobbly legs and helped Ralph up. Ralph appeared visibly dazed. He shook his head and spat out a broken tooth, his first battle wound. Danny and Ralph gripped the railing as they regained their composure. They had to get the fuck out of here, and they had to do it *now!*

Kim suddenly noticed the tension on the gill nets. There was a sharp tug and the boat lurched again. Kim weathered the sudden movement and remained standing. Danny and Ralph almost went down again but held on, cursing. Something was pulling on the nets. The same thing that had pulled Jeff Bowers to oblivion.

Kim pulled the razor-sharp scaling knife from his belt and lunged toward the nets. *"Cut the goddamned nets!"* He yelled to the crew members around him. *"Cut the nets! Cut the nets!"* He scrambled to the railing, which was nearly under water. His head throbbed with pain. He began to hack at the line holding the main net.

Ralph brought out his own knife and hacked at the line. Danny joined them and a moment later a handful of the other crew members were scrambling to sever the lines from various points of the vessel.

Behind them they could hear Dave cursing as he throttled the engine and tried to maneuver the vessel toward shore. A rattled whine was emanating from the engine and Dave yelled "Fuck!" and slammed his fists down on the dash as the boat shuddered with exertion. A cloud of black, oily smoke rose from the engine as the boat moved slowly. It felt and sounded like the engine was dying. Kim cursed himself as he realized what was happening; the engine was flooding. *Goddamn!*

A moment later the mechanisms locked up and the whole thing shut down. The electrical system died, plunging the ship into darkness.

Kim's heart raced madly. The crewmen were yelling to abandon ship. Kim turned to Danny. "Get the life raft!"

Danny scrambled to the cabin as another wave crashed over the deck, bringing the sting of icy salt water.

Kim hacked at the nets, severing another line, preserving their lives for one more precious second. He huffed past Ralph and helped him sever his line. The wind picked up, howling in his ears as the ship tilted even more, slipping farther into the ocean. The howling wind and the shouts of the crew obliterated the sounds of the hull being torn open, flooding the ship further. The icy water flooded up to his knees. He was hardly aware of it. He was so involved in getting the nets cut, getting his men on the life raft and off the ship that he didn't even hear the rising screams of his men. Screams that rose suddenly and were cut off before they had the chance to register in his brain.

Kim's knife slashed through the last line. He heaved a deep breath and turned to Ralph, who was no longer there. Kim blinked and caught a flicker of movement out of the corner of his eye. He turned.

The trident punched through his chest so quickly that he didn't even see it coming. The force of the blow pushed him back into the water. His consciousness ebbed as he felt himself rise to the surface of the water. Kim tried to get up, but found that he was already in motion. He was moving through the water, being dragged down into the murky depths. He caught just a fleeting glimpse of the Lucky Mariner as it went down in the storm, and then everything went black and Kim Isaac knew no more.

1

Greater Northern Maine was overcast and cold as Rick Sychek maneuvered his rusty '73 baby-blue Plymouth Satellite through the snake-like twists and curves of Highway 1.

The patchy drizzle that had been dogging his path off and on during the twelve-hour drive suddenly became a steady rain. Rick turned his windshield wipers on again for the forty-seventh time, this time keeping them on. The rubber blades lurched into rhythm, brushing the water off the plate glass much slower than Mother Nature was dropping her load.

The radio was becoming increasingly fuzzy with static as he drove farther into Boonesville. *Figures.* Rick rummaged around inside a large, green shoebox sitting shotgun. It was crammed with compact discs. *Thank God for modern technology when primitive civilization looms.*

Keeping one eye half glued to the wet road, he was able to procure the disc that his soul screamed for. He snapped the jewel box open with practiced dexterity, honed by years of navigating through the streets of his hometown of Philadelphia with one hand while performing any number of tasks with the other. Rick was positive that he was the expert of eating, shaving, donning a necktie, and changing CDs while navigating dangerous roadwork at eighty miles per hour. It beat being late for everything.

He slipped the disc into the dash-mounted compact disc system his agent had bought him last Christmas. A moment later the rust began to vibrate with the opening bars of Alice

Cooper's *Billion Dollar Babies*, one of his ten favorite albums.

He turned up the volume and resumed driving with two hands on the steering wheel. He bobbed his head in time with the music. He loved CDs. The dash mounted sound job, which was presently engaged in blowing out the Plymouth's tiny door mounted speakers, came courtesy of his agent commemorating the release of his latest horror novel, *Baron Semedi*.

He passed a sign on his left. Phillipsport … 20 Miles. Still a ways to go.

The tall, dark silhouettes of pine trees whooshed by in a wet myriad of rain and sleet as the car maneuvered down the road. This trip up north was going to give him the added boost he knew he needed. He felt good about it. He'd been through a lot lately since his writing career had taken an unexpected turn toward near instant success.

The unexpected runaway sales of *Baron Semedi* had put Rick in a weird situation. When he wrote the thing it was just one of the mainstream horror novels he had written as part of a four-book contract with Diamond Books. There was nothing that differentiated this one from the others. It was another cheesy horror novel featuring a voodoo cult that decapitated women and offered children up for sacrificing, after which they would cannibalize the tots' bodies. Pulp reading designed to be consumed in a single sitting and quickly forgotten by the next day. No biggie. Peter Straub, he wasn't.

He was simply one of the dozens of writers who had a small yet faithful following mainly consisting of bored housewives who picked up his books at the local supermarket check-out stands, as well as the rabid horror fans that showed up at autograph parties with boxes of books to be signed. Like others of his brethren, he'd been undersold and underrated, providing the backbone of the paperback houses that put out his work. His early novels hadn't brought in Fort Knox, but they gave him decent royalty checks that enabled him to live semi-comfortably. Beggars can't be choosers.

As Rick drove he couldn't help but think about the events over the last few years that led to his current decision. His first novel *Shadowbeast* had been a simple connect-the-dots demon-on-the-loose story. Its initial sale prompted Diamond to sign him up to a four-book deal. The advance wasn't bad, but it wasn't exactly a mid-six figure sum either. He'd been working at Sharp Insurance Company for eight years, five of that spent in the company's warehouse where he knew he would be doomed to spend the rest of his life if he didn't do a quick one-eighty and take control of his future. The first novel was written over nine months, during weeknights and weekends. When it sold he was able to quit his job for good. Sayonara nine to five world, hello career move.

Rick settled comfortably into writing for a living. Knowing he'd have to produce a novel once a year to meet the deadlines and the bills, he settled into a comfortable writing schedule. He worked from ten at night till six in the morning. Rose around noon, piddled around the house and did chores. Sometimes he wrote short stories, which he sent off to magazines. Weekends were devoted to the same social life he held before he became self-employed. His sex life improved somewhat and telling women he wrote novels sometimes impressed them. It still wasn't as impressive as, say, being a rock star, but it did the trick.

Rick grinned at the memory as he rounded a curve in the road. His second published novel, *Night of the Devil,* was loosely based on the legend of a beastie dubbed the Jersey Devil. The lurid tale had the monster hack its way through three hundred pages and scores of half-naked teenagers. The sales doubled that of his debut and had even garnered a bullshit award from some know-nothing writer's committee. The third book followed later that year, a vampire novel titled *Night.*

Then *Baron Semedi* was released to the collective masses. Why this book racked up over two hundred thousand sold copies in six months was beyond him. While the book was better written than the first few outings, the story was still another booga-booga piece of exploitative masturbation. The cover art was the most retarded muck-up in publishing history; it was a painting featuring the skeletal protagonist choking a chicken while a near-naked girl was shown draped over an altar in the foreground. The cover painting had nothing to do with the story.

Thinking about that horrible cover made Rick laugh aloud. As best as Rick was able to understand, the fire started when a writer close to the popularity and influence of Stephen King had read the galleys one night on the porcelain reading chair. He'd given it a great cover blurb, which Diamond maxed out in all their promotional shticks. The senior editor quickly made it that month's lead title and ordered an exhaustive marketing campaign behind the book. The month the novel hit an interview appeared in a horror magazine with the writer who blurbed it, essentially saying that he thought *Baron Semedi* was the greatest thing since canned beer. Everything that happened since then had been a whirlwind. The success of *Baron* prompted Diamond to reissue his previous three releases, and he was promptly signed to a two-book hardcover deal with a big house with Diamond to reissue in paperback. The Big Time was coming.

And I thought I was just going to be another hack, Rick thought as he rounded a sharp curve in the road. When Cynthia called him with the news that the hardcover deal had gone down and the combined advances, including paperback rights, were in the mid-six-figure range, Rick had danced around in his underwear. Tribal celebration time. "I'll never be hungry again," he chanted.

Rick frowned as he drove. The emergence of bigger dollars in his contracts had changed lots of things. Writer's Block had set in almost immediately after the deal was signed, and he panicked. How was he going to get out of Writer's Block, and deliver the next two books in his contract? What kind of a book was he going to write as his hardcover debut?

All this inspired his retreat. His friend Shawn Marine, who he'd worked with at Sharp Insurance, had a summer house on the coast of Maine in a little burg that was no more than a speck on the map. There seemed to be a real lack of anything resembling civilization anywhere near the town. The closest city was thirty miles south through a desolate, windy mountain road; most likely the same road he was now commandeering. It would be the perfect place to start anew. New surroundings would bring in fresh ideas.

He made the arrangements, packed his Plymouth and was off to Phillipsport, Maine within the week.

Rick looked out through the blurry passenger's side window at the Atlantic Ocean. The turbulent, churning surface was a dark shade of gray. The sky looked almost ochre from the horizon to the heavens, expanding north and south, east and west. The clouds had moved inland fast with the blowing wind. Rick popped his headlights on. A shade more and it would be nightfall even though it was only two o'clock in the afternoon.

A sudden rupture in the sky spewed forth a dazzling forked bolt of lightning. Rick had to squint, blinded by the flash. He shook his head. A heavy *KA-BOOM!* hit, causing the air to vibrate. It felt like the earth had been jolted by a killer quake. The rumblings issued forth, creating an ominous feeling in conjunction with the already pelting rain and dark sky. A sharp green afterimage of the lightning was still etched on his optic nerve.

He took his foot off the gas pedal and let the car slow a bit. He rubbed his eyes with his thumb and forefinger and gently began blinking them back to normal vision. Better. His sight was slowly refocusing back to normal.

When the afterimages from the lightning faded, he slowly eased his foot down on the gas. He wanted to make it to the house before the storm got worse. Traffic was sparse and he was hoping to make it in the next ten minutes.

He rubbed the condensation from the windshield and peered through the small misty hole of dampness to get a better view. It was getting worse outside.

A sign came into view: PHILLIPSPORT ... 2 MILES.

Great! He leaned forward over the steering wheel to see better and began keeping his eyes peeled for upcoming onramps.

Nothing.

Nothing but trees.

He grinned and cranked the stereo up a notch. Alice Cooper bellowed that he was No More Mister Nice Guy.

The mood the weather was putting him in was perfect; he'd always been a sucker for this type of climate. It was straight out of a Hammer Horror film. He gripped the steering wheel tightly and grinned. The spark was ignited. His mind coalesced into power mode. Creative energy. His fingers itched for the hard, plastic keys of his computer keyboard. The urge to create had hit him with an ugly stick.

He was so into his anticipation for getting into work, letting the mood of the storm take him, that he failed to notice the large crustacean in the road in front of him.

He caught just a glimpse before the car went over it. His mind snapped back as the tires thudded over something large and hard. His foot hit the brake, the wheels locking into a wet skid. He panicked as the car skidded, his hands fumbling at the wheel. *Which way do I turn the wheel? Which way do I—*

Another thud as the tire passed over the object again, this time coalescing in a hearty *crunch.* The rear of the car was buffeted slightly by what felt like a small explosion. It pushed the car into a tighter skid.

Rick gripped the wheel, fighting to gain control of the car. The huge pine trees off the side of the road sped into the windshield.

And everything went black.

2

The buzzing inside Rick Sychek's head slowly brought him out of his stunned shock.

Loud, yet unintelligible, just barely swimming to the surface of his consciousness.

"Eeeeeyyyyybbbbbooooooddddddyyyyy!"

Swimming farther up. Growing more alert.

"Eey Bbddyy!"

A tug. Then a painful shaking sensation. He snapped out of his daze as he broke the surface of the mental quagmire.

"Hey, buddy!"

Rick blinked. He was dimly aware of a warm wetness coating his forehead. His senses began working toward some coherent pattern that resembled normality. His head swelled with the beat of a throbbing headache. Fuck reality. He'd rather sink into the nothingness of unconsciousness and sleep this nightmare away.

He felt another tug on his shoulder. He slowly turned his stiff neck to see what was causing it.

A large, blurry dark shape came into view. It took Rick a second to put the figure into a recognizable form. The figure boomed another thunderstorm of explosive decibels of noise that caused another wince of agony.

"Hey buddy! You okay?"

Stupid question. People always seemed to pop this one when they come upon someone who has just dismantled himself in some way. Rick blinked and stared at the figure. The man's face was framed by a dark bundle of cloth. Rick lifted his hand and tried to rub the sticky wetness out of his eyes. His fingers ached and he felt weak.

He opened his eyes again, this time his vision zeroing in on normal 20/20. Comprehension set in.

The man standing over him was large, hawk nosed and lanky. He was wearing a yellow windbreaker with a hood pulled over his head, draping over a frame clothed in a brown shirt and brown slacks. His feet were encased in black, muddy work boots. His light brown hair was frosted with gray. His skin and facial features bore the appearance of a logger. The man looked at him again with concern. "Jesus, mister but you sure took a fall down this here incline. You hurt anywhere else?"

Rick felt a giggle rise to the surface. An explosion of pain in his muscles stopped it. "Hurt? Of course I'm hurt. Jesus …" He tried to rise to a sitting position. His back muscles groaned in agony.

The man reached out a hand to help him and Rick's mind blossomed in warmth. It felt like a gallon of blood had been pumped into his head. He winced and rubbed his temples. He felt sticky blood in his matted hair.

The booming voice crashed into his ears again. "You gonna need a doctor?"

Rick turned to the man standing over him with a concerned look on his face. He didn't look as weird now as he did before. His nose stuck out on his face like a potato.

Rick blinked at the man again. He noticed for the first time that his clothing was actually a uniform of a Highway Patrol officer. His windbreaker/raincoat was police-issued. His shirt collar was pulled up, framing angular features accented by an unshaven lantern jaw. His voice was rather high-pitched, almost effeminate for his position of authority. A shiny badge was pasted on his lapel. Officer of the Law.

Suddenly the memory of the accident slammed back into his brain. He blinked and quickly turned his head around to see where he was.

He was still resting in the Plymouth Satellite, securely buckled into his seat. It was still raining outside. He was still alive.

And the entire front end of his car was crushed into shit.

It was curled back like a pretzel, exposing bare, scraped metal and wiring. A headlight and part of the grill were now resting on what was left of the hood. The windshield had fragmented into a dozen wavy spiderwebs of cracked, silver lines. Steam rose from the hood in small curly bends like smoke from a dragon's nostrils. The raindrops sizzled when they struck the engine. Still hot.

The object of impact loomed in front of the windshield, large and oppressive. The huge pine looked like it had weathered four hundred years of blizzards, loggers, and mankind, and it had absorbed the impact of the crash quite nicely. It had enveloped the entire front end of the Plymouth. Pieces of bark had splintered off, exposing raw pulp beneath. The tree looked like it was at least seven feet in diameter at the base. Pieces of it were lying on the mangled hood of the car.

His heart deflated in his chest at the damage. *Looks like I'll have to get a new car now.*

The patrolman spoke again. "If you need medical help, I'll have to take you into town. Ol' Doc Jorgensen don't have a radio or ambulance."

Rick nodded again and began to take slow inventory of his body. He moved his arms and legs. No bones appeared broken despite the pain he felt; there was a good possibility that he had wrenched his muscles pretty good. He ran a hand over his head and again encountered sticky blood. He looked at his hand and saw that it was streaked. He was cut somewhere. Shit.

The officer leaned his head in and looked at Rick's head. He nodded with a slight smirk. "Looks a lot worse than it is. Scalp wounds bleed like a bugger, always look fatal. Even so, you might have a concussion. Better take you to town."

Rick started to get out of the car when his legs were hit with a sudden slam of cramps. He went rigid, grimacing in pain. For a moment he thought he was paralyzed, that one wrong move had broken his back. His arms and legs were still moving but his body wouldn't obey his commands to lift itself off his ass and skedaddle. Then he remembered the seatbelt. He fumbled at the buckle, snapped it open and slid out, feeling like an idiot.

The patrolman pretended not to notice Rick's blushing face as he helped him out of his crushed vehicle. The rain drenched

Rick instantly as a bolt of lightning flashed down. The low rumble of thunder vibrated the ground and Rick turned back to his car, his precious belongings still stowed away in the back seat. He looked at the patrolman. "My stuff ..." The patrolman nodded. "Once we get to the Doc's, I'll have someone come back and pick up your stuff. You oughta be happy you're alive. Lucky you was wearing your seat belt. Most folks who run into Ol' Little Feet there ain't so lucky."

"Little Feet?" Rick was curious.

The patrolman nodded toward the tree. "Nickname the locals christened this here tree. On account of she being so damned big."

"Ahh." Rick looked out at his car. He was glad he'd listened to all the public safety advice aimed toward seatbelts. He would have flown through the windshield and splattered against Ol' Little Feet like a ripe tomato. Not a pretty sight.

The patrolman didn't seem to notice the rain. He stuck out his hand. "I'm Deputy Russell Hanks of the Phillipsport Sheriff's Department. Though most folks around here jus' call me Rusty." He smiled a wide, goofy smile and held out his hand. Rick shook it limply and tried to smile back.

"Rick Sychek."

Recognition flitted through Rusty's eyes. He leaned forward questionably. "Rick Sychek the writer?"

Rick almost jumped in surprise. He was used to the recognition at conventions and book signings, but here in the boonies the recognition was surprisingly refreshing. A real reader of his work. Rick grinned and nodded. "Yeah, Rick Sychek the writer. That's me."

Rusty's hand pumped Rick's again with heavy abandon. His face suddenly took on the look of a little kid meeting Santa Claus for the first time. His blue eyes glittered under his yellow hood. "Gee, that's somethin'. Never met a real-life writer before. I've read almost all your books. Shelby's drug store stocks 'em."

Rick smiled and looked back at his car, trying to reconstruct the accident in his mind. He walked around the car, peering under the chassis and inspecting the tires, trying to find an explanation to the mishap while Rusty tagged along behind him like a friendly puppy.

"You spendin' time in Phillipsport, or ..." Rusty's voice trailed into mumbo jumbo as Rick tuned it out. Now was not the time to deal with a star-struck fan. He checked under the front of the car as his mind backtracked to the accident, suddenly remembering the large, red crusty thing sitting in the middle of the road that he had swerved to avoid.

Rusty stopped the fandom banter and knelt down next to Rick, who was checking out the front tires. His expression took on a serious, professional look of the law. "You hit something in the road?"

Rick nodded, studying the smashed front end. He ran his hand down the front of the car, searching for fragments of what he'd hit. "Think so."

"Tree branch brought down by the storm?"

"No, it wasn't that. It was more like some kinda weird lookin' animal."

Rusty's expression turned to idle confusion. As a deputy, he probably had that look from constantly dealing with the mundane, day-to-day small-town stuff. He helped Rick inspect the front of the car. "Deer, maybe?"

Rick wiped the blood and water from his forehead with the back of his hand and rose. "No. The rain was so heavy that I only caught a glimpse of it. But it wasn't a deer. It was smaller." He held his hands out in front of him, forming a small shape. "It was shaped like ..." He gestured vaguely, trying to describe the creature he saw. His eyes darted up the road, tracking the skid marks back up along the wet road where he saw Rusty's patrol car sitting with its red flashers rotating in the rain. The engine was still going and hot exhaust smoke billowed out in gray clouds into the cold mist. The car was sitting on the spot where Rick had begun to spin out.

Rick tried to describe the thing again. "It ... it looked like a big crab."

Rusty looked puzzled. "A crab?"

Rick looked at the deputy. "I think so. It looked like a big red, gargantuan crab."

Rusty put a gloved hand on Rick's shoulder and squeezed it softly. His blue eyes reflected concern. "I think we'd better get you out of this rain and off to see Doc Jorgensen."

Rick wiped his forehead again and nodded. "Okay ..." He looked back at the car. "What about my car?"

"I'll raise Carl's garage on the radio and have him send a man to tow your car in. You can pick up your stuff there."

"I should at least get my computer gear," Rick said. He moved toward the car, now dreading what he was going to find in the back seat. He had completely forgotten about his laptop and portable laser printer until now and the thought of facing smashed equipment was something that he didn't want to have to deal with. He opened the passenger side door of the Satellite and leaned inside. His luggage, which he had stowed in the trunk, could wait. He'd put the laptop and printer on the back seat to specifically keep it from being bumped and jostled in the trunk with his luggage. The dome light on the car's ceiling went on as he opened the door and he sighed in relief: the printer, the laptop and the case containing disks and other equipment were fine. They were on the seats where they should be. He picked up the laptop and unzipped the case he had stored it in. He brought it out and opened it up. It was fine. It might have been jostled a little bit, but it didn't appear broken.

He brought the equipment over to the patrol car. Rusty opened the rear door and helped him store it in the back. His luggage could stay in the trunk; clothes could be easily replaced. Computers couldn't.

He felt better already; everything was being taken care of. With the exception of the scalp wound that had stopped bleeding, he seemed to have escaped further injury. Doc Jorgensen would make the final verdict on that, though.

Once the equipment was in Rusty's car he cast one last look at his own smashed vehicle lying at the base of the tree when a flash of red caught his eye. He stopped and retreated back to the front end of his car. Rusty followed him.

"Anything wrong?" Rusty called out.

Rick knelt down beside the deflated front right tire, peering intently at the rubber. Something was sticking out of the shredded black tire. Something with the color of dark rust.

Deputy Rusty joined Rick at the side of the car and peered down. "What is it? See anything?"

Rick ignored him and pulled out his Swiss army knife from his back pocket and flicked it open. He inserted the blade into the tear the dark object protruded from and began digging around it. After a moment the object came free. Rick grabbed it and turned it over in his palms, studying it intently. Rusty peered over his shoulder and drew a sharp intake of breath. "Jesus Christ I'll be damned!" Rusty breathed.

It was a claw. A very large crab claw.

The deep red pincer had been torn off at the joint. Pale strips of flesh hung from the end. It dripped a milky yellow substance onto the wet ground.

Rick had never seen a claw this big before. It was twice the size of the largest lobster he had even seen. God only knew what the rest of it looked like, much less how big the fucker was. The pincer was tinted various shades of red and magenta. A delicate crisscross pattern of color accenting various shades of red melting beautifully together that ended with the pointed tips blending into a thick shade of black. As an instrument of death, it was quite beautiful.

Rick grabbed the pincer by its claws and gently pried it open. Strong muscle sinew still constricted under the shell, frozen in death. He pried the jaws apart gently. When fully open, the pincer was about eighteen inches from tip to tip. The serrated teeth lining the jaws were razor sharp and inlaid in multiple rows, like a shark's jaws. The hard, crusty shell of the pincers themselves were tough enamel. And heavy. This thing could probably snap off a man's head.

He prodded at the soft tissue at the joint as the claw suddenly snapped shut with a loud *clack*.

He gasped and dropped the claw into the mud.

Jesus!

His heart did a quick pitter-patter in his chest and slowed down. He grinned and leaned forward and retrieved the wet claw from the muddy puddle at his feet. He brushed it off and slipped it into the pocket of his coat. Rusty was already shining his flashlight under the car for more signs of the beast. Rick joined him but the only thing he saw was a large puddle of thick oil pooling under the engine block.

He brushed aside a smattering of mud and grass and lowered his head so he could search for the rest of the crab. Rusty retreated to the car and came loping back unfolding a long, black umbrella.

"Carl said he'd have a tow truck here in about fifteen minutes," Rusty said. He must have put in a call on the CB in his excursion to retrieve the umbrella. "Had the dispatcher relay to Doc Jorgensen that I was bringing you in. He's waiting for us at his office."

Rick nodded and got to his feet. He moved toward the protective sheath of the umbrella and together they headed for the patrol car.

He slid into the passenger side of the vehicle as Deputy Rusty slid behind the wheel. They pulled out with flashing red lights into the rainy downpour.

The driver's side rear tire thunked over the remainder of the crushed crab. Neither man noticed as the car pulled away.

The smashed body was a pulpy mass of broken shell and pale, yellow meat. One of the legs still twitched in a delayed death spasm. The rain pelted down on the pavement, washing the milky blood off the road where it mixed with the mud and grass of the embankment.

A moment later two dark red shapes crawled out onto the road and up to the smashed body. They were significantly larger than the dead creature that had been crushed by the departing patrol car. The claws of the two new crustaceans clicked furiously as they dug into the wet flesh mound and stuffed huge, moist chunks into their mandibles.

Five minutes later there was hardly a trace of the deceased crustacean left. A few scattered pieces of shell remained that would later be washed into gullies by the rain.

The two crustaceans scurried into the bush and headed back down to the beach as a large, battered tow truck pulled up to the scene.

3

Captain Jeremiah Stebble was hating life like a sumbitch.

The old-timer fisherman was doing everything within his power to keep his vessel from capsizing in the choppy gray waters. Never mind that he was the only one on board, or that he was a self-appointed captain. Never mind that his vessel was nothing more than a fifteen-foot, leaky rowboat with no means of propulsion other than the two weathered oars that he now clutched with throbbing hands. The outboard motor had gone out twenty minutes before. He had been cruising steadily inland after checking his lobster pots, and when the massive black clouds of the storm began brewing he gathered the final booty of his catch and started making his way toward shore. The motor gave out three minutes into the journey. He was still another thirty minutes to salvation by motor. With the oars? Probably hours with this storm.

He eyed the distant, dark shoreline and gnashed his tobacco-stained teeth together. *Goddamn.*

Today's excursion had been mired in weirdness from the get-go. Ten minutes after he had cast off, a commotion from the shore caused him to look back toward the sandy beach. What he saw was something that all his years as a fisherman had never seen.

The fish were beaching themselves.

They seemed to be swimming up to shore and propelling themselves onto the sand where they continued to flop in a forward motion, as if their little fish brains were still telling them to keep swimming.

As if to escape from something that was chasing them.

The phenomenon was attracting a smattering of tourists and shop owners who gawked and pointed at the beached fish. Jeremiah shook his head and continued on his eastern trek out to where he'd laid his lobster traps. He would catch up with what was going on later. There was business to attend to first.

The other weird thing was the erratic behavior of the seagulls. They circled overhead, cawing ceaselessly, their tone jittery and nervous. Jeremiah thought this to be rather strange but when coupled with the fish beaching themselves, he dismissed it. The gulls were probably just reacting to the event in typical gull fashion. No problem.

It wasn't until Jeremiah was out to the farthest trap he had lain that he realized that the currents were out of whack too. He could feel his boat drifting southeast in a counterclockwise direction in an area that normally held no currents. Jeremiah knew this section of the Atlantic like the back of his hand, and was accustomed to the normal rhythms of the ocean caused by offshore storms and the seasons. But this was just too unnatural. Despite the odd shifts Mother Nature sometimes instills in things, this just didn't sit right with Jeremiah's instincts.

Now he was making his way back to shore after completing his rounds. He did them hurriedly, wanting to get back before the current decided to do something else unexpected, and before the storm broke.

Suddenly, a sharp sliver of pain wedged into his lower jaw. He vocalized his thought now. "Goddamn!"

His rear molar was throbbing bad with this weather. Impacted. Should have had the goddamn thing pulled when his dentist said. It had to be taken care of soon. If he sold this week's catch to that annoying little asshole who owned that fancy-pants restaurant down in Vermont, he would be okay. The thought of dealing with the owner, a self-righteous fuck named Garcon Dupuis, made him want to chuck the whole thing altogether. And that made his jaw hurt even more.

"Goddamn fucking French faggot!" He hissed, trying to steer the small boat through the pounding ocean. The more he thought about the buttwad, the angrier he got and the more uncoordinated he became while trying to pilot the vessel through the choppy seas. Or was it the storm hindering his progress? The waves it belched forth were definitely bigger, spewing salt spray over him, infuriating him even more. He'd get back to shore, goddammit, and he would deal with that asshole Dupuis his way. Even if he had to rip off the man's cock and stuff it up his asshole to do it. Goddammit!

The boat suddenly dipped and a huge wave slammed into the ocean five feet from his boat. The force nearly ripped the left oar from his gloved hands. His shoulder muscles screamed in torment. Dark, salty water splashed up from the sea, completely drenching Jeremiah Stebble from head to toe. *"Goddamn fucking shit!"*

He quickly used the back of his sleeve to wipe the stinging brine from his leathery, brown face. He was getting too goddamned old for this shit.

The thought of having to fish after this season depressed him greatly. He'd spent nearly all of his seventy-five years on or around the sea. His whole life and everything he had accomplished was linked directly to the ocean, and the life that lay within its depths.

But during the last few years things had changed drastically. Overfishing had killed nearly ninety-five percent of the industry. Large, commercial fishing vessels and their goddamned drift nets had gouged entire species out of the sea. He couldn't remember the last time he'd seen a whale, a dolphin, or even a fucking god-damned great white shark.

Up until five years ago Jeremiah had been able to make a modest living on a large lobster boat, fishing off of Morrow Bay. The only problem hindering business lately was that the lobsters were being caught faster than they could breed. The catches got smaller and smaller every year while the demand got heavier and heavier because of assholes like Dupuis turning stupid, inbred morons on to the delicacy of lobster.

What it all boiled down to was that there were too many goddamned people on the planet eating too much food, using up too much land, and breeding too many illegitimate, stupid squawking babies that nobody could afford to take care of. Much less want.

Jeremiah had used up his savings to buy the dinghy he was now currently navigating. He bought a couple of rusted lobster traps and only recently began to take a stab at it again. To carve out a small living off the sea.

One bad season, that's all it would take to kill off Jeremiah's new venture. The year hadn't been so kind to him so far. He'd been lucky once while chartering a large fishing boat and hooked a swordfish the size of a Buick by accident. That barely made up for the lack of decent-sized lobsters.

Jeremiah squinted toward the shore, making sure to keep it within eyesight constantly. If he lost his bearings in this weather, he'd never make it back to shore alive. The choppy sea was making it impossible to see the buoy where he'd attached the last trap along his normal route. The buoy was the closest to shore, thus, his last stop. Might as well stop by and see if the pickings were any good.

He surveyed the area quickly. Just over a large swell he could barely make out the black outline of the buoy thrashing about like a cork in a Jacuzzi. He groaned and forced his aching muscles to maneuver the boat toward the marker.

The icy rain came down harder.

Three minutes later he reached the buoy. Despite the cold rain and the icy wind, he was sweating from exertion.

Jeremiah dropped the oars in the boat and reached out, grabbing hold of the icy, cold metal framework of the buoy. He caught his breath and ran a gloved hand over the slick metal near the bottom. His hand came across a rusted catch-hook. He managed a small smile.

It was illegal to attach lobster traps to buoys, but he didn't give a rat-fuck. He had to make a living, goddammit. He was glad that the Coast Guard hadn't found the hook and cut the traps loose like they had two years before. Motherfuckers.

He wrapped his hand around the thick wire that was welded to the hook and began to pull the traps up from the depths. The ocean wasn't very deep at this point, and thank God for that. Not much of a haul this far in. Despite that fact, the trap seemed slightly heavier this time around. He smiled. Big old lobsters this time. Maybe life wasn't so bad after all.

Jeremiah Stebble quickly pulled the thick wire from the icy water, wrapping the line around his left hand. He could feel the cold radiating from the wire through the heavy cloth of his coat.

There was a sharp tug on the line that nearly pulled him into the water. "Goddammit!" He pulled harder.

The line tugged again harder from somewhere below.

Some goddamned octopus is trying to steal my catch! Worse than a foreigner moving in next door to your house.

Natural predators were common in this industry. Octopi loved to feed on the trapped crustaceans as they floundered in the steel cages. The rubbery bodies of the octopi allowed them to crawl into the tiniest openings. One time he'd thrown an octopus into an ice chest. He'd caught it in one of his traps feasting on a catch. The octopus squeezed its bulk through a hole in the lid the size of a quarter. Lack of bones made it possible for them to ooze through anything. He could probably squeeze a twenty-foot octopus into Garcon Dupuis' asshole if the French faggot gypped him on another transaction.

He leaned over the boat, trying to peer into the murky, roiling depths. The line tugged again. Jeremiah was ready for another octopus this time, and wrapped the wire around one of the oar spurs attached to the lip of the boat, relieving the tightness around his arm a bit.

A flash of color erupted a few feet below the surface. He pulled harder and the blood red object came into view.

He pulled up a few more feet of line, keeping his eyes on the object below. He could now make out a frantic, scuttling movement. The tugging grew more violent. Jeremiah pulled and spun the line over the oar spur. His heart raced. Must be some pretty big goddamned lobsters.

He brought up more of the line.

The top of the cage was now only a few feet below the choppy, gray surface. He plunged his arm under the cold water and searched amid the bars. His hand touched something hard and cold.

Something felt wrong. It was too goddamned big.

The creature sitting atop the shattered cage felt the man's hand touch the hard shell of its back. The gloved fingers probed, sending the crustacean into attack mode. Instinct took over immediately and its long, segmented tail curled upward over its back in scorpion-like fashion. Its three-inch stinger jabbed Jeremiah Stebble's forearm just below the elbow, piercing the skin and muscle and shattering the radius. Jeremiah shrieked.

He lacked the vocabulary now to utter another expletive directed toward his maker. White-hot pain eclipsed all thought.

He wrenched his arm out of the water with a backward flinching motion, screaming in agony. The creature was hanging onto his arm by its tail, the stinger still embedded in his flesh. Jeremiah felt his heart lurch in his throat and barely noticed the change in temperature as he pissed his pants. He reached for the animal to try to pull it free. The creature arched its back and used its claws to anchor itself to the side of the boat.

Jeremiah's eyes widened as the blood-colored crustacean clicked and writhed on the lip of the tiny vessel. He tugged on the thing's tail again and was successful in pulling the stinger out of his arm. Liquid fire erupted in his arm as dark blood poured down the inside of his jacket, staining the cloth a deep crimson.

Jeremiah Stebble shrieked again, his terror-filled eyes locked on the large creature.

From below the boat in the cage, two other creatures surfaced from the torn prison. They'd just finished devouring the five regular-sized lobsters that had been caught.

The creatures clacked their pincers and scurried onto the lip of the boat to join the other one, which was still locked onto the side of the vessel.

"Jesus Christ!" Jeremiah screamed. *"Oh, goddamn Jesus fucking Christ!"* He tried to cradle his wounded arm but his left was still wrapped with the wire from the trap. He yanked hard, trying to pull free from the line. It caught snugly. The line could take five hundred pounds of pressure and would take a pair of strong wire cutters to break.

He tried to fumble with the line, but his right arm was swelling rapidly from the sting—it stung so much that it was nearly numb. The thought that the creature-thing was poisonous flitted across his mind in a flash and was gone. He had to concentrate on getting out of here before he could worry about whether he had been poisoned.

The three creatures seemed to examine the wounded, screaming man with eyes that looked like small, black ball bearings glued to colored spring metal. The stalks waved like wheat in the wind on a warm Kansas afternoon. They clicked their powerful claws rapidly, as if communicating to each other in Morse code. Jeremiah stood in numbed shock for a moment, watching them. The clicking sound sent another volley of shrieks to issue from his throat. He started fumbling with his left arm again in another attempt at freeing himself from the wire line.

The creatures moved spider-like into the boat and raised their stingered-tails menacingly over their backs. They advanced on him.

Jeremiah looked around for a weapon, anything to fight off those things. His wounded arm had started to pulsate from the toxic fluid that had been injected into his system. Nausea hit him like a sledgehammer. He doubled over and tried to fight back the sickness rising in his stomach. *Jesus Christ, what's happening to me?* His fingers swelled like fat sausages inside his gloves. His whole arm was numb, just like the time he'd caught his finger between a boat hull and a steel support. The doctor at the emergency ward had injected his hand with Novocain and he was numb for days.

There had been so much blood. Just like now.

He shook himself back to reality as the first creature crawled onto his leg. The grip of the thing's claws was incredible, like being caught in a bear trap.

His wire-wrapped hand closed around the wooden club he kept on board to whap sharks on the nose when they got too close. He gripped the club and brought it down on the back of the creature clinging to his leg. The impact caused the animal to retract its eyestalks back into its shell. But then it dug its claws deeper into Jeremiah's leg, drawing fresh gouts of blood.

Jeremiah went berserk. He yelled hoarsely, whacking the creature with the club. The other two creatures made their move and scattered to either side of the man. They hissed loudly, spreading their mandibles wide.

Jeremiah's arm felt like it was on fire. He had never felt such pain in his life. It went past shock and careened into lighting his consciousness on fire, keeping him awake, alert. The heat grew hotter as he watched in horror as the cloth of his jacket sleeve and glove grew taut with growing pressure. The seams on the fingers of the glove began to split and rip under the increasing diameter of the digits. His arm was inflating like a balloon.

The creature to his right advanced on him. He swatted at it with his swollen arm.

The balloon-like limb made contact. What happened next was unbelievable, even to Jeremiah's rapidly-spinning mind.

The swelled arm hit the animal's hard, shiny shell. A loud pop ensued and his arm exploded in a splatter of blood and meat. The spray drenched the creature inside the boat with goo.

Jeremiah was beyond screaming now; he was howling. He raised his ruined arm in front of his face. It looked like the flesh had dissolved off the bone. The bones of his hand and forearm were held together by cartilage and stringy sinew. The muscle-and-skin casing was sloughing off like sludge; it bubbled as the poison of the creature's sting ate the tissue like acid.

Strong enzymes dissolved the cartilage and ligaments.

The flesh and bones of his hand dropped onto the floor of the boat, sizzling in a puddle of black gunk and slime. Jeremiah slumped against the side of the boat, semi-conscious. The three creatures advanced on him, poisonous tails leering forward over their backs.

Their death jabs sent Jeremiah Stebble into a painful St. Vitus' Dance of bubbling venom and flesh.

4

The ride in the patrol car provided Rick Sychek with his first view of his winter home.

It was a five-minute trip through the twisting, turning two miles of bumpy roads to get to town. Towering pine trees stretched to the sky and obscured the menacing, black clouds. As they drew closer to town the trees thinned out, overshadowed by the wide beach and the roiling, blue ocean.

Rick wiped away the condensation on the passenger's side window. He gazed out at the flat horizon through the rain-blurred glass and marveled at how dark it was. Sea and the sky met in pitch black. Far off in the Atlantic Ocean, a bolt of lightning streaked down and hit some unknown spot. The clouds were a lighter shade of gray overhead, with a slight tinge of sepia. It was like looking at a weathered black and white photograph taken a century before. Rick broke his silent reverie. "Pretty big storm, huh?"

Rusty grinned. "Folks at the weather bureau say it's gonna be the biggest storm of this century. The way it looks, it might turn into a hurricane!" Rusty appeared genuinely awed by this spectacular turn of Mother Nature.

Rick grinned back. "I've never been in a hurricane before."

Rusty kept his eyes on the road. "It's gonna be a big one all right. Just you wait."

Geez, doesn't this guy have anything else to say? Rick turned to the view and decided to steer the subject away from the storm. "So Rusty … how many people live here in Phillipsport?"

Rusty's eyes lit up, excited. "Well … let's see …" His brow knitted as the unoiled wheels of thought turned in his brainpan.

"Last week Mrs. Twain had twins ... and Mr. Lewis' brother-in-law is staying with them till April ..."

"Yeah ..." Rick coaxed him along. Rusty appeared to be in deep concentration. Rick waited, watching the deputy as he tallied up the population of Phillipsport in his head. Rick stifled an impending giggle. He was amazed that they let this guy carry a gun. His eyes dropped to the .38 that was strapped to Rusty's gun belt.

Finally Rusty smiled and looked at Rick. "Five hundred and forty-seven!" His face beamed with pride. His eyes sparkled.

Rick smiled and nodded. "Does that include me?"

Deputy Rusty's brow knitted again as the mental wheels clicked another notch. It was amazing this guy even had a brain. After a moment's thought Rusty gave him the final count. "Five hundred and forty-eight!"

Rick laughed. Rusty looked confusedly at him, trying to figure out what was so funny.

Rick gazed back out the window and smiled. Five hundred and forty-eight people was a good number. He'd probably hardly even know they were around.

There were so few of them that there would probably be nobody to hang out with on Saturday nights.

As they drew closer to town Rick craned forward, peering through the pouring rain. The water sliding down the windshield painted everything an uneven shade of gray. The tiny, brick buildings reeked of antiquity. None of the structures looked like they were built after 1900. Everything was of a quaint, Victorian style that made him feel like he had just been transported to a different time zone—like the sixteenth century.

Rusty pulled off the main highway onto the Coast Highway. Five hundred yards to the right, the turbulent ocean slammed onto the beach a few hundred feet from the thoroughfare and the storefront. The streets that bypassed the Coast Highway were narrow, jammed with tiny houses, some of which appeared to have been chopped into apartments. Fords and Chevy pickup trucks lined the street with cars and station wagons. There were few pedestrians out in this weather. Most of them were probably holed up in their ancient tenements in front of a roaring fire.

Rick felt like leaping out of the car and running through the rain-soaked streets, soaking up the history and becoming engraved in its essence. He could hardly wait to see the place he was staying at. "This is great," Rick whispered. He couldn't tear his eyes from the scene. The white, clapboard structures and old brick buildings were just too beautiful.

Rusty grinned and nodded. "Yep! But you ain't seen nothing yet. The best part's up ahead." He raised his chin and smirked at some unknown secret.

Rick grinned with him and wondered what could be better than this lovely little sea town with its Victorian style and character.

Dr. Jorgensen's home office was tucked on a small side street. The neighborhood was quaint, with huge trees stretching their branches over the street. Halloween decorations in the form of jack-o-lanterns and tacked up Universal movie monsters adorned the windows of every other house. Going inside Dr. Jorgensen's office reminded Rick of the family practitioner he went to as a child; the living room was now the waiting room, while the kitchen was the receptionist area and the bedrooms served as the examining rooms. Plastic jack-o-lanterns were placed strategically, their hollowed heads filled with paper wrapped sugary sweets for the younger patients. Paper skeletons decorated the receptionist area. Dr. Jorgensen emerged from the reception area with a friendly smile on his face. He welcomed Rick with the same genuine eagerness and kindness his doctor from childhood days had. Dr. Jorgensen looked to be in his early sixties. His features were kind, smoothly lined, his hair white and thick. His eyes were sea blue and danced with glee. It brought Rick to instant relaxation. He also looked ready to do business.

Dr. Jorgensen peered at Rick closely. "Rusty radioed ahead and said you had been in an accident. From the looks of that scalp wound, it looks like you have, too. Let's get you in back here and have a look at ya."

Once in the examining room, Dr. Jorgensen fussed over the superficial scalp wound. "Pretty nasty lump on the noggin you got there. You feel dizzy?"

Rick shook his head.

"He was kinda dazed when I came upon him," Rusty said. He had followed physician and patient to one of the rear examining rooms. "Like he was in a light shock." His face was still beaming, as if he was proud of himself for finding Rick. He probably thought he'd saved Rick's life.

After the scalp wound was cleaned, dressed and bandaged, Dr. Jorgensen went through the preliminaries. He shined a penlight in Rick's eyes, examining the pupils intently. He clicked the light off and leaned back. "Pupils appear normal. Not dilated." He held up his hand in front of Rick, four fingers standing up. "How many fingers do I got up?"

"Four."

He flashed his forefinger up. "How many now?"

"One."

"And now?" Peace sign.

"Two."

Dr. Jorgensen leaned forward, his features still showing concern, yet relaxing a bit. "You seeing double at all?"

"No."

"Lose consciousness at all?"

"No … I mean, I was kinda dazed for a minute." Rick hoped that his injury wasn't that serious, and the treble in his voice reflected that. "I never lost consciousness, but I did kind of zone out for a while."

"You feel sick to your stomach?"

"No."

Dr. Jorgensen ran Rick through a thorough examination. "Were you wearing a seat belt?" he asked, leaning forward as Rick lay down on the examining table at the physician's instructions. Rick had taken off his shirt minutes earlier at the doctors' instructions and after visually inspecting him, the physician now began prodding and probing his trunk with gentle fingers.

"Yes."

"Feel bruised anywhere?"

"A little sore in places."

"Here?" Dr. Jorgensen pressed slightly on Rick's right side and Rick winced.

"Yeah."

"And here?" Now he pressed down slightly below Rick's right nipple.

"Ah! Yeah." Rick winced again.

Dr. Jorgensen continued along the line that the lateral seat belt would have pressed against Rick's body, holding him in his seat as he was thrown forward from the accident. Rick felt pain all the way up his chest to the base of his left shoulder. Dr. Jorgensen continued his probing examination along Rick's stomach and lower abdomen, asking if there was any pain. There wasn't.

Dr. Jorgensen motioned for Rick to sit back up and then he examined his back. He ran his hands along the back of Rick's neck, asking Rick if there were any areas that hurt. There weren't. He told Rick to get up and follow him into the examining room across the hall and Rick did. The room was equipped with X-ray equipment and once those were taken, Dr. Jorgensen told him to put his shirt back on. "I'm going to take a look at these," he said, holding up the X-ray film in his hands, "just to make sure, and then I'll be right back. You can wait in the other examining room if you want."

They went to the first examining room where Rick had left his jacket and five minutes later Dr. Jorgensen came back out, smiling broadly. "You seem to be okay, so I guess your skull isn't as bashed as you thought it was. No broken bones, no sign of internal injuries. The muscles along your chest and shoulder will get pretty sore, though. You got off pretty lucky there, partner. Just to be on the safe side, though, I'm going to prescribe a mild painkiller that contains a sedative. It'll make you drowsy, but it'll help your body cope with the shock to its system. You may not be feeling it now, but come morning your body is going to wake up feeling like it just went through the ringer. You can pick it up at Shelby's Drug Store." He clapped Rusty on his broad shoulders. "This big lug here will be more than happy to drive you over."

"Of course I will. My favorite author can go anywhere he wants to!" Rusty rose and zipped up his raincoat.

Dr. Jorgensen turned to Rick with raised eyebrows. "Author, huh? Novels?"

Rick nodded, trying hard not to blush. "Horror novels."

Dr. Jorgensen chuckled. "Well I'll be. That's just great. I don't read much horror myself, but I do like science fiction."

"Oh, Rick is the best," Rusty said, as they walked down the hall to the waiting room. Dr. Jorgensen darted behind the reception area and scribbled out Rick's prescription while Rusty rattled on. "He's so good he blows Stephen King away. I've read all four of his books."

"Whoa, wait a minute Rusty," Rick chuckled, putting his jacket on. "Thanks for the praise and all, but Stephen King I ain't."

"Rusty told me that you went down into a ditch off Highway 1," the doctor said as he scribbled the prescription. "What happened?"

Rick turned to the doctor, putting on his jacket and wincing slightly. He was getting sore already. "I went down into a ditch trying to avoid hitting something in the road."

"What was in the road? Animal?"

In all the excitement he had almost forgotten the claw. Rick reached into his jacket pocket and pulled it out. Dr. Jorgensen's eyes widened behind his wire-framed glasses at the sight of it. "My God!"

"Ever see anything like this around these parts?" Rick asked. His heart quickened in beat slightly at the sight of Dr. Jorgensen's reaction to the claw.

"Never," Dr. Jorgensen said. He gestured at the claw. "May I?"

Rick handed it over. "Be my guest."

Dr. Jorgensen took the claw in his hands and examined it, turning it this way and that. He moved his fingers along its edges and probed along the section of meat that hung in strips from the joint where it had been ripped off the creature's body. He looked up at Rick. "Mind if I wrap this up and put it in my freezer? I have a friend at the University of Maine's Biology department who would probably love to take a look at this, if it's okay to you."

"By all means, please do," Rick said.

"What do you think it is?" Rusty asked. He had been

standing quietly the whole time and was just as awed by the claw as Dr. Jorgensen.

"Don't know for sure," Dr. Jorgensen said as he examined it, turning it over in his hands the way a small boy will examine a bug or a lizard he has found while playing. "I've certainly never heard or seen a crustacean of this size before in these parts." He marveled at the claw for another minute, then set it down on the counter.

He wiped his hands on a paper towel and turned his attention back to the task at hand. He slipped the prescription over the counter. "Take two of these tonight when you get home. Depending how you feel tomorrow morning, you might want to take one before each meal. Don't exceed five in one day. You staying in town for a while?"

"I'm writing my next book here."

"Ah." He raised his eyebrows in interest. "Not about us, I hope." He grinned.

Rick laughed. "Not sure yet."

"Well, since you're going to be local and all, I'll know where to find you when I find out about our friend here." He indicated the claw on the table. "As far as the prescription or anything else, if you have any problems come and see me."

Rick pocketed the prescription "Thanks, Dr. Jorgensen."

"Call me Glen."

Rick smiled. "Thanks, Glen."

"Don't mention it." Glen's blue eyes twinkled merrily. "And I'll be looking out for one of your books in the next few days. I can probably use some good old-fashioned horror novel to get me in the Halloween spirit."

"Try *Night of the Devil*," Rusty said at the door. He opened up the umbrella against the pouring rain. "It's great."

"I will." Glen waved from the counter. "Take care, you two."

"Thanks again," Rick said, and then they were heading back out into the rain into Rusty's squad car.

Once in the car, Rusty wasted no time in slipping back into his jostling, happy-go-lucky demeanor. "We'll get you over to Shelby's Drug Store in a jiffy! This is where the best part comes!" Rusty grinned as they left Glen Jorgensen's. The rain had turned to a steady drizzle now.

"What do you mean?" Rick asked.

"What I told you about before." Rusty started the car and pulled away from the curb. "The best part of town is where we're headed!"

"The best part of town is the drugstore?" It was hard to believe that the drugstore could be the hotspot of Phillipsport.

"It's where the drugstore is *at*!" Rusty grinned. His voiced cracked with excitement. "You'll see."

Rusty swerved the patrol car to the left and headed farther inland. Rick looked over his shoulder and out the back window at the receding buildings. He turned his head back to the front and saw what was rapidly approaching. His jaw dropped. He couldn't believe what he was seeing.

Rusty noticed his expression and grinned wider. "Ain't she a beauty?"

Rick's soul crumpled up and blew away.

They were approaching a tan colored myriad of stores with glittering signs and slick banner advertisements. It was the ugliest excuse for a shopping mall he'd ever seen. A huge yellow and pink sign had been erected in the main driveway.

SEASIDE PLAZA
30 Shops for your convenience!
We speak tourist!!!

"God no!" In the middle of history and character there was *this*.

Rusty slowed the car down and looked up at the plastic totem-like sign that advertised the mall. Rusty looked up at it as if it was the shroud of Turin. Rusty's eyes seemed to mist up. "They just opened a frozen yogurt store last week."

Rick sank into his seat as Rusty drove into a parking lot that would probably accommodate more cars than the entire population of Phillipsport. The shopping center was grouped around a K-mart and Lucky Supermarket. Those were accompanied by a Wherehouse CD & Tape store, Blockbuster video, Marshall's, Pizza Hut, and a Subway Sandwich shop.

There was also a Barnes and Noble bookstore. His books were probably being sold there to the vast Phillipsport masses.

"Yes, sir," Rusty said. He was still beaming. "Anything you'd ever want is right here in this center. In fact, I think you could be born, raise a family and die right in this parking lot and never have to leave for anything."

Rick shook his head and grinned. He had never heard anybody get so excited about a shopping mall before.

Rusty nodded as they pulled into the parking lot. "Okay. Shelby's Drug Store is in this mall. Everybody in town usually hangs out here. Well, here and at the Denny's over on Pine Road." Rusty pulled into a slot across the way from Shelby's Drug Store. Rick noticed the items advertised in the windows and Rusty killed the engine.

Rick looked out at the drug store and snickered. It was decorated with pumpkins, black cats, and witches. "Denny's, huh? Home of the Grand Slam Breakfast."

Rusty's eyes lit up. "You like them, too? Oh boy, that's great! My favorite author likes the same food I do."

Rick rolled his eyes at Rusty's excitement as they exited the vehicle.

5

The drug store wasn't as bad as the rest of the mall looked. It had obviously been built in the fifties and had retained its inner design of the old-fashioned drug stores that served milkshakes and fries for the Fonzies and Richies of that era. The mall was brand spanking new; the stucco walls still looked virgin, unmarred by the weather of time and decay. Shelby's Drug Store contained a small coffee shop on the left, complete with white-and-gold-flecked Formica tabletops and sunburst decorations. The booths and most of the seats at the counter were taken up with what Rick assumed were locals. Very few appeared to be under fifty, and they all had one thing in common. They were looking at Rick as if he'd just stepped off a spaceship.

Rick felt himself grow small, as if he was shrinking inside. Deputy Rusty waved to a group of men milling around the counter and led Rick through the coffee shop. A thousand eyes followed him as he walked through the room. *How dare you walk in here looking like* that, *boy! What the hell's th'matter with you?*

Deputy Rusty stopped and turned to Rick. "Why don't you have a seat. I'm gonna go in the drugstore and find Lee. Have yourself some coffee."

"Okay." Rick retreated back into the coffee shop and slid onto a stool at the end of the counter. He could still feel the unmistakable sense of eyes lighting on him and turning away as the men in the room resumed conversation. They were still keeping an eye on him, though. After all, he wasn't from around these parts.

A pretty blonde girl in a pink waitress uniform approached him from behind the counter. She smiled warmly at him. "What can I get you?"

Rick ordered coffee and the waitress served it pronto. "Cream and sugar?" She looked at him shyly. Her hair fell in blonde ringlets over her forehead and down her shoulders. Her eyes were as blue as the sea, her dimpled face punctuated by a smiling mouth and a cute nose. Her body didn't look that bad beneath the waitress uniform; her skirt was mid-thigh length, showing off tanned, muscular-yet-shapely legs. She reminded Rick of Alicia Silverstone; she had the same All-American girl looks. She was blonde, young, cute, but did not give the impression that she was hot-to-trot or flirtatious. When she turned to pick up an order off the counter, Rick couldn't resist a peek at her rear. Nice. Rick sipped at his coffee. It was nice and hot. Just the way he liked it. The waitress came back and flashed him a big smile. "You new around here?"

Rick nodded, grinning. "Just came in town."

"I'm Melissa Peterson. But some folks around here call me Missy." She held out her hand and Rick took it.

"Rick Sychek. Nice to meet you."

"Likewise."

"What brings you to town?"

"I'm working on a book," Rick began. "I'm a writer and ..." And the story came out, an abridged version of how he came to decide to settle in Phillipsport for the winter for his new book. Melissa seemed very interested and when he was finished she smiled.

"That sounds great. I'm a Journalism major at Bridgton Community College. Looks like now there'll be somebody in town I'll have something in common with."

"Absolutely." Rick took a sip of his coffee.

Melissa noticed a customer beckoning to her from the rear of the coffee shop. "Duty calls," she said. She exited the counter and went over to tend to her duties. Rick settled on the counter, drinking his coffee and wondering how much of the day was left that was salvageable to do something constructive.

His thoughts were broken by the arrival of Rusty and

an older, gray-haired gentleman dressed in a red and blue plaid shirt and blue jeans. Rusty patted Rick on the back as he approached the counter. "Rick. This here's Lee Shelby, the owner of Shelby's Drug Store. Lee, this here's Rick."

A round of *pleased to meet ya's* was traded and Lee Shelby scratched his head and scowled. "Rusty tells me that you went down into a ditch off Highway 1. Says you swerved in the road to avoid hitting something."

Rick nodded, suddenly remembering the giant crab-like thing in the road. He took another sip of coffee. "Yeah. It was just right there and I didn't know what it was. I tried to avoid hitting it and lost control."

Lee peered at him curiously. "Looks like you got a bump on the head. Doc Jorgensen take care of you?"

Rick nodded. "It was nothing serious. Just a scalp wound."

"Doug is filling your prescription order," Lee said. He clapped Rick on the back and grinned. "I know it's a helluva welcome to town, crashing into Little Feet and all, but I really do hope your first experience in town doesn't change your mind about staying."

"Accidents happen." Rick shrugged matter-of-factly. "I'm just glad I made it to town in one piece."

Lee and Rusty chuckled, prompting a grin to emerge from Rick's face. "Welcome to Phillipsport, son," Lee said. His grin was wide and genuine. He was truly glad that Rick was new in town.

Rusty took a seat at the counter next to Rick and Melissa came and took his order. Lee joined them from the other side of the counter and the three men chatted for a few minutes while Melissa tended to the other customers. Lee excused himself after a minute and went to attend to some other business. Rusty began talking with somebody in the booth closest to him; his back was turned to the counter, talking in his excited tone as Rick sat at the counter nursing his cup of coffee. Melissa came back and poured him another cup. Their eyes locked for the briefest instant, then she looked down at the counter. "You live around here?" Rick asked.

"I live in town," she said. She began wiping the counter idly with a wash rag.

J. F. Gonzalez

"Is this considered 'town'?"

She laughed. "Rusty sure considers this town," she said, stealing a quick glance at the deputy who was paying them no heed in his conversation with the men in the booth. "He loves it here."

"Yeah, it has all the comforts of a big city mall."

Melissa stopped wiping down the counter and leaned against it nonchalantly. Her eyes locked with his again, more firmly. "To answer your question, I live off Fir Street, which is off the main drag. That's the section the old timers refer to as 'in town.'"

"Which is ... ?"

"About five minutes from here."

"Ah."

"And you?"

"Don't know yet. I haven't even been to where I'm supposed to be settling in for the winter."

They were so involved in their conversation and their flirting with each other that they didn't notice the door to the drugstore opening, the new customer sauntering in. It wasn't until Melissa's eyes moved toward the newcomer and her expression changed from smiling and flirtatious to a look of dread—like a child who has just been discovered misbehaving and knows the consequences—that Rick realized somebody was approaching them.

The neighboring patrons continued on with their drinks, food, and conversation as the new man now sidled up next to Rick with a cold, cocky look. His steel gray eyes flicked from Rick to Melissa and back to Rick again. He was wearing a Highway Patrol uniform similar to Rusty's, but seemed to carry more of a demeanor of authority. His badge read SHERIFF.

Rusty turned at the approach of the newcomer and recognition flickered across his features. He clapped Rick on the back. "Sheriff Conklin, this here's Rick Sychek. Rick's a real famous writer and he's gonna be—"

While Rusty launched into his litany, Sheriff Conklin looked at Rick with stony features. Scrutinizing him.

"—staying in Phillipsport, and—"

"He's the one that wiped out on Highway 1." Not a question, but merely a statement of facts. Sheriff Conklin's voice was gritty. Rick felt the man's gray eyes light on him, marking him.

"Why, he sure did!" Rusty admitted this in a tone that was eager and jubilant. It was almost like Rusty was saying, *Well goddamn, he sure did! And isn't that just great!*

Sheriff Conklin snickered and shook his head. His eyes went from Melissa, who turned away, back to Rick. "Wiped out in a little patch of rain. What the hell were you doing, boy? Playing speed racer?"

"I—" Rick began.

"He weren't speedin', sir," Rusty said, grinning. "No sirree."

Sheriff Conklin acted like he hadn't heard Rusty. He leaned toward Rick, his features set in a perpetual scowl. "Not speedin, huh? Well, then, why'd you spin out, boy? Been drinkin?"

Rick opened his mouth to protest. He looked at Melissa who flashed him a brief smile of encouragement. Conklin caught the brief exchange and his features darkened. A pall of what appeared to be jealousy flickered briefly over his features and then was gone. His features became stony. He huffed. "Speedin' on Highway 1 in a rain storm is a misdemeanor offense. Not to mention crashing into the trees; Little Feet is five hundred years old and you done ruined her." He moved toward Rick. "I got a good mind to write you a ticket for that."

Rick opened his mouth to protest but Lee Shelby beat him to the punch. The owner of Shelby's drug store had heard the exchange and now he was stepping up to the counter. "You've got to be kidding! This kid was involved in an honest accident. He wasn't driving recklessly."

Conklin flashed Lee a smirk. "Did you investigate the scene?"

"No," Lee Shelby sputtered.

"Then keep out of this." Sheriff Conklin turned back to Rick. His features were unemotional. "As for you …"

Rick's heart had begun to beat fast at the mention of a ticket; it began to beat faster at the tone of the sheriff's voice. He had had run-ins with cops like Sheriff Conklin before. If you weren't a middle-of-the-road White Anglo Saxon Male

Protestant, cops like Sheriff Conklin would pull you over for anything, just for the chance to harass you in the hopes of making an arrest. It didn't matter that you didn't commit an infraction, what mattered was that you were either a long haired, drug snorting, hippie-commie scum, or you were an earring-wearing faggot who was a little bit too feminine, or you were black, or Oriental, or Mexican, or whatever. If you fit any of the above, you were subject to unnecessary search and seizures from officers like Sheriff Conklin. Rick had once had two previous run-ins in Philadelphia with cops like Conklin; one of them ended with Rick spending the night in jail for resisting arrest. The charges had been dropped later because there hadn't been any to begin with. The officer stopped him because he had long hair and surely he must be either carrying drugs, or was under their influence. Rick had protested and spent the night in jail.

Ever since that night Rick had thought about the situation and decided that should he find himself in a similar situation, he would handle it differently. He even rehearsed various scenarios in his mind. Now that Sheriff Conklin, the spitting image of the other two asshole cops that had harassed him for similar reasons, was in front of him just egging him on into a similar confrontation, he switched to this tactic effortlessly. His features softened. "Gee, Sheriff Conklin, but I'm really sorry about the accident. I'm even more sorry about the tree. If there's anything that I can do to help …" he shrugged his shoulders. "Anything I can do to help in the treatment of … Little Feet was the tree's name?"

Sheriff Conklin scowled at him. "That's right."

"Well if there's anything I can do to help in Little Feet's treatment, I'd be more than happy to do it." He swept a hand around the counter where Rusty, Lee Shelby and Melissa were gathered, watching the confrontation. "Everybody's been real helpful to me here, too, and I really appreciate everything that the fine people of your town have done to help."

Sheriff Conklin's scowl smoothed itself out. It looked forced. The lawman smiled and stood up. "No need to worry, son. Just wanted to rattle your cage. Make sure you weren't some good for nothing scum bag who was going to cut and run from his duty."

"No sir," Rick said, getting into the act wholeheartedly. "In fact, I'll be staying here in town, so I'd be more than happy to help with the tree."

Sheriff Conklin regarded him with those cold gray eyes. Rick met his gaze and didn't break it. Sheriff Conklin nodded at him. They had a mutual understanding. They had a great dislike for each other, but they weren't going to be uncivil about it. The sheriff turned to Rusty. "I want to see your report on this on my desk tomorrow morning."

"Yes, sir!" Rusty said.

Sheriff Conklin turned to Lee and nodded. He turned to Melissa and his gaze lingered on her a little longer, then he turned to Rick. He nodded, tipped his hat. "Good day, gentlemen." He turned and walked out of the drugstore, his boot heels clicking on the floor.

All eyes followed the sheriff as he stepped outside and climbed inside his cruiser. Rick turned to the others at the counter. Melissa wiped glasses behind the counter, not meeting his gaze. Lee looked reflectively at him. "Well, that there is your first encounter with our asshole sheriff."

Rick laughed. Melissa looked up and cracked a smile. It seemed to break the tension. Rusty grinned at them as he turned back to his conversation at the booth nearby. Lee clapped Rick on the shoulder. "Trust me, we're not all backwoods rednecks."

A guy that looked like a pulp logger who had been seated at the booth closest to the counter sidled up to Rick, eager to compare notes. His chubby face was as red as a fire hydrant. He looked like he was more pissed off about the incident than Rick. "Listen guy, don't worry about Roy Conklin. I'll tell you all about him. Guy's a prick. One day when I was driving down York Road ..."

Lee patted Rick on the shoulder as he turned and walked behind the counter to resume his duties. "Welcome to Phillipsport, son."

Melissa offered to drive him home after he had four cups of coffee and a slice of apple pie with vanilla ice cream. Rusty had stuck around and made small talk. Lee breezed in and out, stopping occasionally to crack a joke. Rick smiled and took it all in good-naturedly. Shortly after the incident with Sheriff Roy Conklin, he had appeared relieved. She smiled at him encouragingly, hoping she could get a moment alone with him so she could tell him the scoop about Phillipsport's sheriff, but Gary Richards was already chewing Rick's ear off. By the time she poured his third cup of coffee he appeared to be doing better. By his fourth he was just fine.

Melissa joined Rick at the counter after her shift for a cup of coffee. During her shift, his prescription had been filled and now he sat with the bag of painkillers on the counter, listening politely to Gary as he carried on a one-sided conversation with Rick. Melissa slid into the stool on Rick's left and that seemed to save him.

He smiled politely at Gary and turned to her. "Hi," he said. His features said, *please make that guy stop.*

He seemed grateful for the attention. She asked him about his writing and he started talking about his book.

It sounded very interesting and after a moment, Gary grew restless. He had tried to hang onto the new shift in the conversation but Gary's idea of entertainment was a night at the local tavern.

Melissa got the idea that while Rick could probably party with the best of them, he would also be content to spend an evening reading an old book.

After a few minutes Gary nodded at Rick. "See you around, man."

Rick turned and offered his hand. "Of course. And thanks for the info." They shook hands and Gary went off to rejoin his friends.

Rick turned back to Melissa. "Now where were we?"

"You were telling me about your book."

"That's right." He picked up where he left off, telling her a little about himself, about his writing, why he had moved to Phillipsport. He told her about his drive to Phillipsport and his accident. "Does this area have really big crabs and lobsters?" he asked her.

Melissa had never really paid much attention to crabs and lobsters unless they were on the menu of a nice restaurant. She shrugged. "I don't have the foggiest idea. Why?"

Rick shrugged, as if dismissing it. "Just wondered." He quickly got past that issue, and related his meeting with Deputy Rusty Hanks, which ended with him being here at Shelby's Drug Store.

She smiled and divulged some vital stats on herself as well. She lived in Phillipsport with her grandmother and attended a community college in the larger town of Bridgton, some ten miles north. She was a Journalism major, with a minor in English Literature. She had a few friends that she hung out with from school but spent a large portion of her time at school, working at the drugstore, studying, or taking in movies at the local theater with her grandmother. Small-town life. Melissa finished her coffee and glanced at her watch. It was almost 4:00 p.m. "I gotta get going. Listen, I can drive you home—"

"I'd appreciate that," Rick said, his features brightening. Melissa smiled back and helped him gather his belongings. Rusty had offered him a ride home, but Rick had declined almost absentmindedly. He'd been telling Melissa about his work and Rusty traded a nodding glance at Melissa before heading back out to duty. Rick grabbed his jacket and followed Melissa out to her car, a 1988 Subaru Wagon. He stowed his belongings in the back and slid into the passenger side.

He relaxed even further as she pulled out of the parking lot and drove toward Carl's garage to pick up his things from his car. "How are you feeling?" Melissa asked him.

"Fine," Rick said. "My head's okay, if that's what you mean."

"I'm glad your head's fine, but that's not what I meant," Melissa said, keeping her eyes on the road as she talked. "I was asking if you were okay after what happened a little while ago back there."

Rick scowled slightly, the memory of Conklin flickering to the surface. "That asshole was just itching for a confrontation, wasn't he?"

"I could see it coming the minute he walked in," Melissa said. "Roy Conklin has been doing stuff like that to people for years."

"Why do people put up with it?"

"Most of the older citizens of town are cut from the same mold: good old boy, narrow-minded racist bigot. They're the ones that keep voting him back into office. He does do a lot of good for the community. We haven't had a murder in God knows how long. I've been living here most of my life and I don't remember hearing anything about murders in Phillipsport. The most that happens out here is the occasional bar fight on Saturday night. Some of the people here don't seem to mind what Conklin does, just so long as he protects their small-town standard of living and keeps out big city influences." She glanced at Rick. "Which is what he and most of the people of this town are going to consider you."

"Lee Shelby and Rusty seemed pretty nice," Rick retorted.

Melissa smiled. "Lee is great. He's definitely a man who doesn't go with the status quo of this town. And he was right about one thing; not all of us are backwoods rednecks."

"You included, I would hope?"

Melissa stole a glance at him and saw that he was grinning. A jokester. She laughed. "I'm far from it. I hate rednecks although I have to admit I have dated a few of them."

"I haven't been too proud of some of the women I've dated before myself."

Melissa swallowed the lump that had risen in her throat and decided to go ahead and confess right now. What could she lose? "I've got to admit that I'm ashamed of the fact that I dated Roy Conklin briefly."

"Really?" His tone of voice suggested that perhaps he had been expecting this, but that he was feigning surprise.

She tried to diffuse the situation with a sheepish smile. "Yeah, I know. Stupid thing to do. I had just broken up a long term relationship and he seemed charming to me. He also reminded me of my father at first. My father had been a cop." She bit back what was going to spill forth next. *He and my mother were killed in an accident.* But she didn't want to go down that route. That could come later. "Anyway I went out with him for three months and I saw the kind of person he was pretty quick. He ... kind of fell for me and I broke it off with him when he started getting too serious. He's been pissed at me ever since."

"How long has this been?"

"About nine months."

"Great! Seeing us talking back there at the counter probably made him jealous."

Melissa was silent. Those were her thoughts exactly.

"Has he ever harassed any other guys you've gone out with?"

Melissa shook her head. "Most of the guys I date are from other towns, guys I meet at school. I don't really like any of the guys in Phillipsport. They're all pretty dense, except for Jack who owns the comic book store out on the pier and he's not my type."

"There's a comic book store in town?"

"Yeah. It's right on the pier." She stopped talking and checked for traffic as Carl's garage was approaching on their left. There was no oncoming traffic, so she made a left and pulled into the garage where his car was and waited while he got his stuff. She helped him load it into the trunk and back seat of her own car, and then they were off again.

Rick gave her the address to the house he was staying at and they made the rest of the trip in silence. He stared out the passenger window as the beauty of nature whipped around them—the tall trees, the thick brush growing everywhere. The rain had stopped briefly, leaving everything rich, green, and dripping.

They were on Highway 1 again, and now Melissa made the turn that Rick would have made had he not spun out five miles back. This road led inward through a thicket of woods. Another turn led down a smaller road and then there was the house, sitting on the right in a small clearing. The rear of the place seemed to overlook the town of Phillipsport and the Atlantic Ocean from a low hill.

Melissa pulled into the driveway and stopped the car. Rick scrambled out and jogged up to the porch and tried the door with the key. It opened effortlessly. He turned back to the car, grinning at Melissa as she opened the trunk and hoisted the first of Rick's belongings out onto the driveway. "This place looks way cool!"

Melissa smiled at his vocal enthusiasms as they moved his stuff into the living room. The minute all his stuff was stowed on the living room floor, he bounded toward the massive windows that opened out onto the back deck. Melissa followed him, a shy smile on her face.

The view from the back deck was wonderful. Sloping down the hill below the deck stretched fifty yards of lush green grass. Melissa followed him inside and was surprised at the house. It was bigger than she expected it to be; she thought it was going to be a simple two-bedroom cottage and this was more like a regular three bedroom house.

Rick turned toward Melissa, excitement on his face. "This is better than I thought it would be."

Melissa smiled. "I'm glad."

"Want to come see the rest of it with me?" Rick was already starting for the door that led to the deck.

"I don't think so, Rick." Melissa said, hesitantly. She was already regretting telling him she'd dated Sheriff Conklin and was fearing that he was only being nice to her now because he was just going through the motions, waiting for her to leave. After all, *she* was the reason Conklin had treated him so shitty. *Stop it,* she told herself. *You can't blame yourself for everything.* But she still had to go. She had an exam to study for the next afternoon. "I've really got to get going."

Rick stopped and turned toward her. He looked like he had just gotten bad news from home. "Oh, I was hoping we could have dinner or something. Are you sure?"

Melissa nodded, a flutter of excitement fluttering through her. *See, dummy! He knows it's not your fault that Sheriff Conklin is a prick.* But still, as much as she would have loved to have dinner with Rick and talk to him, she had prior commitments. "Yeah. I've got studying to do for a final, and I've got to work early tomorrow morning."

"Oh. Okay." He accepted her decline just fine.

Melissa followed him into the kitchen. She pulled out a note pad and pen from her purse and scribbled her number on it. She handed it to Rick, smiling. "Call me sometime, and we'll get together. A friend at school is throwing a Halloween party next week. Maybe you'll—"

"I'd love to." Rick grinned.

"Great!" That was better, but she still felt awkward. "Listen," she said, as they walked out to her car. "I still feel bad about what happened back at Shelby's." She stopped and turned to him, concerned. "Roy Conklin probably would have eventually gotten around to harassing you even if I wasn't there today, but not everybody in Phillipsport is like him. Like I said, there's Jack over at the comic shop, Janice Harrelson and her son Bobby, a few others in town. You'll meet them eventually and I think you'll like them."

"Well if they're anything like you, I think I will," Rick said.

They promised to get together in a few days once Rick had settled in and do dinner and a night on the town. She told him to call her if he needed anything. Rick promised he would, and then she was off. She backed the car out of the driveway and turned to wave at Rick before she headed down the road, which led to Highway 1. She glanced up briefly in the rearview mirror as she piloted the car down the road. She saw Rick receding in the distance, watching her drive off from the porch of his house. A moment later he was out of the picture.

Melissa sighed as she headed down Highway 1 toward home. She wished the more negative elements of today hadn't happened, but she was glad she met Rick. She sensed a kindred soul in him and welcomed it. After living in a small town like Phillipsport all your life it was hard to find somebody in town who had interests other than Monday Night Football, deer hunting, deep sea fishing, or drinking at Bud's Tavern on Highway 1. Jack Ripley, who owned Ripp It Up Comics, was one, and Janice Harrelson was another. But they were so much older than her. She had no idea how old Janice was; Janice used to baby-sit her and when you were little everybody seemed to be old, but now that Melissa was an adult now herself at the ripe old age of twenty-two, she assumed Janice was in her mid to late thirties. Jack on the hand had to be much older—at least forty-five. She got the impression that Rick was in his early thirties, but with a youthful spirit in him. He just *seemed* younger; he liked the same kind of music she liked, and was hip to what was currently happening, and that was refreshing. Not that Jack and Janice were fuddy-duddys, but if a band like, say, Hole came into town, Melissa was pretty much on her own. Jack and Janice were both rock and rollers, but Hole just wasn't within their realm.

The only other person who might possibly be along the same wavelength with Melissa was Stacy Robinson, who was a year older than her and who lived at the other end of town. Stacy was smart, could carry a conversation about things other than farming and football, and she read *books*, not the kind of glitz trash most women in town read. The only thing wrong with Stacy was that she was a fucking waste case who smoked too much pot, drank excessively and had a reputation for taking on five guys at once in bed. The one time she and Stacy had gone out, Stacy wound up going home with some druggie punk. Melissa had been hit on plenty of times herself that night, but Stacy pulling the disappearing act to do the bump and grind with the nameless punk when it was supposed to be their night to hang out together and have some fun had taken the wind out of her sails. She'd gone home alone.

And that was never *any* fun.

Melissa drove home and thought about Rick.

Two miles up the coast from the Phillipsport pier rose the monolithic twin peaks of the GE Power Plant. This facility powered Phillipsport County. It sat roughly two hundred yards from the beach and was bordered by a high chain-link fence. The administrative building was two stories and housed twenty-five employees. The generators and their facilities employed twelve people, twenty-four hours a day. At any given moment there were usually no more than twenty people at the facility. The office staff worked nine to five hours, leaving the swing and graveyard techs to themselves.

This evening, the employee parking lot of the GE Facility was a quarter full. The lot was easily accessible by Highway 1, and the gate had been left open. It was normally accessed by a coded card that was inserted in a slot, which opened the gate— only tonight, that mechanism was on the fritz, which resulted in the security department leaving the gate open. One never had to worry about crime this far out in the boondocks.

The cameras mounted at strategic points along the perimeter of the power plant tracked everything. They were viewed in a small room with seven video monitors set along a bank of security equipment. There were nine guards that rotated shifts and schedules, one guard on each shift. Presently the swing-shift guard was sitting on the porcelain reading chair engaged in a tattered paperback copy of The House on the Borderland and a joint of some primo Acapulco Gold.

The monitors showed everything in stark black and white. There wasn't a soul on the grounds of the GE Plant.

The video screens caught the first wave of crab monsters as they marched past the open gates into the parking lot. By the time the guard rose from his alternate work activities, the creatures had scampered out of reach of the cameras and into the building itself.

6

How the fuck am I going to do this?

Kirk Fischer sat on the cold, sandy beach sipping on a long-necked bottle of Budweiser. The wind had picked up considerably since he came out to the beach two hours ago, and Kirk shivered. He had told his live-in girlfriend Stacy Robinson to meet him here at the beach at two. It was now closing in on four. Late again.

Kirk took a long pull on the bottle of Bud and sighed. He'd taken a vacation day from his job as a forklift driver at the mill. He needed some time to think before his big pow-wow with Stacy. They had to talk. Their relationship had gone from weird to worse in the three months they'd been living together. And while Stacy's behavior tended to cause flickers of concern from time to time, it had descended to downright scary. Up at noon with a toke from her trusty water bong and a couple of beers, and then a hit of acid around three followed by more beers and some more hits off the bong. Her choice of herb was on the exquisite side; sensimilla and hash imported from Acapulco. She sat around the house all day reading science-fiction paperbacks and watching the latest features courtesy of the local Blockbuster Video outlet. Sometimes the mainstream movies were replaced with a few porn titles. He came home from work around five-thirty and they would hang out, watch movies, make love (or fuck, depending on the mood), ingest more herbal and alcoholic vices and keep repeating the process. She drifted to sleep in a stoned stupor. She woke around ten long after he left for work to start the whole process over. It was her daily existence.

Kirk drank his beer and threw stones into the ocean. The wind picked up slightly, lifting his collar-length black hair. He lit a cigarette with a shaky hand and inhaled. He'd gone over the past three months in his mind, picking it apart. Trying to make sense of it. After the third time he'd firmly convinced himself that he wasn't to blame for the way she was behaving. She had been fucked up long before Kirk had ever met her.

He'd met her at the Eastwood Mall near Bangor in a bookstore. He'd been perusing the Science Fiction section where she was browsing. She'd been dressed in low-slung blue jeans, a tattered T-shirt that showed a hint of her flat, creamy belly, and black boots. Her hair had been dyed a deep magenta. It was obvious the way her t-shirt jiggled that she wasn't wearing a bra. Their eyes lit on each other and firecrackers exploded. Kirk felt that familiar stirring in his groin immediately. Her eyes sparkled with inviting lust. They made small talk. Introduced themselves. Stacy broke the ice a moment later by saying she wanted to go out with him.

They went to a bar down on Circle Boulevard and had a few beers. It was apparent early on in the evening that they wouldn't be spending much time in the bar. They found a nice, quiet booth, and Stacy slid in beside him. They talked, hips barely touching. Kirk's arm goose-fleshed every time Stacy touched him lightly. She read the response and a moment later she kissed him. It was impossible to break away from her; her kiss seemed to draw him into another world, a world of pleasure and intoxication. His lust swelled and their kissing grew more passionate. Their hands roamed over their bodies, caressing, fondling. His hands wound up under her T-shirt, his fingers flicking over her nipples, making them hard.

And then a light bulb went off in his head. *If we don't get to a bed real soon, we'll explode. Or wind up fucking our brains out here in this booth.* He broke away from her, panting. "Let's go someplace more private."

They couldn't go to his place. He still lived with his parents, but he wasn't going to tell her that. They walked out to the parking lot hand in hand. She told him to follow her to her place. Kirk followed her black Trans-Am south with a rigid hard-on, just waiting for the moment. A part of his mind twitched nervously. He had never had a woman come on to him so strong in a public place. It was too unreal. She'd been like a bitch in heat, ready to take him right then and there. That had made him hesitate from following through, but his little head ruled out any chance of morality overruling his instincts. He was too horny to be sensible.

They arrived at her place in Phillipsport, some sixty miles northwest of Eastwood. Fucked like jackrabbits. Slept till noon.

And God, it was the best sex he'd ever had. Stacy fucked him with such animal fury that he thought she was going to pull his dick off. Her energy seemed boundless. She never grew tired, and she pushed them through the night in position after position, orgasm after orgasm, until they finally collapsed into each other's arms and exhaustion overtook them.

He'd spent the weekend at her place, in bed, falling for her.

The house was hers. She bought it with the first installment of the inheritance money she'd received upon her mother's death. Car accident. Stacy had been seventeen. There had been a fight. Harsh words. Stacy always had to have the last word in an argument and she made sure her mother got it.

It drove her mother outside and into the car where she peeled away with the fury of squealing tires and burning rubber. She never came back.

Now nearly five years later Stacy still blamed herself for her mother's death. Always would. If it wasn't for her, mother wouldn't have gone storming out of the house in anger. Would have paid more attention to her driving. Would still be alive.

Kirk had listened to her that weekend and tried to pry her out of her self-pitying state. Accidents happen. No reason to beat yourself up over something that not only wasn't your fault, but had happened five years before. None of what he said seemed to have any effect on her. Eventually she'd begin sucking his dick again and all thoughts of mother and her accident went out the window as they began another round of lovemaking.

She told him she loved him that weekend. She said it with conviction, tears streaming from her hazel eyes. The crackling of her voice supported her conviction. The energy and emotion pouring off her was more than enough to convince him. He believed her.

He moved in the next weekend.

Life went on for the next few months. Kirk still had his job at Plummer's Mill, which was a good twenty miles away. Stacy had her house, her Trans-Am, her money, and her time. She was expecting another insurance payment in the summer, but with the way she was spending it now it wasn't going to last long in the future. Next to the lavish gifts she bought Kirk, she spent a good deal of it on escaping from the memories of mother's accident via herbal, alcoholic, and chemical vacations.

Kirk dragged on the cigarette until it was down to the butt. He stubbed it out on the sand and drew his knees up to his chest. Goddamn, but it was cold out here.

At first he didn't mind the drugs. He used pot recreationally and he especially loved getting stoned before they made love. With Stacy it was electrified twofold. They fit each other's bodies snugly. Sex with her was so fucking incredible that he felt like he could die making love to her.

It was most likely the intoxication of her sexual prowess that blinded him for the first three months. The mental part of their relationship that had always been so absent began to make its presence known gradually, until it began overpowering him within the last few days. Little by little, her mental aberrations picked at his brain until he paused and took a real good look at the woman he had moved in with. The woman he told the guys down at the mill that he loved.

Everyday … waking up at noon … the pot … the booze … afternoon soaps … hanging out at Jack's Sugar Shack on Highway 98 some ten miles north, which was the area's lone adult video store (why hang out at a place frequented by men who were looking for a quick release of lust unless she was providing it?) … a tab of acid every couple of days … more pot … sporadic shopping splurges … more pot … heavy sex (the more time passed, the more he suspected that he wasn't the only guy playing hide the salami with her) … and then on to the next day to do the whole thing over again. It was at that point Kirk realized that Stacy was a major nut case.

Kirk sighed and pulled the last long necked Bud out of the bag. He twisted off the cap and drank deep. Goddamn, what a fucking mess. He loved her, and wanted to help her. She needed counseling, AA, psychiatric treatment, rehab, Jesus Christ—anything! She was slowly spiraling into her sea of misery and if he didn't pull her out, she'd drown in it. He needed to get her away from this pissant little town, which was where the source of her pain lay. Make a better life for both of them.

Get her away from her broken past.

A shuffling sound approaching his backside spurned him to look over his shoulder. Stacy was approaching him from the parking lot, a weathered smile on her face. Her magenta hair blew in her face, which was touched up lightly with makeup. Kirk's heart broke when he saw her. She was so beautiful she didn't need makeup. "Hi, baby." Her voice was soft, childlike.

Kirk rose and they embraced. Stacy huddled into him, her check pressed into the leather of his jacket. He stroked her hair, kissed the top of her forehead. She tilted her face up to his and they kissed. He broke it before it could get any further.

"Stacy, we need to talk," Kirk said. He turned and walked away, his back to her. He could sense her behind him, her demeanor becoming confused but knowing what was coming. He turned back to face her, doing his best to keep his feature's stern, yet gentle. Understanding.

Loving.

"What do we need to talk about?" Stacy asked. Her voice lowered to a shaky whisper.

"Several things." Kirk paced the sand in front of her. She watched as he walked on. "I love you very much, Stacy. And I want to help you. I want to protect you, and I want to make things better for you." He stopped and turned to her. "But goddammit, you make it awfully hard when you don't give a shit about yourself. All I see you do is sit at home all day, getting drunk, getting stoned, taking God knows how much acid—"

"What I chose to do with my body is nobody's business but

mine." Stacy nearly spit it out through gritted teeth. She seemed locked into a silent, screaming rage that threatened to break through at any moment.

"What you do with your body is my business." Kirk approached her, jabbing his finger at her. "Because if you continue to fuck up your body, it destroys any chance we have of continuing this relationship."

"Why are you doing this?" Stacy screamed, burying her face in her hands. "Why are you doing this to me, why—" Her face was turning red and her eyes were beginning to leak. She choked the words out in sobs that snapped Kirk into action.

He grasped her shoulders and shook her. "I'm doing this because I care about you! I'm trying to make you—"

Stacy brushed his hands away and stepped back, crying openly now. She held her hands up to her ears as if to stop the barrage of criticism aimed at her. "Stop it, I don't want to hear it—"

"—understand, that you need help, you need to see a professional about—"

"WILL YOU STOP IT!"

Kirk stopped as if he suddenly slammed into a brick wall. Stacy stood her ground, her face red and wet with tears. Her breath fast and heavy, as if she'd just run a marathon. Kirk caught himself before he launched off into another tactical error. He had to bring it all up; the drinking, the drugs, the suspicion of her having affairs behind his back. He would have to proceed slowly and not hit her with everything at once. It was already getting out of hand; he knew she was going to be in some kind of denial, but not like *this*.

"Listen," Kirk said, his voice soothing. He held his hands up, palms outward. "Let's talk this thing out."

"No, we're not going to talk this out." Stacy's tone was charged with emotion. She glared at Kirk, her chest rising and falling. "I want you out of my house."

"*Jesus*, Stacy—"

"I *said* I want you out of my *house!*"

A glimmer of movement caught Kirk's eye as he leaned into the argument. He looked past Stacy's shoulder out at the white sands of the beach. Stacy's eyes narrowed in suspicion. "Did you hear me? I *said*—"

Kirk held his hand up, still looking past Stacy's shoulder. His eyes widened.

Stacy whirled toward the beach. Her scream lodged in her throat in a wretched gasp. *"Oh my God!"*

The creatures were only twenty feet from them. To Kirk they looked like giant crabs from one of those shlocky B-movies. *Nuclear Crabs on the Rampage,* directed by Roger Corman, based on the novel by Guy N. Smith. Kirk had lived his whole life on the Maine coastline and had never seen crabs like this before. They were as big as a fucking St. Bernard.

Kirk grabbed Stacy, who stood rooted in shock. The creatures were advancing quickly and he could hear the clicking as their claws clacked together. He made to spin Stacy around and push her into a run toward the parking lot. *"Run!"* He shouted. *"Jesus, Stacy, run!"*

Stacy went apeshit. She fought against his grasp, screaming at him hoarsely. She slapped at his hands, at his chest as he tried to get her to run. *"Get the fuck away from me, get away from me—"*

She was in panic mode and if he didn't get her out of here they would both be attacked. The creatures were scuttling rapidly toward them, gaining momentum. Getting closer.

Still clutching Stacy's shoulder's, he made to move her forward in his flight to escape. He could hear the hiss of the creatures lunging at them and the clattering of their claws and then suddenly Stacy turned, twisting out of his grip. Kirk teetered on the brink of falling backward, then she pushed him and he *did* fall, flat on his back into the sand. He scrambled on the ground in his haste to escape. Stacy was already running pell-mell toward the parking lot to her Trans-Am. Kirk rose to his knees, stood up to run but was dragged down to the ground from behind. He ate a mouthful of sand as his face hit the beach and then something sharp pierced his ankle.

He had never felt pain so great. It ricocheted up his leg and rocked into his skull. His mind seemed to keel over and his vision blurred for a moment. When it cleared, a pair of stalked eyes were glaring down at him, tiny jaws clicking. And then the agony blossomed as that great, terrible claw came down again and tore a chunk out of his hip.

Kirk yelled and this time he did move. He hobbled forward in a slithering motion and ate sand again. There was the pressure of a tremendous weight on his back as a creature climbed on top of him, poised for attack. Kirk squirmed like a rat caught in a trap. Only pure adrenaline kept him going, surging through his bloodstream rapidly and pouring out of him via the hole in his leg.

The creature at his side seemed too hungry to even immobilize its prey. It dipped its claws into Kirk's back, ripping chunks of flesh and stuffing them into its mandibles. Kirk screamed, squirming beneath the weight of the creature on his back. His eyes glassed over and his mind was drifting. He clawed frantically at the sand.

The last thing Kirk Fischer saw was Stacy's Trans-Am rapidly diminishing in the horizon with the squeal of spinning tires. The rest of the creatures grouped around him and joined their brethren. A few jabs of their segmented tails later, and Kirk was reduced to a bubbling mass of sizzling flesh which they ate their fill of.

Fifteen minutes later the creatures moved inland, leaving the tattered remains of a black leather jacket and an empty six pack of long necked Budweiser—hardly enough to acknowledge Kirk had never left the beach.

7

It was too bad Melissa hadn't been able to stick around, but Rick did have a ton of chores to get through before starting on his next novel. Still, her absence weighed on him as he eagerly explored his house. He had hoped she would have traipsed through with him, sharing his enthusiasm and surprise as he uncovered the dwelling's many features. But he would have to do without her for now. It was time to unpack and settle in.

It was a modest, one-story farmhouse. There was a living room, a kitchen with a dining room, and a den. There were three bedrooms, the largest of the trio tucked in back of the house with its own bathroom and shower. A second bathroom was off the main hall. Rick christened the middle bedroom as his office, and began moving his computer equipment in.

The house was equipped accordingly with worn yet homey furniture. The kitchen had all the necessary tools of the trade; pots and pans, dishes, glasses, silverware. The den contained a television, a VCR and a so-so stereo system. The master bedroom contained a king-sized waterbed with satin sheets. The bed sat across from the walk-in closet with mirrored sliding doors. All the better to watch if he ever got lucky and found a steady honey to do the horizontal bop with.

Rick spent the next two hours unpacking and stowing things. Clothes went into the closet or in the dresser. His computer and laser printer went in the office, along with his files and supplies. The few books and odds and ends he brought along remained in the living room. He'd brought his CD collection and some reading material, along with some VHS tapes. His stay in Phillipsport wasn't intended to be permanent, but the more things he brought from home, the better he felt.

Once he was semi-settled in, he called Cynthia Jacobs. His agent.

He rang her up from the extension in the office. She picked up on the first ring and sounded surprised to hear from him. "So, you made it to Phillipsport?" Her voice came in strong and syrupy, dripping with sex. It instantly reminded him of the first time they'd combined business with pleasure.

It had happened at a convention in Nashville. They'd been conducting business for three years by mail and phone, but that was the first time they had the opportunity to meet in person. They'd both gotten drunk at a party, talking aimlessly. They'd stumbled to their rooms and as Rick bade her goodnight, she swept him up in a sweeping embrace, hug, smooch, squeeze, fondle. They ended up making love in her room. At the time it happened, Rick never thought that it was a wrong thing to do. She made the first move, he was drunk, she was drunk and attractive, and why not take advantage of each other? What else was a man supposed to do when seduced by a drunk, horny, sexy older woman?

He regretted it almost as soon as the convention was over. He knew it was unethical business-wise, but then she had made the first move. Still, it bothered him and he seriously considered dumping her for another agent. When you came right down to it, what kind of agent fucks her client on a business trip? He voiced his concerns to her over the phone one day and they talked about it. She said that she had no interest in pursuing anything relationship-wise and was sorry she'd come on to him. It had been very unprofessional of her and she promised it would never happen again. That made him feel better about the situation.

The problem was that every time they met she slipped. On his first trip to New York they had lunch and in the cab she'd rubbed his crotch and directed the driver to a hotel in Manhattan. Rick went with the flow. In the months that followed they indulged in each other whenever the chance arose, but things never went further. She remained his agent, she handled his publishing affairs and everything was hunky dory. The more time passed, the less he was nervous about it. Maybe it was unprofessional to be engaging in an affair with her client, but their sex life was unrelated to their business life. That was all the justification he needed.

"I got in town late this morning," Rick said, trying to sound casual. He gave her a quick summary of his trip, the accident, and his meeting of a few of the locals. He could tell she was frowning as she conveyed her concern. "Are you okay?" She asked. "You weren't hurt that bad, were you?" Rick assured her that everything was fine, that he'd already made at least one new friend, possibly two others. He quickly told her about Melissa Peterson and at the mention of another woman, he heard a sharp intake of breath on the other line. He quickly changed the subject to what the weather was like in town and she seemed to forget about the blunder. *She's jealous.*

"So you think you'll be able to start working on the book soon?"

"I'm gonna try to get to work on the book tomorrow morning."

"You know, you could have moved to New York for a new locale," she said. She sounded coaxing. "You didn't need to move all the way to the boondocks. How am I supposed to see you?"

"I came up here to get away from the normal, day-today surroundings I had in Philly," Rick said. "I needed a change of pace."

"Like I said, you could have come to New York." It sounded like she was smiling on the other end. "You could have stayed with me."

Rick cringed at the thought. Since the bigger deal had gone through, words that had been absent in her vocabulary began to make their presence with alarming regularity. Words that hinted at marriage entrapment. The last time they spoke she'd ended the conversation with a *love you.* Rick managed a smile. "I wouldn't have gotten any work done."

"Hmm, you're probably right," Cynthia breathed. God, but she had a sexy voice. Too bad she was so goddamn possessive and smothering. It made him not want to have anything to do with her. He hadn't been involved with her sexually for three months, and she was still pursuing him. Business calls always included some attempt at coercion. The vibe he was getting now echoed that their personal life was now crossing over into his publishing deals. Especially since the bigger deal had come through. The minute that happened she began steering him toward a more commercial novel. "Something like what Dean Koontz writes," she'd said. Maybe *now* was the time to switch agents.

"Listen, I'm gonna start the new book tomorrow." Rick began, trying to get the conversation back onto business. "I'll call you." He looked at his watch calendar. "I'll call you Friday afternoon and let you know how far I've gotten."

"Do you think you'll have twenty pages down?" An abrupt switch in tone to business.

"I don't see why not, if I can get ten pages a day done, including rewrites."

"If you do by the time we talk, you might want to send them over."

"Okay."

"And maybe if you get a quarter of the way done by say, the end of the month, you can come down to New York for the weekend. We'll spend it together." Her tone had changed back to that seductive purr again.

Six months ago, Rick would have jumped at the chance. But now that he was seriously thinking about changing agents he knew that wasn't going to be the case. Still, he had to provide an illusion of slight interest until he figured out a way to talk to her about the direction she was trying to take him in. The world didn't need another Dean Koontz. "Sounds good," he said. "We'll see how it goes."

"Okay." Her voice was a throaty purr. "Bye, Rick. Talk to you soon."

"You, too," Rick said, and they hung up.

Rick sighed as he sat at the desk, the caress of her voice massaging his brain. Yep, he definitely needed to have a little talk with her. Pronto. He shouldn't have slept with her in the first place. That had been a mistake. On both their parts.

With that bit of business out of the way, he rose and strode into the kitchen to see what he was going to do for dinner.

Starting work the next morning was tougher than he thought it would be.

He stared blankly at the screen of his laptop. About the most he had done thus far was boot his system and go into Microsoft Word. He'd written the words PROLOGUE in the middle of the page, center space. Now the cursor was sitting at the left of the screen, waiting for the words. But none came. At least not yet.

Rick drummed his fingers on the desk. He'd called out for a pizza last night and chowed down in the den. There was a big screen TV, along with a big, comfy sofa. He'd popped in one of the *Friday the Thirteenth* movies that he found lying around and settled down for a couple hours' worth of mindless, splattering entertainment. Once the pizza was consumed, he raided the refrigerator. Not much to be had, so he hiked to the local mini-market down the road and came back with a case of Black Label beer, two liters of Coke, a loaf of bread, lunch meats, ground beef, and some fruit. He also nabbed some microwave popcorn. He spent the rest of the evening watching VH1, drinking Coke and eating popcorn. He wanted to drink beer, but he'd taken the first of the prescribed painkillers Dr. Jorgensen had given him last night and he couldn't drink alcohol while on them. Tanking up on massive quantities of carbonated beverages was the next best thing.

He fell asleep on the sofa in front of the big screen TV.

After a quick breakfast, a pot of coffee and a shower, he headed straight for his office. Got his files together. Read over some notes he'd made for the next novel. Fired up the computer. And promptly proceeded to stare at the screen for the next thirty minutes.

It just wasn't happening. He had a stunning idea for a ghost story, one that involved past life regression and New Ageism. Cynthia had suggested doing something along those lines. He'd balked at first, but an idea sparked in his head not too long afterward. He'd tried plotting it out, but it wouldn't come together no matter how hard he tried. Great idea, but no meat.

His thoughts started wandering and he fired up the CD player, which he'd set up in the office. Rush's Hemispheres filled the room with its intricate melodies and progressive chord changes. Still, nothing.

He decided to call the garage about his car. He should have heard from them by now. He turned the stereo down and hunted in his wallet for the phone number Rusty had given him for Carl's Garage before he had left the drugstore yesterday. He found it, and punched in the number.

A rough voice answered. "Carl's."

"Hi, I'm calling about my car." Rick gave him the vital stats, and the guy told him he'd be right with him. Rick waited.

"Sorry for the wait," the guy said a few minutes later. "But I'm afraid I've got some bad news. Your car's shot to shit. I'm not only going to have to replace the entire radiator and fan as well as all the belts, but you're gonna need some extensive body work on it. The whole front grill is crushed and the side paneling is smashed. The body work alone is gonna run over two grand, and I'll tell ya right now that your insurance company will probably just write the car off as a complete loss. You call them yet?"

"No, I haven't." He had forgotten all about it in all the excitement.

"Well, I'd check with them before you authorize me to do anything else."

"Okay. I'll do that right now."

"Talk to you later."

Rick replaced the receiver with a sinking feeling in his chest. Great! No car, and he was miles from home. It would be at least two weeks before he could get a new set of wheels after the insurance people started their machine. What a great day this was starting out to be.

Rick rose and went into the kitchen. The mid-day sun brought streaks of light through the curtains. It bathed the kitchen in warmth. No hint at all of the rainstorm that had hit last night. It was too nice to sit in the house all day and work. He had a severe bout of writer's block and he didn't have a car.

The depression he felt over *that* pretty much took the wind out of the writing sails for today. And it really was too nice to stay cooped up inside. He hadn't really seen Phillipsport yet, and he was dying to see what kind of burg he'd settled into for the winter. Besides, a walk might be just the thing to get the creative wheels grinding.

He grabbed his wallet and keys from the desk and stepped outside. He put his black leather jacket on and zipped it up. He looked up at the clear blue sky, blinking as he put his sunglasses on. My, but it was a fine, fine day.

He set off down the road toward town with a contented smile on his face. He didn't even notice the tall, dark storm clouds amassing behind him from the north.

8

Rick decided to head to the beach.

He made the decision after a quick lunch at a cozy little delicatessen near the center of town. He had stopped in for a quick bite to eat and discovered they made the best submarine sandwiches north of New York City. By the time he left the deli, it was a quarter after twelve. The weather was overcast but warm, heavy with humidity. When Rick turned up Highway 1 upon leaving the house, he noticed the big, black storm clouds amassing from the north. *Gonna be a huge storm*, he thought as he reached the crest of town. Hopefully he'd get home before the worst of the downpour hit. The cloud mass looked like it was still a good few hours away.

Now the entire sky was becoming cloudy as the cloud mass moved in. As he hit the boardwalk he passed a few weathered locals and smiled at them. They gave glancing nods or ignored him altogether. They didn't recognize him as being local. They probably never would even if he decided to settle down and live here.

He walked along the boardwalk, noting the storefronts of fish and chips eateries, tourist traps, fish and tackle stores. Halloween decorations adorned the window-fronts of all of them. The wind picked up slightly and the sky turned a sudden gray. Rick's shadow, which had been keeping abreast of him, suddenly vanished in the sepia of the afternoon. Rick looked up at the sky to check the progress of the clouds and noted that the entire horizon seemed to have clouded up faster than he would have imagined. He stopped in mid-stride, gazing up at the sky in wonder as a raindrop hit his eyeball. *Smack!*

He started, both eyes shut tight. He rubbed the offending moisture out of his eye as bigger raindrops began to pitter-patter the boardwalk.

A loud cackle to his immediate right caused him to steer toward the sound. It sounded like a gorilla trying to cough up a furball. He blinked. It was just an old man sitting on a rickety rocking chair on the porch of the Fish and Tackle store. The man had skin like leather and looked like he was eight hundred years old.

For a moment, time seemed frozen. Rick stared at the old man. The old man cackled again, his mouth resembling a cesspool; his handful of remaining teeth were the color of lacquered oak. The man's leathery skin, his moldy-hued gray hair, his weathered face, all looked like it had been chipped from the bark of a pine tree. His sinewy arms and legs were twisted branches that snaked at crazy angles. Stick him out in the woods and he'd be the haunted tree of the forest.

Rick almost expected to see dead leaves dropping off the man as he shifted his weight in the rocker. "Y'know ... only turkeys is dumb enough to look up in a storm." It took a moment for Rick to realize the old geezer was talking to him. The old man cackled again. "Ya look up too long, an' yew'll drown!"

This seemed to tickle grandpa's funny bone something fierce. He laughed until he began coughing violently. The force of the coughs sounded like his lungs were going to be wrenched up his esophagus. He hit himself in the chest with the palm of his hand and raised the cigarette he was holding between two twig-like fingers to his lips. It was the first time Rick noticed the cigarette. A long trail of ash hung from it, defying gravity. The old man took a long drag that seemed to give the ash a new life of glowing orange. A moment later his coughing subsided. Just the right medicine.

Rick managed a weak smile and nodded awkwardly at the man. He continued down the boardwalk taking in every sight, smell, and sound. The rain was coming down harder, not a downpour yet, but a steady spattering of large fat drops. The promise of bigger things to come.

The boardwalk ended at a small, quaint pier that jutted

out over the ocean. It was jam-packed with small shops and restaurants. None of the big, corporate plastic and hype like the shopping center had displayed. All the buildings along the beachfront shared similar, weathered-wood exteriors. This was the real thing. When the rain hit them they gave off a nice, earthy aroma that mixed with the salt of the sea and the slight fish smell that seemed to be everywhere. Now *this* was small town, New England living!

He decided to check out the pier and its shops. A few tourists meandered about, not paying mind to the raindrops that were still spattering leisurely. Some were trying to avoid it like they were rat-poison droppings from the clouds. Rick grinned at the thought and looked up at the sky again. He shielded his eyes to avoid any more kamikaze raindrops and the subsequent ridicule he might suffer from any other billygoat locals. He scanned the sky and the horizon, admiring the beauty of it all.

Then he saw something strange across the beach itself, just over the ocean. Something slightly out of kilter.

Something was upsetting the seagulls.

They were flying in tight circles above the beach, screeching their beaks off. No big deal, seagulls screech all the time. But something about this was different. He didn't know much about birds, but all his life he'd noticed that most birds don't fly around when it's raining and cold. By now the rain was coming down harder, pelting his skin into shivering wetness. He sought the refuge of the covered boardwalk as he gazed out at the ocean. Some of the tourists scuttled off to the safety of their cars or stores. But the seagulls remained, circling overhead and cackling.

Rick watched the birds for a moment, then studied the pier and the beach. There were no seagulls on either. Fifty yards up the beach a family of three was walking along the surf, huddled against the sudden cold and rain. A little girl of six or seven was tossing large chunks of sandwich bread into the air, trying to hit the birds. The food fell back onto the sand, uneaten. None of the seagulls swooped down for a free meal, and Rick noticed for the first time that even the pigeons and the sparrows were absent. He looked behind him, above the storefronts. The pigeons were sitting on the power line, watching the scene with seeming disinterest. It looked like they were stoned.

Back on the beach, the little girl looked at her mother questioningly. The woman shrugged her shoulders and the three continued walking.

A sudden cold shiver unrelated to the weather rippled through Rick's body. This was just too strange.

Seagulls and pigeons were scavengers. They wouldn't pass on a free meal for anything. He looked out at the sea for any sign of distress and saw none. The waves rolled rough in the growing storm, crashing onto the shore with a bit more force than usual. Everything looked normal.

He began slowly walking down the boardwalk toward the pier, keeping a watchful eye on the seagulls' behavior. A faint pulse of music slowly eased the seagulls' weird mannerisms out of his mind and snapped him out of his daze.

He stopped again. Familiar tune, one that had often comforted him in times of stress and confusion. The sound of music. Sweet, wonderful, thoughtful … thrash metal!

The metallic crunch was so alien at first that he didn't believe his ears. It just didn't fit in with this small, coastal sea town. It was probably from the head injury he had suffered in his vehicular mishap yesterday causing him to hear things. But no, he shook his head and listened. Sure enough, it was thrash metal all right. The grinding crunch of the guitar was familiar and he immediately identified the tune as "Speak English Or Die" by the wonderful band Storm Troopers Of Death. He grinned. He was beginning to like this place even more.

His eyes scanned the little sea-front shops as he walked along the boardwalk. The music was getting closer. It sounded like it was emanating from one of the shops at the end of the boardwalk.

He stood in front of the shop, a pleasant surge of surprise running through him. The shop's marquee: RIP IT UP COMICS was the only evidence that the Phillipsport pier was in the twentieth century. The tiny, box-like store appeared like all the other shops on the outside; worn down, dilapidated, peeling paint. A *Superman* Poster, a *Spiderman* poster, and a cardboard advertisement of the latest *Sisters of Mercy* comics were the only things that set this shop apart from the others.

But once inside …

Rick could barely feel his feet as they propelled him inside the store like a moth to the flame. His eyes widened in surprise as they took in the massive rows of comics set in cardboard structures in the middle of the store. The left of the store was filled with used paperbacks and hardcover books, the rest of the wall devoted to specialty-press graphic novels. The right side held the stands, the latest issues of every comic from every publisher, large or small. They were bagged in mylar sleeves, carefully arranged to maximize the display. Science Fiction and Horror magazines sat on the stands with the comics. It was weird to think that such a cool store existed in a town of less than six hundred, complete with goofy deputies and chain-smoking tree-people. He liked this place already.

S.O.D.'s "Fuck the Middle East" was ending and a live version of "Douche Crew" was beginning. Rick started, eyebrows scrunched in confusion. S.O.D. only recorded one album and it wasn't a live one. He stepped farther inside the store to get a further listen to the tape.

A pair of twelve-year-old boys stepped past him, stuffing bags of comics under their coats to protect them from the rain. They both carried beaten-up skateboards with colorful stickers on their undersides. The kids dropped their boards and stepped onto them effortlessly, skating away.

As he stepped farther in the store, Rick saw that more jewels lay within. A display ran along the glass counter where the cash register sat, filled with the rarer comics. Behind the counter itself was an elevated section with even more shelves, and to Rick's practiced eye it looked like the shelves held rare pulps. *Cool.* Standing behind the register was the tallest, skinniest man Rick had ever seen. He was sitting on a stool, perusing the latest issue of *Cinefantastique.*

A young boy of ten was standing at the counter bombarding the man with inane questions. The man rolled his eyes, answering questions as best as he could. "So what's going to be more valuable, *Superman* #298 or the first issue of *Nightshade*?"

From the expression on his face it was obvious the little shit didn't give a damn about reading whatever he bought.

The thin man sighed. "Listen, kid … I'm not a fortune-teller. If you want that, go down the pier to Madame Zondra. Maybe she can divine next year's price guide for you and you can speculate to your little heart's content. Meanwhile, why don't you buy ten of everything just to be certain."

The boy sneered and walked away from the counter as Rick approached. He looked up at the thin man and smiled. The man smiled back. "How ya doin'?"

"Fine," Rick said, approaching the counter. He was still stunned about the live S.O.D. song and wanted answers. "Was that S.O.D. I just heard?"

The man behind the counter smiled, his face becoming a huge set of teeth that nearly obscured his hooked nose and goatee. "You bet it is. It's their live album."

"You mean they got back together?" There was a God.

"Yeah, for one show only. They played in New York at one of the clubs, probably the Ritz. Album's called *Live at Budakon*. Pretty cool, huh?" His Adam's Apple bobbed up and down.

Rick was checking out the store as the man talked, unable to take his eyes off anything. He was in total sensory overload.

"You read comics?" The thin man's eyes were magnified by the coke-bottom lenses of his black-framed glasses.

Rick turned back to the man. "Oh, yeah. I love 'em."

The man leaned back and threw the magazine he was reading back on the counter and smiled. "That's good to hear. Most of the brats who come in here don't give a shit about the story or the artwork of the stuff they buy. They just want to know what books they're going to be able to sell back to me a year from now at an inflated price." He laughed again, his face filling with teeth.

Rick grinned. "This store is great. I thought I was going to have to spend the whole winter without a reading supply shop." Rick wiped the rain from his forehead and grinned. "Phillipsport just doesn't seem to be the kind of place for a shop like this."

"In a way, it isn't," the thin man said. He was leaning

forward over the counter, his grin wide and toothy. "At least that's what everybody has told me. But there are lots of kids in the area, and the tourists usually use my shop as a baby-sitting service while they're enjoying the rest of the pier. Thank God most of 'em slip the little runts a twenty before they dump 'em off here." He chuckled.

Rick chuckled with him. He liked this guy, and was beginning to feel much better about spending the next six months in Phillipsport.

The thin man stood and rose to his full six-and-a-half-foot height. It was astonishing that someone so skinny could still be alive. He looked like a survivor from Auschwitz. The T-shirt he wore caught Rick' s attention; it displayed a field of skulls and a couple of military planes buzzing overhead. It was the Dead Kennedy's *Holiday in Cambodia* album cover emblazoned in bright red and black. Rick admired the choice in clothing. A man of taste, obviously.

The thin man extended a skeletal hand. "I'm Jack Ripley. I own this place."

Rick took the hand and shook it, marveling at his strength. Looks can be deceiving. The name Jack Ripley pulsed in his mind. He'd heard that name before.

It connected. He looked up at Jack Ripley. "Jack Ripley … the Ripper?"

Jack Ripley leaned back and grinned. "You're showing your age, my friend. Most people stopped calling me Ripper ten years ago."

Rick couldn't believe it. Jack Ripley, otherwise known as Ripper in the comic world, was one of the most respected, most widely-imitated artists and writers in the world of underground comics. He had emerged in the late sixties, reached his peak in the early seventies and rode the wave of his success to the beginning of the eighties. He hadn't been heard from since. Rick felt himself glow at the thought of meeting the elusive artist. He had met other comic artists of equal reputation; Robert Crumb and Todd MacFarlane, among others, but this was different. He had become a fan of Jack 'Ripper' Ripley long before he became a fan of other, more well known, comic book artists.

Rick could hardly believe it. He smoothed his wet hair back from his forehead and grinned. "Man, this is great! I love your work."

"Thanks." Jack grinned, obviously smitten with the attention. "It's nice to know people still appreciate what I did even if I didn't work on Spiderman or the X-Men."

"Are you kidding? I grew up reading stuff like *Drugg Buddies* and *Jesus-on-a Stick Comix*. They shaped my life." Rick chuckled. "They made me into what I am. And now I'm standing here with the man who created them. I can't believe it."

Ripper leaned back against the wall of pulp cartons.

His large blue eyes were enlarged and distorted by the glasses. "Yeah, those were the days. You know, I still get royalties from the *All Fucked Up* posters."

"Really? I had one of those in my room for three months before my Mom found out about it and made me take it down."

Ripper laughed.

Rick grinned and laughed with Ripper. Jack Ripley looked to be in his mid-fifties, but obviously took great pains to hide it. His graying, light brown hair was trimmed close to the skull around his temples, long and wild along the top and the back, kind of like a punk rock Lyle Lovett. His large blue eyes turned down at the corners, giving him a sad, hound-dog look, which wasn't helped by the thick glasses. A hooked nose hung down over his upper lip, which was pulled back over the buck teeth. A patch of a goatee sprouted on what remained of his chin. His face was set in skull that appeared long and bony. His body was skeletal, complementing the rest of his bizarre features. His blue eyes radiated a warmth that ebbed like a beacon, bathing his features in a more attractive way. You couldn't help but like the guy the minute you started talking to him.

"So what's the world's greatest underground comic artist doing in a little town like Phillipsport?" Rick wondered if the answer was going to be along the lines of his own reason for moving here. What he got was quite different.

Ripper smiled. "I ask myself that question every morning I wake up." He sighed and drew himself down on a stool in front of the cash register. "I used to live in Los Angeles. Moved there from Northern California in 1973. Everyone thought it was a good idea. A few movie producers were interested in making films based on my comics."

Rick nodded. He'd gotten a few nibbles at *Baron Semedi*, too.

"You ever dealt with movie people?" Ripper asked. He leaned forward over the counter, his features grave.

Rick shook his head. "Not directly. A couple of producers expressed interest in one of my novels, but that was it."

"You're a writer?" His tone changed to sudden interest. His eyebrows raised on his bony forehead in surprise.

Rick nodded. "Yeah. I write horror novels."

Ripper laughed. "Wonderful." He smiled a mouthful of giant teeth at Rick. "What's your name?"

"Rick Sychek."

Recognition fluttered in Ripper's eyes. "Rick Sychek. Yeah, I know that name. Didn't you write a book called *Shadowbeast?*"

Rick grinned and nodded. This was great. One of his adolescent idols recognized *him.*

"I liked that book. Haven't read any of the others though, but I do stock them." He waved a hand toward the paperbacks displayed along the window. Rick followed his gaze briefly and turned back to Ripper. "So, you have bad luck with Hollywood?"

"Not really. Like I said, a few producers expressed interest in *Baron Semedei*. Nothing more, nothing less."

Ripper snorted. "Well, be careful in the future. Most producers are crooks. The good ones mean well, but they'll fuck you over as well. Worst mistake I ever made was believing the bullshit some producers kept handing me about making one of my comics into a film."

Rick frowned, concerned. He was hoping to move to Los Angeles next year and try his hand at screenplays.

"To make a long story short, this guy did make a movie out of *Bird of Prey*, but he stiffed me on the money.

"I took him to court and won, but I still got fucked. My lawyer took a good chunk of the settlement and by then I was in deep debt with bills and the IRS. I had to draw the *Deadshit* series to get myself above water again." He paused for a moment and Rick caught a glimmer of the bad memories passing in his eyes. He could relate. He had been through bad times before. "Anyway, after all that happened, I decided to find the most out-of-the-way place I could and settle down."

"Phillipsport, Maine," Rick said, trying to inject a little humor into his voice.

"Exactly! The gateway to nowhere." Ripper had resumed his horsy-grin and leaned forward over the counter "Anyway, since I knew the comic industry, I decided to open up this place. Been in business for ten years now."

Rick nodded. "And you do all right?"

Ripper rubbed the back of his neck with his bony hand. "I do pretty good. I live."

"Ever thought about getting back into illustrating and creating again?"

Ripper shook his head. "I'm pretty much through with that."

"People *love* your work. If you came out with a new series now it would sell like crazy."

Ripper sighed and shook his head. "Kids don't want underground stuff these days. They want big superheroes in spandex with huge fucking guns blowing people apart. They want guys ripping people's heads off and girls with big poofy hair and big silicone tits. They want the collectible stuff with 3-D wrap-around hologram covers and trading cards … not black and white, black humor."

"What about the small press?" Rick was going to get Ripper back into the business again if he had to stand here all day.

Ripper laughed. "Not enough money and too much stress. I understand your enthusiasm for wanting me to get back into the field, but I really do like where I'm at now. I guess one of the reasons why I like this town is because nothing happens." He nodded toward outside where it had briefly stopped raining. The sky was dark and ugly. It may have stopped raining momentarily, but it would start again soon. The black clouds were promising it. "Unless you count the occasional storm."

Rick sighed, his curiosity satiated. Somehow it felt right that Jack Ripley had really gone underground.

Ripper rummaged beneath the counter. "While I got you here, I was wondering if you could do me a favor?"

"Sure."

Ripper found what he wanted beneath the counter and brought it up. His bony face was broken by a huge grin. He held a tattered paperback of *Shadowbeast* out in front of him in one hand, with a blue ballpoint pen in the other. "Think you could autograph my copy for me?"

Rick felt giddy and proud. His face flushed. "Of course." He took the paperback and the pen and flipped to the title page. "Will you sign all my copies of *Drugg Buddies* for me someday?"

"You got it!" Ripper grinned.

"Great!" Rick bent over the title page of *Shadowbeast* and scrawled a hasty message on the page, his mind in overdrive. He was going to have to make a drive to his place in Philly some weekend and truck his copies over for inscription. A trip that would be well worth it.

Rick finished the inscription, signed his name at the bottom and handed the book back to Ripper. Jack opened it and read it aloud. "To the man who made me into the warped guy I am today, your number one fan, Rick Sychek." Ripper smiled, closed the book and bowed courteously. "I take that christening in honor, Rick."

The lights in the store flickered briefly. Both men looked up at the florescent fixtures as they pulsated. The rain and wind picked up slightly, shaking banners outside, the force of the gusts reverberating in the store with loud clarity. The lights flickered like fireflies and then clicked back on. They remained that way as Rick and Ripper looked up at the ceiling waiting for the storm to knock them out.

Rick shook his head. "Guess we're in for a big storm."

Ripper nodded. "It ain't raining now, but like they always say; 'when it rains, it pours.'"

9

Rick exited Ripp It Up Comics clutching a bundle of comic books wrapped in a bright yellow plastic bag. An ad for the new Robin mini-series was etched in the side. He looked up at the sky in puzzled amazement. Two minutes ago it had been pouring like a flood and now the rain had stopped. The pavement was wet and exuded the aroma of wetness. A nice, clean smell. Rick stuffed the comics into his leather jacket and zipped up tight. Just in case.

He'd bought a trade paperback consisting of reprints of the first six issues of DC's Sandman series, the first four issues of *Hellblazer*, and this month's issues of *Nightbreed, Judge Dredd, Doom Patrol* and *Beautiful Stories for Ugly Children*.

He wanted to rush home and dive into the four-color worlds of wonder. Discovering Ripper's store and buying the comics had changed his mind about his plans for the day. He could explore the rest of Phillipsport tomorrow. He had all winter.

He wandered out along the pier, debating on whether or not to walk along the beach or explore the pier itself. There were a number of stores that looked worth investigating. The pier was dotted with a handful of people; locals window shopping, a few old men standing at the end of the dock leaning against the railing with fishing poles gripped in weathered hands. A woman was leaning against the railing at the far end, looking out over the beach. Not much action. Still, the view from the end of the pier was probably breathtaking. He might even be able to see his house from there.

He strode down the pier as the wind picked up and ruffled his hair. He would go to the end, sneak a quick peek, and head home. He wanted to get back, get a fire going in the hearth, and spend the rest of the day embroiled in fantasy-land. He deserved the time off from writing.

The fishermen were hogging up the south side of the pier. The woman was the only person on the north side, which was where he would be able to get a better glimpse of his house. He approached the weathered railing and leaned against it, marveling at the coastline. Gorgeous. Highway 1 wound like a snake up the coast and disappeared behind a grove of trees. Perched on a jutting cliff overlooking the ocean was his winter retreat. From here it looked way cool.

Rick grinned. He would have to come up here again and get a photograph of the home from this vantage point. It would make a great postcard.

He leaned against the pier for a moment, reflecting on his thoughts. The wind tousled his hair across his shoulders and he shivered. He glanced toward his right and noticed the woman who was occupying the north side of the pier with him. She was gorgeous.

The woman caught his glance and smiled. Rick looked away and kept his gaze toward his house. He could feel her eyes lighting on him, inspecting him. He stole a quick glance out of the corner of his eye. Looking at her made him even more aroused.

Her skin was a rich, golden tan. Brown, shoulder length, curly hair framed a pretty face, punctuated by full lips, large hazel eyes and a nice, smooth face. She was wearing a large cashmere sweater and blue jeans. She had a voluptuous figure. Her breasts were large and full and he could make out their contours quite nicely beneath the sweater. A mouthful. All of this was packaged in a nice, five-foot-five frame.

The woman caught Rick checking her out. He caught a glimmer of a smile on her lips and he turned back. Yes, she was smiling and her eyes sparkled with interest. Rick felt himself blush and chastised himself. The vibes coming off her were strong. It was as if she had a huge Day-Glo sign over her head that read VERY INTERESTED. It would probably be good to take advantage of it.

Only she beat him to it. "Nice weather we're having, isn't it?"

"You bet." Rick glanced toward the house again, feeling like an idiot. It was as if he'd suddenly forgotten how to behave around women.

"You wouldn't happen to be that writer guy, would you?"

Rick turned toward her, surprised by her question. She scooted closer, leaning against the railing facing him. The wind whipped her hair over her face and she brushed it away. Rick felt his heart pound as she smiled at him.

"Yeah, I am." *God, Rick, you could do better than that.*

"I thought so." Her eyes sparkled with deeper intentions. "I heard about your accident." She shook her head.

"That's too bad."

That broke the ice. Rick chuckled. "Yeah, it is." His self-confidence came back.

The woman held out her hand, her smile beaming. "I'm Janice Harrelson."

"Rick Sychek." Her hand felt soft and firm in his. They maintained skin contact longer than most people who are meeting for the first time. Their eyes locked briefly. This time Janice averted her gaze first. She looked away shyly, then looked up again with a smile. "I hear you write horror novels," she said, her voice soft.

"Yeah. I'm working on a new book right now." Rick didn't feel like plunging into the whole story of why he was up here. That could be better left for explaining later. Like over dinner. Janice was his type of woman: she had meat on her bones, but she wasn't fat. Rick never saw the appeal of the waif-like models that had been the rage of a year or so back. Rick loved full-figured women, and Janice definitely fit that bill. She was full-figured in all the right places.

"That sounds really interesting." She looked sincere. He could read it in her features which glowed. Her eyes sparkled. "You'll have to tell me more."

"Absolutely!"

"Where 'bouts you staying?" The sparks of interest and attraction were still spreading.

He motioned out across the ocean toward his house on the jutting cliff. She followed his gaze. "Right out there. The house that's tucked behind those trees on the cliff."

Janice's features dawned in awe. "Wow! Great."

Rick beamed. "Yeah. To tell you the truth, I haven't really checked it out that much."

Janice turned to him, her features brimming with eager adventure. "Well now's the time to do it before it starts pouring. I would have checked it out the minute I moved in. It's gorgeous."

Rick's heart thumped in his chest, stirring his attraction to her. "Thanks." He was beaming like a proud papa.

"You'll just have to have me over for dinner some night," she said, matter-of-factly. Her smile was seductive, holding vast promises. "You can tell me about the book."

"Name a time and a date."

"Eight o'clock, October twenty-second." She grinned.

"That's tonight."

"Nothing wrong with that, is there?" Her voice and features were teasing. Tantalizing him.

"Not at all. Tonight it is."

She leaned forward questionably. "You're sure you're not married or anything?"

Rick shook his head. "No."

"Kids?"

"None of those, either." Rick chuckled. "What is this, the third degree?"

Janice smiled. It was all harmless flirting, he knew that, but he couldn't help detecting an underlying note of seriousness beneath the tone. She confirmed his suspicions with her next question. "You don't hate kids, do you?"

"No, I love 'em," he said, dancing around the subject lightly. He hoped she wasn't one of those women that wanted to get married and have kids the minute you slept with her. "They're okay."

"Wonderful." Her eyes lit on his again and she smiled. The dancing connections they were making through their flirting realigned themselves and hit each other dead on. Straight connection. God, but she was gorgeous.

"Mom!"

He turned toward the voice, noticing the change on Janice's features. Her smile changed from flirting lust to joyful pride. He followed her gaze as the boy's voice echoed toward them again. *"Mom!"*

"Hi, Bobby," Janice called out, waving him over. Rick straightened up and saw a boy of about seven running up the pier toward them. His brown hair blew in the wind as he ran up to them. Janice swept him up in a hug, her features beaming with pride. Her eyes still held that same sparkle of interest toward Rick. "This is my son, Bobby."

Rick smiled and held out his hand to the freckle-face boy. "Hi Bobby, I'm Rick."

"Pleased to meet ya." Bobby shook Rick's hand limply, then turned to his mother. "Can I run up the beach and see if I can find some more shells?"

"Just for a minute," Janice said. "I want to get home soon."

"Okay, great!" He started to break away to run down the pier again before he was snagged by Janice. She grabbed on to the back of his jacket before he could make a getaway.

"One minute," Janice asserted. Firm.

Bobby looked back at Janice and huffed a breath of annoyance. His freckled face bore the slightest hint of rebellion. "One minute," he echoed and grinned. One of his teeth was missing.

Janice released her grip from his jacket and Bobby took a step back. His gaze went from Janice to Rick, then dropped down to the hand that held the bright yellow bag from Ripp It Up Comics. His eyes grew wide. "Cool. You like comics, too? Wadya get?"

Rick shrugged. "Nothing much. The latest *Nightbreed* and *Ugly Stories For Beautiful Children,* a *Sandman* book."

Bobby nodded. He reminded Rick a little bit of Opie from the *Andy Griffith Show.* "Yeah, Ripper is the only cool person in this town. I hang out there all the time."

"Not all the time, buster," Janice said, mocking tone. "You're grounded from comic books for the next two weeks, remember?"

The idea of previous sentencing for whatever childhood

crime had been wreaked in the kid's name seemed to go unheeded. He nodded nonchalantly, as if he knew the appeals would come within the next few days. "I know," he said. "Do you like the *X-Men*?" His attention was riveted back to Rick.

"A little," Rick said, grinning. Ad-libbing. He hated the *X-Men*.

Bobby began spilling inane comic book questions at Rick, totally oblivious to his mother. "I've got number fifty-four, the one that's worth, like, fifty bucks now. I've also got the new *Mutant* comic and—"

"Tell you what," Janice interrupted, patting her son's wind-blown brown hair. "Why don't we go get some cotton candy and get to know each other a little better." She traded a sidelong glance with Rick, her hazel eyes holding greater promises in store.

Bobby saw right through the charade. "Aw, Mom, can't I go play on the beach some more? I don't want to be around you guys if you're gonna be making sucky faces at each other."

Rick sputtered laughter, Janice joining him. Bobby looked at them with bored disinterest, waiting for a chance for his reprieve. Rick didn't feel embarrassed at all by Bobby's sudden burst of honesty; it was pretty god-damned funny. Janice ruffled Bobby's mop of hair. "Go on, but be careful."

Bobby's face erupted into smiles and he set off to run. Rick looked over at Janice and smiled. Bobby started off, but then doubled back and leaned toward Rick. "Hey Rick, if you're gonna be my Mom's new boyfriend, ya gotta know something."

"Robert Alton Harrelson!" Janice's tone changed to authoritative steel. Rick read the glimmer in her features; she knew Bobby was joking and he sensed that they teased each other often.

"What?" Bobby looked at his mother with irritation.

"What does he need to know?" Janice put her hands on her hips. Waiting.

Bobby leaned in close to Rick. "She can't cook!"

Janice leaped toward Bobby, arms out to grab him. He gave out a maniacal cackle and slithered like an eel out of her grasp and ran down the pier. Janice stepped after him and stopped, watching as the little urchin hit the sand and head for the water, laughing all the way. "You wait, Bobby! When you least expect it!"

Janice turned back to Rick, chuckling to herself. "Can you believe that little shit?"

Rick shrugged. "It looks like you two have a pretty good relationship."

Janice nodded. "We do. Sometimes too good. I know where he gets that wicked sense of humor from, too. He's definitely *my* kid." Rick nodded. Intuition told him that Bobby's father probably skipped out of the picture a long time ago.

"Well, Rick, how about that cotton candy?" That flirtatious tone crept back into her voice.

"You got it."

They set off walking down the pier toward Rox's hamburgers, a greasepit burger stand that served everything that was bad for you. Janice got a pink swirl of cotton candy. Rick settled for a coke. They found a deserted table, wiped the settled rain off with some napkins and sat down. Small talk commenced shortly after their behinds met plastic.

Rick answered not-too-personal questions about himself. He told her everything that had happened to him up till now; his brief past in Philly, his decision to move to a new location, the drive to Phillipsport, his accident, his encounter with Rusty and the sheriff, the exploration of his house. At the mention of Melissa, Janice nodded, no hint of jealousy in her face. "Melissa's a sweetie. Believe it or not, I used to babysit her."

Gee, she sure doesn't look that old. Rick originally pegged her to be around twenty-five, give or take a few years. Missy couldn't be more than twenty-one and if you count Bobby in as being around seven, Rick could definitely see that Janice was most likely around his own age. "When she dropped me off yesterday, Melissa mentioned that you and Jack Ripley are kindred spirits."

"She's a sweet girl," Janice said. "I don't see her that much now. Sometimes I'll stop by Shelby's for a bite and we chat, but it's been awhile."

"She drove me home from Shelby's the other night," Rick

mentioned. He cut Melissa out of the loop from that point on. He liked Melissa, but it wouldn't be right to talk about another woman with Janice, even if that other woman was merely regarded as a friend.

He filled the rest of the anecdote with what had happened till he ran into her at the pier. He was surprised that Ripper, one of the most seminal influences on his writing, lived in Phillipsport. Janice nodded, smiling at him. "Jack Ripley plays a good babysitter, too. If you know what I mean."

Rick nodded, catching the glimmer in her eye. What better way to keep Bobby occupied some evening than leaving him with Ripper to peruse comic books while he and Janice got to know each other better?

The one minute Janice had imposed on Bobby quickly stretched to thirty. After a while she rose and walked over to the edge of the pier to check on him. Rick heard her call down to him faintly for a moment. When she came back she looked more at ease. "I told him we'd come get him in a few minutes. He won't scamper off if he knows I'm up here."

Great. That meant they could relax in the pleasure of each other's company. Rick sipped at his coke and listened as Janice related bits and pieces of her life. She was a secretary for the town's only lawyer who was currently out on a Black-lung case in Harrisburg, Pennsylvania. The job itself gave her ample free time when it came to raising a seven-year-old. She somehow found the time for little league baseball games, after school activities, and volunteering for PTA duties. She gave Bobby what he really needed; her undivided attention in her love.

Beyond that she had time for a few hobbies. She liked to read and watch movies—she was a big fan of Alfred Hitchcock films and anything by Stephen King. "It makes sense, I guess," she said. "Being from Maine and all, he really captures the region quite beautifully."

Rick nodded and grinned. Bright woman. He liked her already.

They talked about their interests for a while; Janice liked to take Bobby to New York and Boston to peruse the museums. Bobby was interested in dinosaurs. Rick drew his leather jacket tighter around his body. The wind had picked up considerably, blowing his long hair over his face. Janice noticed the wind and looked out over the horizon. Rick followed her gaze. "Looks like we're gonna be getting a bigger storm."

Janice nodded. The sky from the north was as black as India ink. Forks of lightning flashed through it, creating a rippling effect of electricity. Rick could practically feel the tension in the air. The cloud mass looked like it was still a good twenty miles north. With the way the wind was blowing this new storm would hit them by nightfall.

"Is the weather like this all the time?" Rick asked, his eyes glued to the electrical show unfolding to the north.

"No. It gets pretty stormy in the winter, but I've never seen it like this before. It's really getting black and dreary, isn't it?"

Rick smirked. "I like it black and dreary."

Janice laughed and they slipped back into conversation. Rick was so absorbed in the conversation, in her awesome beauty, that he didn't even notice the storm clouds building in higher masses and moving quickly toward them.

10

Bobby Harrelson looked back toward the pier where his Mom and Rick were. He couldn't see them from this vantage point, but he knew they were there, talking grown-up stuff. He knew Mom wanted to be alone with Rick the minute he saw her making goo-goo eyes at him. He had been around Mom enough times to know that she wanted to be left alone whenever she got that way. His buddy Richard told Bobby that his mom did that to his dad all the time. Whenever Moms did that it meant they wanted to get laid. Bobby had a vague definition of what that meant, but it was still confusing; did it mean they laid down together? How boring.

Bobby turned and scaled the rocks of the beach carefully to avoid the cold, splashing waves. He'd been picking his way casually among the rocks for the past fifteen minutes now and hadn't come across anything. The rocky area held all the tide pools, which was where you found all the cool stuff; sand dollars, tiny fish, skeeters, wriggly things that were unidentifiable to him.

He had scoured all of them, but there was nothing. The waves had probably splashed them all out to sea. Too bad.

Bobby climbed on a large rock and sighed. He looked out at the ocean. The tide had receded for the moment, but it would come in at high tide tonight. Mom said there was going to be a full moon tonight and he knew well enough that the tide rose whenever the moon was full. Hopefully that would bring something up from the ocean. Something cool that he'd never seen before.

One time he'd found a tiny octopus in a tide pool and took

it home in a jar. Mom had put her foot down on that. He'd wanted to keep it till at least Monday when he could take it to school for show-and-tell. Mom wouldn't have it though, and he had to dump the critter back into the ocean. What a bummer that had been. He would have had the greatest show-and-tell exhibit of all time. Instead he had to settle for a crummy piece of driftwood that sort of looked like Ross Perot when you held it up at the right angle.

Bobby jumped off the rock and landed in the cold sand. A huge wave was coming in and he scooted back to avoid getting wet. God forbid he get his new Air-Jordans soaked with sandy sea water. Mom would kill him.

He stepped back as the wave crashed on the beach and rolled up the sand. He watched the tide retreat, exposing shells and sand crabs. He looked up at the gray sky and the vast expanse of ocean and sighed. Nothing much else out here to play with. Might as well go back.

He was just about to turn and trudge back up the beach to the pier when a flash of brown caught his eye. He turned toward his left and squinted down the beach. A brown mass was lying in the sand, tangled in seaweed. Bobby stepped toward it curiously. He trotted over the sand to the object until it was more identifiable, then he started running. A moment later he pulled up to a stop just a few feet from it.

It was a boat. A small one. The tail of the craft was in the water and the gentle lapping waves pushed it farther up the beach. There was a small outboard motor on the tail and a broken oar leaning against the railing. It looked like it had just been cast up from the ocean. In short, it looked like whoever was piloting it had abandoned ship.

Bobby turned around, checking to see if anybody was watching him. The beach was deserted. He looked out toward the pier and could now see Mom and Rick. They were still there, still talking and making goo-goo eyes at each other. Good.

He stepped closer toward the boat, pretending he was a special investigator who had just discovered an abandoned ship. He would have to tread carefully to avoid being spotted by any enemy agents whose only motive would be to discredit his find. Not to mention he had to be extra careful for any enemy spies that might be lurking in the ship. He would just peer inside quickly, assess the situation, then dash off and let his commander know what he had discovered. Headquarters would send reinforcements to aid him right away.

Something about the boat looked familiar the moment he saw it and now it dawned on him. It was Old Man Stebble's boat. But where was Old Man Stebble?

Bobby stopped and checked out his surroundings more carefully. He looked back up the beach, looking for Old Man Stebble. Surely the old fart wouldn't leave his boat on the beach unattended. And what was it doing on the beach in the first place? Old Man Stebble was real protective when it came to this boat. He wouldn't leave it *here*; he would most likely anchor it to the docks south of the pier. Bobby kept his eyes peeled for Old Man Stebble. He didn't want to be caught anywhere near the old codger's boat. Stebble had a nasty reputation of being a total prick when it came to his personal belongings.

But Old Man Stebble was nowhere to be seen.

Bobby kept his guard up as he stepped back to the boat. He was going to assess the situation quickly and hightail it back to headquarters and inform his superiors. But he had to do it before Old Man Stebble showed up or he was dead meat.

The chewed and splintered hull was the first thing he noticed as he drew near the boat. He stepped forward, craning his neck forward to see inside. A few holes had been gouged in the walls of the tiny boat and a few splintered pieces of bark lay on the floor amid dark water. It was a miracle the boat had made it this far. It looked like it should have sunk.

The cawing of the seagulls made him crane his head up. The birds were shrieking up a storm. It seemed like they were sending him messages about the boat, but it was something he couldn't fathom. He reached for his keyring where his special decoder was, and brought it out. He rubbed the shiny black surface and pointed it up at the gulls, pretending he was trying to get a read on whatever the gulls were trying to tell him. Whatever it was the birds were upset about, the decoder couldn't decipher it.

He stepped closer to the boat, his curiosity spurring him on.
Click, click!

Bobby stopped, straining his ears. What was that?

He studied the boat again. It was perched on the sand at a forty-five-degree angle, its hull and a portion of the bottom facing him. The interior lay on the other side of the boat itself. He took another step closer.

Click, click!

His heart jumped. He caught a bright flash of red through one of the holes in the side of the boat, followed by a soft scuttling sound. Bobby's heart leaped in his chest in pure excitement. There was something in the boat. Something alive. Something he could take to school Monday to show off to his friends!

The thought of finding something to show the kids at school propelled him to the boat hull. He stood on his toes and tried to get a better look over the side, but he was too short. He briefly considered circling around the exterior of the boat, but the interior was facing the ocean. Mom would cream him if he got wet.

Bobby sighed, his mouth drawn in a tight, pensive line of grim determination. The only way he was going to catch whatever was in the boat was to face it head-on. He looked around and spied a three-foot section of driftwood lying in the sand. The driftwood looked a little bit like a club. He picked it up and turned back toward the boat. Brandishing the piece of driftwood like a club gave him a new burst of confidence. Nothing would stop his mission now!

With newfound determination, Bobby walked over to the abandoned boat and rested his hand on the splintered edge. Then he carefully lifted himself up and peered over the side.

The dark storm clouds were just beginning to touch down over Phillipsport County when Bobby screamed.

Rick was telling Janice about how he became a published novelist when Bobby's scream hit their ears.

Janice was up in a flash, running down the pier toward the beach. Rick rose and scanned the shoreline, trotting after Janice.

His heart was racing. He spotted Bobby halfway up the beach, near an old boat on the waterline.

Another piercing scream.

Rick's mind slammed into action. He took off after Janice, who was already halfway to Bobby. He chased after her, running as fast as he could till he came to a halt at the boat. Janice was kneeling beside Bobby who was doubled over, howling in pain. Janice was bent over him, her features creased with worry and fear. Rick noticed that Bobby was holding his left hand and shrieking. His hand and arm were covered with blood. Janice was holding his bloody arm, trying to steer it toward her so she could get a good look. *"Bobby, let me see your hand!"*

"Mommeeee!" Bobby was howling with an intensity that made Rick's knees shake. He was at Janice's side in an instant, reaching to see what the extent of Bobby's injuries were.

Janice got a hold of his blood-streaked arm and slowly brought it up. Bobby's face was screwed up in pain, tears streamed down his face. Janice let out a little yelp when she saw the extent of Bobby's injuries. His middle finger had been severed at the second knuckle.

"It hurts!" Bobby moaned. *"Oh, Mommy it huurrttss!"*

Rick helped steady him as Janice bundled him to her bosom and lifted him up. Rick's eyes darted around, trying to catch a glimpse of what could have injured Bobby so greatly. He was running on pure adrenaline now, trying to find out what had hurt Bobby, while trying to help him and Janice at the same time.

"We've got to get him to a hospital," Janice said, her voice trembling. She turned her tear-stained features to Rick. "Will you help me get him to the hospital?"

"Of course," Rick said. His eyes were still roaming over the area, searching for a possible solution. He put his arm around Janice's shoulders to lead her away when a flash of red caught his eye. He whirled around just as—

Click, click!

—they appeared around the side of the boat. He gasped in surprise and stepped back. Janice stopped, her scream lodged in her throat. Bobby caught a glimpse of them through tear-blurred eyes and began screaming uncontrollably. *"No! Don't let them hurt me, don't let them hurt meeee!"*

There were roughly half a dozen deep-red creatures crawling out of the small boat. They looked like a cross between a giant crab and a giant scorpion. Their claws clicked in a frenzy that drove Bobby to insane shrieks. Their small black eyes wavered on eyestalks that resembled something right out of a nightmare.

The sight of them jogged Rick's mind to yesterday ... the crash ... the flashing red thing he hit ... the piece of claw that he'd given to Dr. Glen Jorgensen ...

Jesus.

There was a piece of driftwood lying on the sand. Rick picked it up and wielded it like a club as the creatures advanced on them. He stood in front of Janice and Bobby protectively, sizing the creatures up. Their pincers were menacing, but could probably be avoided. They were low to the ground and could be stepped on. It was their arched, scorpion tails that were going to give him trouble. Anything that looked that lethal was probably poisonous as well.

Rick backed up against Janice and Bobby. Janice gathered Bobby in her arms and managed to drag him back. He howled as if all the hounds of hell were on his trail.

"Janice, get Bobby the hell out of here." Rick brandished the driftwood, ready to swing if one of the mutant creatures got too close.

Janice scooped Bobby into her arms amid his screams and turned to run toward the pier when one of the creatures popped up from under the sand in front of her like a Jack-in-the-Box. Janice screamed and almost dropped Bobby. The creature locked its black marble eyes on her. Rick's heart was racing as he quickly assessed the situation.

Jesus, they were fucking surrounding *them!*

They had to get out of here some way. He reared back and swung the makeshift club Hank Aaron style at the nearest creature. The wood impacted on the thing's armored back, causing it to skitter back. Rick swung again, this time connecting with the arched tail. There was a loud snap and the last two segments of the tail broke free and flopped on sinewy meat.

The wounded creature squealed and backed up, its eyestalks wavering drunkenly.

Its two companions charged them and Rick swung like a madman, hitting the one closest to him straight in what passed for its face.

Pieces of shell and cracked mandibles flew through the air and landed in the wet sand. The force of the blow flipped the creature over on its back and it kicked its eight legs furiously like a dying spider. He backhanded the other one, the top of the club striking the side of its head. It retreated backwards as Janice screamed.

The creature in front of her had dug itself out of the sand and had the loose hem of Bobby's jacket in its claw. Mother and creature were engaged in a bizarre tug of war over Bobby as Janice kicked at the thing with her feet. Rick sprung toward the creature, rose the club over his head, and brought it down on the thing's head. The club hit the creatures' eyes, driving the eyestalks into its head and popping the eyes like grapes. The creature mewled in pain in a deep tone and kicked its legs.

It still had a hold of Bobby's jacket. Its segmented tail jabbed blindly, the stinger missing but coming too close for comfort. Rick brought the club over his head again and brought it down with all his strength. The twin sounds of splintering wood and cracking shell reached Rick's ears like sweet music. The creature twitched on the sand, its head a bashed pulp of yellow blood and red meat.

Rick barely had time to catch his breath when a wave of fury raced up to them.

"Rick, Janice! What happened ... oh Jesus!"

It was Ripper. He had just run up from the pier, probably at the sound of Bobby's screams. Now he scuttled back at the sight of more of the crawling things that were rapidly scuttling over the top of the boat toward them.

Ripper's arrival jarred Rick out of his brief lapse of reason and another burst of adrenaline blossomed in his system. He grabbed Ripper and Janice and spun them toward the parking lot. "Let's get the fuck out of here!"

He herded them toward the parking lot, not looking back

as they ran as fast as they could over the sand. The wind was blowing harder now and it looked like it was going to rain any moment. Rick ran as fast as he could while keeping Janice in front of him; he knew the going would be slower with her since she had Bobby. He debated having them stop so he could take him, but thought better of it. Why did one think of such stupid things in moments of stress?

They reached the concrete boardwalk a moment later. Ripper turned toward them, his Adam's Apple bobbing in his chicken neck. "I'll go get my van." He turned and sprinted toward the van. Rick turned his attention to Janice and Bobby.

Janice was crying openly. Her cashmere sweater was stained a deep maroon with Bobby's blood. She settled down on her knees, laying Bobby across her legs. Rick kneeled down with her, noting Bobby's condition. He had stopped moaning and seemed to have lapsed into semi-consciousness. Probably shock. His freckled face was pale, flushed. His shirt was stained red, the crotch of his blue jeans and the front of his denim clad legs stained with blood. He was holding his wounded hand to his chest, cradling it from further harm. It was still bleeding profusely.

Rick slipped out of his shirt to make a tourniquet to quench the flow of blood. Janice looked at him, still crying. "What's happening, what were those things, what's happening ..."

"I don't know," Rick said, grabbing Bobby's blood-slicked arm. "But we need to stop the bleeding." He wound his shirt around Bobby's wrist, tied them together in a knot. He couldn't remember how tight to tie a tourniquet. He remembered vague instructions on first-aid he received when he was in college, but they did no good for him now. Everything had happened so fast that he couldn't gather his thoughts together for the correct procedure. He just hoped the makeshift tourniquet was right and that it wouldn't kill him.

Janice was sobbing uncontrollably and she straightened up and turned toward the ocean. Her eyes grew wide. "Rick!"

Rick spun around. The creatures were scuttling toward them rapidly. He pulled Bobby up as Janice grabbed her son's arm and helped hoist him up. Bobby was semi-conscious, his face white. Rick scanned the parking lot, looking for Ripper's van. His adrenaline surged as a blue Chevrolet van pulled up alongside the curb. Ripper was at the wheel.

Rick swung the door open as the van pulled to a stop. He helped Janice lift Bobby inside while Ripper clamored out of the seat and jostled to the rear to help. Rick turned to catch the progress of the creatures. They were only ten yards away and rapidly approaching. Ripper eyed them, gauging the distance as he rolled Bobby into the van.

Janice hopped up into the van followed closely by Rick just as a searing bolt of pain stabbed through his left calf. He yelped and turned back to see the blaring eyes of one of the creatures bore into him. It had a hold of his left leg in one large monster pincer. Rick felt strong hands grasp his shoulders and pull him into the van, felt excruciating pain as the skin of his leg was shredded as it passed through the claw of the creature, heard the van door whisk shut, felt and saw the thing's stinger jab him in the leg, and then he blacked out.

11

Rick Sychek was waiting with nervous patience in Dr. Glen Jorgensen's waiting room when he saw Sheriff Roy Conklin pull up.

He felt a sense of dread as he watched the man get out of his squad car. Despite the fact that Conklin hadn't actually carried out his thinly-veiled threat of ticketing him for his accident, the underlying message conveyed that the sheriff would be watching him. Almost twenty-four hours later, that feeling was beginning to bear fruit.

Rick tried to calm the feeling down but he couldn't. He had been on a pure adrenaline rush since that thing attacked Bobby. And between helping him and keeping Janice calmed down and trying to help her, he hadn't been functioning emotionally very well. One little push from this bastard would be all it would take to screw up his time in this town.

He battled the emotions down and when Roy Conklin entered the waiting room, Rick didn't even look up. He was troubled by the ordeal, dammit, and he wasn't going to be made a pawn in this man's petty mind games. Still, he couldn't help feel the rise of nerves as the sheriff's eyes fell upon him as he closed the door. They seemed to be speaking to him subliminally. *Okay … what did you do this time?*

Roy Conklin strode over to the receptionist's window and knocked on the glass partition. It opened and the sheriff leaned forward. There was muffled conversation. Rick couldn't tell what was being said but whatever it was, it was brief. The door closed and the sheriff's eyes lighted on Rick again as he crossed the room. He stopped at the window and gazed out. Rick continued staring straight ahead, his mind numb, heartbeat racing.

"The boy sounds pretty badly hurt," Sheriff Conklin finally said, breaking the silence.

Rick nodded. "Yeah," he said, softly. "He—"

"You were there when it happened." Not a question. Just a statement of the facts.

"Yes," Rick nodded.

"Mind telling me what happened?"

Rick gulped. The incident rose in his mind again, unbidden in the ferocity of it. He told Sheriff Roy Conklin, paying no heed to the credence of the story. Let the sheriff think he'd lost his mind, the man had to know what was out there. He spilled it out; his walk to the pier, meeting Jack Ripley, and later Janice and her son; he related the scream, how he and Janice had raced down to see what had happened and the horror of what they saw; the beast slinking toward them as Rick scooped Bobby up in his arms, the last minute attack by the creature that had almost killed *him*, the flight back to Dr. Jorgensen's and through it all Janice's hysterical voice babbling about her baby, her poor baby boy—

When he finished there was silence. He looked up at Sheriff Conklin, who looked at him from behind his mirror shades. The lawman's features were expressionless. "You don't believe me," he said.

"I didn't say that," Roy Conklin said.

"But it looks like you're going to."

"If you were me and just heard what you said, you wouldn't believe yourself, either." Sheriff Conklin put his hands on his hips and seemed to glare down at Rick. "You say these things that attacked you guys were crab things?"

"Yes, crab things," Rick exclaimed. He held his arms about three feet apart, indicating the creatures size. "They were about this big from head to tail. They looked like giant lobsters to tell you the truth."

Roy looked at him as if he was a new species of insect. "Giant lobster? Listen to yourself, kid. How do you expect me to believe a shit story like that?"

"I don't care what you believe!" Rick was on the verge of

shouting and he mentally checked himself. From behind the nurses partition, movement appeared. A headache began rising in the bony ridge of his nose, right behind the eyes, and he closed his eyes to will it away. When he opened them the sheriff was gazing out the window again. "I'm sorry," he said quietly. "I didn't mean to shout."

Roy Conklin didn't answer. He kept his gaze trained out the window at the lightly falling rain.

Rick Sychek stood in the middle of the waiting room, trying hard to keep his frustration down. He'd been on the verge of telling the sheriff about the claw he'd dug out of his tire the day before, how he thought it might belong to one of the crab things. But after seeing the lawman's reaction to his story, he figured his credibility with the man would slip even further if he told him his theory about the accident. So he kept his mouth shut. Roy remained silent as he kept his gaze on the rain. The sky outside was light gray but it was growing darker rapidly. The wind was picking up again. The silence was deafening.

Rick was just settling back into his seat and psyching himself up to telling the sheriff more about what happened when the lawman broke the silence. "It looks like the storm's going to get worse."

Rick looked out the window.

The storm clouds were massive; coal black and building, they roiled across the sky threateningly. The wind blew briskly, scuttling leaves and grass, bending the smaller trees. From as far as the eye could see the clouds covered the horizon, blotting out the afternoon sun. A few drops of rain spattered on the ground outside and hit the window. Rick retreated from the window and cast a glance at Sheriff Conklin. The sheriff remained at the window, seemingly entranced by the sudden storm. It looked like it was going to be a big one.

Rick was beginning to wonder what was going on behind the closed door to Glen Jorgensen's office when the lights suddenly went out.

With the now absent sun, it cast the waiting room in a grayish gloom. Rick looked up at the lights in surprise, and from behind the glass partition he heard the sharp exclamation of Glen Jorgensen's nurse Barbara. Sheriff Conklin peered out the window. "No lightning, yet," he said. "Strange."

The squawk of CB static came through the radio clasped to Roy Conklin's belt. He unclipped it and raised it to his mouth. "Unit 7 to Unit 12, I copy you. Over."

Deputy Rusty's voice came in, full of static and tin. "Sheriff Conklin, I've got a power outage here at headquarters. I put in a call to the GE plant and didn't receive a response. Over."

"Did you try the CB band, Unit 12? Over."

"Affirmative, Unit 7. I've been unable to raise anybody in all communications, sir. It also appears the power is out elsewhere. It looks mighty dark out there. Over."

"Meet me at the GE Plant in fifteen minutes, Unit 12. Over." Sheriff Conklin headed for the door.

The door to Glen Jorgensen's office opened and the physician stepped out, looking surprised to see the Sheriff. Barbara stood behind him, peering curiously over his shoulder.

"Affirmative, Unit 7," Deputy Rusty's tinny voice squeaked. "Over and out."

"Over and out, Unit 12." Roy Conklin signed out, nodding at Glen Jorgensen as he replaced the CB unit and made for the door. He bade Glen a courteous nod. "Gotta run, Doc, but I'll be back in a few to take a report." He stepped outside and dashed to his patrol car. He backed out of the driveway and headed down the road into the storm.

Glen approached Rick from behind. "What was that all about?"

"It sounds like the power is out all over town," Rick said. "He's meeting Rusty at the power plant to see what's happening."

From behind them, Barbara spoke softly. "I'll go back and check on Bobby and Janice. He got really spooked when the lights went out, poor thing." She turned and went down the hall.

Glen and Rick stood in the waiting room, looking out the window. The storm was growing stronger, the winds blew harder yet the rain was still coming down in drizzles and spits. Lightning couldn't be seen, nor thunder heard. "Did the wind blow the power line down?" Dr. Jorgenson asked.

Rick shook his head and pointed out the window.

"No. Look up there." Glen followed his pointing finger. The power line across the street was intact, the thick, heavy cables resting in their spot as they always did. "And it surely wasn't lightning, either. We would have seen it, heard the thunder right before the lights went out."

Glen Jorgensen was quiet. His heavily-lined face was etched in worry. "I wonder what it is then?"

Outside, the storm grew stronger.

12

Deputy Russell Hanks got to the GE power plant two minutes before Sheriff Roy Conklin sped to a stop at the gates of the employee parking lot.

He'd received a call from the Phillipsport County dispatcher that something was amiss at the power plant. Just what, the dispatcher didn't say. It had been a routine 911 call, most likely from building security. It could be anything from a medical emergency to some wayward criminals holding up inside the plant with a hostage situation. The nearest state prison was one hundred miles south and a good fifty miles inland. If there were prisoners that had made a break it was feasible they could have made it this far north on foot, especially if they had stuck to the heavily wooded areas.

Sheriff Conklin had answered the call on the radio and Rusty waited for him in his patrol car at the entrance of the building. The wind was picking up a bit, and Rusty drew his raincoat tighter around his lanky body. He hadn't seen it rain this hard in years.

A moment later Sheriff Conklin's car pulled up beside Rusty's. Conklin rolled down the passenger side window. The rain had trickled to a steady drizzle. "Let's see what kind of shit this is, partner." Roy sneered. For a moment Rusty wondered what it would be like to step behind Conklin, pull his police-issued revolver, point it at the back of his superior's head and decorate the ground with Sheriff Brain stew.

It was the first time the thought of killing Sheriff Conklin crossed Rusty's mind and the notion downright scared him. The thought of pulling a gun on another human being unprovoked had never crossed his mind, especially in the heat of malice. It wasn't the act *per se* that had him on such pins and needles; rather, it was the fact of actually performing it. He would draw his gun if threatened and shoot to kill to protect himself or uphold the law. But to do so out of malice and hatred? Yes, Sheriff Conklin was an unbearable, smug, racist asshole and yes, Rusty admitted that at times he downright hated the man. But kill him?

Why, that would make him just like Sheriff Conklin.

Rusty tried not to let his unease show as he got out of his car and followed the bigger man to the large gate that bordered the lot. "How's the Harrelson kid?" Rusty asked, trying to make conversation.

"Pretty torn up," Conklin replied. They were standing outside the gate to the power plant. "That Ichabod Crane-looking hippie that runs that comic book store and that new guy brought him and his mother into Doc Jorgensen's. That new guy was there at the Doc's when I showed up."

Rusty frowned. When Conklin didn't like somebody he didn't give them the compliment of calling them by their first name. It was like they didn't even exist. Hell, Rusty was surprised Conklin referred to *him* by his first name.

Before he could stop it from coming out, Rusty let his tongue loose. "Why don't you like Rick, Sheriff Conklin? He sure ain't done nothin' to you."

Conklin reacted as if a bucket of cold water had been thrown on him. He turned slowly to Rusty, a look of dumbfounded amazement on his craggy face. His cold, gray eyes were like flint and they bore right into Rusty's. Rusty dropped his gaze from the sheriff, wishing he hadn't said anything. God, but the man was an intimidating prick.

The ice was broken by Conklin's laughter. Rusty looked up into Conklin's face, cracked by a wide grin as he chuckled. Rusty grinned, feeling the pressure lift from his shoulders. Roy put his hands on his hips, grinning down at his deputy. "Why that's a stupid question, Rusty. You know how I feel about outsiders to Phillipsport. Especially ones from big cities like Philadelphia or New York, and especially ones with hair long enough to pass for a woman. Damn bunch of commie-loving, war-protesting, drug-snorting bastards is what they are. Every single one of 'em. Ain't no better than niggers and faggots as far as I'm concerned." Conklin glowered at Rusty, his intimidating figure seeming to tower over the Deputy. "It shouldn't matter to you what I think of him," Roy said, slow and steady. "What should matter is you knowing when to keep your nose out of other people's business."

Rusty gulped and shuffled a step back. He didn't want to bring Conklin's fury down on him, but then again he'd seen the sheriff violate the rights of too many people. Control was his vice, and intimidation was how he wielded it. He'd born witness to Roy's threats and intimidation since he had been a deputy, and his reluctance to stand up to the man felt like he was tarnishing the badge of law and order.

Only now he wasn't going to take it anymore. He was getting downright tired of it. He stepped forward. "I think that's something you need to follow yourself, Sheriff. Butting into other people's business—like singling out Mr. Sychek for something he ain't even done; now *that's* buttin' into other people's business. And if you're like'n to keep that up, then I guess I'm gonna have to tell the proper authorities."

There. He'd said it. And his belly began flip-flopping in his abdomen as Sheriff Conklin glowered at him with an evil looking grin. "Why Russell ... that's pretty damn good. For a minute there I didn't think you had any balls."

"I got balls ... you can bet on that. Least I don't pick on people the way you do."

Roy's grin faded, replaced by an angry grimace. His eyes narrowed in their sockets. "You better watch your fucking tongue boy. I'll slap you so hard your whole family will die."

Rusty's heart was racing madly in his ribcage and he could feel the adrenaline pouring through his system. He was pumped and ready to go full swing. Might as well go all the way. What else did he have to lose besides this dead-end job? "You know, I have a feeling that the people of this town are sick of you and the way you treat people."

"What are you sayin' boy?" Roy coaxed him on, daring him.

Rusty paused for a moment as the rain pounded steady. "Folks around town don't like the way you do business. Next year's the election and word is you won't be re-elected."

Roy stood still, looking like an animal trapped in the headlights of an oncoming car. It obviously appeared that he had gotten the message loud and clear. He grunted, turned and began heading toward the power plant.

As they strode up the walkway to the power plant, Rusty appeared to let down his guard. Roy noticed this with a smirk. He would have figured it. The feebleminded deputy could talk as much shit as he wanted but it wouldn't do any good. Sheriff Roy Conklin was in control of this town, *not* the taxpaying citizens of Phillipsport. They just better watch it and not pull any funny stuff or they would see how quickly help arrived when the town started going up in flames.

But now his thoughts on his political defeat evaporated as he and Rusty stopped and looked up at the towering monolith that controlled the region's electricity.

Usually the building was lit up like a Christmas Tree. Not so now. There wasn't one light on in the structure anywhere.

Rusty looked concerned. Roy glanced at him with slight irritation and rubbed the back of his head. Much as he hated Rusty, he had to admit the power outage at the GE Plant was pretty weird shit.

Rusty finally broke the silence. "Where is everyone?"

Roy was going to come back with an inane retort destined to put Rusty in his place, but the rain-soaked parking lot and empty windows of the building made him think otherwise. "I don't know," he said quietly. The hostility was gone for the moment. The two men were once again cops.

Roy looked at the security booth next to the gate, which was wide open. Somebody should have emerged from the booth when they drove up. No guard had emerged to meet them, and nobody had emerged from the building.

Roy zipped up his coat, drew his hood up over his head and turned toward the booth. Rusty sighed and quickly followed suit. They walked up to the booth. Roy pulled a flashlight from his belt and flicked it on. He tapped on the dark window a few times, hoping for a response, but none came. He shined the light into the booth. It was empty.

He stepped back and looked up at the fence. The top was covered with spools of razorwire. He looked down toward the beach where the waves were slamming on the rocks with massive power. He turned his gaze toward the cars in the parking lot, the security camera perched on top of the security booth, and wondered why nobody from the control room inside hadn't come outside to greet them when they pulled in.

It was apparent that nobody was manning the control panel in the plant. Roy moved to the front gate, which was wide open. He placed a gloved hand on the chain-link fence. He tugged at the gate in puzzlement. "What the fuck's going on? This thing is always locked."

Lightning flashed in the distance, followed by a steady roll of thunder. The rain beat down harder, as if the sudden thunder had opened a chasm in the sky. Sheriff Conklin and Rusty raced down the lot to the employee entrance and the shelter of the overhanging concrete of the plant.

It was hidden from the security booth and the parking lot, but once they got to the employee entrance they knew something was terribly wrong.

The glass doors of the entrance were smashed to pieces. They lay shattered in the foyer.

They pulled their guns out of their holsters and crept quietly inside. Roy motioned silence. The tiled floor of the foyer was quickly becoming covered with water from the rain and the going was slippery. They crept slowly into the building.

The interior security booth was to the left. They approached it slowly, guns drawn. The steady rain pattering outside was the only sound in the plant.

The booth appeared empty.

Roy stopped just shy of the visitor's window where people stopped to sign in to security before going on to other parts of the building. He could see into the window of the booth and noticed the non-descript items: the desks, the control panels, computer monitors. No lights blinked on the panels. The monitors were blank.

Roy's nose tickled. He sniffed at the air, his nasal passages picking up a strong, acidic scent. His eyes almost watered from the stench. "You smell that, Rusty?"

"Yep."

And it was then that he saw it, just out of the corner of his eye. A patch of blue lying on the floor, between the door of the security room and the employee break room. He motioned to Rusty.

His deputy saw it. "What do you think it is?" Rusty asked quietly.

Roy shook his head. It looked like a discarded shirt, but it was hard to tell in the dark.

"Follow me."

They moved forward. Roy pulled out his flashlight. They made their way over to the spot until they stood over the thing on the floor. Roy trained his flashlight beam on the floor. Rusty gagged and turned away as Conklin tried to figure out what he was looking at. The strong smell was wafting up from it and it took a moment for Roy to realize what he was looking at.

When he realized, he winced. "Jesus Christ!"

It had once been a man. That much was apparent from the few remaining scraps of clothing. A tarnished security guard badge lay amid the tattered, slimy clothing. What remained of him was nothing more than a pile of red, smoking ooze with yellow bone poking out in a helter-skelter of gunk. The head was little more than a skull completely stripped of flesh and skin. The jaw was hanging off at an angle and Roy could see that the left side had been punched in to get at the brain.

The ribcage was collapsed, the bones broken, snapped, and otherwise melted. There were no identifiable internal organs anywhere. What little flesh was left was bubbling and sizzling like it had been doused with acid.

Rusty grabbed Sheriff Conklin in panic. "It's true, Sheriff. Just what Rick says. There's giant crab monsters running around stinging people! We've got to warn the—"

Conklin grabbed Rusty by the collar and shoved his face

to within a hair's breath of Rusty's. "We ain't warning nobody. Not until I find out what's going on around here." He loosened his grip on Rusty's jacket and straightened up. He tried to smile. "There has to be somebody here in the building."

He turned around, shining his flashlight in the gloom. A doorway was etched into the darkness down at the end of the hall that led to the generators. Roy pointed to it. "Let's check out the generator."

Roy began moving down the corridor toward the generator room. Rusty remained rooted to the spot near the break room. The sheriff stopped and turned around; his deputy looked ready to puke. Roy sneered. "What's the matter boy … can't play the big man's game?"

Rusty only looked up at him in revulsion and fear as the sheriff chuckled and opened the door to the interior workings of the power station.

A moment later, Roy felt the other man behind him, following him like the peon he was. Roy grunted his satisfaction, puffing himself up to lead the way.

They slowly made their way to the interior of the power plant. The beam from his flashlight played on a maze of pipes, tubes, and railings that went in all directions; they shimmied up the walls, along the ceilings, and sprouted from the floor. Big monolithic computer equipment jutted up like Egyptian pyramids in sectioned cubicles. Along one wall sat a bank of computer equipment with tape reels. Roy played his light toward them; beyond lay rows of shelving housing more tapes. Probably computerized records of every utility bill within a forty-mile area.

The acidic smell was stronger in this room than it had been out in the main hallway. They moved slowly, their flashlights playing upon computer equipment, pipes, desks, scattered remnants of paperwork that had spilled onto the floor amid demolished office furniture and machines. Something had happened here and the dim light emanated by the flashlights wasn't bringing out the mystery.

Undaunted, Roy pressed forward, ignoring Rusty's faltering steps behind him. He heard the deputy gag at the stench. The poor boy was probably pissing his pants in fear right now. Some cop.

Roy pressed forward toward a large metal threshold that led deeper into the building. The warehouse?

Click, click!

"What was that?" Rusty's voice was loud, scared.

Roy whirled around, flashlight shining on Rusty's frightened face. His gun was clenched tightly in his fist. "It's nothing. You're letting your imagination get to you ..."

"No, it was *something*, it was—"

"It was just the pipes cooling down!" Roy said. "We're in a power outage, remember? When the power goes, the water in the pipes cool down."

Rusty was nearly hysterical. *"That ain't no fucking pipes! It's the crab things that Rick told us about!"*

Roy snorted. "You want to go back?"

Rusty nodded vigorously.

"Did you bring your flashlight?"

Rusty looked down at his belt. It was sans flashlight. The dipshit had left it in the car again. He looked up at Roy with a sheepish expression.

"Unless you can find your way back in the dark, I suggest you shut your fucking hole and stick by me."

Rusty sighed. He might be scared, but he wouldn't dare defy Roy's orders. Not if he wanted to keep his job.

Roy turned back to the threshold and led the way through the rest of the plant. Rusty tagged along behind him. Roy moved slowly, deliberately. He wanted to listen closely to any sounds that might be emanating from the darkness. Sounds would provide good clues as to what may have happened.

Sharp clicks echoed throughout the metal guts of the building.

Roy's fingers itched as it played over the trigger of his revolver. God, he wanted to shoot something.

A soft moan floated from the darkness.

Both cops froze in their tracks. Roy moved the light and his revolver toward the direction of the sound. Beside him, Rusty had pulled his own weapon and was training it in the same direction.

The moan came again. Louder.

Something red moved on the floor ahead of them.

Roy leveled his gun and fired. The shot reverberated through the building, making the pipes buzz. The red thing ahead of them stopped moving. Roy kept his trigger arm as rigid as steel, finger poised ready to fire again.

Rusty leaned close to him. "Is it dead?" He whispered.

Roy slowly approached the thing, puzzled. Rusty trailed behind him cautiously. Roy shined his light on the figure and he heard Rusty draw a sharp intake of breath as his own heart began a quick beat of fear.

It was a man. At least from the waist up.

Roy resisted the urge to vomit even as his partner voided his lunch in steaming splatters on the floor behind them. He willed his hands to stop shaking even as the light from the flashlight wavered in the gloom, creating spotlights around the form that had once been human.

The man appeared to have once been a utility worker, maybe a computer operator. His blue coveralls and plastic name badge told Roy that much. He could also tell that the poor sucker had been in extreme pain before his bullet sheared the side of his head off. Blood and brain matter decorated the floor; a dark, thick pool was expanding under him.

From the waist down it was a different story. All of the flesh and bone below his waist was in the process of being eaten away. The same bubbling acid they saw in the break room was eating at the exposed bone and flesh of the dead man's lower half. Roy let his eyes travel away from the man's body to follow the gruesome trail that led into the darkness. The poor sucker had been crawling toward them on his hands and belly as the acid ate away at his knees. He probably heard them come in. From the amount of blood and dissolved meat it was surprising that he made it this far. The agony must have been intolerable, plus the severing of his femoral artery surely would have allowed his life to escape quicker. Which meant that this just happened to him. Maybe within the last minute ...

Roy took a deep breath, trying to piece it together. He had to stay calm, otherwise Rusty was going to go bugfuck and they would *both* wind up as mush like this guy.

"A chemical leak ... that has to be it. Some kind of acid that eats at the flesh." Roy spoke slowly, as if repeating carefully rehearsed lines. That had to be it. When he served in 'Nam his company once experienced a chemical leak on their base. The effect had been similar on the few hapless souls that were unlucky enough to contact the deadly chemical mixture they were working with. They'd been planning on spraying a Viet Cong village with the stuff when the spill happened. Ten men died pretty much like the poor sucker lying on the warehouse floor in front of him. The chemical testing on the Viet Cong village had been aborted. Whatever chemical this man had been eaten by, it had to be the same thing he'd experienced in Viet Nam.

"Chemical leak? Can't you see that there's something alive that's doing this?" Rusty's voice was a high screech.

Roy brought his revolver up. "I see people being killed by some kind of acid. That's all." His voice was soft. Calm. "I saw something similar in 'Nam when we were experimenting with a chemical weapon. It did the same thing. You see something different, obviously."

Rusty's eyes darted to the dead man at their feet. "I see that you just shot this guy! He was trying to crawl to us for help and you shot him without identifying yourself as a police officer. That's—"

Roy whirled, the barrel of the revolver pointing right at Rusty's face. He clicked back the hammer as Rusty went rigid. All the color drained out of the deputy's face. "That's *what?*" Roy's voice was deadened, his eyes narrowed like cold flints.

Rusty quivered in his uniform. His hands rose in the air. Surrender. "Wh-what ... y-you can't ..."

Roy kept the weapon aimed at the deputy. "I can do anything I goddamn feel like. Especially when it comes to making a loud-mouthed deputy stay quiet. Now ... what I see here is a guy who was killed by an acid leak ... a guy who was dead when I accidentally slipped and dropped my gun, thereby causing the wound in his head. Isn't that what you see, Rusty?"

Rusty was shaking so hard that his own gun nearly slipped from his fingers.

Roy's lips pulled back into a grin. He could smell another acidic stench; that of urine which had no doubt suddenly voided from Rusty's bladder.

Roy lifted the gun from Rusty's face. He had done the trick. "You know ... I'd be careful on these slick floors ... I might just slip again." The gun came back down to sight on Rusty's pale, wet forehead.

Rusty backed up, his body trembling. "No ... don't ..."

Roy's finger twitched. A slight tug and all his problems would vanish in a cloud of smoke and blood.

His finger tightened on the trigger. Rusty screamed.

Roy jerked the gun back and laughed. Oh, to feel the power, to feel others grovel at his knees in fright!

He looked at Rusty, laughing. "You miserable sack of shit."

And then, the noise again ...

Click, click!

Rusty's shriek caused Roy to jump back and nearly trip over the dead man. His heart leaped into his chest and his adrenaline spurned. He gained his balance, tightened his grip on the gun and moved forward. He stabbed his light toward Rusty where the sound came from. "Goddammit, what the hell is going on—"

He stopped, nearly tripping over them. At Rusty's feet were two huge red scorpion-like creatures with their pincers tearing away chunks of flesh out of the deputy's leg. The things were busy stuffing the strips of meat and skin into their chitinous mouths as Rusty screamed at the top of his lungs.

Roy watched in horror, rooted to the spot as Rusty tried to scramble away only to fall to his knees in pain.

Rusty looked down at the creatures. He lifted the .38 and pointed it at one of the creatures' backs. The slug shattered the crustacean's shell and exploded its insides. It twitched and fell over on its back, its legs curling in like a dead spider.

The second creature dug its claws into Rusty's thigh and bit down hard. Blood spurted from the wound, drenching the creature. Rusty's eyes were wide in pain, his face slick with sweat and contorted with agony and what looked to Roy like anger. He stuck the barrel of the gun against the thing's shell between the eyestalks. He pulled the trigger and the shell ripped the creature apart. It grew still with its pincers still embedded in the deputy's leg.

Rusty's energy dissolved and a pall seemed to wash over him. He collapsed back against a layer of pipes and closed his eyes. He whimpered, his breath coming in short gasps. Roy still remained rooted to the spot. He couldn't believe what he just saw. It couldn't be a chemical leak now. It was something far beyond anything he could have ever dreamed.

Roy moved, felt warm moisture on his crotch and the inside of his legs. He had pissed himself.

Ignoring his damp trousers, Roy shined the flashlight on Rusty. The deputy opened his eyes, his breathing harsh and ragged. His leg was bleeding badly. His fingers were still locked on the gun.

Roy turned, checking the rest of the plant. The beam from his flashlight stabbed darkness. He couldn't see or hear anything out there. He turned back to Rusty who lifted his arm, pointed his gun at Roy, and fired.

There was a sear of pain through Roy's right thigh. The sheriff yelled and fell. The flashlight tumbled to the ground and spun, trailing flickering light along the walls. The reverberation of the shot echoed in the plant as Roy howled, eyes squeezed shut, his hands clamped over the wound. *Goddamn sonofabitch shot me!*

The flashlight stopped spinning, it's light shining back toward where they had come. The exit.

Roy began scampering toward a large row of machinery, dragging his lower body behind him just as another gunshot sounded. He felt it pinging right by him. He darted behind the object, groaning as he settled his weight on a portion of his injury. *The goddamn motherfucker is shooting at me! Who the fuck does he think he is?*

A fresh wave of pain flowed through him as he raised his own gun, leveling it toward the ceiling. He was lucky he hadn't dropped it when Rusty shot him.

Click-click! Click, click, click, click …

The metal interior of the plant suddenly echoed with hundreds of sharp clicks. Roy's eyes darted around the plant, suddenly seeing shadows squirm and come alive. His vision barely made out deep red shiny shells scurry about and multiply. A fish-like smell assaulted his nasal passages.

Gritting his teeth, Sheriff Conklin rose, his back rubbing against the cold metal of the shapeless piece of machinery. He hobbled toward the edge of the machinery, listening. Amid the clicking he could hear the scurrying and drag of Rusty trying to make his getaway. The bastard.

Conklin emerged from behind the machine and hobbled toward where Rusty had been. The pain in his leg throbbed, but he could move it. He dimly made out Rusty's form hobbling toward the exit, limping on ravaged legs. Roy raised his gun and fired. The bullet hit Rusty's shoulder, jerking him forward, pushing his body to the floor. He fell, the gun flying through the air to hit the ground. Roy grinned as he limped toward the fallen deputy.

Rusty turned over, making scrabbling motions to get away. His eyes grew wide as Roy limped forward, his gun smoking as it came up again, pointing at him. "You stupid hick fuck. I'll send you straight to hell." He leveled the gun at Rusty's chest and was about to fire when he felt a sharp tug on his leg. He looked down.

One of the scorpion-like things was tugging at his pants with its large pincers. It pulled and the fabric ripped free, exposing his bare calf. Roy reacted instantly, swinging the gun barrel down and pulling the trigger. The shot blew the crustacean into chunky red and yellow sauce.

A barrage of clicking behind him brought six more making their way right toward him. Roy turned his head and saw that the fallen flashlight was pointing at the door the way they'd come in. He shot a glance at the wounded deputy and grinned. Rusty shuddered.

Roy smiled and limped quickly toward the exit. The pain from the gunshot wound hampered his movement, but Roy tried to will the pain away. He would get through this. He made a wide berth around Rusty, chuckling as he did so. He retrieved the fallen flashlight, cast one look back at Rusty. "So long, motherfucker."

Then he left. Moving out the door and closing it behind him, leaving Rusty in the darkness of the power plant.

A moment later all that remained of Deputy Russell Hanks was his badge, gun belt, and high school ring.

The crustaceans wandered through the pipes and machinery, searching for any last bits of edible matter. The vague sounds of a quickly retreating police cruiser barely registered in their primitive auditory canals.

What did register was the presence of something else.

This sent a wave of panic through the creatures as they skittered and crawled into any dark crack or crevice they could find. Their primitive nervous system could register only a few sensations and this was one that they knew better than the others.

They knew it better than the urge to breed.

They knew it better than hunger.

They all felt the emotion as old as time itself.

Fear.

13

Rick was leaning against the receptionist counter as Glen Jorgensen leaned over the transmitter. "… Bangor General, please come in, Bangor General—"

Glen Jorgensen had been trying to reach Bangor General Hospital for the past fifteen minutes. This was the second attempt they'd made; the first had been close on the heels of when Janice and Bobby arrived at his office when it became apparent that Bobby's injuries were much worse than Glen thought. When he was met with static, he darted back into his examination room, barking at Barbara to assist him. Rick had waited in the comfy lobby as the physician worked on Bobby, wondering how the boy was, how Janice was making out through all this. He wanted to be back there to offer some comfort, some support, but he knew he would be hindering whatever Dr. Jorgensen had to do. So he sat in the lobby.

Glen Jorgensen emerged thirty minutes later looking tired and drained. He had worked on Bobby himself, suturing what remained of his finger, splinting and bandaging his hand. Between the time Sheriff Roy Conklin left and Glen began working on Bobby, the storm had grown stronger. Rain pelted the roof and came down in sheets, billowed by the howling wind. When Glen emerged from the examination room he hardly noticed the weather outside; he went straight back to the transmitter and tried again.

It was at this point that Rick got up and sidled up to the reception area. Glen noticed him and nodded. "I gave both of them a mild sedative. They're resting in the room down at the end of the hall if you want to see them."

Rick nodded and walked down, limping slightly from the bandaged wound on his right leg. Barbara was emerging from the room when he approached it. Her features were strained with worry. "You can see them, but not for long. They both need rest."

"How is he?"

Barbara sighed. She was middle-aged and matronly with reddish hair cut to the shoulders. She wore a white nurse's uniform with a blue sweater draped over her shoulders. "We sutured his finger as best we could and got him stabilized. But he's lost some blood and is in shock."

"Will he need an emergency blood supply?" If the kid needed blood now Rick would gladly hop onto an examining table and jab the needle in the vein himself.

"I don't think so," Barbara said matter-of-factly. "But Dr. Jorgensen is trying to raise Bangor General. He needs to be in a hospital."

The rain suddenly drummed harder, and thunder boomed. *KA-BOOM!* Its reverberations shook the building. It was the loudest crack of thunder he'd ever heard, or felt. They both looked up for a moment as the boom faded amid the patter-patter of rain, then back at each other. "How 'bout Janice?"

"In shock, as any mother would be," Barbara said, her features lined with worry. "But she'll pull through."

Rick moved toward the door. "I won't be long," he said.

Barbara nodded and Rick stepped inside the room.

Janice had been wheeled into the examination room on a stretcher, and now she was resting with her eyes closed next to Bobby who lay asleep on the examination table with a blanket pulled over him. Bobby's bandaged and splintered hand was cradled close to his chest. It looked like his hand had grown gargantuan. Janice was drowsy but alert. Rick knelt down by her. He wanted her to know he was here for her, but he didn't want to appear smothering. A slight smile appeared on her face as he knelt beside her. "You're still here?" Her voice was weak.

"Of course," he whispered. "I wouldn't leave you two here to fend for yourselves."

"You're a dear," she said. Her hand reached out, her fingers lightly brushing the top of his hand. A genuine gesture. "How are you?"

"How am I?" For a moment Rick had forgotten that he'd been hurt. "Oh, that …" It was incredible that in light of what happened to Bobby and their scramble to get off the beach and to Dr. Jorgensen's that she would remember, much less notice, that he had been stung by one of the Clickers. "I'm fine."

"Good." She settled back on the pillow, her eyes growing heavier. "God, I'm so tired."

"I know," Rick said. He wasn't very tired himself. If anything, the stress had pumped up his adrenaline. But then he hadn't taken a tranquilizer either.

If there was one thing that surprised them all, it was the attack on Rick. The cuts to his leg from the creature's massive pincer had been deep and ugly but hadn't required stitches. Glen attributed that to Rick pulling away just as the creature locked its hold down on him. If he had hesitated a moment sooner and jerked his leg back, the force of the creature's hold on him would have pulled the meat off his leg the way one pulls meat off a chicken leg.

The creature's stinger had pierced the muscle of his right thigh, creating a nice three-inch-deep puncture wound, almost as if he'd been stabbed by a small knife. Glen had examined him shortly after Bobby was stabilized, and dressed the wound. If the creature was venomous—and Dr. Jorgensen was pretty sure they were from the evidence Rick and Jack Ripley had been able to provide—Rick had received what the Good Doctor referred to as a "dry sting"—when the animal bites or stings, but no venom is injected.

"It happens with rattlesnake bites quite a bit," Dr. Jorgensen said. "You'd be surprised." Surprised he was. And grateful.

Luckily, in the name of science, the thing's tail had been severed when the door to the van slammed shut. The moment they hauled Rick in screaming in pain and slammed the door, Janice saw the tail. She batted toward the rear of the van while Rick clutched at his leg, eyes squeezed shut in pain, tears welling from them, wondering if he was going to die. Jack was driving like a maniac to get them to Glen's and the tail was forgotten until Glen and Barbara were helping them into the office. After Glen stabilized Rick, he got Jack to go back to the van and retrieve it. Jack had brought it to him, holding it by the tips of his fingers as if it were cancerous. Glen took it gingerly and deposited it in the back room, laying it to rest on a shelf in the freezer with the claw Rick had brought him yesterday. For future reference.

Glen was positive the thing was poisonous. But ten minutes after they had arrived at his office, Rick showed no signs that any venom had been injected into his system. There'd been no abnormal swelling, no loss of muscle coordination, no slurred speech or blurred vision, no nausea, cramps, or vomiting. And most importantly, no deterioration of the flesh that was common in the Brown Recluse Spider, and in some cases, rattlesnake bites.

"I'm going to rest for a little bit," Janice said. "Will you take me and Bobby home?"

"Of course." Rick squeezed her hand. "I'll be here."

"Good." Her eyes opened briefly. "Thanks, Rick."

Rick smiled and stood up. Janice closed her eyes again and was asleep in no time.

Back at the reception area, Glen was still trying to raise Bangor General. Barbara was sitting at her desk, looking almost defeated by the fact that there really was nothing for her to do to help the situation. What could one do with a huge storm, a disaster of possible monstrous proportions, and a downed radio?

Glen turned to Rick as he entered the reception area. "Nothing," he said, almost angrily. "I can't even get anything. Nothing but static."

"Have you tried anybody else?" Rick asked.

"I tried raising the sheriff at the station but transmission is out everywhere. It must be this storm." Glen sighed and rubbed his forehead with the back of his forearm.

"The phone lines are down, too," Barbara said.

Great. "What about the local radio?"

Glen reached over to a transistor radio that sat underneath the reception counter and flicked it on. Static on both AM and FM bands, all across the dial.

"Jesus Christ, we should be able to get something." Now Rick was alarmed. He could understand the power going out, maybe even the phone lines going out in a storm, but the lines weren't down. Whatever it was, it had to do with something at the plant. If the power was affecting everybody on a wide scale it would also affect the radio station and the phone company. But wouldn't they be equipped with an emergency generator?

"Whatever is going on, it must have to do with something at the GE plant," Glen said. He rose to his full six-foot height, shaking his head in confusion.

"Sheriff Conklin took off for the plant not long after he got here," Rick said. "Rusty radioed in and there seemed to be some kind of problem out there."

"I just wonder what." The expression on Glen's face didn't look so good. It cast a dreary pall over Barbara and Rick.

Rick tried to break it. He motioned toward the rear of the house. "What happens with Janice and Bobby?"

"He should have gone to the hospital, which was why I was trying to raise them." Glen lowered his voice. "If I could I'd drive them to Bangor myself, but with the way this storm is I don't trust those roads."

"Plus who knows what it's like outside the Phillipsport County limits," Barbara piped in. "It'll be best to just hole up here until this blows over."

Glen nodded. "Barb's right. Bobby's stabilized enough now that he can sleep off the tranquilizer and be okay when he wakes up tomorrow morning."

"Could they both go home tonight?" Rick asked.

Glen nodded reluctantly "If it wasn't for this storm I'd rather Bobby would have gone to Bangor General. But he's stable enough to where he can go home and recuperate nicely. If he rests, his body should be able to regenerate the blood that was lost. I can take them home myself if you'd rather go back to the beach and fetch Janice's car."

Rick nodded. That sounded like a plan. Jack had gone back to the pier to shut down his store and try rousing somebody at the sheriff's station—there were usually two additional men on duty beside Rusty and Roy. There was no telling when Jack would return and there was no way to call the comic shop to update him. Besides, it would be better for him to go to the beach for the car anyway. He surely didn't want the Doc to go down there in the event that those creatures were still around.

"What I'd really like to do is take a better look at that tail you brought in." Dr. Jorgensen looked mighty interested in that. "I gave that claw you gave me last night a good look over. Couldn't identify it for the world. It bore all the similarities of your regular garden variety crab or lobster, but it was ... all *wrong*."

"How so?" Rick asked. How could something that by all rights looked like a crab or lobster claw not be?

"I took a blood sample from it, ran it under a microscope, and while I'm not a marine biologist, the sample didn't match up to any of the DNA samplings I could compare to in any of my textbooks on marine life." Glen Jorgensen shook his head in dismay. "The white blood cells were shaped differently and there seemed to be more of them, a higher count than normally known for that species of crustacean. The DNA itself was ..." Glen appeared to be groping for the right word. " ... just not right. I don't know how else to explain it."

"Maybe we should get it to a professional," Rick suggested.

"I'd like to. The closest University with a good marine biology department is the University of Maine in Orono, a good two hundred miles south. Maybe after this storm lets up, we can pack those samples in ice and get them down there." Glen cocked a questioning eyebrow at Rick. "You'll help me?"

"Of course. Just say the word. Where do you have them now?"

"Freezer in the back."

During their talk, Barbara had slipped quietly away to check on Janice and Bobby. She came back with a more relaxed composure. "They're both sleeping soundly," she said.

Glen Jorgensen nodded. "Good. Janice should come out of it in another hour or so." He looked at Rick. "Suppose I give you a quick lift to the pier to fetch Janice's car. Barb can tend to our patients while we're gone."

"Sounds good. Where are the keys?"

"Janice's purse is hanging on a coat hanger in their room," Barbara said. She had drawn her sweater down over her shoulders, as if fending off the cold. "Her keys should be in there."

Rick went to back to the room they were sleeping in and found the purse where Barbara said it was. He fished amid wadded tissues, a leather pocketbook, a mini-photo album, packs of chewing gum, and the remnants of a People magazine before he found the keys buried at the bottom of the rubble. He pocketed them and went back to the reception area where Glen Jorgensen was donning a coat. "Ready?"

"Ready as I'll ever be," Rick said. "I'll check to see if Jack is still at his store while I'm at it."

"Good," Glen said. "When I get back Barb and I will work on getting these two back to their home."

"Maybe I'll drop her car off at the house then," Rick said. "As long as you can give me a lift back to my place later."

"Agreed." Glen zipped up his jacket and reached for his umbrella. He looked over at Barbara. "I'll be back in a few minutes."

Barbara saw them to the door as the two men went out into the rain, the doctor's brand-new Blazer, and the darkening day.

14

Roy Conklin slammed his foot down on the accelerator as the car slid toward the front gate of the power plant. The road was covered with more than half a foot of water that was quickly rising thanks to the rain. It was coming down harder now, so hard that Roy could barely see out the windshield. He and Rusty had made it to the power plant just in time before all hell broke loose.

Rusty.

"Goodbye, fuck head!" Roy laughed as the front end of the patrol car narrowly missed the gate of the utility plant. Maybe now with that idiot gone, Roy could get some shit taken care of. He was now in complete control. No more fucking townspeople questioning his authority. No, siree. From now on, Sheriff Roy Conklin was the big cheese around these parts.

Those things that killed Rusty were the answer.

Roy formulated his plans as he made his way out of the plant and into the car, pausing only to reload his revolver and blow those overgrown crustaceans into gunk and crab shell. He was able to put down all his weight on the injured leg with only a minimum of pain.

When he reached the safety of his patrol car he examined it briefly and was relieved to find that it was just a flesh wound; the bullet had just grazed his thigh. It was bleeding like hell, but that would stop in time. The important thing was that the bullet had nicked him and not buried itself in his leg. That would have been bad.

As he drove out of the power plant he began formulating a plan. He would roll on into town and organize the men into a good old-fashioned hunting party. He would lead them back here and blow the creatures back into whatever shithole they had crawled out of. He wasn't going to fuck up again—he'd done that once before in 'Nam when his carelessness had caused that chemical spill, but not anymore. He knew what he was dealing with now. Mutant sea creatures. And what better way to deal with mutant sea creatures than to get a hunting party going with some of the boys in town and wipe them out?

Hell, this might just be the ticket out of here. Leading a party of men to kill these things could be a story worth more than the O.J. Simpson saga the tabloids spend so much money on. Roy was sure that the creatures were some kind of rare animal and they were probably something that some fancy-pants scientist will just cream for. He sure hadn't seen anything like them before and he'd lived in these parts of Maine his entire life. Hell, for all he knew this could be an entirely brand-new species. They might even name the fucking things after him.

Yeah ... things were definitely looking up.

He was so wrapped up in his daydream that he failed to notice the big, yellow DIP sign posted at the side of the road. He should have known better, since he'd posted that sign himself after two county employees had knocked it down on a drunk driving expedition a few years back.

Normally the patrol car would have easily handled the dip at the speed Conklin was driving. This time the dip area was submerged under two feet of water and Roy didn't realize anything was wrong until the entire front end of the car dropped down and went under. Muddy water blasted the windshield, causing him to hit the brakes. A jolt of pain slammed through his injured leg as he was slammed into the dashboard. A sense of warm wetness spread down his leg; it felt like the bullet wound had torn open, soaking his pant leg.

He howled in pain and let his foot off the brake, but by then it was too late.

The car lurched to a stop with the front end pointed down into the dip. Water sloshed up the hood and turned to steam. He could hear the engine compartment filling with water and he panicked, fumbling to throw the car in reverse. Before he could do that, the engine gave one last cough and died.

Roy sat in the car, the rain drumming all around him, beating a steady tattoo of sound on the hood of the car. Fear pulsed through his veins as he turned the key to try to restart the vehicle. The starter ground wetly with a grinding sound, then nothing. Even the steady clicking of the solenoid was swallowed up as everything flooded.

"Goddammit!" Roy slammed his fist hard into the steering wheel. It made his leg hurt even worse.

Now what the fuck am I gonna do? He sat in the car and stewed in his thoughts for a moment. He tried to look through the front windshield, but the driving rain was making everything a gray blur. His fingers flicked the automatic windshield wiper but nothing happened. The battery must have shorted out, too. *Great! Just what I fucking need.*

He opened the driver's side door gently and icy cold water flooded in, splashing over his feet and the pedals of the car. He grunted, cursed his ill fortune and with great effort finally found himself almost thigh deep in the puddle. His vision caught the DIP sign and he growled. He struggled and waded to the shallower part of the road near the shoulder. It was only up to his ankles here.

Roy glanced back up the road and saw the twin towers of the power plant about a mile back. He turned south and figured that he had another mile and a half back to town. Not too bad in normal circumstances, but the rain was creating a real danger of flash floods and mudslides. Plus, he was limping on his wounded leg, which throbbed like a sonofabitch. He looked out at the beach. The dark, gray waves were really pounding the rocks and sand of the shore. The tide was lapping at the rocks fifty yards from the road; he'd never seen the water line this high before.

The best way back to town was this road, Highway 1. He'd simply have to go around the puddle caused by the dip and hike it back. Maybe he'd get lucky and someone would come along and give him a lift back to town.

Nope. That wouldn't work. The only people who would use this road on a day like this were those who worked back at the plant. And they were all dead.

Lightning flashed out over the ocean. The thunderclap that quickly followed almost knocked Roy off his feet. His hand massaged the area around the bullet wound, and he started limping down the road.

He had traveled about half a mile when he decided to head toward the beach.

The rushing water made this decision for him. It transformed Highway 1 into a dangerous river of water and mud. He'd almost been knocked down twice by the force of the current and had to grab onto a low-lying tree branch to avoid being swept away. When he got to his feet he clambered up the incline that served as the side of the road and scuttled down the hilly slope that led to the beach. The beach was wider at this point of the coast, and as long as he stuck to the rocks he would be okay.

The wet sand along the beach was easier on his wounded leg and the bleeding had finally stopped. He felt a little light-headed and for the first time since his confrontation with Rusty (*Jesus, I never knew the stupid fuck had it in him. Goddamn, but he shot me!*), he began to worry about blood loss and shock. The thought ran through his head and he shook it out. He gritted his teeth with set, grim determination. No way was he going to let that numbskull Rusty have the last laugh by dying out here on the beach from a wound he'd inflicted.

Fuck him!

He quickened his pace and a moment later was able to make out the dim silhouette of the pier. Another mile or so and he would be back in the warm arms of civilization.

The comforting softness of the sand had created an almost lulling effect on him that when he stepped on something hard in the sand, it jolted him to awareness. He stopped in mid-stride, thinking it was a rock until he felt it move beneath his foot.

"*Yaaahhh!*" He jumped back, arms flayed out. He lost his balance and fell on his butt in the sand—and gasped as the rock grew claws, legs, and a dark, red shell. Roy yelled and scrambled back as the crustacean pulled its body from the sand and waved its marble-like eyes at him. Remembering what those things had done to Rusty, Roy scrambled back farther till his back brushed up against a tree. The creature hissed and clicked its claws at him. The segmented tail arched threateningly and Roy saw drops of yellowish liquid drip from the stinger that he knew wasn't just dirty rain water.

He plucked the revolver from his holster and aimed it at the creature. He'd reloaded before he set off down the road in the patrol car and had packed a box of shells in his jacket pocket. The crustacean became a pile of oozing yellow meat and broken red shell with a single shot.

He sat slumped against the tree for a moment, the recoil of the gunshot echoing amid the driving rain. Slight movement in the distance made him squint and crane his neck for a better view.

His eyes widened. There were more of them. The sound of the gunshot must have aroused the other creatures. The sand was now erupting with red shells and clicking pincers as they rose from their hiding spots in the ground. The clacking of their claws began to rise above the din of the rain as Roy rose to his feet.

He held his gun out before him as his back hit the tree again. He fired the revolver, blowing crustaceans into paste with every shot, but he quickly realized that alone wouldn't help him. He was hopelessly outnumbered, and would soon run out of bullets.

He stood his ground and sized up his advantages. He could make a dash for it back to the car, but Highway 1 had become a river. The car was dead. Heading down the beach in the opposite direction these things were coming from might corner him in more. In short, he was fucked.

The clicking rose louder as he saw them getting closer.

He turned to the tree as his mind lit up. It was an old pine, with its nearest branch five feet from the ground. He cast a nervous glance backwards, turned back toward the tree and jumped, grabbing the lowest limb and hauling himself up. His arms and legs wrapped around the branch, causing it to bend down from the weight of his body.

He became soaked with water and wet leaves. He ignored it, pulling himself up just as the creatures made the base of the tree. His wounded leg dangled as he sat on the limb, dripping blood onto the creatures' backs. It throbbed. The creatures raised their upper bodies and snapped at the air below his foot with their claws. He pulled the tempting leg up and tucked it to his chest, wincing at the pain from the bullet wound. The creatures snapped at the air, straining their scorpion-like bodies upward.

Roy's heart pounded in his chest. His mouth was dry. *Hope these things can't climb.*

One of the creatures ventured toward the base of the tree and was quickly blown to mush by his revolver. None of the others tried that approach. They remained where they were, directly under him. Maybe their tiny brains put two and two together. Or maybe their now-deceased buddy possessed a little more intelligence than his brethren. If they all had any ounce of intelligence they would be able to swarm right up the trunk of this tree and chow down. But as it was, they merely stood on their rear legs, snapping at the air.

One of them broke from the mass and wandered toward the trunk. Roy kept the barrel of the pistol trained on it. He watched as it reached the base of the tree and began to eat its dead comrade. Some of the others joined suit. Roy kept the pistol trained on them, waiting for one of them to make a break and head up the tree. But none did.

As they ate he swiveled around the branch, taking care as to not further hurt or damage his already injured leg. It hurt like a sonofabitch, and throbbed with a pulsing pain. He climbed higher into the tree, ignoring the pain, feeling more comfortable the more distance he put between himself and the creatures below. He finally found a spot close to the halfway point and found a comfortable area. He rested against the main trunk, the limb he was on splayed between his thighs, and massaged his wounded leg as he thought about his predicament.

Everything that was happening was his second chance at redeeming himself. After that accident in 'Nam, when he'd been dishonorably discharged from the army after having spilled that experimental chemical that was intended for the Viet Cong village, he had come back to Phillipsport a bitter man. He'd joined the army willingly at the height of the Viet Nam war. Serving his country was his duty to God and country, contrary to what the niggers, hippies and faggots were bellowing during that time period. He'd enlisted and made his father and the other men that hung around Sapp's General Store proud. Those boys were all Korean War and World War II vets. But the accident, innocent as it was, had been the straw that broke the camel's back. He had come back disgraced, discharged. And what added insult to injury was that no sooner had he stepped foot into U.S. soil when he found himself in the middle of a Viet Nam War protest.

He'd flown home with a slew of servicemen who had either already served their time, or who were being honorably discharged from service. Over half of them had suffered injuries during the war. A band of protesters had set up camp outside of the airstrip where a welcoming party had been formed. As the soldiers marched past amid the cheering of the crowd, a group of protesters strategically positioned themselves in the crowd along the path of the returning veterans. Just as Roy passed the junction where the parade ended, he found himself caught in the middle of a fray as protesters rushed out and began calling them baby killers. A few of his fellow soldiers had yelled back and then all hell broke loose.

Roy gritted his teeth against the pain and the memory. He could still remember it vividly. How a pair of long-haired punks had rushed him, knocking him to the ground. He'd fought them hard, breaking one of the commie punks' noses from the sound of it, and then a few niggers and gooks joined them and he was being assaulted by four of them, beating him with their fists and then he was knocked to the ground. His last memory was of a long-haired, bearded man drawing back to kick him and then an explosion of pain.

He woke up in a VA hospital with a fractured skull and various other injuries.

He hadn't trusted people like that since then. Especially when many of those long-haired hippie commies began cutting their hair, donning suits and blending into mainstream society to poison it. Every five years or so another band of long-haired radicals would crop up to replace those, and by the dawn of the Reagan years the country was shot to hell. Everybody was doing drugs, fucking each other in the ass, pissing on the flag, and worst of all, society began becoming more tolerant of it. What was worse was that people like himself, hard working men and women, were now getting the shaft in favor of blacks, women, chinks, and Mexicans. People who possessed less intelligence, less civilized behavior. The kind of people who had beat him down upon his arrival home in the states after serving his stint in the war were now the kind of people who had taken over. And they were determined to carry on until Sheriff Conklin and his kind were eradicated from the face of the earth.

All Roy Conklin had ever wanted was to serve his country with pride and dignity. He'd wanted to uphold the law of God and Country. Make the world a better place. And what had it gotten him? A broken head and a beaten spirit.

So he'd come home to Phillipsport, enrolled in night school at the college down at Bridgton, and began working for the sheriff's department a few years later. He had married once, but that ended in an early divorce; she couldn't take the criticisms he leveled against her brother, who was a faggot. So she'd left him and married a lawyer from Orono, one of those liberal lawyers who defended child molesters and murderers. No sooner did honest men like Roy get scum like that off the street, then men like his ex's new husband were working to get them let go so they could do it again. Where was the justice in that?

His thoughts were abruptly cut off by the rustling of branches over his head.

He turned his face up, lifting his gun as he saw a dark form climbing in the branches above. He aimed and fired. The branch exploded into splinters, sending the thing tumbling down.

It hit the branch he was sitting on and extended a claw. It gripped the branch as it came down, stopping its descent. Round, black eyes locked into his and it hissed.

Roy's eyes shifted as he drew the gun up, ready to fire again. The creature regained its grip and pulled itself on the branch and Roy chuckled, relaxing.

It was a raccoon. It gripped the limb, its black eyes locked on him, watching his every move. It hissed again and bared a mouth full of needle-sharp teeth.

Roy's chuckle turned to a snicker as he lowered the gun. He regarded the raccoon the same way he regarded everything else in the world. If it didn't fuck with him, fine. If it was a bother or an inconvenience then it needed to be destroyed. If the creature came any closer to him, scratched him, he might fall and tumble out of this tree. And since those goddamn Animal Rights assholes would most likely save the raccoon before they would lift a finger to help a human being, he knew what had to be done.

He needed to save what shells he had in the gun for himself, no question about that. There were other ways to deal with this critter. He kicked out with his good foot, connecting with the animal's head. The raccoon skittered back, claws digging into the bark, hissing loudly. Roy kicked it again. The animal hissed again, grasping for a tighter hold. He kicked it again harder, this time succeeding. The raccoon fell.

It landed in the middle of the pack of crustaceans at the base of the tree. They swarmed over it, arched tails stabbing downward amid squeals and howls. It sounded eerily like the sounds of a cat fight. Roy looked down, grinning as the creatures swirled amid garbling yowls and bubbling, frothing flesh.

It was dead within a minute, reduced to melted flesh.

Roy Conklin watched from his lofty vantage point. The crustaceans wasted no time in scooping the dissolved flesh into their jaws and partaking in what was theirs.

He watched the creatures clean up the remaining traces of the raccoon. They picked that puppy clean, leaving no tidbit uneaten, no morsel undigested. Once they were done they began to crawl back toward the beach. No more snapping their claws around the base of the tree, straining upwards. Guess their memory span wasn't that great. Roy's heart raced as he watched them scuttle back to the beach, digging themselves into the sand. He grinned. They'd forgotten him. The momentary diversion of the raccoon had been enough to satisfy them.

He smiled. As soon as they dug themselves in, he would

quietly climb down and head back to town.

He looked out at the pounding surf and saw more of the things crawl out of the sea like so much grunion beaching themselves to spawn. The minute they hit the beach, they burrowed in the sand. His eyes scanned the beachfront, noticing similar movement. They were digging into the sand all up and down the shore. His mind calculated the numbers; if you estimated a forty-mile stretch of beach that was affected, than it was going to take a lot of work to destroy them all.

Roy was just about to start his trek down the tree when he noticed that the newly arrived creatures were burrowing into the ground more frantically. Some seemed so agitated that they tried to dig into the bare rocks along the beach, tearing off their own claws. Those behind them clambered over their brethren only to repeat it, or find soft soil. Weird ...

A sound broke his reverie. A moan.

He tilted his head, trying to find out where it was coming from. It came again, closer. Roy shivered, feeling suddenly cold in the rain and driving wind. His flesh goosepimpled at the sound; it was hollow, terrifying. It chilled every ounce of his being. Combined with the weather and the creatures below, it was enough to give anybody the willies.

A bolt of lightning burst over the water as the moan abruptly ended.

By the time the accompanying roll of thunder died, Sheriff Roy Conklin had dropped out of the tree and began moving in a brisk, limping run toward Phillipsport.

15

Rick's first stop after Glen Jorgensen left him off at the pier was the sheriff's station.

He approached the darkened facade slowly, trying to formulate in his mind how he was going to broach the subject to Sheriff Roy Conklin that they needed help. The man rubbed him the wrong way, but he needed his help. Now their very lives, the very lives of the entire town, rested on everybody banding together to fight these things. Rick hoped that his fears toward the sheriff were unfounded.

He approached the front door of the sheriff's station and peered inside the windows. The interior lights were out but there was enough light outside for him to get a good glimpse. The front office was empty.

He stepped back, standing under the awning of the building, avoiding the rain that was falling. Sheriff Conklin was probably still with Rusty at the power plant trying to get a handle on whatever it was they had been called up there for. Rick turned and headed down to the pier to find Jack Ripley.

There were no signs of the creatures anywhere but that did little to ease his anxiety. He wished he had a firearm with him. Going to the scene of the confrontation without one made him feel naked, but where was he going to get one now? Besides, if he stayed in the middle of the street and kept a lookout, he should be able to run away at the first sign of danger. The creatures could be outrun.

He looked out onto the pier and saw Ripper's car parked on it in front of his store. He started jogging toward the pier, heading out in the downpour. The puncture wound in his leg twinged a little and he slowed up. Even though the sting had been a dry sting, producing no venom, it still hurt like hell and would probably leave a nasty scar. Ditto for the cuts the creature's claws had gouged into his leg. His only reminder of them now was the bandage that covered them beneath his tattered jeans.

Rick was almost to the edge of the pier when he saw Jack exit his shop, locking up. Rick raised his hand and shouted. "Hey, Jack!"

Jack looked up and smiled when he saw Rick. Rick jogged the rest of the way to the entrance of Jack's shop.

Jack nodded. "How's Bobby?"

"He'll be okay," Rick said, panting slightly. "Doc's driving him and Janice back to her place. I came back to get her car. What about you?"

Jack grinned wide. "Everything's fine. None of the little brats raided the place even though the door was wide open." They chuckled over that and Jack looked at Rick's leg. "How's the leg?"

"Hurt's like hell," Rick said. He lifted his right leg and gave it a shake. "Doc says he won't have to amputate, so I guess I'll live. Seen any more of the crab things?"

Jack shook his head. "Nope. Can't find the sheriff, either."

Rick briefly told him of Sheriff Conklin's visit to Dr. Jorgensen's office and his sudden call to the power plant to join Rusty in some investigation. Jack nodded, stroking his chin. "That would explain the power outage. It surely isn't downed lines."

Rick looked down the deserted pier. All the other shops were vacant and dark. The black and orange Halloween decorations reminded Rick that the holiday was next week. If felt like they were living it now.

A barrage of screams mingled with clicking sounds from the south parking lot snapped their attention away from finding Janice's car. They bolted toward the sound, rounding the row of shops, stopping at the edge of the pier and looking out over the parking lot at where the sounds had come from.

A family of tourists back from an outing that had obviously

been interrupted by the rain were surrounded by the creatures. Their main attention was diverted to the boy—he was in the middle of a tug-of-war by the creatures who had grabbed onto each arm with their large pincers, pulling him. His parents were screaming in fright. More of the creatures came running up the beach to join in the fracas; one approached the boy, stinger raised high, and nailed the boy in the stomach. The boy howled in pain.

Rick felt numb with shock, rooted to the spot as the fracas went on. For an instant the scene below took him back to two hours before when he and Janice had run down the pier to the sound of similar screams of pain coming from Bobby. The sound of the boy's screams intermingled with the clicking of the creature's claws created an eddy of mad cacophony in Rick's ears. *Clickers*, he thought. *What else can we call them?*

The man rushed forward to save his son only to be stung by in the stomach by a clicker. The force of the blow sent him reeling on his butt. The man sat on the sand for a moment, eyes wide open. His hands clutched at his full belly as he moaned in pain. The creature advanced on him and popped him again, this time stinging his neck. The man shrieked as the venom inflated his neck like an inner tube and simultaneously dissolved the flesh. His stomach expanded and finally burst like a ripe melon. It looked like a balloon filled with sausages soaked in barbecue sauce exploding.

Rick watched the action as it went down in slow motion before him.

The boy's chest began expanding, the flesh bubbling as he fell to his knees. The clickers swarmed around him, stuffing pieces of his flesh in their mandibles.

The woman remained standing in the sand screaming as more clickers surrounded her and took her down. Stingered tails rose and fell and the audible clicking of pincers snapping at flesh rose in Rick's ear.

The man sat on the sand, his inner organs spilling out of his split belly, covering the creatures in a sticky, red mess. The man continued screaming and kicking out at the feasting crustaceans even as he was being eaten alive before his very eyes.

Jack bent over and vomited into the wet asphalt of the parking lot. Rick stared at him as if in a fog. This was far worse than he could have imagined. There were dozens of the things scurrying up out of the water now to get their piece of the late tourist family. There were God knew how many more farther along the coast, scurrying farther inland. He didn't want to think about what was happening to other unfortunate people the creatures came across. The clicking sounds hurt Rick's eardrums.

He grabbed Jack by the shoulder, pulling him to his feet. "We've got to get the hell out of here and warn everybody!"

Jack focused on Rick with fear in his eyes. He looked like he was going to be sick again. The nausea seemed to pass over his face again and watching it made Rick want to throw up.

Finally Jack gained his composure. "How? The phones are out ..."

Rick thought for a moment. "We'll have to go door to door ... there aren't that many people in this town—"

"Not many people?" Jack panted. "There's close to a thousand ..."

"Compared to Philly that's nothing," Rick said. But he knew what Ripper meant. "If we could get some help—" The clicking cut him off as it intensified. They looked toward the beach as dozens and dozens of the things came bubbling out of the surf. It looked like the entire beach was alive with the red things. It looked like there were thousands of them making their way onto the shore.

Rick grabbed Jack by the coat and pulled him along down the pier, leaving Janice's car forgotten. They headed back to town, toward the mall.

16

Glen Jorgensen was sitting in the rear examining room, the one where the freezer was kept, examining the remains of the two creatures that Rick Sychek had his run-ins with.

He sighed and sat back from the desk he was working at. The severed claw and tail segment were resting on carefully placed trays, which, in turn, rested on two towels. He had stowed both samples in the freezer the moment they'd come into his possession, both to preserve them for better study later, but also because they fascinated him. And with good reason.

Glen had been born and raised in this town. Had walked its beaches at night, swam in the ocean, fished off the pier. And he'd never seen, nor heard of, anything remotely resembling the monstrosities that emerged from the ocean that caused so much fear and bodily damage. When Rick brought the claw to his office yesterday he'd racked his brain trying to come up with a plausible explanation. He'd searched through all his textbooks on crustaceans, arachnids, Atlantic sea life, Maine wildlife, everything he could find. And he'd found nothing.

And then today—the scene at the beach, Bobby's hand …

Glen Jorgensen shuddered at the thought that was skittering in his mind.

He stood up and walked out of the room toward the receptionist area. The waiting room and reception area were brightly lit against the darkness that was raging outside thanks to two battery-powered lanterns placed on the reception counter. The rain was coming down in hard torrents, the wind howling, ravaging the trees outside, making the big oak tree outside the house scratch its branches against the north side of the building.

The screeching sound the branches and leaves made against the wet glass of the windows was enough to give anybody the willies. Couple that with what lay in the metallic trays in the rear office, and—

But no. To think about that now would be to go mad.

After dropping Rick off at the pier, Glen had trudged back to the office. Janice was already coming out of sleep and Barbara was tending to her when he arrived. Glen told her that Rick had gone to fetch her car and he would be dropping it off at the house. Janice had nodded groggily and asked if he would take her and Bobby home. Glen had given her a quick look-over, pronounced her fit yet exhausted due to stress and prescribed a night in bed. Bobby was still passed out. With Glen's help, Janice got out of bed and hobbled to the bathroom while Barbara helped him bundle Bobby up for the trip.

With Barbara's help he got Janice and Bobby into his car and drove them home. He carried Bobby upstairs to his room and helped Janice set things up; his favorite blanket, his X-Men comics at his bedside should he feel the urge to delve into comic book world when he awoke.

Glen had left a bottle of tranquilizers with Janice with explicit instructions not to exceed two every six hours. Janice nodded, saying she understood, she'd get some rest, she was going to take care of her little boy and thank you. Glen smiled, told her to call him at home if she needed him—she had the number—and then he and Barbara left.

After dropping Barbara off at her modest little cottage on the outskirts of town, he'd driven back to the house. He'd double locked the front and back doors of the house and shut himself up in the office where he proceeded to study the segmented tail and severed claw again.

The comparison to the claw and the tail fit. Both pieces looked to have come from an animal roughly the size of a badger; something approximately three feet long, a foot and a half to two feet wide. The stinger at the end of the tail was a good three inches long and needle-sharp with no barbs. Smooth. Like the stinger of a wasp. It could sting again and again and again.

But was it venomous?

In his opinion, it was. Every critter he had ever run across with a stinger had been venomous in one form or another. During his initial examination of Rick Sychek's right thigh, he'd looked for tell-tale signs of a venomous sting; redness around the wound, swelling, nausea, blurred vision, sweating, shortness of breath. The only symptoms present were the redness and swelling around the wound and those could have been caused by the wound itself—after all, nearly three inches of a sharp, protruding objected *had* been jabbed into Rick's thigh. But the other signs of a venomous sting—the nausea, dizziness, abdominal cramps, stiffness of the joints, corrosion of the flesh—never showed up. After his cursory examination of Rick, he had immobilized the leg and let him rest up in examination room number one while he turned his attention to Bobby. He waited for something to show up, but Rick had been fine.

Once Bobby was bandaged up, he asked Barbara to draw a blood sample from Rick. He would examine a sample in his lab at the office and send a smidgen of the blood to Bangor General for further analysis. After he sutured Bobby's fingers, he'd given Rick's blood sample a look under a microscope. In short, a healthy sample, with no trace of a foreign substance.

He'd mentioned this to Rick on the ride to the pier. He'd brought up the dry sting theory and Rick agreed. If the creatures were poisonous in some way, he was damned lucky. No telling what they would be up against if it had injected its venom.

Glen stood for a moment, letting these thoughts run past him. If he could only get these samples to somebody in Bangor, they might—

Something rose in Glen's mind, eclipsing all thought. He turned and made a mad dash up the stairs to his private living quarters, all thoughts to the specimens downstairs in the metal trays forgotten. He ran to his study and began searching for a book, all the while his mind racing, putting together pieces of a long-forgotten puzzle.

He remembered reading something about a fisherman pulling up a giant lobster like the one Rick had come across back in the 1930s. The story had made the local paper, as well as a book on local superstitions. The fisherman had been casting for trout when he and the men he was with hauled a net to the ship with a giant lobster trapped in the mesh. The captain of the ship stated it had been the most gigantic lobster he'd ever seen— well over three feet long—but also unlike anything he had ever come across. It wasn't really a lobster—he didn't know what it was. His men had been dumbfounded and watched in shock as the thing clipped through the sturdy mesh and splashed into sea. They'd tried casting for the creature again, but it failed to turn up in their nets.

There hadn't been a sign of anything remotely resembling it since then.

Until now.

Glen found the volume on local folklore he was looking for and turned to the story. He scanned it quickly, confirming the events. Late fall, 1935. Ten miles off the coast of Phillipsport.

And then there was another story—

He flipped through the book, excitement spurring him on.

He found it in back of the book. An artist's sketch of the creature that had attacked Bobby, Janice, and Rick.

Homarus Tyrannous had been a prehistoric crustacean that lived in the Northern Atlantic Ocean in the latter part of the Paleozoic period, but there was evidence that they survived till at least the middle of the Mesozoic Period. Not much was known about them save for the few fossilized remains that were found embedded in stone and ice in Greenland in the early 1920s when they were discovered. From what scientists had been able to surmise, they bore a strong likeness to modern day crabs and lobsters, and were most likely the linkage between those species' primitive beginnings.

They'd been extinct for over two hundred million years.

This was what sent Glen's heart racing, what sent him racing toward the shelf in search for another volume as another thought exploded in his mind. Sent his hands shaking as he found the book, a slim chapbook published by a local tourist curator shop, and began thumbing through it.

It told the story of the Lost Village ...

He'd happened across this little doodad in a tourist shop on the outskirts of town. Amid trinkets of hand-carved figures carved by the local Indians, arrowheads, taxidermied animals, jewelry, postcards and T-shirts bearing the Phillipsport banner, travel brochures and local history books, Glen Jorgensen had found this booklet.

It was written by Paul Hackett, a member of the local Micmac Tribe. Hackett held a Ph.D. in American Literature and Urban Folklore from the University of Maine at Orono and was well versed in the stories handed down to him from his family elders. He was also the owner of the curio shop Glen had bought the booklet from. Glen remembered being interested enough in the booklet to inquire as to where Dr. Hackett was so he might speak to him, but the author was out of town on business. Perhaps if Dr. Jorgensen stopped in again another time? Glen had paid for the booklet anyway, making a mental note to stop in and speak to Paul Hackett himself at some point, but he never got around to it.

Now he flipped through the little booklet, scanning it rapidly.

In 1605, late in the month of October, the entire village of an early English settlement vanished without a trace. The settlers had landed in the area now known as Phillipsport that summer and settled in the area, befriending the Micmac Tribe. While they settled, the ship that had brought them set sail for England for supplies and more of their brethren.

When the ship arrived the following spring they found the village deserted and in ruins. Weather hadn't been the cause of the destruction; the village had been torn apart by something malicious. There hadn't been a trace of the settlers anywhere. Only a few scraps of clothing and the ramshackled structures of their modest settlement remained.

The local Indians denied any involvement or knowledge of the whereabouts of the settlers. Despite some intense interrogations, the Indians held fast to their denial. They had seen nothing, heard nothing.

The one tell-tale sign that the settlers met with a fate other than hostile Indians was a hastily scrawled message on a piece of stone. What seemed to start off as the simple lines to mark off the days spent in settlement ended as squiggles culminating in a fragmented sentence ...

… demons from the s—
And a rough sketch …
The sketch was reproduced in the booklet in pencil for the reader alongside a grainy black-and-white photograph of the original stone etching. Glen stared at it for a long time.

The first, a rough sketch of the thing Rick found. It looked like a cross between a giant crab and a scorpion. The severed tail and claw resting in his downstairs freezer would match a beast like this perfectly.

The second … a hint of a message, preserved in time in the grainy black and white photograph, the message cut off suddenly when the unknown artist met with a sudden, unknown fate.

Glen Jorgensen read through the rest of the booklet with amazement. Phillipsport County remained largely uncolonized until the early 1700s. The crew that landed in the area one hundred years before had taken their tale back to the mother country and the tale became a legend, handed down from generation to generation.

And it had remained as such. Until Paul Hackett dug up the story and published it for the local tourist trade.

Glen had heard a rough version of the story when he was growing up in Phillipsport. It was told around a Boy Scout campfire when he was eleven or twelve. An older kid told it in all the spooky tones and gestures of campfire story telling. "And legend says that the Wendigo came down from the sky and ransacked the village, destroying all its inhabitants and pulling them back with him into the air, never to be seen again. And even now, four hundred years later, the Wendigo waits for the right moment … when an unwary boy might stray alone into the forest … like … *us!*"

The story had always ended on a melodramatic note, designed to shock. And it had spooked him back then; it held all the reverence of those urban legends that are handed down from generation to generation, from older brother to little brother and his friends, in turn handed down to smaller kids in the neighborhood where it grows, mutates into a story with horrifying proportions. They were the kind of stories that the teller proclaims was steeped in the truth, and he or she believed it; it had happened to his cousin's sister's boyfriend's best friend. There were similar tales of woe. Bloody Mary, who appeared in the mirror—after you gazed into it in a dark room and chanted her name three times—to rake your face with her long fingernails. The Hook, who hung around lover's lanes and decapitated young fornicating couples. It bore similarities to such a legend, with the possibility of more. The Wendigo was more than just an icon in this tale; it was also an Indian legend, centering in New England, the northeast coast of Canada. Indian legend described it as a monster—a god, if you will—that roamed the woods of greater Canada and Maine, devouring human flesh and ravaging everything that crossed its path.

Glen chalked the Wendigo legend up with that of the Loch Ness Monster and Bigfoot—unproven, undocumented fairy tales. At least there were photos of Nessie and Bigfoot. He had always regarded the Wendigo legend as a pile of shit in comparison to the former two.

Glen closed the slim volume, his brow creased in reflection. The lost village story and the creatures they were dealing with now had a common thread—Paul Hackett reported in his book that shortly before the settlers vanished, there'd been an invasion of giant crabs from the ocean. The villagers had scampered inland, horrified at the sight. This had been documented by a tribe member who'd been near the campsite when it happened. The Indian darted back to his tribe to spread the word. Legend had it the tribe retreated farther inland *en masse*, as if escaping the wrath of a rival tribe on the warpath.

They'd waited until the following rise of the next full moon. Just as their forefathers had done, many times before the white men had ever come to this land to build their villages. Then they returned.

This time the white man's village was ransacked. Not a soul had been spared.

Glen Jorgensen pursed his lips in thought, his mind running on autopilot.

A mass exodus of giant crabs. The excited shock of the villagers.

And then the town is ransacked, the villagers vanished.

The hastily scrawled message in stone ... *demons from the* s—

Demons from the sea? That would be the most plausible deciphering of the message. The settlers had obviously seen the giant crabs come up from the beach. In those times of religious persecution, when possession by devils was taken seriously and a mole on a pretty girl's cheek meant she was a witch, they very well could have thought the overgrown crabs were demons from the sea. They could have very well been scared out of their wits when the crustaceans had washed ashore. Panic had probably ensued at a greater level than was happening now. Somebody could have scrawled the message and then been interrupted to join the fray to beat the creatures back to the ocean. But why would the creatures have come up in the first place, just as they were doing now?

"Goddamn," Glen Jorgensen murmured as it came to him. He'd just put two and two together when the thought occurred to him to take a peek outside and see what was happening.

He placed the chapbook on the shelf and hurried out of the study and up the stairs. The attic took up the entire floor of the house and had been renovated into a recreational room. Glen had done all the work himself. He moved across the room, past the pool table and wet bar, to the telescope perched by the port window that looked out over the east side of the town.

He moved the telescope over the horizon, his right eye up against the lens, scanning the scene. The storm was still unleashing her fury, blowing rain against the window, blowing the trees into a frenzy. He scanned the town over the peaked roofs of the Victorian style buildings and homes, over trees and telephone poles to the beach and pier.

To the scene that was unfolding below.

17

Rick and Jack hit the first house they could find, a cute little white bungalow with blue trim perched on the corner of Main Street and the entrance to the pier. Rick pounded on the door until the occupant opened it with a grimace. "What the hell is going—"

"We have to get out of here," Rick almost shouted. "They're invading the town, they—"

The man at the door was middle-aged, late forties, balding with strands of long gray hair spilling off the back of his head and down his back, stained white T-shirt over a huge paunch. He was wearing horn rimmed glasses with lenses that were so thick they resembled the bottom of coke bottles. "What the fuck are you—"

Jack interrupted him. "I know it sounds crazy Earl, but the beach is being invaded by a mass of huge crabs."

"Huge *what?*" Earl looked at the two as if they were experiencing a bad acid flashback.

Jack cocked a thumb toward the beach. "Take a look."

Earl peered over their shoulders. His eyes widened.

"What the *fuck?*"

Rick risked a glance behind him. The Clickers were cresting the sand and had reached the parking lot of the beach. They were heading right toward them.

He turned to Earl, pushing his way inside the house. "We've got to get out of here now."

Earl scrambled back as Rick and Jack fumbled inside. Jack slammed the door shut as Earl moved toward the window, his eyes as wide as saucers. *"What the fuck are those things?"*

"Clickers," Rick said, moving to the kitchen. It ended in a laundry room, which in turn led to the backyard. A white picket fence lined the backyard, which led presumably to the neighboring house. "Got any guns in the house?"

"Earl? What the hell is going on?" A short, squat woman wearing a yellow-stained, white nightgown emerged in the hallway. Her gray hair hung in greasy clumps over her eyes. She was fat. She wasn't wearing a bra, and her tits hung down her chest like pendulant udders beneath the frayed nightgown. Her bloodshot eyes moved from Rick to Jack. "Who the fuck are these guys?"

"Shut up!" Earl barked to the woman, his gaze still trained out the window. "Jesus Christ, them things is heading this way!"

"Don't tell me to shut up you fucking asshole, fuck you, Earl, you fat fucking slob of a pig," the woman bawled. Rick moved past the woman to the bedrooms, looking for weapons, a gun, anything that would help fight these things off. Moving past the woman was scary enough; the heavy smell of body odor and booze permeated the air around her.

Jack found a deer rifle in the hall closet. He opened the slide. Five rounds left. He joined Earl at the window.

"This thing work?"

Earl seemed to notice Jack for the first time. "Yeah. Hey, I got more guns in the bedroom."

"You ain't gone go shootin' critters in this storm!" The woman yelled at him.

Earl turned his jiggly bulk toward the woman and screamed at her. *"Shut yer trap, Maggie, just shut up! There's things out there coming at us and—"*

"No, you shut up Earl, you fat sack of slime shit!" Maggie was screaming, blowing snot and crying at the same time. Rick emerged from the bedroom with two rifles and a box of shells. He nodded at Jack, who was gritting his teeth. Why the hell did they pick this house? Christ, he felt like shooting both of them.

"Gimme that rifle!" Earl barked. He took three heavy strides forward and plucked one of the rifles from Rick's hands and

turned back toward the window. He opened the window and cradled the rifle to his shoulder, aiming at the beach. The barrel of the rifle kissed the mesh of the screen. Maggie was screaming hoarsely next to Rick. If she didn't shut up soon, by God, he'd blow her stupid brains out himself.

"These fuckers are all over the place!" Earl said excitedly, and then he fired.

The shot blew a hole in the screen and made Rick jump. Earl cocked the rifle and aimed again. Rick moved over to the window just as Earl squeezed off another shot.

Earl's front lawn was overrun with Clickers. Two of them lay on the walk, their shells mashed and exploded, drawing a circle of feasting Clickers. Others scurried past and scuttled up the walk toward the house. Earl fired at them, yelling *"Look at them fuckers go! Jesus Christ!"*

Rick motioned to Jack and the two men moved out of the living room and into the kitchen, away from Earl's yells and Maggie's hysterical jig. Earl continued to shoot the Clickers outside, following each shot with a hysterical cackle of triumph. He seemed to be oblivious that they were storming the town and were probably scuttling up Main Street this very second. "We need to get the fuck out of here."

"You said it," Jack said. He was still clutching the deer rifle. He handed Rick an extra box of shells he had salvaged.

They exited the house through the backdoor, leaving Earl to his muttered cursing as he fired the remaining rounds into the Clickers.

Rick and Jack had just crested the fence of the house behind Earl's when they witnessed another civilian fatality.

A young man had ventured out of his home to investigate the gunshots that were coming from Earl's house. Rick saw the Clicker on the sidewalk before the young man did, and yelled. *"Hey! You! Watch out, on the sidewalk!"*

The young man looked up at Rick, confusion across his face, and then he looked down on the ground and saw what was already attacking him. Stinging him.

He screamed. Scrambling back, he tried to run, but the Clicker climbed on top of him, pinning him down. Rick and Jack stood rooted to the spot, watching in fascinated horror.

The creature's barbed tail jabbed downward, stinging the man's back. The young man screamed again as the Clicker began digging into the man's back, tearing away bloody strips of flesh with the man's shirt still on it. It stuffed the bloody meat into its mandibles as the man's skin began to stretch, expanding his abdomen. Jack turned away and grabbed Rick's elbow, moving him on up the street. "I can't watch this." His voice was choked. It sounded like he was on the verge of being sick again.

They trotted down the street with the man's dying screams echoing in their ears. Rick was still holding on to the rifle and the box of shells. People came out of their homes as they ran past, looking confusedly down the street. As they passed, Rick and Jack shouted at them to stay inside. A few wandered off into the sidewalk, saw the Clickers and turned to scramble back into their homes. Rick and Jack moved farther inland, threading their way through the neighborhood, pounding on doors, admonishing the occupants to take arm and defend themselves. Most people took their advice. Others ... simply didn't.

Through it all, the amount of Clickers they saw was relatively few. Rick surmised that they were rampaging in one solid mass, hitting one end of town—the beach presently—and going on to the next. The few Clickers they saw and managed to blow up with the rifles were probably stragglers.

But eventually they would come. All of them. And they would engulf the entire town.

As they headed farther inland, moving toward the shopping center, it suddenly occurred to Rick that they needed to get to Janice's house to warn them.

Oh God, what am I gonna do?

This thought ran through Stacy Robinson's head as she paced her quaint craftsman style home on the outskirts of town. It massaged her brain as she went from bedroom to living room to kitchen, oblivious to the storm that was now wreaking havoc on Phillipsport and causing such a thunder and shower spectacle. She ignored the crashing boom of the thunder as she went to the bedroom and dragged out a suitcase, wrenching open the drawers, pulling clothes out and dumping them in the suitcase. Her mind roiled with the same thoughts of *what am I doing? What is going on?* and then she'd stop packing and move to the kitchen, wishing none of this had ever happened.

When she got home last night she'd gone immediately to the closet and brought out her suitcase. She packed, throwing clothes in blindly, not even thinking about what she was going to do, where she was going to go. All she could think of was that she had to get away. She'd pushed Kirk away from her and he'd fallen right into those … *things* … and that was equal to murder and she had to get out before— She'd stopped, taken a deep breath and let it out. Calm down, she told herself. *This is what got you into this mess in the first place. So just calm down.*

She had gone into the kitchen and taken out a bottle of Jim Beam and poured herself a glass. She smoked a cigarette and sat at the kitchen table while she drank the bourbon, trying to get a handle on her thoughts. Before she knew it the glass was empty, and she'd poured herself another. And another. And another.

So she'd gone into the living room, feeling pleasantly buzzed and filled the bowl of her water bong. She took a few hits off the bong, letting the smoke settle in her lungs before she exhaled. There. That felt better. Now she could think this through calmly and rationally. Think it through one step at a time. First she needed to rest her body and her mind. She'd just gone through a terrifying experience and she needed to be on her guard and thus, needed to have all her energy. That meant she needed to get some sleep. Come tomorrow she could decide what to do in a calm, rational manner. Perhaps she'd leave town, but if she did she would do it the right way. She would go through it calmly and rationally.

She stopped her pacing at the kitchen counter, wishing for a cigarette. She'd smoked them all last night. Outside, the rain lashed against the windows and the sky over the ocean was as black as pitch. Stacy was still wearing the worn, black leather jacket she'd worn to the beach the day before. Below that she was wearing a cranberry-colored sweater and no bra. Cold air seeped through the holes in her jeans. She moved toward the refrigerator, thinking she might have left a pack of cigarettes inside, but stopped, suddenly remembering. It had been Kirk's turn to make the beer and cigarette run today. And Kirk was—

She couldn't bring herself to think of that word. Because that would equate Kirk with what had happened to her mother and—

Stop it!

Stacy felt on the verge of screaming if that word so much as invaded her cerebral cortex. Because that word, the dreaded D word, was the perfect way to describe mother's current state now. She had witnessed Kirk's ... that *word*, and had she not been such a bitch he would be here with her now, holding her, comforting her.

But no, she always had to have the last word. It had been that way with Mom when they'd argued. They'd been living together at the time. Stacy was seventeen. She realized now that Mom was just trying to raise her right, was trying to guide her through the turbulence of adolescence. Either way, Stacy didn't like it. Didn't like Mother's constant nagging, her constant criticism, her frequent questions of *where did you go? what are you doing? who are you hanging out with? do you really have to do* that?

The day she killed her mother had started like any other; an argument, mother began hitting the booze a bit too much, only escalating her emotions further. Stacy still didn't remember what it was that set her off. But in any case, the facts remained: Stacy had screamed at Mother, told her that she hated her, that she never wanted to see her again and that she hoped she rotted in hell. Mom's face had turned to stone, the alcoholic twinges that erupted like facial tics whenever she grew angry suddenly gone. *Fine*, Mom had said, her voice as cold as black ice on a pond in winter. She'd stormed out of the house and slipped inside the car, peeling out like the hounds of hell were on her tail. She never came back.

While driving through a winding road at a high speed, she'd

lost control of the car. It flipped three times and went over the embankment—it didn't explode, but it didn't have to. Mother was killed instantly.

And then, yesterday afternoon, Stacy telling Kirk to get the fuck out of her house. Kicking him out of her life on the spot. And why? Kirk had done nothing to deserve being kicked out of the house, to be treated that way by her. He had been looking after her. He'd been concerned about her drug use. A common concern.

She realized the only reason she reacted the way she did was because she was running from her problems. She'd rebounded from the death of her mother to the warm comfiness of herbal intake. This psychological habit was burdened by spreading into alcoholic and chemical indulgences. Sexual interludes were interspersed between them. For five years she had gone from lover to lover, going through friends the way most people go through underwear, and going through the hefty insurance settlement that had been bestowed on her like it was water.

And where had it gotten her?

Stacy's bottom lip quivered in the beginning stages of a cry. She stomped out of the kitchen into the living room, hoping its warmth would relieve the mood. The room was decorated quite nicely; an Oriental throw rug, crème-colored sofa and love seats, and an oak coffee table piled with magazines and tattered paperbacks which rested in the middle of the room. A Michael Whelan print occupied the wall over the sofa, and posters of Motley Crue and Guns N' Roses took residence in the entry hall. A stereo was set up next to the forty-five-inch screen TV, the entertainment center housing hundreds of videocassettes and compact discs. Because this room was catty-corner to the refrigerator, it was her sanctuary. TV and music all day, and beer and food in the fridge just a few steps away. She even kept the water bong right by the sofa.

She stood in the center of the living room, trying hard not to cry. If she hadn't been so goddamned afraid to face up to her problems, face up to what Kirk had been trying to tell her, this wouldn't have happened. She wouldn't have thrown such a fit and tried to storm away the way mother had. She wouldn't have fought with him, sent him reeling to the sand to be attacked by those things—

At the mere thought of the things that had come crawling out of the ocean her hands began shaking with fear. God, she needed a drink.

She spun back toward the kitchen and rummaged for the Jim Beam that she had partaken in last night. She found it in the liquor cabinet. Still a third left. Good.

The amber liquid cast a warm glow down her throat, warming her chest. Another shot brought the warmth further, settling in her bones in a nice, peaceful ambiance. The third shot calmed her nerves down to the point that she felt better. Back in tune.

She stood at the kitchen counter, the bottle of Jim Beam in front of her. The rain pelted the house, the drumming of it filling her eardrums. Far over the Atlantic Ocean, thunder boomed. The wind brushed the trees against the windows, creating a spooky atmosphere. This would be a great night to cuddle up with Kirk with a great horror flick in the VCR; *Night of the Living Dead, Halloween, Psycho*. He would be there to comfort her through the scary moments of the film, his arms draped around her shoulders, one hand in her lap, caressing her thigh. And after the film was over they would make-out, and then he would peel her clothes off and go down on her and she would open herself up to him, open herself to his manhood, open herself to—

But not anymore. Kirk was gone now. For good.

Instead of bursting into tears the way she thought she would have, she stalked back into the living room, her green eyes on fire.

It was her mother!

Mother did this to get even with her, for making her rush out of the house in anger and get in the car and drive off that cliff. Mother had followed Stacy to the beach, had witnessed the argument, had seen the monstrosities coming up the beach before she and Kirk even felt their presence. And she'd acted upon it accordingly. It had been Mother who possessed Stacy, made her fight with Kirk, made her struggle in his grasp, pushed him away from her, sent him falling to the sand, smack-dab into the clicking horror of the monsters that picked him apart and devoured him while she ran like a coward to her car.

Stacy stood in the living room, her senses tuned to everything around her: the creak of the house as it shifted on its foundation; the moan of the wind as it blew around the eaves; the patter of rain that drummed on the roof; the crackle of lighting that flashed on the horizon, followed by the slight boom of thunder in the distance; the ticking of the clock above the mantelpiece in the living room; the hum of the gas burner in the furnace when the thermostat kicked in, heating the house. Stacy stood rooted in the center of the room, watching, waiting, all senses peeled for any extra activity. Any presence, any outward signs that Mother was here and watching.

Nothing.

Stacy smirked. She wouldn't be fooled though. Mother was trying to drive her crazy. But two can play at that game.

Stacy went up the stairs to her bedroom and rummaged in her dresser drawers for the blotter acid she'd picked up from Brent last week. There were five hits left. She took it downstairs with her, went into the kitchen, took out a bottle of Rolling Rock and went into the living room. She rummaged inside her purse for the dime-bag of pot and her pipe, fished them out. She filled the bowl of the pipe, lit it and inhaled. The herb burned, curlicues of smoke drifting up. She took two hits before she extinguished the pipe and cracked open her first beer of the evening. She wasn't going to let Mother beat her at this game. No way. Mother wasn't going to drive her crazy with guilt, drive her to stew and cry in the house while Kirk lay dead and mangled outside. No, she was going to sit in here, collect her thoughts, trip for a while and figure out what to do. Come up with something positive. That was the ticket.

She took another swig of beer and moved to the stereo. She found a battery-operated boom box, rummaged among her tapes, and found Pink Floyd's *The Wall*. She put the tape in and turned up the volume. She placed the boom box on the coffee table, settled back in the sofa and went for a hit of acid. She took it with a shot of Rolling Rock. She'd deal with this problem and

she'd find a solution for it *her* way. Not mother's.
Comfortably Numb.

18

Janice Harrelson looked out the kitchen window of her modest three-bedroom home on Elm Street, trying to fight off the drowsiness brought on by the tranquilizer Glen Jorgensen had given her. She'd tried to sleep after Glen dropped her off and could only toss and turn in bed. She left her bedroom door open so she could listen for anything that might emit from Bobby's room, but her son slept soundly. The shock had probably helped add to the tranquilizer Glen had given him. Poor baby.

She slipped downstairs and tried brewing a pot of coffee only to discover that the power was out. She went around the house, trying the lights. Damn!

The storm had probably knocked out the power somewhere, or had probably affected the GE power plant. She pulled her hair back into a ponytail and rummaged around for her boots and a jacket. She'd have to go outside to find the circuit breakers; she didn't remember what electrical items she had left on before she and Bobby left this morning, but she didn't want to take chances and burn the house down should the power suddenly come in. Better safe than sorry.

She found a heavy windbreaker with soft down insulation and a pair of rubber boots. She rummaged in the closet for an umbrella, found a red one, and took that with her. She opened the door, stepped outside, opened the umbrella, and prepared to step off the porch to go around to the side of the house.

And stopped dead in her tracks and stared down the street.

A dozen or more of those creatures that had attacked Bobby were scuttling toward her, clicking their powerful claws. A few of her neighbors had ventured outside out of morbid curiosity and now most of them were running back into their homes, their mad cries coming through loud and clear. The things were just as fast, chasing after their human prey, some of them overpowering them.

Janice stood rooted to the porch in fear as she saw old Mrs. Smith, the eighty-five-year-old widow who was so sweet to her and Bobby when they took afternoon walks, being attacked by three of the monsters. Their barbed tails jabbed downward, bringing shrieking cries of pain from the old woman. Janice's limbs shook as giant claws dipped down, ripped flesh, stuffed them into their mandibles. Her stomach roiled as Mrs. Smith's abdomen began to swell, her housedress splitting from the intense pressure. Her body expanded and blew up like a hot water balloon, inflating to almost double her size before the skin split and reddish, meaty goo splashed over the crabs, drenching them in Old Woman Sauce. More eruptions over her body exploded in blood and gristle and the crabs feasted on the sizzling, bubbling flesh. Janice turned her head away, her breath heaving.

God, one of those stung Rick, what if they had stung Bobby?
Click, click! Click, click!

She whirled around at the sound, her heart jumping into her throat. Four blood-red creatures were scuttling up her walkway, their insane eyes wavering on their eyestalks. With the darkening sky moving in fast, she didn't notice they were coming up the sidewalk toward her house. She turned and scrambled to the front door, the sole of her right foot slipping. Her arms reached out to break her fall, grasping the doorknob, her feet slipping as she fought to regain her footing. She panted, struggling to get up, her ears barely registering the *click click* sound of their claws as they scrambled up the walkway and steps that led to the porch. Her mind reeled with panic as she regained her footing, her hand turning the doorknob, the weight of her body pushing the door open, her fear propelling her inside the house ...

She slammed the door behind her, threw the umbrella down on the floor and scrambled up the steps, taking them two at a time. She ran down the hall to Bobby's bedroom, adrenaline spurring her on.

Bobby was sitting up in bed cradling his hand to his chest when she bolted in. He started, his face streaked with tears, his eyes scared, afraid.

"Mommy ..."

"It's okay, honey." Janice went to him, hugging him. Bobby buried his face in her shoulder, the tears flowing more freely. Janice cradled his head, comforting his cries. "It's okay, honey, it's okay ..."

"What happened to my hand, Mommy, what happened?"

"You had a bad accident," Janice said, the lie slipping out effortlessly. Her mind worked on overdrive: get him out of bed and in some warm clothes and shoes just in case she had to get them out of the house. What did she have for a weapon?

"What happened, Mommy? What were those things that hurt my hand?" He was clearly crying over the realization of what had happened earlier in the day. He'd probably blocked everything else out of his memory.

"They were ..." *They were what? Giant crabs from the ocean that came to devour the town, and don't worry honey, you were lucky. They only clipped off half of the middle finger of your right hand.*

She didn't answer him. Instead, she pried his fingers off her neck and moved away from the bed, heading toward the hallway.

"Mommy!" Bobby wailed, arms stretching out to her.

"It's okay, honey. I'm just going to check on something." She left his bedroom and headed back to hers, heading straight for the end table by her bed. She opened the bottom drawer and took out the flashlight she kept stored in there for emergencies. She turned it on; it emitted a strong beam of light. She left the bedroom, using the flashlight to light her way, and made her way toward the stairs, trying to listen to any alien sounds above the steady drum of the rain. The first floor lay in darkness; with the power out it seemed to be even darker since her porch light, which was on an automatic timer, now sat silent and dark. She took the steps down slowly, one by one, ears cocked for anything out of the ordinary. Above her, Bobby called out, shattering the atmosphere and rippling through what she thought was a sound. She turned toward the second floor. "It's okay, Bobby, hush! I'll be right back."

"Don't leave me here alone!" Bobby wailed.

"I'm not leaving you alone, Bobby, now will you please be quiet." She said this with a little too much anger in her voice and instantly regretted it. A choking sob emanated from his room; it sounded like he'd been on the verge of letting loose another wail when she told him to be quiet, stopping it in its tracks. He sniffled, choking back the sobs in that hitching way children do when they are trying to stop crying. Janice felt the gloom of guilt flow through her as she continued her descent down the stairs. She hated to be stern with him because he was always such a good boy. But now ...

Now she was trying to make out whether she'd heard something unnatural before Bobby's scream cut it off.

She stood still on the staircase, straining her ears to catch anything above the din of the rainfall.

Nothing but the wind.

And the rain.

And the slight scratching sound that was coming from the bottom of the front door.

Janice froze, every cell in her body freezing up. The sound was very clear above the soothing drum of the rain on the rooftop.

Scritch scritch scritch scritch ...

Janice took a step forward, peering into the darkness. The front door was built of heavy, solid oak. There was a small stained-glass window set at eye level in the door which served as a nice porthole. It usually allowed a small beam of light to stab into the house, illuminating the floor immediately below the door and the first three steps of the staircase. Now it was pitch dark. Janice stabbed the beam from the flashlight down at the spot and looked at the bottom of the door to where the sounds were emanating from and her heart lodged in her throat again.

The door was being picked apart from the outside.

Omigod!

She knew it was those things even as she turned and

scrambled back up the steps, knew it was them as she burst into Bobby's room, her expression stopping another wail set to burst forth from his lungs as he looked at her in stunned shock. She moved toward his bed. "C'mon honey, you're going to have to get up out of bed."

"What's wrong?" All traces of tears had left Bobby's face, replaced by utter confusion.

"We have to get out of here." She set the flashlight down on the nightstand by his bed, its beam casting a warm glow toward the ceiling. She stooped toward the bed and cradled Bobby carefully in her arms and picked him up, blankets and all. He put his arms around her neck and clung to her as she moved toward his bedroom window, which overlooked the south side of town. She thought she could dimly make out the scratching sound of the crabs picking their way through the door downstairs. They'd burst through any moment now ...

"Think you can stand up for me, champ?"

Bobby nodded, a brave expression on his face. Janice gave him a quick smile and kissed his forehead. "Atta boy." She set him down carefully and he was standing next to her, still swathed in the blankets from his bed. Outside, the rain beat harshly against the house.

Janice scooted toward Bobby's nightstand and rummaged through, searching for the painkillers Glen Jorgensen had left her with. She found the bottle and pocketed them. They would come in handy later.

She turned just in time to see Bobby moving toward the bedroom doorway. For a moment her heart leaped in her chest as a vision of Bobby crossing the threshold and being overwhelmed by dozens of the giant, snapping crustaceans tearing his young body apart, flashed through her mind. The vision got the best of her, prompting her to leap across the room. "Bobby!"

He stopped at the sound of his name and turned to her. The expression on his face made her feel slightly stupid for jumping to conclusions. "What?"

She held her tongue and herded him back to the window. "Nothing," she said. "Put your shoes on and stay here. I'm going to get my coat."

Bobby raised his cast encased hand at her as if to say *you expect me to do* what? Janice got his drift and sighed, smiling. "Okay, stay here and wait for me while I find my jacket. When I come back, I'll help you put your shoes on. Okay?"

Bobby nodded and sat down on the bed. Janice smiled and ruffled his hair. "I'll be right back."

She stepped quietly in the hall, her ears straining for the slightest sound. Despite the darkness of the hallway, she could see pretty well. She went into her bedroom and found her heavy wool coat and donned it. She found a pair of thick gloves in her dresser and put them in the right pocket of the coat. Then she walked softly out of the room and tiptoed down the hallway back to Bobby's room.

The scratching sound from the front door was getting louder. She stood at the top of the stairway, her body frozen, straining to listen as the creatures continued their mad frenzy at trying to claw their way inside.

Surely they couldn't claw their way through two solid inches of heavy oak …

But she surely couldn't stand up here all night to find out. She went back into Bobby's room and closed the door. Bobby was sitting on the bed, his features questioning. Trying to be brave. "Those … things are coming back to get me, aren't they?"

Janice picked up his Converses and knelt in front of him, putting the left shoe over his foot and knotting the laces. "We have to get out of here, Bobby." She couldn't bear looking in his face.

"They *are* coming to get me, aren't they?" Bobby said, with all the demanding conviction a seven-year-old could muster.

Janice finished knotting his left sneaker and moved to the right. "Nothing is coming to get you."

"Then what is that noise?"

"What noise?"

"The one downstairs." That sarcastic tone of voice again. God, but kids could be such little shits.

She finished knotting his sneaker and put her hands on both his knees, her green eyes locking onto his. "Everything is going to be all right. Okay?" Her tone of voice told him otherwise. It said, *don't argue with me. Do exactly what I say and don't argue.* She hated to be so stern with him when he was so tuned into things, but she was dealing with the situation as things were occurring.

Bobby got the message and nodded. He stood up as Janice rummaged through his closet and took out his parka. He put it on while Janice double checked everything; gloves, painkillers, keys, wallet. Everything was in place. Now for the escape.

She went to the window and opened it. A gust of cold air blew in through the screen, blowing rain through the sill to splash on the floor. The cold air and fresh atmosphere began evaporating the mist that had fogged up the windows from the heat of the room. Janice threw her weight into the window and heaved it all the way up. She looked out the window, her body blocking the view from Bobby for his sake.

It was now fully dark outside but she could see surprisingly well. There were scattered flashlights waving back and forth in the distance; people in the streets were assessing the situation. She could also make out beams of light coming from darkened houses. The street directly below appeared deserted. Through the heavy rain and wind, she could make out the clatter of people running amok, car engines revving, and what sounded like gunfire to the north. A dozen men in hunting gear ran down the street, rifles in hand, shouting excitedly to one another. It was true then. Something was definitely up.

The men turned the corner and began running down the street, rifles ready. Janice leaned forward till her face was kissing the screen and screamed at the top of her lungs. *"Hey guys! Up here! Hey guys! Hey!"*

Lightning flashed amid the downpour, briefly illuminating the street below. She screamed again. *"Heeeyyy!"* It was drowned out by the booming thunder.

She winced as the thunder rolled. She turned back to look at Bobby. He was still sitting on the bed, his expression grave. His brown eyes looked up at her, seeming to say *don't let them get me, Mommy. Please don't let them get me.*

She gave him a smile that she hoped was enough to put his mind at rest. "Everything's gonna be okay, sport."

He smiled back.

She turned back to the window. The men with the rifles were out of sight, but now another pair was in sight. And they were moving toward her house.

"Hey!" She yelled. *"Heeeyyy out there!"*

The figures were closer and grew familiar. Janice felt a sense of relief pour through her as recognition set in. One was tall and gangly, the other of medium height, long, dark hair flapping behind him. Rick and Jack ...

"Hey, guys! Rick! Jack! I'm up here!"

And as they picked up their stride and dashed up her street to her house, she felt a strange sense of relief despite the fact that she felt like it was the end of the world.

19

"They're at the front door!" Janice shouted down as Rick and Jack ran up to the house. "They're trying to get inside—"

They stopped in their tracks, catching sight of the creatures tearing apart the front door of her house. Rick only paid them a glance before he darted up the lawn to the side of the house beneath the second story window of Bobby's bedroom. He held his arms out. "Come on, let's get you out of there."

Janice reached for Bobby and lifted him up onto the windowsill. She gently prodded him. "Go on, honey, it's okay."

"Come on, big guy, I'm right here," Rick said, his heart pounding. The rain was drenching them. He held his arms out to the frightened, injured boy. "Just climb out onto the ledge and I'll catch you."

Janice swung herself out the window and edged down the shingled ledge. Bobby scooted farther, his face blank, as if his system was blocking the fear out and he was on autopilot, doing what he needed to do to survive. He swung his legs over the sill and Rick held his arms out. *"Come on!"*

Bobby jumped. Rick caught him, the boy's sudden weight slamming into him and giving the pain in his right leg an added burst, only to be replaced by the rush of adrenaline that pumped through his system at the reaction of the act. He swung the boy down on the ground and Jack hustled him off to the sidewalk. Rick stole a glance around the side of the house; those things were still occupied at the front door, but should they catch wind of what was going on here, on the other side of the house—

He turned back to Janice who was now perched on the ledge. He motioned for her to jump. She jumped.

She landed in a forward roll and was on her feet in a flash, moving toward Bobby who was standing at Jack's side. "You okay, baby?" Bobby nodded.

Rick grabbed Janice's arm. "We've gotta get out of here!"

She nodded and together, in a closely-knit pack, they headed down the street, away from the Clickers at Janice's front door.

They hit the corner of Sycamore and Elm and made a left. Janice held Bobby's hand as they darted down the street. It was deserted and dark with no signs of the Clickers anywhere.

Rick stopped and motioned to Jack. "What now?"

"We gotta find the sheriff," Jack said, panting. The rain had let up slightly but it was still drizzling. He wiped his wet brow with a large, bony hand. "There's a radio at the station, one with a stronger signal, and somebody should be back by now. If they are, they've no doubt radioed in for help. Plus, we can get flashlights there."

Janice winced. "I had a flashlight upstairs I was using. I forgot it."

"That's okay," Rick said. While it was fully dark now, they could still see fairly well. Up ahead of them, bobbing lights moved urgently. The streetlights themselves were dark.

"It won't be like this for long," Jack said. He motioned toward the sky where the clouds were moving at a fast pace with help from the wind. What little light they had from the moon was soon going to be obscured by more heavy clouds.

Rick nodded. "Then let's go."

They headed down the street, past silent houses settled back in comfy lawns. They reached the end of Elm, turned left on Spruce, and zigzagged their way through the residential section of Phillipsport, braced for any sign of a Clicker. Bobby kept up with the spirit of a trooper; he held onto Janice's hand with a firm grip and an equally grim determination.

At the town center and along the beachfront shops and pier, the town was out *en masse*. Those who lived close to the beach who'd witnessed the initial uproar had either gathered their firearms and ammunition to begin the battle from windows, or braved the rainy weather and fought on the front lines. They lined up like soldiers in battle, guns cradled in their arms, ammunition ready for reloading, lanterns and flashlights illuminating the darkness. Gunfire sounded even as Rick and Jack rescued Janice and Bobby, and its faint echo was a constant reminder of the threat they faced as they threaded their way to the center of town. Along the way those that saw what the uproar was about either beat a hasty retreat—some scrambling into their cars and making a beeline for farther points inland—or gathered their own firearms and held down the fort to protect their respective homes and families. Many Clickers that managed to make it past the front wave of people shooting them were killed by those that lived farther inland. However, quite a few managed to survive and do what they came to do: breed and forage for food.

And eat they did. Most of what went down their gullets were hapless pets that got caught up in the ruckus: dogs, cats, some pot-bellied pigs, the occasional hamster or guinea pig. A pair of Rotweillers chased down several Clickers, attacking them with their jaws, and were quickly swarmed and overrun by more. The cats were usually able to escape, but some weren't so lucky; a mother cat nursing her nine kittens underneath the porch of one house was ravaged by a pair of Clickers, her meows of pain reduced to sizzling fur and flesh. For the most part, however, those cats that were outside were able to escape where most cats escaped to—up the nearest tree. Local wildlife was infected as well: a group of foxes nestling in a burrow were torn apart and devoured; squirrels and other rodents made small appetizers. One Clicker invaded the den of a hibernating rattlesnake and began chowing down before the slumbering reptile could gather its senses. By the time it did it was too late.

There were human casualties as well, but these numbered less than the animals and pets of the area. A dozen Clickers invaded a home and descended on the owner, a portly woman of fifty-five and her thirty-seven cats. They left the house ten minutes later, leaving a mass of goo, fur, and bubbling flesh. A handicapped man who had been rendered paralyzed from the waist down in an automobile accident fifteen years before in

Atlanta, Georgia, was attacked as he tried to hoist himself up the stairs of his home; the Clickers swarmed through the pet door he'd installed for his dog and they found him halfway up the stairs. He screamed, trying to scoot up the stairs faster, but he was no match for their numbers. Five minutes later what was left of him sizzled on the green shag carpet of his steps. They left his dog in the same condition on the back porch.

The Clickers that beached themselves by burrowing into the sand were forgotten as others scuttled up the shore, heading toward the townspeople now lining the pier with rifles, shotguns and semi-automatic rifles. Billy Ray Wilkeson, the town tough who hung out at Juke's Bar on the outskirts of the city—and was a frequent lover of Stacy Robinson when her boyfriend was slaving away at work, and who sometimes accompanied Sheriff Conklin on rides through backroads on the lawman's off time to beat up niggers and faggots—let out a bloodcurdling scream and dropped the rifle he was firing at the Clickers. A large one had snuck up on him right below his line of fire and clamped down on his ankle with one blood-red pincer. Billy Ray screamed again and stepped back as the Clicker's segmented tail rose and jabbed. The stinger plunged through the paunch of his stomach and Billy Ray promptly fell down on his ass. The Clicker lunged, tore out a chunk of his face with a mandible and began eating even as Billy Ray's stomach expanded and sizzled.

But for the most part, the people were winning.

Glen Jorgensen was watching the action from his third-floor attic, viewing it all through his telescope as his opinion became clear. He stepped back from the telescope as the realization dawned on him: he was in a relatively safe place, so long as they didn't go by human scent. He had three guns in the house—a Luger semiautomatic with a ten-round clip, a .45 Magnum Long Barrel, and a Winchester thirty-aught six hunting rifle with a scope—and he had several hundred rounds of ammunition. All the guns except for the Luger were kept in the attic; the Luger was kept in his bedroom, in the top drawer of his nightstand. An old habit he'd never broken when he was completing his residency at St. Mary's in Yonkers, New York. His one room apartment had been a five-minute walk from the hospital, and he often passed by patients he worked on who had come into the hospital after having been stabbed, shot, or beaten up in domestic disputes, gang turf wars, or Saturday evening barroom brawls. And more often than not, he was accosted at the hospital itself for his cash by some gun-toting junkie who would snake through the busy hospital corridors, shaking down anybody and everybody. He was glad when the residency was over; he didn't know if he'd eventually face the barrel of some hood breaking into his apartment, or if he would go crazy himself from the eighteen-plus hour days.

Now he gathered the weapons together, breaking open the rifle. He sat on his desk loading the rifle, all the while keeping his attention to the window and what lurked out in the rainy darkness. He could hear the sound of gunfire and from the sounds of yells and jubilant screams it sounded like the citizens of Phillipsport were going to be mounting some strange-looking trophies over fireplace mantels in the weeks to come—not to mention bringing the scientific community down on this little seaport haven in droves. But that wasn't what worried Glen.

It wasn't over. Not by a long shot.

He finished loading the rifle and turned his attention to the Magnum. He opened the chamber and began loading it. He was lucky to find a window between two trees on the northeast corner of his home where he could train his telescope. Once there he had a great view of the beach, and he'd been watching the action on the shoreline for the past two hours. Those crabs weren't just hurtling themselves en masse to wreak havoc on the town; they weren't just beaching themselves to forage for food. Glen witnessed the intensity of their scramble to shore and their haste to breed in the sand. He noticed as the last wave hit the beach that they were more frantic, more concerned about scuttling up the beach and away from the sand, than with mating. They barely even noticed the threat of the men on the shore blasting them away with their guns. They continued to scurry up the beach even as others were blown to mush. They were scuttling inland as fast as they could.

It almost looked like they were fleeing from something.

Glen Jorgensen's features were grim as he began loading the rifle. What was going on outside was confirming the fear that was now pulsing through his veins. It was confirming the theory he had formulated through his reading of the past few hours.

Something was hunting the crabs. Something that had taken the village settlement nearly four hundred years ago.

Glen Jorgensen finished loading the rifle. He set the weapons by the window near the telescope. Then he went downstairs to his bedroom, found his heavy-duty flashlight, and with the strong beam lighting his way, headed to the first floor. He checked the front door, making sure it was double-bolted, then went around the lower floors checking the windows and the rear door. He strode down to the basement and made sure the windows down there were shut and locked. Then he headed back upstairs, gathered some food and water from his second-floor apartment kitchen, reinforced the windows there, and headed back up to the attic.

Glen set up his watch command by the window. He hefted the rifle up and lowered it on the mantelpiece that sat near the window. Then he sat down, keeping a watchful eye out the window, looking out for what he knew in his heart was left to come, but praying to God that it wouldn't.

They wound up at the center of town by pure fate. They'd run back toward the beach and decided to try making a grab for Janice's car. Just when it seemed like they weren't going to get the chance to get the car because it was surrounded by Clickers, opportunity knocked when Janice's neighbors, a young couple in their mid-twenties, blew a couple of them away with their hunting rifles. That was when they seized the opportunity to make a mad dash for the vehicle. Rick took the wheel while Janice stayed in the back with Bobby, who remained curiously mute throughout the ordeal. Several Clickers came across their path, yet Bobby showed no physical reaction. Instead of numb fear or hysterics, he simply looked at the creatures in awe, as if wanting to know more about whatever it was that had hurt him.

They drove through town, tearing down the streets as the headlights of the car picked up what was going on: people running madly, hysterically; other people brandishing rifles, pistols, baseball bats, running into the street in rage, beating and shooting the Clickers who seemed to scurry unheedingly. Rick had to take care not to swerve into either people or Clickers. Driving through Phillipsport on this night was almost like driving through downtown Los Angeles at rush hour.

They hit the center of town and Rick pulled up in front of the sheriff station. People were running along the beach front with rifles, shotguns and handguns, shouting enthusiastically at each other. *These fucking people are acting like it's a goddamn war or something,* Jack thought. But then he mentally checked himself. It was a war; one against mankind by what he termed an alien invasion. Alien because as far as he could tell, he and everybody he had come across had never seen creatures like this before in their lives.

"Radio should be inside," Jack said.

Rick nodded, looking around. There wasn't any sign of Clickers anywhere. The only Clickers around were dead.

Rick turned around toward the back seat. "If the radio here doesn't work—"

Jack tapped Rick's shoulder and motioned out the window. "Sheriff's here."

Rick turned toward the window and saw Sheriff Conklin heading toward them. His clothes were slightly disheveled and damp, his grin cocky and malevolent. He looked pale, panicked. The sheriff limped toward the car and for the first time, Jack noticed that the right leg of his pants was stained a dark maroon. *Most likely a Clicker,* Jack thought as he traded a glance with Rick and shrugged. Both men exited the car.

Roy approached them, his grin fading as Jack noticed that most of the townspeople seemed to be ignoring the arrival of the sheriff. They were all off on their own little worlds.

"Sheriff Conklin—" Rick began.

"Put your hands up!" Conklin barked.

"What?" Rick began, but he got no further than that when

Conklin abruptly spun him around and shoved him against the car. Rick was momentarily stunned as he hit the side of the car with his chest, making it rock a little on its springs. Inside, Janice gave a startled cry. Rick moved to turn back and Conklin had him in a chokehold, one muscular arm around his chest and throat, holding him. Rick struggled. "Hey, what the fuck's wrong with you?"

"Stay the fuck down," Roy muttered, throwing his weight into the hold, which pinned Rick to the car. Janice scrambled across the seat and emerged from the other side while Jack stood in numbed shock beside the car, his bony hands curling into fists as Roy brought his handcuffs out and snapped a cuff on Rick's left wrist.

"What the hell are you doing?" Jack yelled. His Adam's apple bobbed up and down.

"You shut your face or I'll haul your ass in, too," Conklin said as he relaxed his grip slightly and pushed Rick against the car with his knee pressed into his back.

Janice was livid as she stormed up to the lawman. *"You cocksucking pig!"*

Roy calmly snapped the second cuff on Rick's right wrist. "You want to join him, Miss?" Roy looked at her with eyes cold as flint. It was like looking into the eyes of a shark.

Rick was still stunned. "What the hell is going on here? Why are you—"

"Shut up!" Roy said as he hauled Rick up and began moving him off the street to the sheriff's station.

Jack followed him a few feet behind. "What are the charges?"

"No charges," Roy said. "There's a war going on and last time there was a war, men like him," he shook Rick's shoulder with the tight grip of his hand, "were the reason we lost. We're not losing this one." He opened the door of the station and marched Rick inside. Jack stopped at the curb, staring vacantly at the gray facade of the building as Bobby's voice rose in the air. The boy was crying again.

Jack turned back to the car. Janice was in the back seat comforting her son who sniffled and sobbed. "What did Rick do, Mommy?"

"Nothing, honey," Janice said, trying to soothe her son. She stroked his head with her hand, smoothing hair back from his forehead.

Jack caught her attention and motioned inside. Janice nodded. Jack turned and strode into the office, more pissed off now than when those things had stormed the beach.

He entered the lobby just as Roy was leading Rick down the hall to the cells. "Okay now, will you please tell me what the fuck is your problem?"

Roy stopped and slowly turned his neck, casting Jack in his cold gaze. "What was that?"

"What the fuck is your problem? Have you lost your mind?"

Roy took his pistol out of its holster and pointed the barrel at Jack's face. He cocked the hammer. His eyes narrowed in cold slits. His face was stone. "You know, Jack, I believe I have. Do you have any suggestions on how we can alleviate this problem?"

The rest of what Jack intended to say dribbled out of his mouth, spiraling away into nothingness. He raised his hands as if to ward off any anticipated blows. His legs felt rubbery and his body suddenly felt light. He took an involuntary step backward.

"It's okay, Jack," Rick said. "Go back outside with Janice and Bobby."

"Yes, Jack," Roy said, keeping the weapon trained on Jack's face. "Go outside and keep that slut and her little brat company."

Jack stood his ground for a moment as if rooted to the spot. He looked at Roy closely. The lawman's clothing was damp, almost sopping wet. It was disheveled, and his hair was even more matted. There was a tear in his slacks, the clothing itself stained badly. From within the tear he could see blood. The lawman's face was white, almost pasty, and his eyes were haunted and livid. His lips twitched as he stood before him, training the gun on him.

For the first time, Jack noticed that Rusty wasn't with the sheriff. Where was he? The heavy sound of Roy Conklin's breathing and the mad, livid look in his eyes told him that something caused the sheriff to become unglued mentally. There was no trying to reason with the man now.

He backed up slowly until he was at the door. Then he eased out the door outside onto the sidewalk.

Only then did Roy lower his gun.

Jack watched the rest of it from the sidewalk. Janice stood by the side of the car, calling out to him. "What happened? What the hell is going on?" He held up a hand to silence her and watched as Roy ushered Rick to the rear of the sheriff's station. A moment later Conklin reappeared and headed toward a room off to the side.

It wasn't until Sheriff Conklin was out of sight that Jack went back to the car and told her that he thought Sheriff Roy Conklin had finally lost his mind.

"So you're sure you'll be all right here?" Jack had asked her this question for the third time and she was getting tired of it.

"I'll be fine, Jack," Janice said. "Now will you please go find Doc Jorgensen so he can try to clear this mess up?"

Jack nodded and glanced inside the car at Bobby. He smiled and waved. Bobby returned the wave. The smile took a bit more effort.

It had been Janice's idea for Jack to find Glen Jorgensen. If what Jack Ripley told her was true, then Sheriff Conklin had been injured worse than the flesh wound on his leg. She, too, had seen the mad expression in his eyes, and it scared her. She'd read about people who'd gone mad, and in the descriptions in all these works, usually the novels of Stephen King and Dean Koontz, the madman's eyes were livid, haunted somehow. Hollow, yet alive with some insane lust. Sheriff Conklin looked like that now, as if he was possessed by some hidden force that had suddenly taken root. She'd never liked the man much, had always found him to be odd—but harmless. That oddness was now blossoming into something dangerous. And if the problem was medical—psychological from some hidden dementia, or physical from the loss of blood—she knew Dr. Jorgensen would be able to help.

"Are you sure you'll be safe?" Jack asked with growing concern on his features. "Those things—"

"Bobby and I will be fine," Janice said. "If any more trouble happens, I'll get in the car and drive us over to Jorgensen's. Until then, I'm staying here until Conklin comes out. If he's lost it, maybe he'll listen to me. I've known him almost all my life."

Jack nodded. She could see that she'd scored a point, and Jack knew that what she was saying made more sense. Jack had been living in Phillipsport barely fifteen years, which still made him an outsider in these parts.

She'd known Conklin since she was six or seven. He might have become temporarily unbalanced, but she was hoping their personal history would cut through that and speak some sense into him.

It took some convincing but Jack finally took off, darting across the street, moving cautiously as he headed toward Glen Jorgensen's.

Janice watched him go, then checked out her surroundings. The Clickers seemed to be gone; several townspeople were heading back from the beach bearing hunting rifles, talking enthusiastically as if returning from a bear hunt. Another pair of men walked up the street, three of the Clickers hung on meat hooks like fish dangling from their mouths. The Clickers' bodies were broken and blasted away, but they still resembled the monstrosities they were.

A sound behind her made her whirl around. It was Sheriff Conklin emerging from the station. He was carrying an semi-automatic weapon and had a pump shotgun draped over his back. There were now two pistols hanging from holsters around his hips. He was limping rather badly and she noticed his wound. Was it a gunshot? He glared at her with that look of madness in his eyes, then turned toward the pier. Janice stared at him, jaw agape. Looking at him gave her the creeps.

She fought the urge to yell after him, to try to stop him and make him see reason. Roy kept walking in that dragging limp toward the pier, his gait illuminated by the sporadic headlights of pickup trucks parked haphazardly in the street. His gait was so purposeful, the look in his eyes so maddening, that she thought if she did try to say something he would snap even further and use the firearms he was carrying. He looked like he was already past the breaking point.

Jack was gone, having trotted off to fetch Dr. Jorgensen five minutes before Conklin came out of the station. The sheriff's limping gait receded as an idea took root in her mind and she moved back toward the car, her mouth set in a tight grimace. She opened the rear door. "Come on, Bobby. We're going inside."

Bobby scrambled out of the back seat, his bandaged hand cradled to his chest. Glen Jorgensen had equipped it with a makeshift sling, and now Bobby had the hand in it. "Are we going to get Rick out?"

"Yep." Janice closed the back door and herded her son through the sheriff's station. She closed the door behind her and motioned Bobby to stop, then listened, trying to catch whatever sounds could be emanating from within the building. The sheriff's station was small, the first room consisting of a makeshift lobby/office. It was equipped with a small waiting area and four desks. Beyond the office to the right there was a little corridor lined with closets. Directly behind the office was a long corridor that was dark. The cells, she assumed. The place was silent.

"Rick!"

From faintly down the hall, his voice. "Down here."

She paused, waiting for the tell-tale signs of another deputy emerging from the jail, or from one of the side rooms telling her she had to leave. But none came.

They were alone in the sheriff's station. Just as she expected.

She locked the door behind her. Then she herded Bobby ahead of her and made her way down the darkened hall to the jail where Rick was incarcerated.

By the time Roy reached the pier, most of the work appeared to be already done. A group of twenty men were blowing the beached creatures to mush, while others stood poised at strategic points on the beach, keeping their eyes peeled for further invading creatures. The few stragglers that made their way to shore were quickly shot. Roy saw Barney Corabi, who appeared to have taken charge. Barney was a bear of a man, tall and beefy with black hair, who favored lumberjack attire. Roy approached him, waving. Barney saw him and waved back. "What we got here, Barney?"

Barney motioned toward the beach. "We got most of it under control. Tried raising you at the station. Where were you?"

"Rusty and I were over at the power station when they came," Roy said. He still didn't know what to call these things. *They* seemed to be the best way to describe them. "They took us completely by surprise. I'm damned lucky to have gotten out of there alive."

Barney looked concerned. "Jesus, Roy, what happened?" He looked down at Roy's injured leg. "What the hell happened to your leg and where's Rusty, is he—"

"Dead." Roy's voice was deadpan as he looked at Barney and shook his head. He sighed, trying to inject some drama in the narrative. "Those things were all over the power plant when we got there. A swarm of them attacked us and Rusty was in front of me when they came. We both backed up, pulled our guns and started shooting but they got him. They stung him ..." He let that trail off, avoiding Barney's eyes as he looked at the sand filled with so many of the broken shelled, bloodied creatures. "I tried to save him and in doing so Rusty's gun went off and I was shot. By then it was too late ..." He shook his head.

"I know," Barney said. "One of them stung Ritchie Wilkeson during the first wave. It snuck right by us and got him right in the hip. He—"

Roy held his hand up, stopping him, eyes closed against what Barney meant to say next. *His hip swelled up, the skin split and began bubbling. Then his hip just ... exploded.* He knew about that. He'd seen what those things had done to the men in the power plant and to Rusty after he shot him. He'd seen that, but he hadn't been horrified by it. No way. Those things had their purpose in life, and Roy had seen it on the way back to Phillipsport. They were his chance to redeem himself. "What's happening now?"

Barney seemed to have forgotten about asking Roy how he'd managed to get out of the power plant. The burly man nodded toward the men making rounds along the shore shooting the crustaceans, others snaking along the streets that led farther inland, hunting rifles drawn. "Quite a few of them escaped our front lines and made it farther inland. I got Harvey Fisher and had him call on the guys from the Lodge to load their guns and try to corner these things. Harvey got his boys on it while he rounded the rest of the boys up. A couple of them who came out to the shore moved back inland to meet the other team. We've killed maybe fifty of those."

"Any escape even farther?" Roy asked.

"A few I think. We're concentrating our team on making sure no more come in from the ocean as well as keeping the town reinforced."

Roy nodded. He patted Barney on the shoulder. "Good work. I'll keep watch over here if you want to take a break."

"Think I will," Barney said, shouldering his rifle. "Madge Young made a pot of coffee using propane in the Hot Dog Hut on the pier. You want some?"

"I wouldn't mind a cup of coffee," Roy said, gazing up and down the shore.

"Back in a minute." Barney turned and made his way down to the pier.

Roy beamed. He turned his back to the ocean, a grin on his chiseled face. Everything was going to go just as he planned. Now that he was in control and on top of things, he'd make sure these creatures were dead, then organize a simultaneous clean-up crew and medical team to help the injured. Taking control of the war. Something he should have done before, in that other war, the one that he—

He bit down hard on his bottom lip. Blood squirted into his mouth. The pain rocked the thought out of his mind. *We're not going to think about that. Everything is under control. Rusty is gone. That Rick Sychek longhair is in a cell where he won't interfere like he did last time and this time I'm going to do it. I'm going to do it!*

He turned toward the beach. The shore was lined with dead crab-creatures. The men who were walking the beach, making sure they were dead, had departed for points farther inland. Not a living thing moved on the beach. There was no reason for any more men to remain at the beach.

Roy turned his back to the ocean again, watching as the men moved down the streets, heading inland, checking to make sure the dead creatures were really dead and others weren't roaming. He grinned wider, fully satisfied with himself and his plan.

Barney came out of the Hot Dog Hut holding two steaming cups of coffee. Roy moved away from the strand and met him on the sidewalk. He took a cup of coffee. The heat from the drink felt good in his cold, wet hands. He felt good now that things were taken care of. "All those things on the beach are dead. The men are moving inland."

Barney nodded. "Let's go."

They went.

They didn't notice the large, man-like shapes a few hundred yards north rise from the sea and begin heading toward shore.

20

There were screams coming from the beach.

Rick turned toward the sound. Janice stepped back from the bars and turned to her son. "Stay here," she told Bobby, who was sitting on the floor in front of the cell. She exited the jail and went to the window along the north side of the building in the office. A moment later, Rick heard her say: "Holy shit!"

"What?" He didn't like the way she said that.

She hurried back into the jail, her face flushed. "I'll be right back."

"What is it?" He moved to the cot set against the north wall of the cell, directly underneath a small window that was near the ceiling.

Bobby stirred, making as if to get up. "What is it, Mommy?"

"Stay here, Bobby. Don't move." Her voice was stern. She meant what she said.

Rick stood on the cot and stood on tip-toe to catch a glimpse of what had so riled Janice. He was startled by what he saw.

Dark shapes moving forward swiftly down rain-soaked streets, man-like in their gait and walk, but strangely alien. Faint shouts of men, the sound of gunfire. Rick squinted, trying to make out what he was seeing in the gloom; the rain had picked up again, and a darker mass of clouds had moved in, making the atmosphere outside almost black. The yelling outside intensified, and he heard a terrified voice screaming *"No, no, no aaaaahhhhh!"* And then it was cut off.

A sound from behind him made him whirl around. Janice was back, rifles slung over her shoulders. She put them down on the ground and headed back into the station. Rick looked out the window again, ignoring Bobby's persistent inquiries of "Rick, what's outside? Mommy, what's happening?" He tried to get another glimpse of what he'd seen, but couldn't make anything out. Just a few shapes moving to and fro in the darkness.

Janice came back with more guns: semi-automatic weapons, pistols, and boxes of ammunition. Rick stared at the ammunition. "Jesus, what's gotten into you?"

"Come here a minute," Janice said. She inched herself up along the bars of the cells, leaning against them.

Rick stepped forward.

"Closer." She leaned the left side of her face to the bars, pulling her hair behind her ear.

He stepped closer. She reached between the bars and grabbed him by the shirt, pulling him closer. With her other hand she grasped his face lightly and turned it so the right side of his face was facing her, his ear to the bars. She leaned close to him and whispered in his ear. "There's something out there killing people, Rick. I didn't want to say this out loud with Bobby here, but I saw them."

He nodded and whispered back. "I saw them, too, but I couldn't tell what they were."

Her voice sounded scared now. More scared than it did earlier in the evening when he and Jack had rescued her from the roof of her house. Her breath whispered in his ear. "I only caught a glimpse of one and ... it was ..." Her voice shook slightly. " ... green ... and all *scaly* ... I thought I might be seeing things and wanted to look more, but then I thought about those giant crabs, and figured if those were *real*, then these—"

"Are just as real," Rick finished the sentence for her.

Janice nodded. Her eyes seemed to glow luminously in the darkened jail. They reflected deep worry. "I ducked down because I figured ... if they were real, they might see me ..."

"Good thinking." Rick was learning that, in light of the arrival of the Clickers, the fantastic had to be dealt with on the level of everyday reality.

"The front and back door of the station is locked," Janice said. "Maybe if we stay here they'll ..." she shrugged. At a loss for words.

Rick attempted to finish that sentence for her, but dropped it. What he was going to say—*maybe they'll bypass us*—fell short as well. Wishful thinking. If they were going to survive, they were going to have to be alert and quick thinking. "Turn off the flashlight," he said. She nodded, and moved to extinguish the big flashlight she had brought in from the office earlier. She had turned it on a few minutes before to see what she was doing as she made Bobby comfortable on the floor, and had forgotten to turn it off. It had cast its warm glow over the hallway of the jail, making long, dark shadows along the bare, gray walls. She shut it off, and they were plunged in darkness.

"Mommy, what's happening?" Bobby had gotten up and was at the bars. His voice startled Rick and he jumped.

Janice was startled as well; she flinched, her breath caught in her throat. She closed her eyes, hand on her breasts. "Jesus, Bobby, you scared the living shit out of me."

"Sorry," Bobby said. His hand was still in the makeshift sling, cradled against his chest. He looked up at the two adults in the darkness with what looked like curiosity.

Janice knelt down in front of him. She smoothed out his shirt. "We're going to have to stay in here a little while longer, honey."

"I'm hungry!"

"I know. I'm hungry too. But we have to wait here until Jack comes back for us."

"Where did he go?"

"He went to go find Doc Jorgensen."

"Where's that dipshit sheriff?"

Rick laughed aloud. Janice giggled herself. "Bobby, don't say that."

"Why not?"

"Yeah, why not?" Rick asked, feigning seriousness.

"*Rick!*" Janice looked up at him, making a slashing motion across her throat with her finger. *Cut it out!*

"Jack will be here any minute now, and we'll be out of here," Rick said, trying to steer the conversation away to something more constructive.

"How will he get you out of the cell?" Bobby asked. That

was a good question. Fortunately, Janice was acting to help the two of them formulate a plan for that one by herding Bobby down the hall, toward the rear of the jail.

"We'll get him out somehow," she said, herding him down to the end of the hall in front of the next cell. "Now let's sit you down on these cots I brought in from the station so you can take it easy. You know what the doctor told you."

"I know ..." The voice of dread.

While Janice settled Bobby down on the cot and gave him his pills, Rick turned his attention back to the window. He climbed up on his cot and looked out the window again. It was a good thing the walls were thick in this place, and the glass was just as thick and strong. That probably muffled the sound, which helped shield them from the carnage that was going on outside.

The dark man-like figures were running amok now. Despite the fact that it was dark outside and it was hard to make things out, he could tell what was going on. It was easier to tell them apart from normal people; while they might have been mere shadows, these things were bigger than men, and moved much quicker. Besides, they were attacking everybody they came across and tearing them apart.

Rick watched in numbed shock as one grabbed a short, squat middle-aged woman whom he recognized as one of the waitresses at Shelby's drug store. The thing throttled her, its claws sinking into her throat until her head was lolling on strips of flesh. Blood fountained from her neck, gushing black. The thing put its green, scaly face into the flow and drank, eating at the flesh.

Dark Ones, Rick thought. *They're like the Dark Ones out of a Lovecraft story.*

Similar events were happening along the two-block view Rick had from his jail cell window.

Two Dark Ones played tug of war with a teenage boy, one eating him as the boy screamed, their tugs finally pulling the boy's arms from their sockets with a ripping of flesh and cracking of bone. Blood gushed from the cavities as the boy continued screaming, even as more of the Dark Ones gathered around him and began feasting.

A group of four Dark Ones were feasting on the remains of what appeared to be a man dressed in military gear. His rifle lay useless next to him ...

A Dark One chased a man up Main Street, finally leaping through the air to catch him, bringing him down, strong claws ripping his back open as the man squirmed a dance of death.

Rick turned away from the window. His breathing was harsh. Sweat dotted his forehead. *Jesus Christ, what the hell were they going to do now?*

Janice finished tending to Bobby. He approached the bars again. She came up to him, her features downcast, heavy with stress. "Maybe he'll rest a little bit now."

Rick nodded, mustering a smile. "He'll be fine."

She smiled back, though it was strained. "I'm worried."

"I know."

"Jack should have come back with Doc Jorgensen by now," she said, looking at him. "I just hope that ..." She looked toward the entrance of the station, obscured by the corridor that turned into the jail ward. " ... those things weren't out there when Jack left, and ..."

"I know," Rick said. He reached his arms through the bars of the jail and took her hands. She returned the gesture and they held hands for a moment, content with just reassuring each other that they were there. The physical contact was welcomed. They needed each other.

"We have weapons, right?" Rick asked. "I mean, this is a police station. We've probably got a whole arsenal here."

Janice nodded. "We do."

"Then we should be able to hole up in here until these things go away."

"Maybe I could shoot you out," Janice said. She gestured toward the lock of the jail cell door. "You know, take one of those Magnums or something to that lock. Blow it away."

Rick nodded. "Good idea, but those things might hear or sense the reverberation of the gun going off."

Janice sighed. "You're right."

"You're sure the key to the cells are nowhere to be found in the office?"

"I looked everywhere. Went through all the drawers and desks, went through clothes in the closets. Nothing."

"And it's likely that if any of the other off-duty cops have keys, they would have them with them," Rick said. "And we don't know where they are."

"Maybe I should get the rest of the weapons from the office," Janice suggested. She let go of his hands, moving to step back.

"*No,*" Rick said, almost a little too sharply. He looked over at Bobby to make sure he hadn't startled him. Janice followed his gaze and held it a bit longer to make sure her son was still resting. He was. She turned back to Rick who sighed, and grasped her hands again through the bars. "We should move around as little as possible. I don't know what those things are outside, but they came from the ocean and it's obvious that they're amphibious. They probably track things in the ocean by movement, and they can probably do the same on land. So, let's stay put."

Janice nodded. She looked afraid. "What if they do come in, though?"

Rick looked glum. "Then," he said, his voice lowered, "I guess we have a problem."

21

The Dark Ones were on the rampage.

Those that were lucky escaped with their lives. Those that had been shooting the Clickers and turned to gape at the seven-foot-tall Dark Ones emerge from the ocean turned their weapons on them only to get eviscerated even as they scrambled to escape. One third of the population of Phillipsport went out that way; gutted by razor sharp claws, limbs torn off, gullets sliced open and devoured as their hearts still beat. Ten percent of the population of Phillipsport was killed as they stopped to help those that had been initially attacked by the Dark Ones. For the most part, guns were no match for them. Even hollow points did no damage, but were only a minor inconvenience to the large creatures, like bothersome flies. Bullets didn't really do much except make them mad.

They mowed down Main Street, destroying anything that got in their way. By now everybody that came in contact with them was running for their lives. As word spread through Phillipsport, those that were beginning clean-up from the Clicker's invasion quickly retreated. Even then, some weren't so lucky. The Dark Ones had moved in rather quickly and most people ended up running and screaming while a Dark One was in hot pursuit, only to be ambushed by another that had been waiting behind a corner or a parked car. The dark of the night didn't seem to hinder the creatures at all. It was as if they were used to the lack of light and the heavy darkness of shadows.

Some people ran into the presumed safety of homes or buildings, only to be chased by the Dark Ones. The concrete walls of most structures were no match for them; they merely

J. F. Gonzalez

burst down the doors and waltzed right in, wreaking havoc inside until they had their prey.

At the town's center where the shopping mall lay, more pandemonium ensued. The Dark Ones were making their mark, chasing people in cars and on foot. A team of men hunting Clickers turned their rifles on the large, amphibious creatures heading toward them, then quickly fled as they realized the bullets were having no effect. They ran into the shopping mall with the Dark Ones in hot pursuit. The creatures chased the men in the shopping center and others joined them for the hunt. The men were eventually caught and killed. More Dark Ones joined them in the feast.

Sheriff Roy Conklin watched it all from what he hoped was a safe vantage point; he was perched on a ledge in the alley that ran between the coffee shop and the Barnes and Noble bookstore. The alley ran out into the parking lot of the shopping center, and from where Roy sat huddled behind a trash bin he could see the things slaughtering everybody they happened upon.

Twenty minutes ago Roy had been riding high. He had taken over the hunt for the crab-things and had quickly taken control of the situation. Now he was simply quaking in his boots.

He'd limped down Main Street with Barney, sipping his coffee, supervising the end of the hunt and barking orders to several teams to get a clean-up crew started. Barney had finished his coffee and suggested they head to the shopping center. They could round up the work crew from the store's warehouse and utilize their equipment in a clean-up. Roy agreed, and they headed toward the shopping center on foot. They arrived not a moment too soon.

Roy had gone into the supermarket to find Arnie Sumner, the manager, when a scream made him turn around. One of the men who had been paired into a hunting group—Ritchie Mercury, who ran the War Horse Saloon on Harbor Street—had been attacked by a large, man-like green thing. It looked like the *Creature From the Black Lagoon*. The thing sank its jaws into Ritchie's neck and blood flowed as the man squirmed. Roy automatically took a step forward, drawing his gun and getting ready to aim when several more things appeared from Main Street. All at once a series of images kicked in, registering several things: screams coming from where he and Barney had just come from, the sudden increased sound of gunfire, and the rapid footfalls of large, heavy bodied things moving quickly through town.

Roy stepped outside, gun drawn, and that was when he saw Barney, who was near the edge of the parking lot. Barney had watched the coming of the things with a sort of numb, amazed shock—now he let out a yell, which seemed to snap him out of his shock, and turned to run. One of those things was on him in an instant, throwing a huge, taloned fist through the back of his skull with such force that his eyeballs ejected out of the sockets. The rest of his face split like a pot cracking down the middle and then he was down and the thing was on him.

Holy Jesus fucking Christ! Roy thought, breaking into a halt. More of the giant green things were coming in a steady stream from the beach.

That was when Conklin turned and ran like hell.

He quickly realized that he had nowhere to go; the only way out of the shopping center was the main thoroughfare, which was now crowded with the green monsters. No matter which way he ran, he would be seen and chased down. He hesitated for a moment, heart beating rapidly in his chest. The entrance to the shopping center was blocked off, along with the surrounding perimeter of the parking structure that could easily be accessed by the monsters. The only theoretical way out was through the back. Conklin circled the building and ducked down the first alley he saw—the one between the Barnes and Noble and the coffee shop. He hit the end of it and clambered onto a garbage bin, his leg smarting with pain as the gunshot wound was roused from its dull throbbing. Then he made his way along a wall that bordered the book store, gritting his teeth against the pain that was rocketing up his leg. From there it was a quick hop to a ledge that served as the barrier to an outside generator that supplied power to the supermarket during power outages. Conklin climbed on top of that, his leg howling in agony again and he bit back a scream. He paused briefly and touched the wound. His hand came away damp with blood. His breathing was harsh, his forehead dotted with sweat. He had to break past the pain barrier if he wanted to stay alive. Gritting his teeth, he reached for the roof of the store. It was too high.

Damn! He looked back over his shoulder. The things were swarming *en masse* over the parking lot, slaughtering everybody they came in contact with. It looked like World War III down there, and he couldn't retrace his steps now. To do so would put him right in the battlefield.

There was a small cubbyhole between the generator and the supermarket. He crawled inside, still perched on the generator and crouched down. The pain in his leg sang loudly, and he huddled in the darkness, biting his lower lip to stave it away. Fresh blood ran down his lip and chin. He closed his eyes and waited for the throbbing in his leg to subside. After a while it did.

He opened his eyes and looked out of the cubbyhole. From this vantage point he could see a portion of the parking lot from the mouth of the alley. Despite the darkness of the night, he could see quite well. Most of the men that were out killing the crab things had been equipped with flashlights and lanterns, and he assumed that most of the men that were killed by these new monsters had dropped them, still blazing. Their feeble beams stabbed the darkness, illuminating the parking lot well enough to see what was going on. And what he was seeing didn't look so good.

The sound of people screaming was maddening to his ears. He covered them with both hands and lowered his head. Those screams were driving him mad. He couldn't bear to listen to them as they screamed on and on and the thick, heavy sounds of the things grunting, and roaring, and biting, and slashing intermingled with them. It reminded him too much of that other war, the one far away in the South Pacific jungles where he'd tried and failed. He closed his eyes against the memories, trying to will the sounds away.

In time, the smell of blood and death rose in the air.

Roy retreated as far as he could into the cubbyhole. For a moment he thought he was a goner when one of the creatures pounced on a man right at the mouth of the alley and began tearing into his soft belly. More creatures joined it, and Roy huddled farther into the cubbyhole, trying to drown out the thick, wet, slurping sounds of the creatures feeding. His heart accelerated rapidly in his chest; any moment now and they would finish with whoever that poor guy was and make their way down this alley, sniffing for prey. Their senses would lead them to the back of the alley, over the garbage bin, onto the ledge, into the cubbyhole where they would find—

No! Don't think like that, he told himself. He grit his teeth. *Don't think like that, they aren't going to find you, they aren't going to find you, they AREN'T GOING TO FIND YOU!*

He remained crouched that way for what seemed like hours. His body trembled in anticipation of those claws digging into his back, pulling him out. His skin was sweaty, ridden with gooseflesh caused by the combination of the cold, wet air and the heat his body was exuding. He pulled his gun out of its holster and gripped it, finger resting on the trigger. They might come down this alley and find him, but he would be ready for them when they did. Bullets may not do much harm to them, but if they found him here wedged in this little space, and pulled him out, he would plant the barrel of the gun right in the first creature's eyeball and pull the trigger. They may take him down, but he would get a lick or two in before he went. He wouldn't go down completely defeated the way he had before. No way.

Roy sat crouched in the cubbyhole, the anticipation dying down. After a while the fracas in the parking lot died down as well.

Roy looked out down the mouth of the alley. No sounds of struggle issued from the parking lot. No sounds of death and screaming rose to his ears from the shopping center.

The shopping center was as dead as a tomb.

Roy listened for a while. The rain had let up and the wind had died down. Dark clouds still hung heavy in the sky, and the only sound that came to him was the sound of trash rolling in the wind along the parking lot. Other than that, there was nothing.

Wait. There was something else. Something faint was now coming to his ears. Roy cocked his head and listened before he was able to make it out. It was the tread of those things, moving farther away. They were leaving the shopping center.

He waited until their steps retreated farther and farther in the distance. When he heard nothing for five minutes, he began to breathe a little easier. His heartbeat slowed to a more normal rate. He remained in the cubbyhole for another ten minutes, ears primed and ready for other sounds: sounds of life in the parking lot or farther; more intrusions from more of those large, scaly monsters. All he heard was the wind.

Satisfied that the things were gone, he replaced his gun in its holster and cautiously crept out, pausing every so often to listen for any new sounds. He climbed on to the generator, the wound in his leg reawakening to pain, but he ignored it. He made his way to the wall to drop onto the garbage bin; he tried to put most of his weight in the landing on his left leg, but the right still bore some of the burden. It exploded with pain. He cried out, then cut it off. He leaned against the wall, gritting his teeth against the dull ache of the pain and waited for it to subside.

When the pain dwindled to a dull roar, he stepped forward and listened. Nothing.

This time when he jumped to the floor of the alley, he did it carefully. He sat on the ledge of the wall, his legs dangling over the side, then gently lowered himself to the ground. The few feet he had to drop to the ground weren't as bad this time. The pain that went up his body was bearable. He checked the wound again, saw that it was bleeding again, then wiped the sweat from his brow. He felt light-headed, almost faint, and he paused again, waiting to regain his senses. After a few minutes he felt good enough to venture down the alley and check out his surroundings.

There wasn't a sign of life anywhere.

He drew his gun again and walked slowly toward the mouth of the alley, keeping to the left wall where the darkness was pitch black. At this vantage point, he would be able to see anything coming from the main highway and Main Street, but would be hidden from the creatures that had just left. He crept along the wall, his body tense until he reached the mouth of the alley.

He looked out over the parking lot. It was a vast sea of black tar with white and yellow painted lines designating parking spaces and driving routes. All of this peppered with body parts, blood, and crushed vehicles. The smell of blood hung wet in the air.

Conklin gulped and took a tentative step forward. His boot stepped in something gooey. He looked down. His boot had sunk into the torn open belly of a man he *thought* was Al Farmington, the President of Phillipsport Bank. The way the man's skin was torn off his face, it was hard to tell. He made the identification from the faded tattoo on the outside of the left forearm that he remembered Al telling him he had gotten when he served in the Army.

That arm was now severed and lying near his groin. The man had been wearing faded jeans and a plaid, long-sleeved shirt that had been shredded along with the rest of him. His once portly body was now ripped open and gaping red and raw; all the internal organs had been scooped out. He looked like a Thanksgiving turkey that had just been gutted.

Roy winced as he lifted his boot out of Al's now carved-out stomach. He peered around the corner, toward the south side of the shopping center where the creatures had gone. All was clear.

He stepped out into the parking lot. There wasn't a sign of anything, anywhere. He was safe for now. The trick now was to get the hell out of here.

He began crossing the parking lot, heading toward the main highway when suddenly three figures burst from the shopping center and began running toward what cars were left standing. Roy stopped for a minute, his gun drawn and trained on them and he almost fired off a shot before he realized they were people. They must have been hiding deep within the bowels of the supermarket when the things struck, and now they crept out pretty much as he had just done. The only thing that differed with them was the look of panic-driven fear that permeated off them like miasma.

They reached a car—a white Subaru station wagon— and began piling into it. Roy ran toward them, waving his arms. "Hey! Wait a minute!"

The sound of his voice didn't break their pace. One of them—white male, middle-aged, and presumably the male figurehead—looked up briefly as what Roy assumed to be his wife and teenage son opened the doors and piled into the car. The man opened the driver's side door.

"Wait!" Roy yelled, running up to the car. "You have to take me back to town!" If he could get back to the station he could equip himself with more armament.

The man looked at Roy as if the sheriff was crazy. "Uh uh, no way, we're getting the hell out of here." He fumbled in his pockets for his keys as Roy leaned against the driver's side window.

"I am the sheriff of Phillipsport County and I demand that you take me into town *now.*"

The man got his keys out of his pocket and jammed them in the ignition. His hands were shaking. "Fuck off."

The man started the car and was about to pull away when Roy stepped back and drew his gun. He pointed it at the man. "Get out of the car now, *sir!*"

The man looked up at Roy with an I-can't-believe-this-is-happening look. He raised his hands off the steering wheel in a gesture of surrender. The woman next to him began screaming epithets equating police officers with pork products. The boy in the back seat looked like he was in shock.

Roy pointed the gun at the man's head. "Get out of the car."

"Okay, okay," the man said. He opened the door as his wife screamed.

"Carl no! Don't get out of the car!"

Carl was out of the car. The woman fumbled open her own door and tumbled out. She was in her late thirties with wavy black hair streaked with gray. Her face was bright red with white-hot anger. *"What the fuck do you think you're doing, you goddamned pig!"*

Roy felt a tingling rise along his arms. His face felt flushed, his mind flashing with heavy images, his leg throbbing with pain. His heart was drumming rapidly. He had to get back to the station where the weapons were. He was down to only a few bullets. The volume of the woman's voice, combined with the family's initial yelling and screaming were sure to carry. If those things could hear the way humans could hear ...

Roy motioned for Carl to step aside. Carl did. The boy was still in the back seat, making a feeble attempt to exit the vehicle. Roy motioned with his gun. "Come on, let's hurry it up."

Carl's wife was screaming right next to him. *"I'm going to get you, you redneck backwoods piece of shit—"*

Roy turned around, pointed the barrel of the gun at the woman's face and fired. Her face exploded in a cloud of bone, tissue, and brain. Her body dropped instantly and began flopping convulsively. Carl stood in numbed shock, his jaws opening and closing, a whining gasp escaping from his mouth. Roy grimaced and moved over to the passenger side where the boy had stopped in mid exit at the sound of the shot going off. He grabbed the kid and shoved him away from the door to the pavement. "Move your ass, you little twit."

He slammed the door and moved over to the driver's side. Carl was still staring at the body of his dead wife. The tingling along Roy's arms was now joined by a nervous twinge in his spine, as if he could sense that somebody was approaching him. The feeling spurred him on as he slid into the driver's seat and slammed the door. He put the car in gear, popped the headlights and pulled out. Carl looked up at the sound of the car pulling away and he made a feeble attempt at running after Roy as he pulled away. Roy gunned the engine and sped through the parking lot as Carl ran after him, waving his arms and shouting.

Roy sped toward the entrance to the shopping center and paused once to check Carl's progress in the rear-view mirror.

Sometime during the initial moment it took Roy to arrive at the parking lot entrance, Carl and his son were besieged by half a dozen of the scaly green things. Roy's eyes were riveted to the rearview mirror as he watched Carl being gutted on the parking lot pavement by two of the things. Farther back, his son was buried beneath three more of the creatures. Roy would have stayed there mesmerized by the scene had it not been for that prickly feeling rising in his system again, that sixth sense that told him that something was coming—

Roy turned his head back and saw the creature rapidly approaching from his blind side. It was running toward him, reptilian arms outstretched, mouth bared in a menacing grin full of razor-sharp teeth. Roy yelled and put his foot down on the accelerator. Tires squealed and the car bolted forward. Roy made a hard left and felt something smack against the rear right side of the car. The force of the blow caused the car to be slightly buffeted, as if whatever hit it lightly bounced the car. Roy didn't care to take a look, remaining fixed on the open road before him as he gunned the engine and sped down the main road, his breath coming faster as his adrenaline flowed through his veins. *They almost got me*, he thought.

He sped down the road, doing ninety the whole way. He was forced to slow down once he reached the older section of town, and he made his way through the center of town, tires screeching on the pavement as he made turns too fast. His senses were on alert now after that near-fatal attack, and he kept his eyes peeled for any signs of movement. There was none.

The town itself was deserted. And littered.

With bodies.

Roy drew in a breath as he slowed the car to a crawl. All up and down Main Street, sprinkling the sidewalk, streets, and lawns of houses and businesses, the bodies lay glistening amid the newly fallen rain. The headlights of the car picked out the littered streets of Phillipsport like a battlefield; torn, ripped bloody limbs, torsos and heads lying like discarded broken dolls. The glistening colors of internal organs lay strewn amid the blood and torn flesh, as if a gang of psychopathic children had come along and strewn the innards around like playthings. Roy drove through slowly, trying to fight his gorge down as he felt the car's tires thunk slowly over bodies. Blood and death was heavy in the air, along with the smell of rain.

Everywhere he looked there was no sign of life. Not a tree stirred. Not a bird chirped.

He reached the station and pulled the car in front of the

curb. He glanced up and down the street, his foot on the brake, ready to peel out if anything moved. But there was nothing. The town was deserted.

He put the car in park and turned off the ignition, keeping the headlights on. He wouldn't be too long. It would take less than three minutes to gather more firearms and ammunition and head back out. The sound of the engine cooling was like a loud, annoying clang that sent his nerves running high. It sounded like anybody within a five-mile radius could hear it. Roy looked around, trying to catch a glimpse of any movement. But there was none.

He grabbed his gun and opened the car door slowly.

The air outside was still. The sky was overcast and dark. Dark clouds loomed over the ocean, looking ominous in the distance. Another wave of heavy storms. From the way the breeze was blowing, the storm would be moving inland within a few hours. Round two in Mother Nature's onslaught against Phillipsport. Roy stepped away from the car, leaving the driver's side door open as he made his way slowly to the station. His gun was drawn, ears perked for any sound. He walked slowly to the door, his goal on reaching the station and bolting himself inside where the cache of weapons were and—

He didn't even see them spring from behind the car they were hiding behind as he put his hand on the doorknob to open it. They came at him like crocodiles charging a herd of wildebeests along the Nile and he turned suddenly, the gun dropping down onto the pavement as the first one slammed into him. His back hit the wall and he smelled the fishy scent of the thing's breath. It leaned forward and clamped its jaws on his face, holding him down while the second one came and grasped his arm with sharp talons and began pulling him away from the building. Roy gave one violent kick before his body went limp as the creatures dragged him away. The last thing he thought was that in the end he never had the chance to make his amends. He never had the chance to turn things around and be the hero. They'd moved too fast on him and they—

He wasn't conscious long enough to finish that last thought.

22

Most of the people they saw from Dr. Glen Jorgensen's third story adobe were now all dead.

Jack Ripley sat on a dining room chair that Glen had hauled upstairs a few hours back. He looked out the window, cradling the thirty-ought six. A crate of shells lay at his feet. Glen sat opposite him, cradling his firearm. They'd been watching the activity and talking for the better part of three hours, and things had died down outside. The rain had stopped and all appeared still. The brief reprieve of rain allowed a few stars to poke between the clouds, giving a little light to the dark night. Glen leaned forward slightly and peered out the window, scanning the street below.

"Bad?" Jack asked.

Glen nodded and settled back in his sitting position. "If anybody's alive out there, they're not coming out."

Glen had seen Jack Ripley snaking through the streets, making his way to the house and he knew in an instant that it had something to do with Rick, Janice and Bobby. He'd crept downstairs, clutching his pistol, and answered the door the minute Jack began pounding on it. He thought he'd almost given the man a heart attack when he opened the door; one look at the gun with its humungous barrel and Jack almost turned and bolted back the way he came.

He'd hustled Jack upstairs and learned what happened; Sheriff Conklin's arrival in town, Rick jailed, the status of the Clickers. Jack had been insistent in getting back to town for Glen to try to talk sense into the sheriff, but Glen hesitated. If what he believed was true, if what he surmised from his research of the old Lost Village legend was indeed accurate, the next wave could happen any minute. And if they were caught while in the middle of town, then what? Try and hightail it back? Somehow Glen didn't think that would be an option.

But another part of his mind nagged at him, the ethical part that told him that there was still some time before all hell broke loose. All he had to do was drive to the station, talk some sense into Roy in letting Rick out due to the emergency status the town was under. And if he could, try to treat Roy's injuries. From the way Jack described him, it sounded like the sheriff was injured and in shock. From the description of his behavior, he might even be experiencing post-traumatic stress. He was very strongly inclined to let that part of him win, to go with Jack back into town and fight the good fight, when a chorus of screams and cries erupted from where Jack Ripley had just come from.

"My God, what's happening?" Jack's face had gone pale.

Glen had gone to the window, gun raised. Jack stood next to him and gasped at the scene below.

Glen knew it would be bad, but he still didn't know what to expect. The scene below resembled something out of Spielberg's *Jurassic Park*; a horde of man-like, reptilian creatures were running amok among town, lunging at the residents of Phillipsport as they were commencing clean-up of the Clickers. The new creatures had obviously taken the people by surprise, since by the time Glen laid eyes on the scene they'd pretty much already overrun the town. People ran, scrambling to get away from the monstrosities, yelling at the top of their lungs. The creatures chased people down like cheetahs nailing Impalas. When the creatures took them down they ripped into the flesh of their hapless victims with sharp claws, burying their jaws into shoulders, necks, and abdomens, tearing chunks of flesh. A few of the creatures appeared to be carrying some kind of weapons—spears, or what appeared to be tridents. That was something he hadn't expected; that meant they might possess some form of intelligence. Glen stood transfixed, horrified at what he was seeing. Yet a tiny part of him was ecstatic, pleased and actually quite surprised that his deduction was right. His

only regret was that he hadn't come up with his theory a day—
even a few hours—earlier, instead of within the last hour.

"What the fuck are these things?" Jack asked, horrified. His
bony fists balled up, the knuckles growing white. His eyes were
wild, and Glen thought the man would bolt and head down
the stairs to try to get to the other three to perform an act of
heroism. And that couldn't happen—shitty as it was.

"No, Jack," Glen said, his hand resting gently but firmly on
Jack's shoulder. "We can't go out there now."

Jack looked back at the physician. "But ... we can't just stay
here and—"

"If we go out there now we'll be slaughtered," Glen said. He
motioned out the window. "There is an army of those things
out there, marauding the way Norse invaders would an English
village."

Jack looked out the window. The slaughter seemed to be
moving as the creatures moved up Main Street and up the
road that led to the shopping center—out of visual proximity
to Dr. Jorgensen's third floor viewing spot. Scattered creatures
moved up the side streets, snaring people in their paths as they
tried to make a getaway. Some of them paused to scoop up the
dead Clickers in their reptilian mouths. Gunshots peppered the
area below as those with guns tried to make use of them. With
the lush greenery of trees on every block, the steepled roofs of
houses obscuring the view and the darkness of the night, it was
hard to tell if the gunfire was having any effect. By the sounds of
the screams of the people below, it appeared they had no effect.

"But ..." Jack began. "Rick ... Bobby ..."

"We can only hope and pray that they're somewhere safe."
Glen didn't want to think about what was probably happening
to them. He'd known Janice since she graduated high school, and
had been her and Bobby's physician since the boy was an infant.
He'd liked Rick the instant he'd met him, yet despite that he had
to keep a clear head. This was an emergency, possibly one of
regional proportions. In working in an emergency triage, it was
critical that emotions were kept to a minimum. The primary
concern was in helping those with the least critical injuries;
those with life-threatening injuries were delegated at the end

of the triage in order to save those who had a better chance of surviving. To the layman's way of thinking that might sound cruel, but it wasn't a wasteful effort. To fight these things off and survive they had to adopt the emergency triage tactic and assume that anybody who was outside, or in near proximity to these creatures, were as good as dead. To assume otherwise and attempt a rescue would be wasting one of the only good resources the town had: a Medical Doctor.

Glen explained all this to Jack slowly and methodically. He looked directly in Jack's eyes as he spoke, boring home the message that they needed to keep calm and not flip out. For the sake of those that might need their help, for the sake of the town, for the sake of the communities outlying Phillipsport, they had to keep calm and act reasonably if they expected to survive.

Jack appeared to get the message. He sat in the chair by the window and stared down at the floor. He refused to look outside. Glen checked his pulse, felt his brow with the back of his hand to check for shock. Jack appeared fine; if anything he was just trying to deal with what was happening emotionally. Glen asked him if he wanted some water and Jack nodded. He handed him a bottle of Evian and Jack opened it and drank it nearly empty. That seemed to put the kick back into him.

So Glen and Jack sat at the window and talked. And Glen watched the progress of the things as the creatures snaked their way through town just in case they strayed down the street below them. A pair of them did, shuffling along, their dark forms vaguely hulking in the shadows as they skittered down the middle of the street and past the house. Glen exhaled as the Dark Ones reached the end of the block and turned left, heading farther inland. He was not aware that he had been holding his breath until he let it out.

"What are they?" Jack asked. Jack had gotten over his initial nervousness and Glen had given him a weapon, a Winchester rifle. He sat on his end of the window, his features still bearing some shock of what they had just witnessed yet composed of a yearning to know more of what was happening.

Glen moved from his spot at the window and crossed over to the table in the middle of the room. He picked up a book and opened it to a spot he knew by memory. "I'm an amateur paleontologist, and my main interest is in prehistoric life forms. I've been reading and studying about it since I was a kid. Anyway, when Janice and Rick brought Bobby in earlier today and I had the chance to examine the claw Rick brought in yesterday, I had a hunch. A wild one, but a hunch nonetheless."

"A hunch that the dinosaurs have come back to take over the world?" Jack asked. He grinned and Glen smiled back. It was nice to see that Jack's sense of humor had returned. It meant he was holding up, coping. "No, not quite, " Glen said. "For one, it would be physiologically impossible for dinosaurs to come back to life. Our present eco-system wouldn't be able to provide for them. Second, because there is still no scientific method of regenerating dead tissues or cells, or even perfectly good cells or DNA preserved in tree sap."

"Like what they did in Jurassic Park?"

"Right. The whole idea of being able to clone DNA that closely matches that of dinosaurs with something like, say, a frog, is pretty far-fetched—not impossible, because in science anything can be possible if we make the right discoveries—but far-fetched nonetheless. What made that novel work was Michael Crichton's background as a scientist. With the knowledge of the science of cloning DNA and regenerating cells from their dormant stage, all it takes is the wide speculation and far-out ideas which he utilized in his novel. This is fine for fiction, but what makes this story so great is that until recently this was theoretically impossible. The reason is that until now, perfectly preserved dinosaur DNA has never been found one-hundred-percent perfectly preserved as described in *Jurassic Park*."

"Until now?" Jack was curious.

Glen smiled slightly. "Yes, until now. About a year ago, dinosaur DNA was found preserved in tree sap that was one-hundred-percent perfectly preserved."

Jack's eyes grew wide. "No shit."

"Yep. Of course, that whole deal about cloning DNA with a present-day living organism to match the DNA of tissue millions of years old still can't be done. But in ten years? Five?" He shrugged. "Who knows?"

"You think these things could be—"

"Not cloned." Glen shook his head. "No way. These babies have been with us for a long time. Take a look at this."

He motioned to the book. Jack looked at the picture Glen was pointing to. The picture was a sketch of a Clicker, pretty much as he'd seen it along with the dozen or more that attacked Bobby at the beach. It was a crustacean with the upper body of a crab, with large, powerful pincers, black marble-like eyes that stood on stalks, and long protruding antenna. The back of the creature resembled a lobster, ending in a segmented tail that tapered into a stinger, very much like a scorpion. It had eight legs. It was very ugly.

The italicized name below it was *Homarus Tyrannous.*

Jack looked amazed. "That's it. That's our culprit."

Glen pulled the book back. "This particular species began life about four hundred and thirty-eight million years ago in the Paleozoic era. There's evidence they survived till about the middle of the Mesozoic era. They predate man by about ..." He stopped and chuckled. "Well, by about four hundred and thirty six million years."

Jack appeared to catch the humor in that, as well as the implications of what they were dealing with. "Holy moly."

"Basically they were an ancestor to our modern day crabs and lobsters, although the bit about the stinger is strange. Probably tells us a lot about where scorpions came from— scorpions originally did come from the ocean, you know."

Jack shrugged. It was obvious he didn't know much about paleontology, but he appeared interested nonetheless.

"Anyway," Glen continued, tapping the book with his index finger. "Not much is known about this particular species, since fossils are scarce. It's believed that they survived the Jurassic period and quite possibly the early Cenozoic period. The latest fossilized remains were dated some fifty million years B.C."

"If that's the case then what the hell are they doing here?" Jack asked. He hefted the rifle in his arms, taking a cautious peek out the window.

Glen raised a finger. "That is where it gets interesting." He walked over to a large wall-sized map of the world that he had tacked over a desk. He pointed at the area bridging the coast of Maine, up through the Canadian coast to Greenland. "Fossil remains have been found in this region, but they've also been found on the shores of Iceland, the Soviet Union, the United Kingdom and the South of France. Which lends believability to the theory that the land masses that we now have were once joined together."

Jack nodded. "Okay. That makes sense."

Glen continued. "Nobody really knows how or why the dinosaurs died off. Many theories abound and one of the more plausible ones is that a meteor struck the earth's surface. The resulting shifts in the earth's ozone layer, as a result, tipped the ecological scale. If the dinosaurs were used to living in a lush, humid area, a sudden shift from that to an atmosphere that was cloudy, dark, and cold could have wiped them out. And remember that this change most likely occurred within a short period of time for the dinosaurs to have died off so suddenly. Like maybe … a few months' time, probably more like a few days."

"Yeah I read a book about that once," Jack said, grinning slightly. "It was a novel in which World War III happens and we're wiped out. Kaput. And it described the ecological changes as happening within the space of days. One minute everything was normal, the next bombs were destroying everything, whipping up firestorms, hurricanes, the works. And it just sent everything in a huge tailspin. The sun was blotted out by thick clouds of nuclear shit, and things were all fucked up for like, years. And it got real cold, freezing temperatures. That book scared the crap out of me."

"I can imagine. And we can assume something similar happened in this case with the dinosaurs. The resulting changes wiped out the dinosaurs; that much we know. Along with Allosauraus and Brontosauraus and T-Rex and thousands of other species, paleontologists have lumped *Homarus Tyrannous* as extinct. Why? Because none have been seen, and the only remains of them are the few fossils we've found. But they've survived, and they're still here."

"How is that possible?"

"Two things." He tapped the map again, indicating the area of the North Atlantic. "This area millions of years ago was rich and fertile and lush and humid. The temperature was most likely very warm. I think paleontologists have only unearthed maybe two remains of our little friends here, and those were partial shells. The rest were fragments imbedded in rock, but they were enough for us to piece together. That's considerably fewer than we've found of, say … Mamenchisaurus, of which we've only found one complete skeleton, and that's scarce indeed. Paleontologists have only found one complete T-Rex skeleton since that particular species' discovery in the 1920s. Anyway, the theory for this is probably because *Homarus Tyrannous* lived along the ocean floor, and this area"—he tapped along the North Atlantic— "is fairly deep and largely unexplored. It is also my theory that they probably only migrated inland for mating purposes."

"If that's the case, wouldn't they have left fossilized remains on shore?"

"They have, in the areas I've indicated," Glen said. "But there hasn't been much. That can be explained by … what we're seeing today."

Jack's features grew grim. "The Dark Ones."

Glen was taken aback by the description of the creatures, but it fit. He nodded, stroking his chin. "Yes, the Dark Ones. Fitting, isn't it. And very Lovecraftian, too."

"Do you think they're some … I don't know … prehistoric relic from our past?"

Glen shook his head. "I've never come across anything fitting their description anywhere. Not even in folklore—" He stopped himself and held up his hand as if stopping himself. "Except for today." He darted over to the table where he plucked the chapbook he'd poured through earlier and flipped through it. "There's an old legend in this area about the Lost Village—"

"Right!" Jack exclaimed. "I've heard that one. Didn't that happen near Fort O'Brien?"

Glen nodded. "Exactly. It was a little town where Fort O'Brien is now; in fact Fort O'Brien's main tourist attraction comes from the Lost Village."

Jack appeared to be putting the pieces together. "The Clickers came up to breed, as they probably always did, and were followed by the Dark Ones for food."

"Just as they always did," Glen picked up. "They followed the Clickers inland much in the way Nile Monitor lizards follow female crocodiles in the hopes of eating their young. Which probably explains why we haven't found that many fossilized remains."

"If the Dark Ones destroyed all of them, how were they able to breed?"

"Nature probably allowed a certain number to survive, just as she does with other animal species. Look at the example of crocodiles again; females lay as many as ninety eggs, but in the end only ten ultimately survive through their first few years. The rest are eaten *in utero*, or within a few weeks or months of hatching by other predators."

Jack was nodding. He seemed to be taking this all in stride. "So a select lucky few survive, do their thing, and scuttle back to sea. What the hell is their breeding period then? Every ten million years?"

Glen had an answer for that, even though it was still unsubstantiated. "They could breed yearly or bi-yearly. They could also breed less frequently than that. Every ten years, or fifteen. Every fifty. Every hundred. Cicadas go through a seventeen-year gestation period. We can't really tell what the breeding period for these things is without study, but my guess is more like every hundred years. This could explain why we've never heard of them till now. They probably come ashore on some remote area ..." He pointed to portions of Canada and Greenland. "Somewhere where they aren't seen by man."

"If that's the case, what the hell are they doing here now?"

Glen grinned. "That's a matter of geology and astronomy. And I'm not an expert at either, but the position of the stars and constellations does have an effect on not only our lunar system, but our geological one as well. My guess is that every four hundred years there is a change in the earth's ocean currents, particularly those in the Atlantic. And they shift in directions that they normally don't flow ..."

"Thus bringing whatever might normally drift along their currents down to us," Jack said. He shook his head, leaning the rifle against the wall under the windowsill. "What I don't get, though, is why we hadn't picked up on this before."

"Oh, we have," Glen said, holding up the chapbook. "Only four hundred or so years ago, the only human population in this area were American Indians who witnessed this excursion over the last few thousand years. They traded the tale orally from generation to generation, and I'm sure that in 1605 when the Lost Village incident happened, those Indians that were here knew the tale only as something of an urban legend. An urban legend that was very true."

"And the Lost Village was comprised of settlers, right?"

"Exactly. European settlers wouldn't have known about the legend since they'd just settled on these shores. They were, as they now say, in the wrong place at the wrong time."

Jack wiped his brow with the back of a bony hand and stared out the window. It was beginning to cloud up again, although the air appeared still.

Glen walked over to the window and stood to the side of it, looking down at the now-silent streets. His voice was low as he spoke. "So what you and Rick call Clickers, which are in reality a form of crustacean long thought extinct, are still alive somewhere deep in the bowels of the Atlantic. And they come up to breed and every four hundred years, when the earth's position in space shifts, the ocean currents shift with it, bringing them to these shores. And every time they drift on shore to breed, they are followed by their natural predators which modern man never knew existed—The Dark Ones."

There was a short pause as both men stared out the window at the ravaged town, taking in the aftermath of the Dark Ones' destructive path. The few bodies that could be seen from the window resembled nothing but piles of cloth-covered, bloody slabs of meat, but Glen thought he recognized one, a man lying face up across the street from Gerber's Drug Store on the Corner of Main and Hill. That would be James Hemsath, the local preacher. Glen had recently referred James to a Gastroenterologist in Bangor that specialized in ulcerative colitis. Now Reverend Hemsath was dead.

Glen turned away from the window, putting James Hemsath out of his mind. Couldn't let the emotions get to him now, not while the town was still in danger. He needed to teach Jack the basics of what they were up against. The more they both knew about the situation, the better they would be equipped to handle it.

"So the whole Lost Village legend stemmed from the last— and ultimately fatal—incident of the last time the Clickers came to these shores to breed," Glen said. "The Indians at the time knew what was happening, and retreated inland. While the settlers ..." he shrugged. "Well, you know the story. The closest description we get that anything horrific is happening is that hastily scrawled message."

"'Demons from the sea,'" Jack said, quoting the message verbatim. "Exactly." Glen said. "And because it was so long ago and the village was essentially wiped out, the settlers that came afterward and made the discovery of the Lost Village treated the Indian legend as nothing but a tale designed to scare children." He sighed. "But every legend has its basis in fact."

"What do you think happened to those settlers?" Jack asked.

Glen was about to answer when a faint noise from the east caught his ear.

He perked up, grabbing his firearm and moving back to the window. Jack rose clutching his weapon and the two men crouched in the shadows, barely breathing as the sound grew louder. It sounded like footsteps, only these were different. They were a kind of wet, shuffling gait that got closer.

And closer.

And closer.

23

Multi-colored bolts of lightning shot up from the nearby hillside and danced through Stacy Robinson's living room window.

Stacy squirmed in her torn and stained easy chair as the thunder rolled. She hugged the terrycloth robe she was wearing tight to her body and, for perhaps the tenth time that evening, thought about getting dressed in something warmer. At one point Stacy started to get up when she realized her clothes were wet. The power had gone out while they were in the rinse cycle in the washing machine, and she didn't want to rummage around in the closet for something else. It was too dark. She thought she had a flashlight around somewhere, but it was nowhere to be found. She'd been trying to remember where the flashlight was while she sat in the chair listening to the lightning flash and the thunder rumble as the latest storm rolled in from the ocean.

She settled back into the warmth of the chair and thought about calling the power company when another lightning flash flickered across the ocean. The acid she'd dropped thirty minutes before accented the effect nicely; more multicolored electricity bolts erupted over the sky. This time the colors were psychedelic. They swirled and became huge walking pumpkins with glowing umbrellas and big smiles. The last forty-eight hours were forgotten as Stacy looked out the window at the rapidly darkening sky and laughed as the walking pumpkins began to dance and sing. She smiled and thought briefly about getting dressed. But then another lightning bolt flashed and the colors sparkled again, merging into even more dancing pumpkins. Life was sure grand!

Things were better today then they'd been last night. The terrifying memories of the crab-creatures and Kirk's death had yet to be forgotten in her confused maze of a mind, but she wasn't as hysterical as she was last night. She'd been convinced that the things that killed Kirk would come to get her. This morning she actually had a chance to think. She had chilled out in the living room, listening to Pink Floyd's *The Wall* as she thought about what to do: get some laundry done, pack some things, close out the bank account. Then take what was left of her money and take off in her Trans-Am. Fuck the house and the rest of her stuff. That was the ticket.

Only that hadn't happened. She'd dozed in the living room and woken up at one in the afternoon. She took a leisurely shower, then began rummaging around for clothes. She stopped intermittently for hits off her bong, a few beers, another tab of acid. By the time the storm really hit and all those gunshots started going off (*don't those fucking redneck assholes know that hunting season starts next week?*) she was peaking and starting the laundry. So she was behind schedule. Stacy always found that things worked out best when she worked at her own pace and that when shit happened, it happened. When you rolled with it, you came out still rolling.

She'd put a Nirvana CD in her boom-box, began doing laundry, singing along with Kurt Cobain and mirroring his tortured voice perfectly, his angst matching hers, his pain touching hers. And just as the clothes were in the rinse cycle, the power went out.

She screamed, threw a box of Tide at the washing machine, spilling powdered soap all over the washer and dryer and the floor. She cried hoarsely, her chest hitching with a frustration that came so deep within her that she didn't know how to quench it.

When the crying fit subsided, she flicked the light switches off and on. The power was definitely out. *Great! Just fucking great!*

She crossed the darkened living room and picked up the phone. No dial tone. *This is just my fucking day.*

Might as well make the most of it. The hit of yellow-blotter she'd taken earlier that afternoon had worn off, so she took another. Then she retreated into the living room dressed in the terrycloth robe because all her good jeans and sweaters were in the fucking washing machine, and she popped another top off a bottle of beer and sat watching the lightning roll across the ocean.

It was a nice way of escaping. She learned early on that the best way to make problems go away was to alter her perception of them and their effects on her. This especially became useful after Mother died (*you mean after you killed mother. Isn't that right?*). Through some metaphysical teachings she learned from an old boyfriend, she'd come to the conclusion that problems and negativity were caused by people who were not in tune to her world view, which was almost everybody.

She tried altering other people's way of thinking, but that hadn't worked. They just weren't worth the trouble or hassle. When the act of denial was too difficult, she discovered that LSD helped; by dissolving other peoples' personalities and reaffirming her sense of righteousness. Dissolving ... just as Kirk had dissolved.

Stacy sat back and smirked as the realization of Kirk's disappearance became crystal clear in her mind. He hadn't died. She'd simply dissolved his negativity and thus, removed him from her world.

She sat back in her chemical haze and let the pumpkins finish their dance and take their bows.

After the finale, the pumpkins did a very strange thing. Stacy wasn't sure if it was her imagination, so she rubbed her eyes and looked out at the mass of clouds again. The pumpkins had lost their electric sheen and grown dark and wet. They twisted and became hunched and ugly. She squirmed in her chair, wondering what the pumpkins were up to now. They'd put on such a great show, but now the act was definitely lagging. The new pumpkins were sort of hopping and clawing through the muddy hill behind her house, making strange bleating noises. The rain melted away the last of their disguises. A strong musty odor rolled in through the cracked side window. Not only were the pumpkins now ugly, but they smelled bad too.

Stacy sat and waited for them to do something fun and exciting, but nothing happened. They continued to rummage through the mud. She sighed, suddenly feeling cold goose bumps rise along the flesh of her exposed forearms. The pumpkins were still being boring, and she'd had enough of their lagging performance. She stood up, marched forward to the window and pounded her palm on the inside of the window to get their attention. "Hey! What's wrong with you guys?"

The creatures turned and Stacy saw red eyes glow a deeper shade of crimson as they focused on her. The bleating croaks rose once again, this time filled with a tinge of excitement, and then they began to slither toward her.

The rational side of Stacy's consciousness suddenly jumped into the driver's seat. The primal emotion of terror ripped through her body. She took an involuntary step back as the nearest Dark One banged its scaly nose on the window glass.

Stacy stumbled back, her breath hitching in her throat as her terror rose. Needle-sharp nails scratched the glass as the creature seemed to study the transparent barrier with a scaly, webbed claw. The sound reverberated through Stacy's ear painfully. The creature gave a firm push and the glass shattered into thousands of wet, razor-like projectiles. Stacy jumped back from the sound of the blow and fell on her skinny ass, looking dumbfoundedly at her naked legs. A few small glass slivers had lodged in the smooth flesh and blood was quickly running down her limbs in tiny red rivers. She stared in numbed amazement at her legs, as if trying to make sense of why this happened, when the pungent fish smell wafting in from outside hit her like a sledgehammer. She looked up to see the creature curling back its lizard-like lips, hissing through rows of serrated teeth. A few of the glass fragments from the window fell to the floor from the upper frame as the creature stuck its head through the opening and began pushing its bulk through.

Stacy screamed and scrambled to her feet. She turned and began running out of the kitchen, down the hall, trailing blood from her cut legs behind her. Terror drove her forward as she rounded the living room, tripped and almost fell sprawling on the floor, up the stairs, down the hall to her bedroom where she ran to the window and looked out at the mass of creatures that were assembling on her back lawn.

The window was open, bringing in the cold air along with the smell of the ocean and the musty aroma of the creatures. The combination of the cold air and the intermingling scents had driven the effects of the LSD and the beer out of her system; she was cold sober. Four more of the creatures were making their way from the beach, and one of them appeared to be carrying some kind of long, thin object. A stick? A piece of driftwood?

A muffled whimper rose from her chest as she raced out of her bedroom to the second-floor landing. She peered over the balcony, getting a clear view of the living room and the kitchen. The monster that smashed the window was now in the kitchen and moving toward the living room. Two more were squeezing their scaly bodies through another window in her living room, the sound of the destruction crashing through the house, drowning out the sounds of the pouring rain outside. The couch was positioned beneath that particular window, and the creature trying to enter swiped at the furniture with its claw. Suede fabric and stuffing flew through the air as the seat cushion was disemboweled. It swiveled its head toward Stacy and grunted. She stiffened like a rodent freezing in the sights of a bobcat, and the creature swatted the sofa aside with one arm, batting it against the wall where knickknacks fell with a crash. Stacy screamed and bolted back into her bedroom, then shut and locked the door behind her.

Omigod what am I gonna do now? She backed away from the door and tried to think. Downstairs she could hear one of the creatures crashing through the living room and down the hall toward the stairs. She backed toward the window and stole another quick glance to check the status of the creatures outside. The backyard looked deserted now. Maybe she could edge out on the roof, climb down the trellis and escape across the beach.

A heavy crash thundered downstairs. It sounded like the creatures below were making progress in their search for her. Their fishy odor was already seeping under the locked door, assaulting her nostrils. She opened the window all the way and was about to scamper onto the roof when she saw three more of the hulking beasts make their way to the backyard.

One had torn down the fence connecting to Mrs. Caulder's yard. Stacy had never liked Mrs. Caulder; the old lady always complained about the music being too loud, and the kind of people she had at her house, and all the men coming and going, and she thought she could smell them smoking pot over there. *This is a peaceful town and no place for hooligans to run rampant*, she was fond of saying. Stacy wondered what Mrs. Caulder would think of *these* hooligans.

Speaking of Mrs. Caulder, one of the creatures was clambering over the demolished fence dragging a bloody corpse behind it. Stacy knew it was Mrs. Caulder before she got a glimpse of her. One look was enough. The elderly woman had been savagely mauled, several large bites taken out of her body. The creature stopped, lifted the body up to its face, probing and sniffing it. Its jaws opened and it tore a massive chunk out of the dead woman's head. Thick gray matter oozed down into the muddy puddle that covered most of Stacy's backyard. The Dark One gulped and the flesh slid down its gullet, smearing the scaly face with dark crimson gore.

Stacy backed away from the open window, gagging loudly. She would never be able to erase the picture of Mrs. Caulder's brains sliding out of her skull. No matter how much acid she took to dissolve the image.

She backed away and gagged again, almost throwing up. Downstairs she could hear the creatures crashing and blundering their way up the steps. Her heart beat wildly in her chest and she was about to scream again when her mind flashed—the closet! There was a small crawl space above this room, and the entrance was through the top of the closet. If she could just get up there she could hide until the monsters got tired and went away.

She dashed to the closet, opened the door and tugged at the chain of the lightbulb. When it did not go on, she realized the power was still out. "Fuck," she muttered. She began pushing aside clothes on their hangers. The small closet was nearly filled to the brim with old clothing, a vacuum cleaner, boxes of science fiction magazines, paperbacks, old bedsheets, a battered Les Paul imitation electric guitar, a crate of old porn magazines and assorted videos. She heaped the clothes down to the floor, moved a box over that contained some stereo equipment and stood on top of it, feeling along the ceiling for the panel. She felt it yield at her pushing hand, and she pushed harder until it plopped over. She scrambled up through the opening, wriggling her legs through and then hurriedly replacing the panel into the slot just as she heard them tear into the upstairs hallway.

Once inside, she held her breath and tried to keep still. It was pitch dark and cold in the crawl space. The roof of the house was only three feet above where she sat, so she couldn't stand up. She scooted down the crawl space over what she assumed was the center of her bedroom. The fishy smell became stronger as the things hammered at the door and walls of the bedroom. She thought maybe if she crept along the attic crawl space, she would reach the other opening into the guest room. She knew the things probably couldn't hear very well (what little she knew about reptiles and amphibians, which she assumed they were, stemmed from two snakes she used to have; a Boa Constrictor and a Burmese Python that an old boyfriend helped himself to when he left her). Even then, she was still careful to evenly distribute her weight on the plasterboard so it wouldn't come crashing down through the ceiling. Every time she shifted her weight, tiny creaks and bumps echoed through the enclosed space, but these were muffled by the sounds of the destruction below. She got no farther than the center of the space when she heard the door crash open.

She froze. They began moving through her bedroom, tearing apart furniture in their search for her. She remained frozen as the skin on her face prickled; she recognized the sensation of a spiderweb across her face. She bit her lip, a tear rolling down her check. She hated spiders, and the thought of not being able to move because those things might sense it made the ordeal even more frightening because what if the spider in question was one of those large garden spiders that she detested and it was now crawling around in her hair?

Don't think about that!

She remained motionless, trying to quell her fear as the crashing below suddenly evaporated into total silence.

The creatures had destroyed everything in the room and were now silent, sniffing at the air. The scent of blood was in the room, and it was strong. The squealing prey was still somewhere in this space, and they could sense it. The scent of it was strong, its blood scent was strong, its—

One of them raised its webbed, scaly hand and pointed at the open closet. The others followed it to the small opening.

Stacy heard the creatures move below her toward the closet door. She shivered, her brain telling her to move now. She obeyed, crawling again toward the inner reaches of the attic.

The creatures hissed at the bloodstains dotting the floor and clothing in the closet. They tore through the clothes in search of the squealing prey, knowing that nourishment was there somewhere. One of the creatures carried a rusted whaling harpoon it had carried from the ocean floor, and used the sharp instrument as a prod, poking it into the boxes and clothes, tearing the contents to ribbons. The squealing prey wasn't hiding amid the rubble.

The creatures turned to each other and bleated, their communication strong and singular. The one clutching the harpoon looked toward the ceiling and spied smears of blood around the square panel. Its olfactory senses picked it up even keener, the taste of the blood on its Jacobinson organ creating a mad blood lust. It reached up and touched the panel, pushing it up. It opened and fell into the crawl space. A grunting of what appeared to be satisfaction welled from the rest of the creatures and they surged forward ...

Stacy was almost where she thought her bedroom ended when she heard a sound behind her. She stopped and turned around. The door to the panel had been flung aside and she gasped in horror as she saw a green-scaled hand clawing at the edges of the tiny trapdoor. She squealed and scrambled frantically down the crawl space, heading into the farther recesses of the attic.

The Dark Ones sniffed at the cold air, grimacing at the open space in the ceiling. They could sense the blood stains around the opening, but their heat sensors weren't picking up the prey. It had moved elsewhere.

The Dark One that thrust its arm up eased itself down and grunted. The creature with the harpoon jammed the instrument through the hole, stabbing at the air. There was nothing up there. The prey had moved away from the opening. They moved away from the closet, eyes trained on the ceiling, trying to get a read on any heat that may be radiating out, as well as the taste of blood …

Stacy saw the harpoon poke through the attic entrance and she whimpered. She scuttled along the attic, her back aching from the confinement of the crawlspace. The splintered wood from the crawlspace floor barely registered in her brain as she crawled along her stomach. The dripping blood from her leg wounds mingled with the dust and cobwebs underneath her. A small drop of blood found a tiny crack and seeped in.

The creature with the harpoon sensed it first. Tiny dots of blood, barely discernible to the naked eye, were sensed by the Dark One's immense olfactory nerves. The trail was faint and led away from the bedroom. They followed it, and the creature with the harpoon stopped and stood underneath the scent, staring up.

Nostrils dilated and gills slapped like wet leather. They could sense that the prey was right above them. A chorus of eager croaks and hisses rose in the air.

The Dark One with the harpoon hissed and thrust the weapon up into the plasterboard ceiling. Chips of paint and plaster dust rained down on the pack of slithery beings.

As well as something warm and wet.

Stacy didn't have time to react as the sharp end of the harpoon came punching up through the floor of the crawl space and into her stomach.

She started, trying to crawl away. There was no pain, but she felt paralyzed. She couldn't move. She tried to scream but no sound issued from her throat. She felt her mid-section grow numb, as well as the slight sensation that her mid-section had been snagged on something sharp. The taste of bile rose in her throat and her energy was momentarily zapped as she tried to move away ...

The Dark One yanked the harpoon down violently and was rewarded by a red-hot shower of delicious human body fluid. The creatures crowded around, webbed claws scrabbling up, lapping up the blood that poured down. The creature with the harpoon moved the tool around as if it was stirring a vat of food and tugged. A smidgen of blood-crusted pink emerged from the hole the harpoon had punched through, and the Dark Ones emitted a throaty chorus of approval.

The creature with the harpoon noticed it and tugged again, revealing the object to be a piece of intestine. Webbed claws shot out and gripped the hanging morsel tightly. The creatures tugged and fought over the intestine, pulling it down as they scrambled for it, some yanking pieces off and stuffing them into their mouths.

The largest one looked up at the quivering rope. More of the organ came spilling through the ragged six-inch hole with each tug. The Dark Ones bleated and croaked in frenzy. The large creature pulled again. More intestine slithered down like a bloody, skinned snake.

Stacy screamed as her guts were yanked painfully from the wound in her belly; the numb sensation had now turned into a fiery burn that was hot and painful.

She managed to get up on her hands and knees, looking down in horror as more of her came sliding out and down the hole. It looked like a huge piece of spaghetti going down a drain.

Razor-sharp pain exploded in her body. Her senses fought for control with the residue of the many acid trips she'd taken over the years. It was as if her synapses were exploding in bright ranges of colors and sensations all at once, only to be overruled by the here and now. She wanted the acid side to win, wanted to retreat into the nice, colorful world that the drug created. She wanted to nestle in the electric fields with the dancing pumpkins and friendly clockwork animals.

Unfortunately, the other side won.

Stacy felt each rip and tug with crystal clarity. Each jolt of pain shot through her like a bullet. The coppery taste of her blood filled her mouth as the overpowering stench of rotted fish, seaweed, and excrement invaded her nose.

In a final desperate attempt, Stacy grabbed onto the rope of intestine with both hands. The gushing blood made her fingers too slick, and the organ wiggled through her fingers like a soaped-up eel.

A few agonizing seconds later, the last few feet of her small intestine left her body. She felt empty, the pain becoming white hot, then blossoming into another feeling, one of numbness again. She marveled at the amount of guts tucked into her small frame and wondered if a doctor would be able to pack it back in. An involuntary giggle died as blood spilled from her mouth.

The connecting tissues in her body pulled taut. Stacy felt her body lurch forward, and then she was abruptly jerked face-first into the dust. A moment later there was a snap as the tissue broke.

Her senses began to dim. She heard the plasterboard under her crack and give way. Another pull. Her spine snapped as her body folded in backwards. She felt herself falling, and the muffled feeling that was coming over her blossomed with bright flashes and colors and muted sounds. A face swirled in the fog that was rapidly swirling around her, enveloping her like a blanket.

Kirk.

He was smiling.

She smiled back.

The shadows from the fog engulfed her.

24

A t some point he must have fallen asleep.

Rick awoke with a start, eyes blinking rapidly as he took in his surroundings: the gray walls of the cell, the grimy bars that kept him from the outside world, the huddled figures outside the cell ...

He lurched up, swung his legs over the cot and rose to a wobbly stance. The air was still and cold. It was still dark outside and he had no idea what time it was. How long had he been asleep? He rubbed his eyes and made his way to the bars. Janice and Bobby lay huddled together on the floor on the other side of the bars. Rick checked them out, fear rising sharply as he realized that they could be dead. He'd fallen asleep and the Dark Ones had broken into the office and slaughtered Janice and Bobby. They'd tried to burst through the bars of the cell to get at him, but the stainless-steel bars thwarted them. That's why he was still alive and Janice and Bobby were—

Lightly dozing.

Janice sensed Rick standing there and got to her feet. She rubbed her sleep-crusted eyes. Her features were heavy with fatigue, yet she offered him a smile. "I must've dozed off."

Rick returned her smile. "Guess we all did. I didn't think that was possible, but ..."

Neither of them thought it possible they would sleep last night. They'd remained huddled on the floor of the jail, Rick inside the cell, Janice and Bobby on the other side as the Dark Ones pillaged and plundered through the town. Every once in a while screams arose from somewhere outside, sometimes gunfire, but for the most part the noises were coming from the

Dark Ones as they destroyed.

And fed.

Luckily Bobby *had* gotten to sleep. He remained at the rear of the hallway, bundled up in some spare jackets Janice had found in the office. His sleep had been deep, too; not once had he woken in fear of the noises and screams from outside. Those sounds contributed to Janice and Rick remaining awake, sitting next to each other on the floor of the cell, holding hands through the bars, talking through the night about what they could do to escape. What they *should* do to escape. Whether anybody was going to recognize their plight and send somebody to rescue them—the army, the National Guard, anybody with enough guns and firepower to blow these green, scaly creatures back to whatever water-logged hell they had come from.

After a while, that end of the conversation meandered onto other subjects. It was hard to tell how much time passed, especially with the storm raging outside and the night so dark and brooding. The sounds of destruction retreated farther inland for a while, and they relaxed slightly, still on alert status. Janice slid a nine-millimeter pistol and several boxes of shells through the bars of Rick's cell should they suddenly be embroiled in a war; she kept a large cache of the weapons she'd snagged by her side, like a camper guarding provisions. Fortunately the creatures outside didn't seem to sense that they were inside the sheriff's station. They were pretty much left alone.

So they talked more. Rick found himself continuing the conversation he'd begun with her earlier that afternoon when he first ran into her on the pier, back when things were innocent, when the future seemed brighter. When it seemed that he might have the extreme hots for her and was anticipating a future with her. He remembered that she seemed to share his attraction and they had played off it at the pier, flirting like they were teenagers. And then that had been broken by Bobby's screams—

Rick found himself intrigued by Janice's background as she spun the tale. She'd grown up in Phillipsport an only child. When her parents divorced, she remained in town with her father, who succumbed to lung cancer five years later, the year she graduated high school. With no one in town left that she could call family, she left and headed to Bangor where she eventually drifted into college. She stuck with it, getting a degree in Liberal Arts five years later. Midway through she met Kevin Murphy, Bobby's father and her future husband. Kevin was an economics major. They married a year later and settled in Bangor and for once Janice thought she would be happy. She had a husband who loved her, a job she liked—she had gotten a job as a secretary at a securities firm—and she was pregnant with Bobby. She couldn't have asked for more.

The first five years were great, but she began to sense that Kevin was drifting. The hours at the office grew later, the business trips grew longer, became more frequent. He began spending less time with her and Bobby and worse, became less interested in raising their son. She forged on and the truth slapped her face brutally one Sunday morning when she was doing the laundry. She was putting Kevin's shirts in the wash for a cold cycle when she lifted one of them up and examined it closely. She checked out the collar. There was a smudge of red lipstick on the tip of the collar.

She confronted Kevin with it. He denied knowing anything about it at first, but after she nagged him about it, he broke down and confessed. She hadn't expected a confession. She expected he would deny it all along and the confession caught her off guard despite the fact that she had already convinced herself that he was having an affair. Hearing it from his own lips seemed to confirm the suspicions. The woman was a secretary at the firm he worked at. It was nothing serious, but—

Besides gaining full custody of Bobby, she got the house, which she sold after the divorce was final. And she moved back to Phillipsport for a more quiet, more serene lifestyle. She wanted something more peaceful, especially for Bobby, but most of all she wanted to escape the past. Coming to Phillipsport did that for her.

Rick listened patiently, sympathizing with her. He had been burned by girlfriends and old lovers in the past too, and he emphasized this. He gave her examples. He tried to make it sound like his own excursions were funny and she laughed. She seemed to appreciate the humor he injected into the conversation. Sometimes the human spirit needed to laugh to break up the monotony of life.

She brought the story to a close: she found her present job as a secretary at the law firm, enrolled Bobby in school here in Phillipsport, and bought the nice little house Rick and Jack had rescued her from about eight hours before. She had known most everybody in town before she left, and she blended back into the community again with ease. She hung out with Carol Bradford and Sue Banali, who were secretaries at the Phillipsport Bank. Bobby had his friends from school. She worked her nine to five with a pause to pick her son up from school around two, although lately he was walking home by himself. They spent the evenings together, with Carol and Sue coming over sometimes for an evening of television. She usually spent her weekends with her son, but when the need arose to be with her friends, or spend a night on the town, there was always an available sitter in the parents of one of his friends. She hadn't dated much after the divorce, but she did drift into an affair with a coworker that ended much the same way it began. Her life had pretty much been the way she described it until she ran across Rick at the pier.

There was an uncomfortable silence, as if both of them were waiting for the other to begin something new. During the talk they sat on opposite sides of the bars, but during the last five minutes they had drawn closer. Rick's hand strayed out from the cell and Janice's found his, her fingers clasping it. He felt a surge of electricity run through him as their eyes met briefly. He supposed if things hadn't happened the way they had he would be sleeping with her right this minute. He almost voiced this observation, thought that he probably shouldn't jump the gun, and shifted the conversation to other topics.

But then somewhere along the way, they must have fallen asleep.

Now Janice shrugged sheepishly. She turned and went down the hallway to check on Bobby. Rick looked out the window; the sky outside was a dark gray—it was morning now. He wondered how long they'd slept.

"I wonder what time it is." Rick said.

"Quiet!" Janice was standing over Bobby, poised over him as if something was about to pounce on the building. Her head was cocked at a questioning angle, as if she were listening to frequencies he couldn't pick up. Rick couldn't hear a thing.

He managed a whispered query. "What is it?"

Janice looked at him. "Do you hear anything?"

Rick listened, trying to pick up whatever noise she was hearing. Whatever it was, he couldn't. He didn't hear a thing.

"I know," Janice said. She looked almost elated. "It sounds like they're gone."

Rick listened. She was right. He detected no sound. None of the roaring and bleatings the creatures made as they plundered the town. No screams or moans from maimed and dying people. No gunfire, crashings. Nothing.

The silence was so still it was almost deafening.

Rick walked over to the window and looked out. His mind had mentally prepared him for what he saw outside but even then, it was still disturbing.

Main Street was deserted. And totally littered.

With bodies.

They lined the street three and four deep. They lay scattered about like soldiers on a Civil War battlefield. Despite the stark horror of the scene, Rick made out some familiar faces; George Cleaver, one of the countermen at the Diner where he had met Lee Shelby and Melissa Peterson two days before; William Reynolds, a man he'd met in Dr. Jorgensen's waiting room yesterday who was an Arrowhead Springs deliveryman who had come into Doc's office to make his drop and collect the empty. There were others. All of them people who'd fought to protect their town. And their loved ones.

Broken crab shells lined the bodies of the dead.

The Dark Ones were nowhere to be seen.

Rick turned away from the window and approached the bars. "I don't see the Dark Ones anywhere. It's pretty dead out there." He paused, realizing the remark he just made. "Literally."

Janice looked grim. She looked down at Bobby, who was still asleep. He was curled up in the jackets, his arm tucked under his chin, his bandaged hand cradled to his chest. She looked from Bobby back to Rick, a grim realization in her face. "We've got to get out of here."

"I know."

Janice moved out toward the main office of the sheriff's station and stood in the middle of the room. Rick couldn't see her from the cell but he guessed she was looking out the big plate glass window at the carnage. He looked at Bobby, who was sleeping deeply. Poor kid had gone through a lot in the past twenty-four hours. No wonder he was conked like that.

Janice came back into the jail area. She picked up her jacket from the floor and put it on.

"Where are you going?" Rick asked.

"I think I see Sheriff Conklin outside," Janice said. Her face was grim.

A weird sense of elation swept through Rick. As much as the trouble Conklin had put them through, it would be the best news in the world right now if he was here bringing in the calvary. "He's alive?"

Janice shook her head. "I don't know." She stopped and looked at Rick. "He's across the street, and ... he locked you in here. He probably still has the keys with him ..."

Rick got the message. It sounded like the sheriff was dead. He nodded. "Be careful."

"I will." She started to walk out but Rick reached through the bars and grabbed her arm, holding her back. She spun back, surprised, the expression on her face saying *what did I forget?* "What?" She asked.

Rick didn't answer. He grabbed her face gently with his right hand and moved it toward the bars, guiding it so her lips met his. She offered no resistance once she realized what he was doing, and kissed him back. He released his grip on her and smiled at her. "Be careful, Janice."

"You bet I will," she said. Her eyes sparkled, her smile flashed wide and bright; she looked like the happiest person on earth at that moment. She squeezed his hand briefly, then set off down the hall.

Rick heard her footsteps retreat slowly through the main office, then pause by the front door. She was checking out the area before she stepped outside. Smart girl. Rick's heart pounded faintly, partly from fear, but a large part due to their emotional and physical connection. He was feeling a very strong attraction to her, and the thought that the feeling was reciprocated produced a strong burst of emotion through him that was so great that, if he wasn't sitting in this cell, he'd be singing. Her kiss was still on his lips, faint now, but sweet, and despite their predicament of life and death, that simple kiss had sent the area below his belt into a raging hard on.

Her footfalls shuffled beyond the hallway. A moment later he heard the click of the front door, and then the latch of the knob as it shut behind her. She was outside.

It was, in a sense, incredible.

Janice stood on the sidewalk in front of the Phillipsport sheriff station, her mind boggling at the sight before her. All up and down Main Street, the bodies of Phillipsport's finest lay on the streets, in the sidewalks, sprawled in doorways. The carnage continued to the pier due east and all the way to the T-intersection that bridged the town square to the west. Broken Clicker shells littered the streets. Janice thought she would be sick to her stomach at the sight of all those bodies— some of them so horribly mangled that they hardly resembled human beings—but surprisingly, she coped well. Perhaps it was Bobby's run-in with the Clickers the day before that had mentally prepared her for what was at hand. What he'd gone through was nothing compared to the carnage that lay before her.

Most of the bodies she saw were ripped and mangled; chests ripped open, arms and legs torn off, decapitations. In some cases all that remained were bloody, lifeless, hollowed-out trunks. But in most cases the dead she saw were somewhat intact. The streets were soaked with blood and water from the rain. The air was thick with the smell of death.

A slight wind picked up, lifting Janice's hair and blowing it. It blew dead leaves and scraps of paper down the street, rustled her jacket. The darkness of night was slowly giving way to the gray of early morning. It was very foggy and the clouds overhead were dark and gray. It made Phillipsport seem more like a ghost town now, with nearly all of its inhabitants dead.

Janice took a deep breath and looked up and down the street. There was still no sign of life, human or otherwise. She looked across the street and down a ways, toward the pier. What she perceived to be Sheriff Conklin was nestled on top of a slew of bodies. She could make out tan slacks and a shirt that looked like it could be brown, but was probably a deep maroon from blood. He looked tall and lean, much like Conklin had been, but from here, as inside the station, it was hard to tell. What clinched it for her was what appeared to be the police-issue belt with a holster the man was wearing.

Janice set off down the street, keeping a steady pace, but trying to keep her footfalls light so as not to attract unwanted attention. She had to hopscotch her way around bodies, Clicker shells, and body parts. She felt her gorge rise briefly when she almost stepped on a severed forearm, hand still attached. An image of Bobby rose in her mind as she stepped away from the limb and she put her hand to her mouth, feeling her throat constrict. She stopped, fighting it back, and black spots began to dance in her vision. She closed her eyes and took a deep breath. The wind was blowing the scent of blood away and she caught a whiff of good old fresh air. That felt better.

She opened her eyes, her composure gained, and set off down the street.

A sound startled her, a skittering sound that came from her right toward an empty car. She whirled around, taking a hopping step backward, her foot landing in a small puddle of blood-soaked rainwater. Janice's heart lodged in her throat, the flight instinct almost set to propel her back to the station and lock the door when she realized it was only a piece of paper flapping in the breeze. It was stuck between the windshield wipers of a car.

She sighed. *God, I'm going to be a nervous wreck by the time I get down to Sheriff Conklin or who I hope is Conklin and—*

A Clicker suddenly came scurrying from behind a car parked diagonally across from her and began scuttling down the street, heading toward the beach. This time Janice did jump back and actually took a few running steps back the way she came before she realized the creature didn't seem to care she was there. She stopped, muscles tense, watching the Clicker scurry toward the pier. It grew smaller as it receded from view.

Janice stood frozen in the middle of the street, unable to decide whether to continue down this road. What else lay in store? More Clickers hiding out, waiting for their escape, much like she was? Would they attack her? It didn't seem likely. The one that just scurried down the beach had been eight feet away from her when it suddenly broke cover and ran for the beach. She imagined that the only thing on their tiny crustacean brains now was survival. Escaping into the ocean.

Janice started back on the path she'd retreated from, more boldly now. She meandered her way past bodies, over severed limbs and bloody pools of viscera. She kept her gaze straight ahead, all senses tuned in around her to catch the slightest noise, the slightest change in the atmosphere. She was surrounded by bodies, some stacked one on top of the other, some stuck to utility poles like grotesque trophies. Her main goal grew closer with each step she took. Recognition filtered through her brain as what she had thought to be Sheriff Conklin revealed to be the local lawman.

She stopped, breathing heavily. Conklin's eyes were open. He was lying on his back, his face bloody. His chest was mangled, his shirt ripped and horribly bloodstained. He was lying on top of a bank of newspaper machines. His right hand dangled over the side limply. Conklin looked deader than a door nail.

Janice's eyes locked on the belt around his waist. It contained an empty clasp that would normally contain his flashlight, but his handcuffs were still in place. His service revolver was missing, and Janice surmised it could have been knocked out of his hands by strong claws swiping the air to knock the lawman on his ass. Besides, she wasn't interested in the gun. What interested her were the keys, which were dangling on his belt from a thick key ring clasped to his belt loop.

Janice reached forward and grasped the key ring. It was bloody, the garment the ring was attached to even bloodier, but she had to get it. She moved her thumb up to the clasp, pushed it, and wriggled it through the belt loops and off the dead man's pants. The keys jangled in her hands as she grasped them. She took a step back, her fingers tingling from the brief contact with the bloodied husk of what remained of Sheriff Conklin, and now she turned and threaded her way back to the station. Her gorge began rising again. It was just half a block up which had seemed miles on her trip out, but now it seemed much closer, more close to normal and it was, she was getting closer to the station, passing bodies, fighting the nausea that threatened to overtake her, jumping over them as she ran back to the station and then she was inside, shutting the door behind her and racing to the rear of the building where the jail was, jangling the keys in her hand, barely able to contain her sickness as she fumbled with them in her hands, trying to find the right one to fit into the lock. Rick stood in the cell behind the bars, his voice soothing and low. "Take it easy, Janice, take it easy ..."

She took a deep breath and forced herself to go slower. She closed her eyes. Black spots danced in her vision. She felt sick, but she could fight it. She'd get him out. She had the keys now, and she'd get him out and they'd be out of this mess. She took several deep breaths, and once she felt the sickness subside she opened her eyes and looked at Rick through the bars. He looked concerned. "Feel better?"

She nodded. "I will once you're out of there." She began inserting keys in the lock, taking her time so she wouldn't drop them or, worse yet, break one in the lock when a thought occurred to her: suppose this wasn't the right set of keys? Suppose they weren't the right set of keys and none of them fit? Suppose that—

But then her fears were eliminated as the key she was currently trying slipped in the lock effortlessly. She turned the key, heard the familiar tumble of locks disengaging and then the door was open. Rick was in her arms, hugging her close. She wrapped her arms around him and as fast as he was in her arms, he was out, moving down to the end of the hall to where Bobby lay sleeping. "Let's get going. We need to get out of here and fast."

Janice took his lead and knelt down over her son to wake him up.

Rick moved into the sheriff's office and checked the status outside. Still dead. It was getting light outside, the sky overhead dark and sullen. He turned to the cache of weapons Janice had pilfered the night before and began taking stock. There was a stockpile, everything from high-powered rifles to semi-automatic pistols. Boxes of shells were stacked neatly on shelves in the storage area. He stuffed four boxes in his jacket pockets, found a holster and also equipped himself with a Remington .30-06. Janice was outfitting herself as well. "Make sure the shells you get match the guns you're taking."

"Right," Rick said. He actually hadn't thought of that before. He checked, saw that the shells he had were for .22s, and put them back. He was still hunting around for the right ammunition when something caught his eye in the corner.

It looked like a rocket launcher. The barrel was huge and heavy. Rick picked it up, noting the body of the weapon, marveling at its weight. He saw a box near it and bent down to examine it closer. He noticed with amazement that the box contained ammunition for the rocket launcher. *What the hell is a small-town police force doing with something like this?* he thought. But then he realized the obvious. Sheriff Conklin had seemed like the type to have a weapon like this around. Why not?

A few moments later, he had everything he needed. He also took the rocket launcher and some ammunition for it. Janice's eyes grew wide when she saw it. "Jesus, where did you find that?"

"In the back," Rick said. "We may need it." Janice already had Bobby in tow. The boy was still sleepy-eyed and cranky, but at least he was walking. "Hi sport," Rick said. "Sleep good?"

"Yeah," Bobby said. He looked up at his mother. "Are we going home now?"

"Real soon, babe," Janice answered. Rick set the rocket launcher down and handed her a semi-automatic pistol and a holster. She put the holster on her hip and stuck the gun inside it. Rick was already made up. Janice took some shells and put them in her inside jacket pocket. She picked up a rifle she had taken down the night before and an extra box of shells. Bobby watched all this with slow dawning wonder.

"Are … things still weird?" he asked.

"Don't know yet," Rick answered him. He was ready and he darted to the door and checked out the vicinity outside. All was clear. He picked up the rocket launcher and turned back to Janice and Bobby. He reached into his pocket, took out a black hair tie and pulled his hair back into a ponytail. "I'm gonna go try and get a car. I want you to stay here with Bobby."

Janice opened her mouth to protest, then closed it. It was the only wise thing to do. As it was, Bobby had no knowledge of the carnage outside. If Rick could find a vehicle that would start—preferably with keys in the ignition—and wheel it around, he could pull it directly in front of the station and she could usher Bobby in without him seeing most of the carnage.

She leaned forward and planted a kiss on Rick's cheek. Rick smiled and kissed her back. He ruffled Bobby's hair. "I'll be right back."

"Be careful," Janice said.

Rick exited the station.

The first car Rick saw was a battered Plymouth parked in front of the post office next door. He went around to the driver's side and stopped. The door was ripped off its hinges and lay hanging by a strip of metal on the street. The front seat was empty, but the seat was slick with blood. Whoever the Dark Ones had dragged out of this vehicle, it would be safe to assume they were dead now.

"Next one," Rick said. He moved up the street to the next vehicle, which was empty and seemingly intact. Rick hoisted his rifle up and was about to ram the butt through the window when a low moan rose from the deserted street.

He looked back down the street toward the beach. That moan sent a shiver of fear through Rick's spine. His first thought was that it was a Dark One lumbering down the street toward him. But there wasn't anything coming down the street at all.

Just a bunch of bodies lying helter skelter all over the road.

The moan rose again. Distinctly human.

All the color ran out of Rick's face. "Oh, Jesus!" The tone of that voice sounded familiar.

He walked down the street toward the sound of the moan, which was rising more reverently now. The sound of the moan carried him over to the mangled figure lying on top of a bank of newspaper vending machines, the same man that Janice was convinced was Sheriff Conklin, the same body where she'd retrieved the keys from.

Rick stopped in front of the mangled remains of Sheriff Roy Conklin. The lawman's eyes were open, his bloodied face staring upwards, mouth open. His eyes were blinking, and Rick realized the lawman was still alive before Conklin let out another bloodcurdling moan.

God, how could he still be alive? Rick thought. He looked at the battered lawman's body. His chest had been ripped open; he thought he could see a portion of his bloody ribcage. His clothes were shredded. There was a gaping wound in his right leg that looked like a huge chunk of flesh had been taken from it. His face was shredded. Sheriff Conklin was horribly mangled, but he still lived. He must have been passed out when Janice retrieved the jail keys from his body; in her fright she probably paid no attention whether he was alive or dead.

Roy's eyes crawled over Rick, their light gray showing slight fear, but now they held the realization of what had really happened to him. He looked like he'd been through hell and back. The sheriff's mouth moved. Rick leaned forward to catch what the lawman might say. Another low moan escaped his lips. He was trying to say something, but it was hard to make out. "*Cccccc* ..."

Rick leaned forward. "Take it easy, guy."

Roy clung stubbornly to that "*Cccc*" sound. He lengthened the vowel so that it became a drawn out "*aaaaa*", then added a "*eeerrrr*". Rick picked up on it immediately.

"Car?" Rick asked. "Where?"

"Blue," Roy spit this word out almost effortlessly. He pronounced it "*blphew*", but Rick guessed the significance to color almost as immediately as he had deciphered the lawman's first word. Rick stood over Sheriff Conklin, encouraging him.

"A blue car."

Roy slowly nodded. Sweat rose on his face in rivulets. *"Kkkk ... eeeee ... sssss ...* in ... in ..."

"The keys are still in the ignition?"

Conklin closed his eyes, breathing heavily.

That was all Rick needed to know. He took a hesitant step back then stopped. Sheriff Conklin had opened his eyes again and was looking at Rick. His breath was coming in harsh and fast. Rick could see the rise and fall of his ruined chest. His face was simultaneously riddled with fear, and expectant of what was coming to him; to Rick he seemed like a man coming to hard grips with the approaching reality of his own death. Rick couldn't just leave him like this, much as he didn't like the man. Sheriff Conklin himself seemed to have metamorphosed from a man with such personal demons that he'd been the most disliked man in town, to a man who had come to grips with the sins of his life and his existence as a human being. It radiated from his blood-streaked face, which was wide-eyed, almost apologetic. Now was a bad time to be making amends to yourself and your maker for your faults, but—

Roy Conklin's breathing became more labored, his mouth gasping as he struggled for breath. Rick moved forward, lightly placing a hand on his shoulder. Roy grasped Rick's hand and squeezed it as his breathing grew more labored, painful sounding, then slowing ... slowing ... slowing. The rise and fall of his chest slowed with it, and Roy's eyes moved from Rick to stare at the ceiling of the awning above him. His breathing grew fainter, fainter ... fainter ...

Then stopped.

Rick stood over the sheriff's body for perhaps two full minutes, waiting for a reprieve, another go-round as the lawman began another round in the fight for life. But there was no movement. Sheriff Conklin was dead.

Rick pried Conklin's fingers from his wrist and placed the hand back at his side. The limb fell over the side of the vending machine, then hung there, limp. Sheriff Conklin's mouth was still open as if straining for that last gasp of breath, his eyes still open and gazing at the ceiling. Staring at nothing.

Rick turned away from the sheriff and began looking for a blue car. As he searched, he felt a small burst of pride at his reaction to Sheriff Conklin's death; he thought he would have turned away from the man who had caused him so much trouble upon arriving in town. But he was better than Sheriff Conklin—he'd offered some measure of sympathy for the man as he lay there dying. He felt better as a human being, and he hoped Roy Conklin had felt some measure of peace before he passed on.

Rick traveled fifty yards down Main Street, heading toward the beach when he saw it. A little blue Datsun, late eighties model. He ran toward it, being careful to jump over the bodies sprawled in the street. He got to the car and flung the door open. It was empty—and the keys were dangling in the ignition.

"Hot dog!" Rick exclaimed. He climbed in, slammed the door, keyed the ignition. The engine cranked to life and Rick felt a huge weight drop off his shoulders as he put the car in gear and made a U-turn, headed back toward the sheriff station. He tried slaloming around the bodies in the street, but that wasn't always possible; a few times he ended up having to drive over them. Rick's stomach turned queasily in his abdomen as he felt the cars' tires thump over the bodies, imagining their slickness becoming further mangled by the tread and weight of the car. After the third one he didn't think he could continue for this long without being sick, and then he was at the station.

He pulled up to it, driver's side against the curb. He could see Janice and Bobby hovering behind the plate glass window, watching him as he made his way down the street. When he pulled up to the curb the door opened, and Janice ushered Bobby out. Rick reached over and opened the passenger side door for her. She herded Bobby in the back seat and closed the door. Rick stepped out and together they transferred the weapons they had gathered into the car, then slid inside, slamming the doors behind them. "Drive," she said.

Rick drove. They pulled away from the curb and Janice cradled Bobby to her bosom, shielding the boy's face from the carnage outside. Rick could tell that the boy wasn't sleepy anymore, that more than anything he would want to lift his head from his mother's protective shield and look outside, but he wouldn't. Janice had probably told him not to look as she herded him outside and into the car. He surely was making no attempt to do so now. Smart kid.

"Where to?" Rick asked. They had just reached the intersection of Main Street and Elm. The carnage here appeared to have thinned out, but bodies still dotted the streets and sidewalks.

"Let's try the town center and the mall," Janice said.

"Okay." Rick drove, heading toward the center of town, leaving Main Street behind them. Leaving the beach and the Phillipsport pier behind them.

Where a dozen dark shapes emerged from the ocean and began making their way up the beach, heading inland.

25

They didn't see a single living soul on their drive through town.

Driving down the empty streets reminded Rick of an old ghost town; streets were vacant, cars parked haphazardly. Bodies lined the streets, although not in the numbers they had toward the pier. Rick surmised that the Dark Ones' emergence caught a lot of people by surprise, especially since most of the town's population was near the pier and the beach fighting off the Clickers. Farther into town, the carnage didn't appear nearly as bad as it did along the beach front and the first five blocks into town. There, it looked like a war zone. Here, it just looked deserted.

They drove past city hall, Carl's Grocery Store (which was the oldest grocery store in town, having first been established in 1843), Cliff's Books, Mabel's Antiques—all deserted. Janice was silent, looking out the window as they drove by. Rick kept his eyes on the road, watching for any sign of life, human and unhuman.

"Let's try the shopping center," Janice said. "If we don't find anybody there, we'll hit the interstate."

"Okay." Rick turned down Elm, cruising slowly. He paused to look at Doc Jorgensen's as they approached it. For a moment Rick was tempted to stop and try to see if Glen was home. But that wouldn't do— *suppose you do and a Dark One is lying in wait and it comes rushing out, and suppose there are others lying in wait, just waiting for the chance for you to leave the car so they can get you and Janice and Bobby—*

He shook his head, clearing the thought from his mind. He

drove past Glen's house, turning left on the next street, heading toward the shopping center.

They were silent as they headed down the road. Rick saw the shopping center in the distance, the parking lot dotted with cars, an occasional body here and there. The sky was dark, but not as dark as it had been when the storm broke. It still looked like they were in for another bout of rain.

They pulled into the almost-empty parking lot, cruising past the storefronts; the Piggly Wiggly, Shelby's Drugstore, Blockbuster Video. Rick was looking into the windows, trying to catch a glimpse of life, thinking maybe people may have run into stores for refuge.

Janice gripped his arm and pointed out the windshield. "There's somebody here!"

Rick whirled around, bringing the car to a stop. A man was running toward them, waving his arms. He looked familiar from a distance. Rick accelerated and cruised, bringing the car to a stop as they drew closer together. The man ran up to them and now Rick recognized him as Glen Jorgensen.

Glen ran up to the window and Rick rolled it down. "Thank God, you're alive," Glen said.

Rick threw the car into park and let it idle. "What's up?"

Glen motioned toward the supermarket that he had been standing in front of when they first glimpsed him. "A bunch of us have been holed up in the freezer of the supermarket. It's a long story. We haven't heard anything for the last several hours, so I decided to take a look and see what was going on. I had just stepped outside when I saw you."

"Who's in there?" Janice asked. She still held Bobby on her lap. Bobby was no longer hiding his face. He was looking around the parking lot in rapt awe, as if trying to deal with all that had happened the only way an eight-year-old could.

"Lee Shelby, Melissa Peterson, my nurse Barbara, Fred Logan down at Huskies Sawmill, a few others." Glen leaned against the car, looking in through the window at them.

"Everybody okay?" Rick asked.

Glen nodded. "No major wounds." He looked in at Bobby. "How you doing, Bobby? How's that hand feel?"

"Fine." Bobby suddenly cradled the splintered hand to his chest, as if suddenly remembering it had been injured.

"Why don't you come back with me to the store," Glen suggested.

"Hop in." Rick opened the driver's side door and reached for the lever to move the seat up to allow the physician entrance. Glen scooted inside and Rick shut the door. He drove them all back to the Lucky's Supermarket and pulled the car up against the large front windows near the double doors. He killed the engine, then got out. The others followed, Janice setting Bobby down on the ground. Rick moved around the hood of the car, Glen in tow, when he caught a glimpse of movement at the end of the road that led to the town center. Something green. Moving.

The others didn't see it. Glen was pushing open the doors, and Janice was retrieving her rifle and jacket with its pockets of ammunition when Rick suddenly tapped her on the shoulder. "Let's get going quick," he said softly. She looked up at the sound of his voice, noticed his gaze extended toward the highway and followed it. Her eyes grew wide when she saw what he was looking at.

The Dark Ones. Heading inland. Toward the shopping center.

Glen had the doors open. Janice grabbed her weapons and Rick herded Janice and Bobby through the doors, then motioned for Glen to go on through. Glen read the urgency in his eyes and slipped through. Rick grabbed the rocket launcher and the ammunition, patted his jacket to make sure he had the other weapons, then went in after them. Once inside the two men slid the doors shut. Rick grabbed Glen's arm and motioned outside. "Looks like we'll be having company."

Glen looked outside and his face grew pale. He turned and motioned down the dry foods aisle. "Freezer is directly in the back, past the seafood department." He herded them down the aisle and around the seafood department and reached the freezer. It was tucked behind the seafood department at the end of a short hallway near the employee breakroom and lockers. A pair of double doors opposite the freezer led presumably to the warehouse. The freezer door was a large fortress of steel. Glen rapped on the freezer door three times—one short rap, two long ones. A moment later there was a shuffling from behind the door, the sound of something being slid back, and then the door was opening. A burly man with curly blonde hair and a scraggly beard stood behind the door, his blue eyes reflecting relief when he saw Glen with Rick, Janice and Bobby. "Thank God, you're back." They darted inside the freezer and the man shut the door behind them. He slid a long metal rod through the handle of the door, wedging it against the doorway jamb. A makeshift lock from the inside.

Rick stood inside the freezer and rubbed his arms. It was still cold inside despite the lack of electricity for the last twenty-four hours. The freezer was large and filled with rows of hanging slabs of beef flanks, shoulders, legs. The meat was red and moist, still fresh. If they had to stay in here for another two days though, the cold would be gone and the meat would begin to spoil. Rick looked at the group of people huddled against the far wall and noted with relief that they all appeared to be fine. Melissa Peterson recognized him and got up from the circle of people and approached them. She was wearing faded jeans and a long-sleeved T-shirt. Rick smiled and Melissa smiled back, embracing him. "I'm so glad you're all right," she said.

"I'm glad you're all right, too," Rick said. Melissa looked up at him, her smile warm, and a little laugh escaped her lips. She caught Janice's eye and her smile grew wider.

"Janice!" she exclaimed. Janice's features broke into a smile and she met Melissa halfway. They embraced as if they were sisters who hadn't seen each other in years. Rick grinned. He looked over at the other people huddled against the wall. He recognized Lee Shelby, owner of Shelby's drug store, who had been so nice to him when he first came into town, which all seemed like ten thousand years ago. Glen's nurse Barbara Schob had joined them and was conferring with the physician. Rick traded a weary smile with her; her gray hair was in disarray and there were dark circles under her eyes, but otherwise she seemed fine. She was dressed like the others in the room: blue jeans, a heavy long-sleeved shirt and boots.

Lee walked up to him, extending his hand. Rick shook it, gripping the man's hand tight. "Good to see you again, Rick," Lee said. "Although I surely do wish the circumstances were more pleasant."

Rick laughed. "I agree."

Introductions were made. The blond, bearded man was Fred Logan. The others who had now joined them were Annette Berger, a middle-aged matronly looking woman, and a husband-wife team Charley and Anne Dennings. Lee found some extra empty crates, which everybody had been sitting on, and some heavy wool blankets they had been using to keep warm. Melissa and Janice were setting them up, chatting with the others, while Rick drew Fred and Lee aside. "There's more of them coming," he said. He quickly recapped their arrival at the supermarket and told of his seeing several of the Dark Ones making their way down the highway toward the shopping center. "Did any of them break in here last night?"

Lee shook his head. Like the others, his features bore the battle-wounds of fatigue in the lines and creases on his face. "I don't think they knew we were in here. I was manning the store yesterday with Missy when all hell broke loose. Charley and Anne were at the counter, and Barbara was having a prescription filled when Fred burst in and relayed the news about the crab things."

"The Clickers," Rick said, nodding.

"The what?" Fred asked.

"Clickers," Rick explained. "It's what I call them on account of the sound their claws make when they click them together. They surely aren't regular crabs."

"Right," Lee said. "Anyway ..." He turned to Fred. "Why don't you tell him."

Fred's blue eyes still reflected the fear of what he saw. "I had been over at John's junkyard looking for a fuel pump for my Chevy when all the commotion started on the beach about those crabs ... Clickers, or whatever the hell they are. I ran down and helped Bill Hawkins and Sheriff Conklin fight some of 'em off, then I saw these ... *things*," He held his arms out wide, as if describing their size. "They were huge, green slimy things.

Walked like a man. Looked like something out of that movie *Creature from the Black Lagoon*. Anyway, I could hardly believe what I was seeing. I was a bit farther up the shore than Roy was, closer to Main Street when I saw them coming from the south near Ralph's sport shop. Anyway, I yelled for Roy, but he didn't hear me. Then they were coming up the beach and one of them attacked Bob Price, the minister at the First Presbyterian Church. It just grabbed him and ..." Fred's voice cracked. " ... it ... bit his head clean off. It just leaned forward, opened its mouth and chomped on him, like a kid eating a popsicle." Fred looked at them, his features grave. "I broke into a run and just kept on running, screaming about them monsters coming out of the ocean, trying to warn people, but ... they wouldn't listen. I just kept running till I got here." He sighed, his face blank. Lost. "I'd be dead now along with the others if I hadn't took off." He looked at Rick. "They're all dead, aren't they?"

Rick nodded.

"It wasn't until I was halfway here that I saw that Sheriff Conklin was running along with me," Fred continued. "When we got to the parking lot here, there were more of them. I panicked and ran in here. Conklin went the other way, toward the Blockbuster. I haven't seen him since."

Rick told him what he had found near Main Street. Fred's features were grave, as if already prepared for the news. Still, he appeared a bit surprised. "I wonder how he got back to Main Street?"

Rick didn't have an answer to that mystery.

Fred looked at him with his empty gaze, the confirmation breaking through. "All dead. All of them ..."

Lee took over the narrative. "When Fred came in he was screaming about monsters, I thought I knew what he was talking about. We'd been seeing these Clicker things and we were inside watching them. They never really came that close to the mall, just sort of wandered around in the parking lot and went off into the woods. After a while it got real quiet. We all went out to take a look and that's when Fred started running toward us with his rifle from the beach screaming about monsters. Missy, Barbara, Charley, Anne and myself headed toward the store. I saw Annette and got her into the store with us." His features furrowed, as if trying to remember important details. "There were still people all over the place, kids jumping into their cars to rush over to see what all the excitement was."

"I kept telling them not to," Fred broke in, his features still blank and grave.

"By then a young couple, a couple of kids, had come through and yelled that there were these things, just as Fred described them, raising holy hell," Lee continued. "I grabbed Missy and herded her into the supermarket as a bunch of people were on their way out. We stood in the store near the magazine racks that overlook the big plate glass windows and looked outside. By then the place was mostly deserted, people had left to go into town to see what was happening ..." Lee shrugged. "I don't know what happened to them. I pray for them, but I think they're dead. All I know is when I saw those things, those that were left—me, Missy, Fred here, Annette, and Charley and Anne along with Dr. Jorgensen and Barbara, who'd just gotten here—we all went to the back where the freezer was. Fred found a metal bar to lock the door from the inside, and we just sat in there and waited. Till now."

Rick took this all in. He had his run-in with Sheriff Conklin around ... four? Five? He tried to remember what time yesterday he met Janice. He'd left the house around one for his walk, met Jack at—

Jack! Where was he? Rick went over to Glen Jorgensen, who was inspecting Bobby. He looked up at Rick as Janice smiled up at him. "Bobby seems to be doing fine," she exclaimed happily.

"Yeah," Bobby said. "Dr. Jorgensen said I was almost as fit as a fiddle."

"And he's absolutely right," Rick said. To Doc Jorgensen: "Have you seen Jack?"

Glen shook his head, trying not to display his thoughts for Bobby to read. "Afraid not."

Rick was alarmed by this fact. The last he'd seen Jack Ripley was when Conklin had taken him to jail. Janice told him that Jack later left to find Glen Jorgensen in the hopes of the physician talking sense into the lawman. Had he ever gotten to

Glen's? He posed this question to Dr. Jorgensen as the physician joined him, Lee, and Fred near the door. "Yes, he did get to my place," Dr. Jorgensen said. "Only I didn't want to upset Bobby back there."

"Did something happen to him?" Rick's stomach felt empty with dread.

"Hold on, hold on, one thing at a time." Glen Jorgensen looked amazingly calm for someone who had seen and been through so much in the last twenty-four hours. "I was upstairs in my little attic study when I saw the beginning invasion. Jack did come and I somehow guessed he was coming to see me. I went downstairs to open the door and ..." He related the story of ushering Jack upstairs, their vigil at Glen's attic window, their conversation, and Glen's theory of the origins of the Clickers.

"We saw the Dark Ones converge and start coming up the street, finally coming to the house, but they never came to the door or tried to get in. We watched everything from my window and telescope. Finally we ventured out about two hours ago when the storm lifted. By then they were heading back to the ocean."

"So they did go back into the ocean, then?" Rick asked.

"Oh, definitely. I watched them. They started diving into the water pell-mell as dawn became light. I think they have an aversion to the light due to their living in the ocean. When they came up yesterday, remember, there was a raging storm, and the clouds were extremely dark. Almost black. Remember?"

Lee and Rick nodded.

Glen continued his narrative. "Anyway, when I knew they were all gone, we went outside. We got into my truck and headed straight here. I didn't want to risk going to the shore even if there might have been survivors; would have been too risky for me if a few of the Dark Ones had stayed on shore and hidden away in houses. Then if I was killed, what use would I be to any survivors? Anyway, we came here and started hunting around in the stores and finally came here, into the grocery store." He grinned, looking at Fred. "I was walking up and down the aisle, calling 'is anybody here?' when Fred opened the door of the freezer. I've been here for the last few hours."

Rick couldn't stand the excitement. "And Jack?"

"Jack wanted to take the truck and try to head south by the secondary roads," Glen said. His features became grave. "He said he knew where there was an Armory Post near Fort O'Brien. We had been talking about Fort O'Brien last night. It was the site of the Lost Village incident in 1605."

Rick had no idea what he meant by that, and he pressed on the subject of Jack. Glen shrugged, as if at a loss for what happened. "I told him it was a stupid idea, that we would be better off in here, but he insisted. I was afraid my truck was the only vehicle we had, but Fred told me he had a car out in the parking lot in good working order and Jack seemed to take that as a yes. I was still holding the keys to the truck in my hand and he snatched them from me and headed outside. I went after him but Lee and Fred held me back. I was furious." For the first time Rick saw the anger surface in Glen's face, his eyes clouding over in anger. And then just as quickly, the physician got himself under control. He shook his head ruefully. "Jack got into the truck, told us he would be back with help, and took off. That was two hours ago. We haven't seen him since."

There was silence for a moment among the men. From behind them in the farther recesses of the freezer, the women were clucking over Bobby and amongst themselves.

Glen broke the silence. He motioned toward the middle-aged woman. "Annette had a mild case of shock and I treated her for it. Had her lie down and take a nap. She seems stable enough now to move her. Everybody else here is fine."

Lee picked up where they were thus far. "We were planning on going back to Glen's and holing up in his attic again where we could see everything, being he's got a radio, guns and the medical facilities if somebody needs it. He went outside to check things out when you pulled up."

Rick turned to Glen. "Guess we'll probably have to put off going back to your place for another day."

From beyond the big steel door of the freezer, the Dark Ones began crashing through into the supermarket.

They sat huddled against the back wall of the freezer as the Dark Ones burst through the supermarket. From inside the freezer it sounded like the store was being torn apart by a tornado; the sound of shelves being knocked down, canned and boxed goods being spilled to the floor and plundered, reached their ears from within the locked confines of the freezer. The destruction grew closer, and for a good ten minutes the sound of a serious destruction—rumblings, tearings, crashings and the wet sounds of ripping and chewing—reached their ears, peppered with guttural roars. Rick assumed they'd hit the meat department and were consuming T-bone steaks, ground beef, and chicken. The sound of destruction and pillaging moved from the meat department and spread to other parts of the store.

Through it all, they remained quiet. Rick stood against the wall, Janice at his side, holding her while she held onto Bobby, who had his arms wrapped tightly around his mother's waist. Glen Jorgensen, Barbara Schob and Lee Shelby were on either side of them, Melissa Peterson cringing against the noises outside. Lee put a comforting, fatherly arm around her and she drew close to him. The others sought comfort from each other in their own way, Charley and Anne clinging together as couples will do, Fred and Annette standing by the corner, both of them equally rigid. Nobody made a sound or moved a muscle. The Dark Ones didn't appear to realize that they were in the meat locker, and to make the slightest noise or move about to cause their own commotion might alert them. Rick had explained his reptile/dinosaur theory to them briefly while they assembled in the rear of the meat freezer. They understood the concept clearly. They remained as quiet and still as a mouse about to be attacked by a snake.

And beyond the locked door of the meat locker, the destruction of the supermarket by the ravaging Dark Ones continued.

26

They'd started up from Boston two days ago on October 21 and the weather had been great; clear skies, brisk winds, temperatures in the mid-sixties. By the time they reached Vermont it was raining, and Brenda told Gladys that maybe they should pull over and spend the night in Lewiston, Maine once they crossed the state line. The radio said the storm was going to be bad and Gladys was inclined to agree. The two women and their sons had taken a vacation from their jobs at Blue Cross to spend a week at Brenda's mother's cabin in Maine. They needed it; both of them were mid-level executives in the company, and were the two most successful African-American women in the organization. Brenda and her son came up to Maine every season, and Gladys had never been and wanted her son to experience what life was like in the great outdoors. All the boy really knew was the streets of Boston, which she didn't want him experiencing any more than he had to. He was twelve going on thirteen and in the seventh grade. Both women had taken their sons out of school this week for the trip, hoping to bond closer to their offspring and each other.

Both boys had been friends for a year now, and hung out together all the time. Brenda and Gladys, on the other hand, had been friends for the last three years, lovers for the past nine months. If the boys knew what their mothers did while they went off and did the kind of things pre-teenage boys did together, they never brought it up.

They'd stayed in Lewiston in separate rooms, boys in one, women in the other. The boys stayed up all night watching cable TV while the women sat up and talked and made love.

The morning of October 22 had dawned bright and sunny, and they rose late. They took in breakfast at a Denny's on Interstate 95 and as they were leaving to go back to the hotel and pack, Brenda motioned to the sky overhead. "Looks like it's clouding up again. Maybe we should check the weather report before hitting the road."

Gladys agreed.

By the time they reached their hotel the sky had been spitting big, fat drops of rain. Gladys turned on the radio and flipped across the FM band, finally finding the weather. "The storm that brought nearly five inches of rain along the coast of Maine yesterday and last night is expected to return today, bringing hurricane conditions along the entire eastern seaboard that should last till tomorrow ..."

Gladys turned off the radio. "Maybe we should stay here another day. After all, we have at least two weeks."

That much was true. Gladys was Brenda's boss at Blue Cross. When your boss was also your lover you could get away with anything.

So they'd stayed. They watched the clouds roll in across the horizon, ordered out for pizza late in the afternoon, watched TV with the boys as the storm thundered outside. The boys went to their room at eight to play Damon's portable Mortal Kombat game, and the women took a bath, ending their foreplay in bed where they made love again for hours.

Gladys was up early on the morning of October 23 getting dressed when Brenda woke up. She rose slowly, rubbing the sleep from her eyes. "Is it still raining?"

"No," Gladys said from the bathroom. "It's stopped but it's still cloudy outside. Weatherman says it's not supposed to start again till later this afternoon, so if we wanna get going we better go now."

"Girl, you better believe it." Brenda headed for the shower to get ready.

They were on the road by eleven. They had another four hours to go by Brenda's estimation, and she tried to make the best of it. Halfway up Interstate 95 they were forced to take a detour down a secondary road due to flooding. Brenda cursed under her breath as she maneuvered the Blazer over the bumpy road.

In the back seat, Damon and Terrence played *Mortal Kombat,* exclaiming with delight whenever one of them chopped the other one's head off or ripped his guts out. God, but kids were little psychopaths nowadays. Gladys gave her a warm, understanding smile, as if reading her thoughts and agreeing with her. Brenda smiled back. In just a few hours they'd be at the cabin and they could unwind, but for now she had to keep her mind on the driving.

An hour into the drive they hit Route 1, another secondary road and another detour. They pulled over and consulted the road map; Interstate 1 skirted the coast and went through Harrington, Jonesboro, Fort O'Brien, and Phillipsport. Mother's cabin was ten miles north of Phillipsport, a two-hour drive according to this map. She put the map in the glove compartment and turned onto Route 1.

An hour later it began to rain. By the time they reached Phillipsport it was coming down hard. Brenda had to turn the windshield wipers on high and turn the headlights on. The wind made the rain beat down even harder, blowing great sleets of water on the road. She slowed down, cruising slowly down Route 1, just skirting Phillipsport. Gladys was looking out the window when Brenda yelled "shit!" and begin to slow down.

They were approaching another roadblock. The detour sign stated that the next ten miles of Route 1 was closed due to flooding and to proceed through Phillipsport and take Route 191. Gladys rested her hand on Brenda's thigh. "We're almost there."

"I know," Brenda said. "This is just getting to be a real pain in the ass." She made the exit and headed through Phillipsport.

"Do you know your way to Route 191?" Gladys asked. The Mortal Kombat game made a bleating noise and an eruption of cheers rose from the back seat. Gladys turned to the back seat. "Shut up back there."

"Not really." Brenda answered. They were approaching a large shopping center, a big-city, suburban open mall. A few cars dotted the parking lot. Brenda swung the blazer in and drove through, headlights picking out a Blockbuster Video Store, a Barnes and Noble, a Lucky Supermarket. The usual strip mall fare. "Maybe we can get directions here. Besides, I've gotta pee."

They pulled up to the supermarket, headlights flashing in its darkened interior. "Looks like the power's out in this place," Gladys said, looking outside curiously. It was nearly three o'clock and it was already almost dark. The lights in the parking lot weren't on at all.

Brenda pulled the car up to the parking stall closest to the store and killed the engine. She swung to the back. "Okay guys! Pit stop. Last time to pee before we hit the road again." They got ready to clamber out in the rain.

It had been quiet outside for the last few hours and they all stood at the door and put their ears to the wall to listen. The muffled patter of raindrops hit the roof above them and they could make out the sound faintly outside. There were no other sounds.

They'd spent their time in the freezer huddled together in the rear of the compartment. There was a brief sharing of stories and experiences as to what brought them here. Fred, Melissa and Lee's stories were already known, as was Glen's. Barbara had stopped by on her way home from Glen's to Shelby's Drug Store to pick up a bottle of Excedrin. She'd been having such horrible headaches lately and they were the only thing that gave them any kind of relief. Lucky for her, she'd been at Shelby's Drug store when the Clickers came marching up the promenade.

Annette Berger had been walking back to her car after a trip to Blockbuster. She'd seen the Clickers come and ran into the video store. She'd watched in horror as the large crustaceans swarmed over the parking lot, heading into the woods. Finally she set foot outside with a few other people and was about to head to her car and go home when the other things had come. Had Lee Shelby not been herding Melissa, Barbara, and Fred out of the drug store and down to the Lucky's, who knows what would have happened to her. She saw them, changed direction and darted in the doors after them. Charley and Anne Denning had been grocery shopping when all the commotion broke out; they joined other gawkers at the magazine rack and watched in horror as the large, crustaceans made their way into the shopping center.

After that was out of the way the conversation broke up again into various circles; Rick found himself in a conversation with Glen and Lee about Glen's theory of the creatures. Fred talked with Charley and Anne about hopefully getting out and escaping through one of the back routes he knew of—they could take Route 73 to a dirt road in Cumberland County that would take them right to the Interstate. Melissa stayed with Janice and Bobby, who were joined by Barbara and Annette. Annette had just come around from her slight shock. Glen examined her briefly, smiled and patted her shoulder. "You're doing fine," he said. "How do you feel?"

"I feel tired," Annette said. She looked it. The dark circles she had under her eyes had gotten bigger.

"Try to rest as much as possible," Glen said. "If you feel the need, pull up one of those blankets and lie down in the corner and try to get some sleep."

Annette nodded and said that maybe she would a little later.

Glen joined Rick and Lee back in their informal little group. Rick looked at Glen. "What do you think?"

"I think they've left," Glen said. "And I think we should at least take a look outside to check the status."

"Okay." Rick grabbed the metal bar that ran through the handle of the door frame in a makeshift lock and started to remove it.

Janice stepped forward. "Rick, no."

Rick removed the bar. "Somebody's got to check it out." He turned to Janice and read the fear in her eyes. The others looked equally fearful, but a little relieved at the same time. He had jumped into the task without a vote taken that somebody should go out to check out the parking lot. He had done it without thinking, because he knew it had to be done, because he had to see. But most of all, he did it because he also knew there would have been a period of awkwardness after Glen's proclamation that it sounded like the Dark Ones had left. People would have shuffled their feet and cast their gazes around, as if searching for a candidate, yet at the same time trying to be conspicuous and invisible. Because they wouldn't want it to seem that they were trying to finger a candidate without asking. Plus, they wanted to be passed up by their peers and he was still a relative stranger.

Rick placed the metal bar on the ground and grasped the door handle. Lee and Fred stepped forward, and now Melissa joined them. Glen nodded, his features showing no emotions. "Take it slow. Just go through the store slowly and if you hear, see, or smell anything out of the ordinary, run like hell back here."

Rick nodded, then turned back to the others one last time. Janice looked like she was showing the strain of the last two days; her face was worn, fatigued. She looked like she was going to break down and cry any minute. Rick leaned forward and kissed her. "I'll be fine. You take care of Bobby."

Janice wiped the tears from her eyes, mustering a smile. "I must be stupid crying like this every time you have to go out and make sure it's safe."

Annette came forward. "No, you're not stupid, dear. We all feel this way." She placed a comforting arm around Janice and looked at Rick. Her features were strong and honest. "God bless you for taking the risk for us," she said. Then she smiled, as if reassuring herself that all would be well. "We'll be right here," she said, as if telling him and everybody else that they would be waiting for him when he came back.

The fear began to build in Rick's limbs as he turned to the door. Now he didn't want to go out, but there was no other choice: they couldn't stay locked in here forever.

Glen opened the door and Rick slipped through, feeling the heavy steel door close softly behind him with a silent click of the lock. He heard the metal bar going back through the door handle. It sounded like his fate was being sealed.

He was in the store.

And he was alone.

He stood at the door to the freezer for almost a full minute, letting his senses grow accustomed to the store's surroundings;

the cold atmosphere, the darkness, the smell of the sea and of something else, something slightly fishy. He almost took a step back but then he saw the smell for what it was. The meat aisle was littered in plastic wrap and white Styrofoam, strips of meat dotting the floor. He took a step out into the aisle; to his right were the meats, to his left was the seafood department. Both had been plundered. There was hardly anything left of either, and what was left hardly amounted to much. The scent of meat and fish hung in the air and now Rick knew where that smell was coming from.

It was chilly in the store's interior due to the power outage and the cold wind blowing from the broken windows and doors. Lack of fluorescent lighting made it appear darker than outside. The air was cold and wet, but clean and crisp smelling. A faint smell of mixed fruits came to him, wet and cloying, and he saw its source a moment later—a spilled aisle of fruit juices. The entire store would be smelling like a mixture of foods along with the cold wetness of the rain.

Rick started moving slowly and quietly down the aisle toward the cash registers. He didn't hear anything unusual. The only sound he heard was the steady fall of rain outside.

He paused once before reaching the cash register just to catch his bearings and try to get a sense of his surroundings. He stood beside a rack of canned tomatoes and spaghetti sauce, letting his ears pick up all the sounds around him; the falling rain, the wind blowing and whistling around the corners of the building, the steady drip of water from rain blowing through the windows of the store. That was it. He didn't hear or sense anything else. He didn't catch the gooseflesh prickly feeling of another life form in the store with him, didn't get the feeling that something was just a little more off-kilter. The place was deserted.

He crept out of the canned goods aisle, flanking the registers. Past them were the large plate glass windows and the dual double doors that opened out into the parking lot. The sky showed through several panes of broken glass; it was dark, bruised clouds blotting the horizon. The rain was falling hard on the empty parking lot.

He almost didn't believe his eyes when he saw the Chevy Blazer pull up in front of the store.

The vehicle parked in the closest parking slot; the only space between the Blazer and the store was the twenty feet of median strip. Rick moved forward slowly, cautiously, through the checkout stands and crept to the plate glass windows. The Blazer was red and from this distance he couldn't tell who was in the vehicle but he thought he made out a woman in the driver's seat. He was about to step outside to warn them of the possible danger when he caught a flash of movement out of the corner of his eye.

It came from the immediate right, around the corner of the store. A huge, hulking green figure crept from the alley between the Lucky's and the Barnes and Noble next door. It crouched there and watched them, right at the mouth of the alley and enough behind the Blazer to avoid detection. Rick froze. He was firmly convinced that the Dark Ones pretty much went on motion similar to snakes, and moving now might alert this one, if not others, to his location. So he stayed put, watching as the creature began creeping toward the Blazer followed by three smaller Dark Ones.

Rick squinted, trying to get a glimpse of the occupants of the Blazer. He thought it was two women and two other people in the back, but he couldn't be sure. They looked to be of African-American descent. Either way, he had to warn them, he had to do something—

Scream! If their senses are like reptiles or amphibians they probably have limited hearing. Scream at the people in the Blazer. You've got to try something!

The Dark One in the lead began creeping forward faster. It was now thirty yards from the Blazer and the women in the vehicle still didn't see it. They were gathering purses and getting ready to clamber out.

With no real plan of action in mind, Rick stepped through the broken pane and outside into the cold, stormy parking lot and began waving his arms and screaming.

Brenda had just gotten her door open and was halfway out when she saw the man with the long, dark hair come out of the grocery store waving his arms and yelling like somebody had stuck a pitchfork up his ass. "What the hell is wrong with him?" She asked aloud.

"What's that?" Gladys asked on the other side of the Blazer. She was climbing out, too, and suddenly everything seemed to slow down. Brenda slowly clambered out, her mind registering the man's screams which were unintelligible, the wild waving of his arms. She looked at him dumbfoundedly, wondering what in the hell this crazy white boy would be screaming at, when movement came out of the corner of her eye so fast that the pain of the Trident slashing through her abdomen came after she saw it pass through her body in a wet stream, her blood spurting out in a huge geyser followed by the red and purplish mass of her intestines. Then the pain came, the ringing in her ears, and she could barely hear Gladys screaming before she saw the large green thing open a maw of yellow jagged teeth and then she knew no more.

Rick continued screaming even after the small Dark One—which loped past the bigger one who'd led the attack—swung the Trident in a deadly arc that sliced through the woman's midsection. Her face went ashen and she went limp as the creature swooped in and buried its maw over her face.

The large Dark One reached the other woman who'd exited the passenger side door and before she even realized what was happening, the creature leaned forward, mouth opened wide, and bit her head off in a hearty crunch. The other Dark Ones moved toward the rear of the vehicle, and Rick saw now who the occupants in the back seat were: two pre-teenage boys screaming their heads off.

Rick snapped out of his sudden fear. The commotion seemed to have awoken the Dark Ones out of whatever retreat they had taken within the last few hours. Rick could see them emerging from Main street, from around the north corner of the parking lot, from the alley where the first wave of Dark Ones had come from. They all converged on the Blazer and swooped in, wolves to the kill. Each victim now had two or three Dark Ones chowing down on them; some of the creatures resorted to a mad sort of tug-of-war. Rick could make out the first woman being the object of such a tug-of-war between two Dark Ones, one tugging at her legs, the other at her upper body before the strain finally gave way and she came apart in a sudden spray of blood and guts. There was a wet *plop* as she spilled onto the wet pavement. Rick turned and began running back the way he came, past the registers, down the canned goods aisle, and he could hear the sound of pursuit as footsteps pounded after him, footsteps that came with a heavy stride, their sound wet and strong, accompanied by a click as claws hit linoleum, and then Rick was at the frozen foods counter, then he was skidding around the corner, hitting the wall, rebounding back up, crashing into the steel metal door of the meat freezer, pounding on the door with his fist as the running footsteps grew louder, louder, the thumps as the creature made the turn, the sudden bang as it hit the wall and Rick felt his breath whoosh in and out of him, his hair standing on end, his body light with adrenaline, he felt and heard the lock give way as somebody disengaged it from inside, felt the door give way from under him as he propelled himself in the meat freezer as the door opened, dived inside as he sensed the creature rebound off the wall behind him and charge after him with such a force that the steel door was pounded back so hard that it knocked Fred, who had opened the door, on his back.

Rick dived through the hanging slabs of beef, feeling the creature behind him pause briefly in its pursuit to assess its new surroundings. He felt the instant rise of alarm among the people in the meat locker, and he dived toward the rear of the freezer where he and Janice had made a stockpile of the weapons and ammunition. He pounced on it, yelling all the while at the top of his lungs: *"Watch out! There's more of them outside!"*

Glen moved toward the open freezer door and slammed it shut. Charley slid the metal pole through the door handle, locking it. Rick rummaged through the weapons, looking for the rocket launcher he and Janice had looted from the sheriff's station. Why the hell that thing was among the cache of weapons at the sheriff's station, Rick didn't know, but he was glad it was there. Melissa, Annette, and Anne screamed and quivered in the corner. Rick wished he had time to reassure the women that they would be all right, but he didn't have time for that, or for their hysterics. If he could only find that goddamn launcher—

The Dark One moved from side to side, checking out its surroundings. It stood easily seven and a half feet tall—big by normal conventions, but small compared to some of the other specimens Rick had seen. The Dark One was greenish blue and appeared more reptilian than amphibious; it bore scales and a frilly ridge of skin that protruded along its backbone, starting from the top of its head and extending down to the base of its hips like an iguana. Its forearms were both large, human-like and reptilian in form and structure; it seemed to move and grasp things like a man, but Rick saw that its forearms could also be used to go down and crawl on all fours if need be. The toes of its front and rear claws were webbed. Maybe they were still evolving, Rick thought. Maybe they were still evolving and—

The thing swept its eyes across the room, its mouth a grin full of razor sharp teeth. Very crocodilian. Then it tipped its head back and roared. Fred, who was slowly regaining his composure, jumped back at the sudden, ferocious sound of it. Charley moved back into the corner between the steel door and the wall. Annette screamed at her husband. "Charley! Oh Charleeyy!"

The Dark One regarded them briefly and stepped forward.

Now Janice was beside him, Bobby behind her, cowering in fear. Rick felt a need to sweep them both in his arms and protect them, but with no handy weapon around, his efforts would prove futile. If only the rocket launcher was where he'd left it …

The Dark One roared again, fixing its sights on Melissa, Annette, Anne and Bobby, who was cowering with his mother next to Anne. The monster charged and Lee Shelby stepped in front of it, seeming to debate whether to join the fracas, then launched himself at the creature.

The Dark One picked Lee off its chest. It grasped him in its sharp talons and lifted him in the air, holding him at eye level. Lee screamed, his legs kicking frantically. The Dark One seemed to smile through all those teeth, and then it leaned forward and with a quick motion it bit Lee's head off in a clean bite.

It lifted its head from Lee's body. Blood fountained up from the neck stump like Old Faithful.

The women screamed. The Dark One chewed as if it was dining on King Crab at a fine seafood restaurant. Outside, beyond the steel door, Rick could hear more of the Dark Ones converging upon the frozen meat locker, pounding on the walls, trying to find a way in. The Dark One dropped Lee's headless body and advanced toward them. Its mouth was a bloody maw. Rick grabbed a rifle from the stock of weapons; surely an ineffectual weapon. He raised it and pulled the trigger.

The heavy resounding shot reverberated through the air, the force of it knocking him back against the wall. Half of the Dark One's head exploded in a spray of scales and mush. It tipped back on its hind legs, flailing its arms wildly; Rick could see its mouth through the blown away portion, could see the craniofacial system as the creature bellowed in rage and pain. He looked down at the rifle in amazement. Surely he hadn't blown the creature away with this!

Janice stepped forward, the smoking rocket launcher in her hands. She looked like a woman ready to go into war; her mouth was drawn in a hard line, her eyes were cold flints. She lowered the weapon, reached down for another rocket, inserted it, then raised the weapon over her shoulder, the stock against her cheek, and pulled the trigger. This time a chunk was taken out of the creature's chest in a spray of bone and gristle. The shot knocked the creature on its back. The creature flopped to the ground and Glen and Charley darted out of its way so as not to be hit by its wild thrashings. It thrashed around for ten seconds then stopped, stiffening in death.

For a moment there was silence inside the meat locker.

With the exception of the wild pounding from outside the locker. Where the Dark Ones were now converging in their attempt to get inside.

Janice collapsed against Rick, the rocket launcher falling to the ground. Rick held her and motioned to Glen, who skirted the headless body of Lee as he made his way over. Rick motioned toward the rocket launcher. "Take that and make sure nobody hurts themselves with it."

Glen picked up the smoking weapon and handed it to Fred, who took it and moved toward the door to assume sentry duty. Glen knelt down beside Janice, Rick and Bobby, concern showing on his face. "Are you all right, Janice?" he asked. "Do you feel okay?"

Janice nodded, her features tired, strained. She looked like she was going to sob but she was so tired that her body couldn't muster up the energy. "I'm … I'm …" and then she did sob, falling into Glen's arms with a loud bray. *"I'm so tired, Glen. I'm so tired!"*

"I know," Glen said, holding her as she sobbed against his chest. He looked at Rick over her sobbing form and mouthed the words *how's the boy?* Rick made a circle with his thumb and forefinger. Glen nodded, soothing Janice as she cried, the strain of all she had gone through finally taking their toll.

Rick led Bobby over to Annette and Barbara. "Can you take care of him for a minute, please?" he asked.

"Most certainly," Barbara said, transforming into a Mother Hen. She held her arms out to Bobby who went into them effortlessly. "You come here darling and have a rest with us. Your Mommy will be with you in just a minute."

Bobby's features were blank. He looked up at Rick with solemn brown eyes. Rick smiled and winked. "That's my boy," Rick said. "I'll be right back."

It was hard to say a thing like that when the sounds of the Dark Ones slamming themselves into the metal door could be heard above all else. Their roaring and gnashing came through sounding like effects from some B grade horror movie. Fred stood back, the rocket launcher loaded again, resting on his shoulder, ready to fire the instant the door burst open. Rick grabbed a semiautomatic rifle from the pile of weapons and loaded it. Others began to stock up, too; Melissa armed herself with the remaining semi-automatic rifle, while Annette picked up the another rifle and began to load it. Charley and Anne had reunited from their brief separation and were now standing in the corner, holding each other. Rick bent down and selected a Smith & Wesson .357 magnum from the two remaining handguns, and a box of shells. He got the cylinder open with no difficulty, and with fumbling fingers began to load it. He watched Melissa and Annette out of the corner of his eye as he loaded his weapons; both women seemed surprisingly adept at firearms and Rick felt embarrassed to even be in their presence. He was fumbling with his Smith & Wesson like a preschooler while they loaded and stocked their weapons with the accuracy of a professional.

Melissa gave Rick a bemused smile. "My father was a cop," she said. "He showed me everything he knew about guns."

Rick nodded. "That explains it. The way you handle that thing makes you look like you could kill me."

Melissa chuckled.

The onslaught against the freezer door continued with more frenzy. Melissa darted up next to Fred, braced for whatever might come through the door. Rick checked Janice's progress; her sobbing had stopped and Glen was still with her, checking her pulse. She was lying down on a pile of jackets. Rick walked up to them, making special effort to point the muzzle of the Smith & Wesson to the floor and not hold it by the trigger. God forbid he should trip and the gun go off.

"How is she?" He knelt down beside Janice, who was lying down with her eyes closed. At the sound of his voice her eyes opened, and she looked at him with a smile.

"She's mostly exhausted," Glen said. He maneuvered his overcoat over Janice's figure, tucking her in. "She and Bobby need to be in a hospital."

"Rick." Janice motioned him closer.

Rick leaned over her. "I'm here, babe."

Janice grasped Rick's hands in both hers. "Please watch Bobby for me, Rick. Take care of him."

"You know I will." He brushed a lock of hair from her brow. Despite the coldness of the freezer there were beads of sweat on her forehead.

"I mean it Rick." Janice's features were serious. "If it comes down between him and me, *take care of him!*"

The words hung in the air with their obvious implication. They reeked of dread. Rick tried to lighten the mood. He smoothed back her hair with a gentle brush of his fingers. "Everything's going to be all right, Janice."

"Don't dance around the issue, Rick." Her voice was stern, commanding, yet gentle. She meant business. "If it comes between me and Bobby, protect Bobby. I know how you feel about me, Rick ..." Her hands grasped his, her fingers interlinking with his. "... I feel the same way about you, too. But please, just watch after Bobby."

Rick felt a lump rise in his throat. He bent over her and kissed her forehead, quelling the lump back. "You have my word," he said, his voice husky. "Now you lay down and get some rest."

Janice locked her gaze with his for a moment as if confirming his promise. Rick found it hard to break away, but he did. He rose and stepped away from her and Glen, fighting the lump in his throat and wiping at his eyes. He almost burst into tears right in front of her and he couldn't do that, couldn't lose control now when there were so few of them left. He took a deep breath, regaining his composure, and walked over to where Annette and Barbara were watching Bobby.

They were huddled at the far end of the freezer behind the last row of hanging slabs of beef. They were seated on the floor on their jackets. Bobby was sitting between them, his face droopy with sleep. Rick knelt down beside them. "How's he doing?"

"Sleepy," Annette said. She put her arm around the tired boy. "He almost conked out when you went to check up on Janice, but he came back to again."

Bobby regarded Rick through sleep-heavy eyes. His features were slack with fatigue. Rick watched as Bobby's eyelids grew heavier and heavier, closing like shades being slowly drawn. A moment later his chest was rising and falling in sleep.

The sounds of the Dark Ones outside still reached even this far into the freezer. Rick looked at the two women. Annette was armed, a semi-automatic pistol lying at her feet. Barbara was unarmed, but with Annette near her and Bobby, the three of them should be fine.

Rick rose to his feet and went back to the front of the freezer.

For a while it looked like the steel pole they'd erected in front of the door would split. The repeated poundings against the door began to throw little dents in the door, then bend it inward. The pole itself began to bend and Rick thought the screws holding the doorhandle that the pole was run through would be pulled from their bearings, causing the pole to snap back with one hearty smack. But neither happened. The door took one hell of a pounding, and the paneling and wall that held up the doorway took a beating, becoming splintered and cracked. But it held. It held fast.

Through it all, Fred, Rick, and Melissa stood at strategic angles; Fred directly opposite the door some twenty feet back, rifle aimed and ready; Melissa thirty feet to his right, flush against the wall, and Rick thirty feet to Fred's left, forty-five degrees from the wall. They stood and waited as the creatures roared and gnashed and pounded at the freezer to get in. They knew they were in here now; they could no doubt smell them in here, if not their fallen comrade in scales. Thank God they hadn't been in hot pursuit behind the one that managed to slip through or they'd all be dead now.

Glen left Janice's side briefly to examine the dead Dark One and was astonished. They could hear him muttering from behind them excitingly. "My God, it's incredible. It's the most primitive looking reptile I've ever seen—if you could call it that. It's also ... vaguely amphibian. Jesus, just *look* at it!"

"So what the hell is it? A reptile or an amphibian?" Fred asked from his position. He allowed the rifle to drop from his shoulder.

"It's a little of both," Glen said. "It has both gills and scales," He moved around the fallen Dark One, pushing and probing at the dead creature with all the excitement of Darwin discovering the missing link. "The only thing I can't understand is their locale; a cold-blooded animal would die in such frigid temperatures as the North Atlantic Ocean. How do they thermoregulate themselves?"

"What do you mean?" Rick asked.

"There are reptiles such as the large sea turtles and the venomous sea snakes that live entirely in the ocean," Glen explained. "However, the oceans they thrive in are in the tropical coasts of the Indian Ocean and the western Pacific, which are relatively warm waters. Most reptiles generally begin to freeze at 37 degrees Fahrenheit. Those that live in cold winter climates thermoregulate themselves by simply burrowing underground for the winter where it's warmer. But how do you do that in the ocean?"

"Maybe they go to a secret cave, or something," Fred suggested.

Rick thought that could be a likely answer himself. Glen didn't appear to hear the possible explanation, and continued in his rapt examination.

The minutes passed by. The onslaught outside seemed to subside a bit, and for a moment it died down completely. Fred stepped forward cautiously, cocking his head toward the door. "Did they go?"

A sudden barrage of blows rained upon the door and Fred jumped back. Rick nearly pissed his pants. The volley of blows resumed, accompanied by the roarings of blood-thirsty beasts. Rick raised his gun up, ready to blow away whatever stormed through that door. The barrage of blows continued, then subsided again.

They're doing this to fake us out, Rick thought. They'll quiet down, then when it gets too quiet one of us will venture forth and then—images of Fred opening the door after several days of silence and lack of food sprang to mind. Fred opening the door slowly, poking his head out, turning back with a look of joy and happiness on his face. *They're gone,* he would shout back. *They're gone, let's go!* He steps forward and the others crowd behind him; Glen, Annette, Charley and Anne, Barbara, Melissa, Janice and Bobby. Rick. They follow Fred out and lying in wait around the corner near the frozen food counter and the canned goods aisle is a Dark One. With a bloodthirsty grin on its face.

Rick shook the image out of his mind.

Now it was silent outside. Dead silent.

Rick stood still, body tense, listening. *I mustn't think what I just thought. I mustn't think that or we'll never get out of here.*

Behind him and around him the others stood as silent as he, listening.

Outside the Lucky's Supermarket, the terror continued.

27

Hurricane Floyd was in full swing by seven p.m. that evening.

He came with a force that was stronger than the previous two storms that hit within the last two days. The past few days' storms dropped ten inches of rain, had been responsible for widespread destruction throughout much of the Eastern Seaboard and New England, and had hit as far east as New Castle, Pennsylvania and as far south as Alexandria, Virginia. Mass destruction was reported in most of the eastern seaboard towns: Portland, Boston, New York, Providence, Hartford, Baltimore. Most of the destruction was along the shipping docks; hundreds of private boats had capsized, many of them hurled with such force that they were driven into shore-front structures. Waves crashed along the beachfronts taking down piers, flooding stores, parking lots, and streets. The water ran down through the centers of towns, causing more flooding, and combined with the rain this made things more hectic; major intersections miles from the beach became rivers as motorists navigated through town on makeshift boats and canoes. Some got stranded on top of their cars and in some cases, their houses. Towns that were lower in elevation got the worst of it, of course.

Those that were a little higher up didn't fare as badly, but they still bore the brunt of the storm, mainly from the fierce winds, some of which were clocked at one hundred and twenty miles an hour at their strongest. In New Castle, Pennsylvania, the storm produced three fierce tornadoes that decimated the eastern part of town and completely demolished a train depot. The tornado hurled boxcars and flatbeds like matchbox cars over a twenty-mile radius—one boxcar was found across the state line in Ohio, crumpled near a train track that went to Youngstown, which was where it had come from. A tornado in northern Virginia tore the roof off a barn and took the cows and horses with it—only to set the animals down safely five miles from where they'd been picked up.

But most of the winds came from the hurricane itself. The wind howled and blew rain and the waves of the ocean fiercely. It hurled down signposts, blew cars over, picked up people and animals and hurled them against buildings and trees. It blew houses down, blew roofs off buildings, and knocked down utility poles. It forced the rain down harder, making it pour from the sky in buckets.

On the evening of October 22 the President of the United States declared most of the New England region a disaster area and promised federal assistance. He told a nation of viewers and listeners that his office would do "all within their power to meet the emotional and financial needs of every American affected by this terrible tragedy." He backed his words up by dispatching the National Guard and the United States Army to help in disaster relief and to aid local law enforcement in stopping looting.

Much of the electricity in the area was down, null and void. The storm had destroyed three major power stations along the eastern seaboard: one, outside of New York City, another in Boston, and yet another in Bridgeport, Connecticut. Along with those three, a smattering of smaller outlets were knocked down, ranging from the GE Plant on the outskirts of Phillipsport, Maine to the north, to the GE Plant in Moonrock Virginia. All totaled, some fifty million people were left without power.

The death toll was another matter. The previous evening, forty-six deaths were attributed to the storm. These ranged from drownings and heart attacks to people being crushed by falling objects. One person was struck by lightning standing in a puddle of water trying to rescue a cat from a tree. A woman in Bridgton, Maine was swept away by a flood that broke through a makeshift dam erected by the town's finest. A man in Baltimore drowned in his car when it stalled in traffic; thinking he would be rescued, he settled down in his seat and promptly fell asleep. When he awoke two hours later the water had risen to roughly three and a half feet, just brushing the lower portion of the driver's side window. He opened the door to exit and was crushed by the torrent of water that rushed into the vehicle. He drowned trying to escape.

The National Guard and the United States Army made their presence known in all the major cities of the disaster area. They began showing up in most areas in the early morning hours of October 23. By ten o'clock that morning they were firmly entrenched in the major cities. More were dispatched to the rural communities. They began assisting local law enforcement and went about on rescue missions. Emergency shelters were set up in fire stations and schoolyards and whatever buildings could hold the stricken that hadn't yet fallen victim to the storm. By eight-thirty p.m. the shelters were full to capacity and began to divert people to surrounding cities and towns for assistance. Most people were able to make it through the heavy, driving rain. Others were forced to turn back; the storm had closed off many roads to other towns. Some communities were cut off from major and local highways, CB transmitters, and telephones. One such community was Phillipsport.

And while people in small communities worked together and managed to weather the storm, the people of Phillipsport couldn't because most of them were dead.

The people in the smaller communities knew that as long as they helped each other, they would eventually be rescued. Once that happened, things would begin to move smoothly. People would be whisked to hospitals. Food and water would arrive. All they had to do was batten down the hatches and wait—it would just take a little longer for the help to reach them due to their being cut off from major metropolitan areas.

The same was true in Phillipsport as well. The remaining population of the town was holed up in the meat freezer of the local grocery store and had no idea of the severity of the problem that lay outside.

By five o'clock the following morning, a plan had been made.

They huddled inside the meat freezer, sitting on the floor, wrapping blankets around themselves and keeping the guns ready and loaded beside them. Somebody always tended to Bobby, who was sleeping in the rear of the freezer, usually Barbara or Janice. Hunger set in around eight-thirty, and two hours later they were all growing very uncomfortable. Psyches began to crumble. Charley started a campaign to see who would venture out into the store to bring back some food. This started an argument between himself and Fred, who felt they should remain where they were. "Well, what the hell are we going to do about food then?" Charley yelled. Fred got up, his face flushed, his wavy hair plastered back over his head. They probably would have gotten into a brawl had Rick not stepped between the two men and broke it up. He was hungry too, but it wouldn't do any good for them to fight about their predicament. They would have to sit down and talk about it rationally like civilized people.

And talk they did. They talked, argued, and reasoned with each other. And while the arguing broke out sporadically they all generally agreed upon three very basic principles:

1) They couldn't sit in the freezer forever. While help might come, rescuers might not realize anybody was trapped in the freezer for perhaps days after any rescue mission was launched.

2) They couldn't just blunder out of the freezer to scope things out or get food, yet they couldn't remain inside from fear. There hadn't been any sounds outside the freezer for the past eight hours, and even if a Dark One was curled up outside sleeping, it most likely wouldn't hear the door opening. As Rick explained, if they were reptilian and Glen appeared to be convinced they were, their hearing was very limited. They apparently went by scent, sight, and movement. It was unsure if they went by heat receptors like pit vipers or pythons, so the sudden change in temperature such as the freezer door slowly opening and letting out some of the cold air might not register to them the way scent would.

3) It was obvious that they didn't like the light. This much was evident from yesterday when they seemed to retreat

when the clouds broke up briefly. Glen explained that this was probably due to the fact that they spent the majority of their time submerged in the ocean at such a depth that the sun didn't reach them. Thus, they lived in continual darkness.

While all this seemed plausible, it did have its logic problems. Fred Logan voiced this as he leaned back against the wall, rifle cradled in his lap. "If they live so far below the ocean's surface like you think, how come the sudden release of pressure on their system didn't cause them to explode?"

Barbara looked queasy at the thought. Charley and Annette looked confused. Melissa seemed to stare off into space, her pretty features heavy with fatigue. Glen shrugged. "They could have a system that allows them to ascend to the surface of the ocean slowly. That could explain why they're able to operate on land so fluidly. You've got to remember that the idea of them living so far in the ocean's depth is still a theory."

But it was still a plausible one.

Fred suggested staying in the freezer until daylight broke. His explanation was that if these things were more active in the dark as Glen and Rick suggested they were, they would be more prone to attack if an escape was attempted now. They mused over this. He had a point, and a good one, but then suppose the day turned out to be just as cloudy and sullen as it had been the day before?

"And another thing," Rick said, choosing his words carefully. He was exhausted, sitting down on the floor next to Janice, his back slumped against the wall. The pain in his leg from the Clicker wound only added to his tiredness. "We have to remember that the Dark Ones first came on land when it was broad daylight. It was very cloudy, the sky was dark with clouds ... but it was three or four in the afternoon. And they were pretty active yesterday as well."

Fred muttered and turned away, his head down. Rick had made a good point, one that could still be argued against, but nobody wanted to do any arguing now. All they wanted to do was get the hell out of here.

In the end, after much discussion and cajoling, a simple plan was made. None of them were entirely comfortable with it, but they all agreed it was the most sensible thing to do. Rick and Fred volunteered to do the honors and Janice protested feebly, but stopped when she realized that it was really the only way out for them. The others remained silent as the two got to their feet and collected their weapons. They all walked to the door of the freezer with them and paused briefly.

It was still dead quiet outside. The light patter of rain drummed on the roof, but beyond that it was as silent.

Glen regarded them solemnly. It looked like he'd aged ten years in the past forty-eight hours. "Are you sure you guys want to do this?"

Fred nodded. Rick nodded and said yes.

Janice stood behind Rick and he turned to her briefly. He tried to muster a smile, but her features were grave, her eyes filled with the knowing that this had to be done. She leaned up and kissed him lightly on the mouth. "Be careful, Rick."

"I will," Rick said. He wanted to tell her that he loved her, but that seemed trivial now. The war hero telling the woman he loves how he feels was the romantic thing to put in a story; it was necessary in every novel or film where the protagonists reached this point. That way, when the good guys go out to fight the good fight, they get in a terrible predicament but ultimately save the day.

Then the hero goes with the girl he loves and they ride off into the sunset together to live a happy life.

But that was for the movies. This was real life. And while he did have strong emotional feelings for Janice, he had tripped over that little emotion called love once too often. He certainly thought he felt it for her, but now was not the time to proclaim it. It would either hold him back, or blow up in his face.

Instead he just kissed her back.

Glen nodded as if accepting their decision, and moved to remove the metal bar that locked them inside.

He turned the handle of the door. Rick and Fred braced themselves for any surprise attack that might come in the form of a hiding Dark One, guns cocked and ready. Glen opened the door slowly, revealing a darkened grocery store littered with trash, crushed cans spilling goo, food wrappers and other plastic and household goods. It looked like a huge frat party had been held in the store and nobody had cleaned up. Fred and Rick looked out into the store for a moment, noting the quietness of the place, then stepped out over the threshold.

The minute they did, the door to the freezer was closed. The metal bar was drawn back through the door handle, locking them out. They were out of the freezer.

The store was silent. It felt exactly the way it felt when Rick had ventured out previously. Aside from him and Fred, there wasn't a living thing in the store with them.

He looked at Fred and the other man seemed to read this in his gaze. Fred nodded. They'd talked about heading straight to the front of the store to check the parking lot, see if there were any Dark Ones abound, but Glen had nixed that one. "Time is of the essence here," he said. "Besides, if there are any outside and they see you, that would be defeating our purpose. Just do what you have to do, and do it as quickly as you can, and if God's willing, we'll be able to get out of here."

With that sentiment on their minds, they set about to do just that.

As a resident of Phillipsport, Fred stocked up on canned goods, frozen TV dinners, and plenty of beer at this grocery store at least once a week. He sometimes bought household goods and at times, automotive equipment. In fact, two months before, he'd bought a pack of flares in this grocery store just in case his truck ever broke down and he had to use them to warn oncoming motorists. The automotive section was on the north end of the building, four aisles up from the women's toiletries and the infant items. Fred led the way, moving quickly but quietly through the fallen rubble with Rick behind him. The lack of sufficient lighting made identifying the correct aisle by the signs that hung overhead almost impossible, but Fred seemed to know his way around the place like the back of his hand. He turned down an aisle and then they were standing by the relatively unscathed automotive rack.

Rick's nerves were on edge. A few items from other aisles had been strewn over into this one, but for the most part the automotive and households goods aisle was untouched. A few boxes of laundry detergent had been dumped, and bottles had leaked the blue soapy fluid onto the floor to mix with the water that seeped in, creating a slick, soapy look. But for the most part the goods on the shelves were intact.

Fred's gaze crawled over the cans of STP, windshield wiper fluid, and makeshift first-aid kits till his eyes riveted on a nondescript gray package. He seized it and groped for another one—the last one on the shelf. He handed one to Rick and began tearing his open. Six flares fell out of the gray wrapping and Fred clutched them in his left hand as his right dove into his jacket pocket for his cigarette lighter. Rick got his flares out and the two men looked at each other. Fred looked ready for action. "Okay, let's do it."

They headed out the doors of the supermarket. Once outside, the cold wind caressed their bodies, the sky still spitting rain, but the parking lot itself was silent.

Empty.

There wasn't a Dark One in sight, much less anything else resembling life.

Rick's eyes scanned the parking lot. His first target told him that they would have to revert to Plan B.

The blue Datsun he'd driven to the store with Janice and Bobby was a crushed mass of metal. The Dark Ones had had a field day with it. It looked like it had been hit by a train.

He shifted his gaze to the other cars in the parking lot. A few sat empty in the lot, lonely and desolate; two of them resembled the blue Datsun. They were parked closest to the store. The red Chevy Blazer that had once pulled up with the two black women and their sons was now standing silent and empty, its windshield shattered. Dark stains of crimson covered the pavement near the driver's side of the vehicle. Beyond the Blazer, only six other cars were in the parking lot that appeared to be in working order—a yellow Datsun, a green Subaru, two Scouts, and a white Chevy pickup truck. Fred pointed at the truck, which was one hundred yards from where they were standing, almost in the middle of the parking lot. "That's my truck there."

Rick nodded and they set off toward the truck in a slow jog.

The barrel of the rifle brushed against Rick's butt as he ran, its shoulder strap reassuring him with its comforting weight as it lay slung over his back. Fred was clutching the flares in one hand, his handgun in the other.

Before him the cars lay scattered about. At the far end of the parking lot, almost at the edge of the lot itself that ended in thick woods, stood a generator-powered spotlight of the kind used for evening beacons. Rick's mind registered it briefly and then it was gone.

The sky overhead was dark with thick clouds. If it wasn't so fucking cloudy, the sun would be coming up in another hour or so. Fred was slightly in the lead as they approached the truck from the passenger side. Rick headed to the passenger side door, one hand on the handle waiting to climb in as Fred scurried to the driver's side. What happened next happened so fast that Rick remembered it later only as a series of images.

Fred's short exclamation of breath, his sharp cry of "What the fuck?"

The guttural grunt of some beast. The sudden rush of air as something lunged. The rocking of the truck as it was hit with incredible force.

The image of a Dark One was the first thing that sprang to his mind as he started running away from the truck as soon as those first images hit him. He slowed his run down to a sort of sideways scurry as he turned to see what was happening. It was then that the truck tipped over with a crash to the pavement and Rick saw the cause of the mayhem.

A Dark One was straddling Fred, who now lay over the driver's side door on his back. Fred was struggling wildly, his arms flailing as he tried to bring his weapon up. Rick brought the rifle up, aiming at the creature and screamed. *"Fred!"*

The Dark One lunged forward in its assault, the weight of it tipping the truck over on its side. Fred screamed as he slid down the side of the truck with the creature on him. He fell to the pavement, the creature still on him, tearing into him with its claws. The force of the truck rolling over a third time dislodged some of its inner workings, and the exhaust pipe came free. Rick saw the creature lean forward, its mouth open wide, sharp teeth gleaming. Rick screamed again. *"Fred!"* Then he began shooting.

The first three shots went wild. The second and third hit the body of the truck; he could hear them pinging off the metal of the body. The next three went wild, one hit the pavement, ricocheted off, and hit the truck again. He wasn't sure which one hit the gas tank, which caused the truck to explode.

The explosion was sudden, instantaneous. Rick threw his arms over his face and fell back. Flames mushroomed in a loud *ka-boom!* as metal pieces and shrapnel flew everywhere. Rick dropped to the ground, covering his head and neck. Heat rushed over him in a deadly wave and he could feel metal parts and chunks of the truck raining down over him. He risked a peek at the truck and his eyes smarted at the sight and brightness of the flames. The truck was an inferno, flames billowing, sending out clouds of black smoke. Rick couldn't spot Fred anywhere in the blaze, but he did pick out the bulk of the Dark One crouched over the underside of the truck. The creature was a motionless, burning husk.

Debris rained down, then stopped. Rick scrambled to his feet, horrified, yet numb to what had just happened. It had all sounded so easy: they were just going to get in either the car he'd driven in or the truck, drive over to the entrance, honk the horn once to sound the all-clear, pile everybody in and drive away. Simple, but now thwarted by one single mishap, one that had been anticipated but not dealt with because there was no dealing with it. They'd known the risks of the possibility of Dark Ones lying in wait. And they'd all agreed that they couldn't stay cooped up in the freezer forever. Somebody had to take that risk. And now that was shot to shit.

There were burning chunks of metal all around him. The rain began to fall harder again, dampening the flames. His hair felt singed, his eyes smarted from the smoke. He took a step backward and stopped when he heard a sound from behind him.

He whirled around. The explosion had attracted the attention of the other Dark Ones. They began to approach him but were stopped by the fire. They stood roughly forty yards from him, shielding their eyes from the intense flames. They mewled and growled in rage; it was obvious that the fire was holding them back and for a moment the line from the film *Bride of Frankenstein* came to mind: *fire—baaaddd!* He almost burst out laughing, it was so comical. They were reacting just as any typical monster would, and while it was true that fire would probably kill most anything, the scenario he was in surely lent weight to the credo that art imitated life.

Rick caught movement beyond the line of Dark Ones stopped by the fire. He craned his head up. Beyond the Dark Ones, another wave of the creatures was making their way to the shattered front of the supermarket. They would go back in and begin their assault on the freezer door again, perhaps this time finally breaking it down.

He had to think of something. The creatures in front of him roared their frustration. One took a tentative step forward and howled as if in pain. Rick saw that they were shielding their eyes more than they were shielding themselves from the intense heat and it suddenly hit him: *It's the light from the fire that they can't stand.* Glen's theory of their sensitivity to light sprang forth and rang true more than ever. The Dark Ones were able to venture out because of the huge mass of clouds and the dark of the night, yet the intense light from the fire, and probably the heat, too, were driving them back. As long as he stayed within the realm of the fire, the ones that had been trying to approach couldn't touch him. Now if he could only drive them, and the ones entering the store, out.

He turned around and his eyes fell on the generator-powered spotlight.

He rushed toward it, hoping that what he just thought of would work, hoping that the generator was working, that when he reached it and turned on the switch and revved it up, it would do the trick. He reached the spotlight, opened the control panel of the generator and saw that it was indeed shut down. He flicked the on/off switch, and the generator began to hum; Rick surmised it was an electrically-powered generator, and hoped that it was charged up. If it wasn't, he was in some deep shit.

He looked out across the parking lot and saw that the Dark

Ones were casting a wide berth around the fire and were now making their way toward him. The generator began to whine into action and he reached along the control panel of the spotlight itself, finding the switch. He flicked it on.

The parking lot was suddenly bathed in light. The advancing creatures cringed and threw their arms over their faces, shielding their eyes from the bright light. Rick felt a tinge of excitement run through him. The spotlight rested on a small cart with four wheels. Rick pushed it. It moved easily and he turned the spotlight around, getting the monsters in the path of its beam. They cried out and cringed, scurrying backwards. Rick felt a rise of triumph, then quelled it. He hadn't won the battle yet. It was just beginning.

He pushed the spotlight forward, keeping its glow trained on the monsters. They backed up, skirting around the burning truck. Rick stopped once, turning around to see if any of them were circling around the light to sneak up on him from behind. The blaze of the truck fire was now on his right, slightly behind him, and its glow cast a wide arc. To his left, the spotlight had them and none were trying to skirt around the far edge for a sneak attack.

The light danced across the broken front door of the supermarket, catching the entering Dark Ones in its path. They stopped as if sprayed with pesticide and staggered back, shielding their faces, roaring in rage and frustration. They staggered around, bumping into each other. Rick continued pushing the light, shoving its brightness forward. It drove the Dark Ones more insane.

The sharp cries of the creatures outside must have attracted more, because now more began to crawl into the parking lot. As soon as the light hit their eyes they cringed back, hiding their faces. They remained frozen in the doorway, unable to move forward but unable to move back due to the others behind them. Rick was afraid they would retreat inside. He reached toward the control panel, planning to maybe turn the light off briefly to allow them to come outside, then switch it back on when they were out. But suppose the generator died before he could get it turned back on again?

His fingers brushed against the control panel and lighted upon a knob. It was pointed at FULL LIGHT. The other selection was FLASH. Rick turned it to FLASH.

The spotlight began to flash in slow, even strokes like a strobe light sputtering to life. It affected the Dark Ones immensely. They became less drunken by the high glare of the spotlight, but more disoriented by the flashing light. They moved around, their eyes open and glazing, their arms rising periodically to their eyes to guard them from the strobe. The creatures at the door of the grocery store stumbled out and began to wander around drunkenly. Rick stepped away from the spotlight and watched them, debating on whether he should dart through the throng to the store.

He hadn't even made up his mind yet when it was made up for him. Rick saw Charley's face peering out the shattered glass of the front door, Annette's strained face beside him, scoping the lot out. The creatures were oblivious to them. Rick stepped out from the spotlight, waving his arms. Charley saw him, motioned to Annette and pointed. She saw him, turned back, as if speaking to the others. *What the hell are they doing out of the freezer?* Rick thought. *Are they nuts?*

Charley and Annette exited the building followed by the others. Glen crowded behind them, followed by Barbara, Anne, Melissa, Bobby and Janice bringing up the rear. The eight of them crowded in front of the shattered doorway of the Lucky's Supermarket and watched the Dark Ones stumble around blindly. The creatures were moving away from the store and the spotlight in large circles, their human prey seemingly forgotten. Rick stood where he was, watching but not daring to dash forward until he was absolutely sure it was safe. He prayed that Charley or Glen or any of the others decided to take a chance and take a mad sprint across the parking lot toward him. He was still a good ten yards away from them—a three-second run, but three seconds too long.

Charley took a tentative step forward, watching the retreat of the Dark Ones. Rick was sure now that Charley was going to chance it. But then Charley turned around. He looked toward Rick but his eyes were focused somewhere beyond, past the parking lot. His eyes widened, and a moment later Rick heard what the other man saw approaching.

28

The twin orbs of headlights were heading straight for him and for a moment Rick was dumbfounded by their appearance. Then he heard the roar of the engine and realized it for what it was: a giant Ford pickup truck. Help was on the way.

The truck stopped abruptly beside him with a squeal of brakes and Rick jumped onto the bed. The others clambered on with him and it wasn't until he was in the truck that he recognized the driver from the rear window. The driver waved at him with his skinny arms, his bony face grinning wildly. It was Jack Ripley.

"Way to go, Jack!" Rick yelled. Jack made a thumbs up sign and drove forward, the headlights of the truck stabbing into the dark parking lot before them. The Dark Ones scattered at the new invasion of light and Rick could now only barely hear them as the truck pulled into the covered awning. The spotlight and the burning pyre of Fred's truck still cast sufficient light in a nice arc to keep the Dark Ones at bay, and now the twin orbs of the headlights from Jack's vehicle brought more protection.

But not forever. They would have to get the hell out of there fast. The truck pulled up to the shattered doorway and Rick leaned forward over the metal side of the bed and began helping them up into the back. Glen and Annette made it up effortlessly, Glen muttering "Thank God he made it back." Rick looked for Janice, found her, and went over to help her and Bobby up. Janice was carrying Bobby, her face bearing a sense of urgency, fear in her eyes. She handed Bobby up and Rick took him and set him down in the bed of the truck. He turned back to help Janice and she was already climbing over the side, Melissa and

Barbara right behind her. Rick helped them in, and a moment later they were all on board, Charley and Anne huddled in the rear of the truck.

Jack gave a war whoop from within the cab and surged forward. He made a wide U-turn, driving right in the light. The creatures were now hovering toward the edge of the parking lot. The Dark Ones hadn't retreated fully, but were somewhat disoriented, still turning their faces away from the spotlight. The creatures were far enough away for them to make a clean getaway. Jack completed the turn and drove back the way he came, passing the spotlight and the burning truck out into the parking lot and beyond.

Rick looked over at Janice feeling as if a sudden amount of weight had been taken off his shoulders. They'd made it out to safety. They were *safe*. He scooted across to embrace her but was startled by a sudden sound and then he was jerked slightly. The truck took a heavy blow on the side, causing the rear end to skid. Rick held on to the side, trying to keep his balance and looking around. Barbara began screaming.

Charley's head was missing.

What remained was a stump gushing blood. It shot out of his neck, drenching Barbara and Anne who were on either side of him. Anne began screaming then stopped abruptly, turned around and threw up.

A lumbering dark shaped receded in the distance as the truck plowed down the highway. It was hunched over, as if set upon devouring something it had caught. Panic rose in Rick's mind and his arms went around Janice instinctively. His eyes darted around the rushing landscape around them, trying to pick out anything unusual lunging toward them. The rain was falling down harder now, and the sky was getting blacker with the heaviness of the clouds. The wind was picking up again, pushing the truck across the road, threatening to tumble them out of the bed of the vehicle. The front of the truck's bed became increasingly cramped as Barbara and Glen, who had also been on that side of the truck, scurried away from Charley's headless form to seek safety. Anne was hysterical, screaming her husband's name over and over again, her voice hoarse.

"Charley! Oh my God, oh Charley! Oh Charleee!" Her arms flew out toward him as if she desired to hold him. Melissa reached across and grabbed her, holding her back as the truck lumbered on.

Rick kept his eyes peeled at the scenery around them. The others kept their heads lowered, crouching down in the bed of the truck, all of them sensing the danger still present. Rick raised his head up slightly, his face taking a sudden rush of cold air blowing from the sky and tapped at the rear window to attract Jack's attention. "The Dark Ones are still around. Watch out!"

Jack's head bobbed up and down, but Rick wasn't sure if it was a nod of understanding or the jostling of the truck. Rick checked the shotgun seat of the cab and saw that it was empty. He wondered what Jack had gone through to get this far, wondered what horrors he might have experienced when he had dropped Glen Jorgensen off at the supermarket and left to get help. He wondered if he had been able to get up the road in order to *find* help.

Rick's eyes lighted briefly on the people he had spent the last twenty-four hours with, and saw that they looked beaten but still had that spark of life in them. Glen's face was long, drawn and sallow. He hadn't even bothered trying to attend to Anne, who was in obvious shock. All the zeal for being the medical man of the bunch—saving and preserving their lives—seemed to have been zapped from him. The others looked equally drained; Melissa's eyes were vacant and haunted, Annette looked morose and uncomprehending, Janice, Bobby and Barbara looked simply scared. Charley's body remained propped where it was like a grisly mannequin. Rick grimaced. If only whatever it was that had taken a bite out of him would have taken *all* of him. They'd all seen too much death and destruction, more than they'd been primed for in their lifetime. Rick wondered when it would all end.

The truck began to slow down slightly and Rick craned his head up, looking through two panes of glass to peer out the windshield at what lay ahead of them. In the truck's cab, Jack gesticulated wildly, throwing his arms up as if to say, *what the fuck is this?* Rick thought the same thing as what lay in the road appeared to be a mass of crimson-colored rocks that littered the road and sides of the highway. But as they drew closer he saw them move, undulating in a mass and he recognized them for what they were: Clickers.

Jack stepped on the accelerator and the truck surged forward, plowing through the mass of Clickers. The tires crunched over the crustaceans and the truck began to jostle on its shock absorbers, as if they were in a four-wheel-drive truck going through rocky terrain. Sharp pinging sounds struck the sides of the vehicle as if rocks were flying from beneath the wheels to strike the undercarriage and sides of the truck. Rick knew what they really were—the Clickers hitting the sides of the truck with their bodies.

One orange-and-magenta-stained claw was clinging to the side of the truck, followed by another one. A moment later the creature pulled itself up, its black eyes swimming on its stalks through the heavy wind and rain. The creature was poised right over Barbara and Glen. Rick fumbled in his jacket pocket and pulled the first weapon his fingers closed on—the barrel of the Smith & Wesson. He pulled the gun out and pointed it at the creature. "Get down!" He yelled at them.

They flattened to the bed of the truck instantly and Rick raised the pistol. He fired and the creature exploded in a spray of shell and crab meat. The blast took off the top portion of the panel the creature was perched on, sending metal shrapnel down on Barbara and Glen. Rick checked for more of the crustaceans. There were none that he could see, and as he looked out toward the road ahead of them he saw that the road was still covered with the creatures. They appeared to be moving back toward the beach. *Where the hell did they all come from? Rick thought. I thought the Dark Ones killed them all, and they'd either been eaten or had gone back to the ocean.* Apparently not.

The truck pulled up to the center of town and stopped at the intersection of Main and Harbor. Jack looked up and down the street both ways, as if deciding which way to go. The carcasses of the town's human inhabitants were still littering the street, and Clickers were moving about freely, seemingly ignoring the truck and the occupants inside. Most of them were scurrying toward the beach. Others were taking their time in heading back to their watery homes, pausing every so often to sample a bite from a corpse. Many of the bodies were now partially devoured, their flesh gleaming red, raw, and bloody in the falling rain.

The truck paused briefly and then Jack made a right down Harbor, heading south. Harbor led to Route 1. Rick felt a momentary sense of relief flood over him as the truck picked up speed, and the others seemed to share this sentiment. The Clickers were dwindling in numbers, their appearance less threatening. Rick still wouldn't feel one hundred percent safe until they were within the safety of several hundred people far from this wet, watery hell; preferably in the company of the Army, Navy, and Marines. But for now he felt a little safer. But he wasn't going to let his guard down. Not for an instant.

For one, they weren't fully out of danger yet. They were still in the vicinity of Phillipsport, and more Dark Ones could be around. Secondly, he still felt some sense of responsibility for Janice and Bobby—especially Bobby, who had seen and experienced more terror and pain than he will probably experience in a lifetime. He'd promised Janice that he would protect Bobby if anything happened to her, and to prevent anything from happening to her, he had to protect her. That meant he had to be on his guard and be alert to whatever might be lying in wait ahead of them.

Rick raised himself up slightly, checking out the road ahead of them through the windshield. He held the gun firmly, ready for anything. The others remained crouched down in the bed of the truck as if sensing that it wasn't entirely safe yet, either. They travelled down Harbor, sending sprays of water through the street, into gutters and over dead bodies. Empty houses, buildings, and cars sped past them and then civilization seemed to grow thinner ahead. To their left lay the beach, silent and deserted, and to their right the woods and the highway.

Freedom.

Jack turned down the highway, plunging into the woods. It was darker within and the truck's headlights stabbed ahead of them, picking out the road and the trees bordering it. The sky was beginning to lighten from pitch dark to gray. They were going along at a steady pace, not too fast in respect to the storm, and not too slow, either. The others seemed to feel a sense of relief, and raised themselves up a little bit. Rick kept his eyes peeled on the road, nerves braced for anything that might come leaping out at them from the woods.

Nothing did. Instead, it came from directly in front of them.

The truck's headlights picked out two cars lying nose to nose, blocking the highway. It came up at them from a sudden curve and Jack had to stomp on the brakes to avoid hitting them. The truck skidded slightly as the tires locked, spinning on the rain-soaked road. The skid spun the rear end of the truck to the right, knocking Rick backward onto the bed. Charlie's body fell forward in a sickening thump, his upper body coming down on Barbara, who began screaming and batting it away. Her hand smacked the red meat of Charlie's neck stump and this seemed to make her scream louder. The others were dislodged from their positions, sending them to the bed on each other in a mad helter-skelter of arms and legs. Rick held onto the gun, praying it wouldn't go off. The truck ended its skid and Jack spun the wheel, righting the truck back into position and coming to a stop. Barbara was still screaming and trying to get Charlie's headless body off of her.

Rick scrambled to his feet, gun raised, his adrenaline pulsing through his veins just as he saw the harpoon plow through the windshield, impaling Jack through the seat.

From his angle it was difficult for Rick to tell exactly where it hit Jack, but it didn't matter. He could see Jack in the front seat, convulsing like an insect speared by an entomologist's pin.

For a fraction of a second he was stunned, but then the rolling motion of the truck jarred him out of it. Jack's foot had slipped off the brake and since the vehicle was still running and in drive, it began to roll forward. And then the thing that had lunged the harpoon swooped in through the windshield, rocking the vehicle back in a shower of glass and crunching metal.

From beside and around him, the sounds of screaming

rose and Rick turned to Janice and Bobby—they were cringing against each other, Janice's arms cradling the boy in her arms, shielding him as he screamed and pushed his legs against the bed, pushing himself and his mother against the side panel of the truck. Glen leaped over the side of the truck, followed by Annette and Barbara, who was still screaming. Anne sat on the bed of the truck, her eyes open in a faraway look that told Rick she'd lost her mind.

Dark shapes moved in the shadows of the woods coming toward the truck and Rick raised the gun. Annette was swinging her legs over the panel of the truck and a Dark One reached out and snatched her in its grasp. She screamed. A spray of crimson rained briefly as her jugular was severed, drenching Janice and Bobby, and then the Dark One retreated with its prize.

Rick stood, facing Janice and Bobby, ready to blow away anything that dared show its scaly face. On his right Melissa cringed against the rear of the truck's cab, mouth opened to scream. Beyond the truck and out to the woods where Glen and Barbara had fled to, screams of agony and pain shrieked from the darkness. Large hulking shapes throttled smaller ones in the dark woods.

Their screams died down as a dark figure lunged out of the dark.

Melissa saw it and scuttled toward Rick in fear. Rick stood up, aimed and yelled, "Janice! Get out of the—"

His words were cut off by her scream as a taloned hand grabbed her shoulder and lifted her up. She clutched Bobby tighter, hugging the boy to her side. The creature lifted her off the bed of the truck, Janice's grip dragging Bobby up with her. Bobby's legs kicked frantically, trying to escape. Rick froze, debating on whether to fire but afraid of hitting Janice or Bobby or missing altogether, but he had to do something to save them, and things were moving so fast now that his finger barely had time to curl around the trigger when the Dark One opened its mouth, engulfed Janice's head in that maw of jagged teeth and bit down.

The sound of her neck snapping between the thing's serrated teeth was deafening; it sounded like ice cracking on a pond on a cold winter day. The Dark One lifted its head after taking Janice's head in its mouth and chewed, like a child eating the top of a hot dog. Blood fountained upward, spraying over her and the creature, drenching Bobby who fell to the floor of the truck. Bobby scrambled to the other side of the bed, screaming hysterically: *"Mommy!"*

All of this happened within seconds as the truck rolled toward the two cars road blocked in the highway. The creature walked alongside the cab as it chewed, still clutching Janice's body. It swallowed.

And then it turned toward Rick and seemed to grin.

Its teeth bloodstained with Janice's gore, it tipped its head back and roared. The sound of it sent Melissa scrambling over the side of the cab, screaming hysterically. Rick scooped up Bobby and vaulted the side of the bed after Melissa, running after her. They rounded the front of the truck, heading toward the woods that lined the beach when a thudding sound erupted, and the Dark One that killed Janice was suddenly standing in front of them.

They stopped, Melissa screaming as she did so. Rick dropped Bobby, who scrambled back and cringed against the cars blocking the road. The creature stepped forward, swatting Melissa aside casually, causing her to tumble down the wooded incline that led to the beach. Rick could hear Melissa screaming as she fell all the way down and the creature stepped up to him, its bulk seeming to tower upward. Behind him, Bobby was screaming for his mother. The creature fixed Rick in its gaze, as if sizing him up.

The creature opened its mouth, a maw of teeth that gleamed with Janice's blood. The Dark One was easily twelve feet tall and looked older, more refined, more mature than any of the others. It walked upright like a man instead of hunched over like the others. Its yellow eyes regarded Rick, the pupils tiny slits that gleamed like evil diamonds. Its nostrils flared as the tips of its mouth and upper lip curled back in a sneer. It opened its mouth and roared, bending forward to scoop Rick up in a similar head-biting motion that would leave him lifeless.

But Rick anticipated the move. His finger curled around the

trigger of the Smith & Wesson. He moved the weapon up as the creature's head descended down. The arc of the Dark One's bite descended down over the barrel of the gun, heading straight for him. All Rick had to do was shove the gun up farther, his arm up the creature's mouth to his elbow, and pull the trigger.

The back of the creature's head exploded outward in a spray of green skin, blood, and tissue. The creature reeled back, roaring in pain. Rick cocked the gun and stuck the barrel up beneath the creature's chin and pulled the trigger again. The blast sent that part of the creature's head exploding in a showering mash of bone and brain. It teetered on its hind legs for a moment, arms waving drunkenly before it toppled over on its back.

Rick reacted instantly. He ran over to Bobby who was cringing against the car, still screaming for his mother. Scooping the boy up, he ran down the incline toward the beach where Melissa had fallen. The stretch of woods was small, and he thought he could hear the cracking of weeds as more Dark Ones crashed in the woods behind him. He skirted around some trees and reached the bottom where he found Melissa getting to her feet. She appeared dazed. Rick helped her up and motioned down the beach. "We've got to get the fuck out of here!"

Melissa nodded. Rick set Bobby down, but the boy clung to his legs, his sobs hoarse and dry; all the tears seemed to have run out of him. He clutched his injured hand close to his chest and Rick knelt down before him, looking into the boy's eyes. "Come on, big guy. Gotta be brave for me now. Okay?"

Bobby nodded, still sobbing. "I want my mother."

"I know," Rick said. "But we gotta get outta here, okay?"

"Okay." Bobby sobbed. The kid looked like he was in deep shock, running on autopilot. He had witnessed his mother's death, had felt her blood rain down on him, had one of the Clickers take half of his middle finger and almost kill him, had seen the big Dark One kill his friends, almost kill Rick, and he still wanted his mother. He probably just wanted the whole nightmare to go away, wanted to go home, get into his pajamas and be tucked into bed by his Mommy who would smooth back his hair, kiss his forehead and tell him everything was going to be all right.

Rick felt a painful lump rise in his throat, and he swallowed it down. He wanted it to go away himself but it wasn't. It was only going to get worse.

He got to his feet and propelled Bobby forward. "Let's go." With Rick bringing up the rear, he herded Bobby and Melissa back up the incline through the little stretch of woods, then parallel with the woods. And as they ran through the woods, Rick thought he heard the sounds of pursuit behind them as the Dark Ones crashed through the trees. He also thought that it felt slightly warmer and it was just a little bit lighter.

They ran. Through the trees up ahead, Rick could make out the first telltale signs that it was morning. The darkness of the night was gone, being slowly replaced by the gray of the clouds. They were moving fast, the wind blowing hard and cold. Rick still had the unmistakable feeling that it wasn't as cold as it had been, that it was slightly warmer, that—

Melissa screamed and Rick was startled. They stopped in their tracks as a Dark One leaped from behind a tree. Melissa instinctively leaped to the side, and now it was he and Bobby in front of the creature. Bobby didn't stop as fast as he should have, and the thing picked him up in one swoop of its powerful arms. Rick yelled *"Noooo!"* just as the creature brought Bobby's screaming form to its face and began gorging amid the boy's screams and struggles.

It began to eat Bobby alive while the boy's lifeblood splattered to the ground at the Dark One's feet.

Rick was so shocked at the sight that he stood rooted to the spot. All he could do was watch in horror as the Dark One devoured Bobby in greedy chomps and gulps. The boy's screams abruptly died off.

He didn't even realize he was screaming until he felt rough hands turn him toward the road and begin pulling him toward it. Only then was he aware that it was

Melissa, who'd stumbled back to grab him and push him back on the flight to escape. Only then did he realize that he'd been standing in one spot, screaming his head off, and that the Dark One that was devouring Bobby would soon be lunging at him.

Still screaming, he ran after Melissa as the wind blew the storm clouds across the sky.

29

Rick was convinced they would be dead meat as they ran pell-mell through the woods. He could hear the crashing in the woods behind him as the Dark Ones gave chase. He didn't know if it was the same creature that had killed Bobby, or if there were others, but it felt like more than one. It *sounded* like more than one and—

Slowly but surely, the pursuit behind them was slowing down. It hit him when they reached a crest in the woods that led to the main highway that had been blocked off. Rick stopped abruptly, not hearing anything behind him now and Melissa stopped and turned, looking confused. And then it hit him.

The storm was over.

The clouds were breaking.

Sunlight was shining through the dissolving clouds.

He could see it on the small crest they had stopped on, and he tilted his head up and grinned. The rain had stopped, and while it was still cold, the slivers of sunlight that stabbed through the dark clouds brought a sense of joy to Rick's face. Over the ocean, the storm clouds dissipated, revealing blue sky. The wind was pushing the clouds inland in a slow, steady pace. A few more minutes and they'd be bathed in sunlight.

Melissa was laughing, clapping her hands together and looking up at the sky in victory. She looked like she had just won a million dollars. Rick turned back where they'd come from, catching a fleeting glimpse of huge, dark shapes scurrying to the ocean as if trying to escape a deadly plague. Rick watched as the beasts ran to the beach and dived into the ocean, back down to their watery darkness. He wanted to be happy, but he was still in a state of shock over just losing Janice and Bobby.

Watching the creatures slip into the ocean, it was hard to believe that any of this was still happening, that he'd gone through all this only to remain virtually unscathed.

"*Yes!*" Melissa yelled. She laughed, and to Rick it sounded as if she was teetering on the brink of madness herself. "*Go back to the hell you came from, motherfuckers!*" She was laughing hysterically, tears streaming down her face.

The sound of her laughter brought their triumph back to reality. They were momentarily safe for now, but the creatures could still come back. They had to get the hell out of here and go to where there were other people.

Rick pulled at Melissa's arm. She turned to him, her grin wide, and for just an instant Rick wondered how Melissa was doing mentally. "We've got to go, Melissa."

Melissa nodded, her grin fading. "Where should we go?"

"Follow the road I guess. Somebody should come along eventually."

"Okay." They walked up the incline that led to the road and stopped, looking down its twisting, winding expanse. It would lead south to another secondary road that would go in a northwestern direction, which would eventually lead to the Interstate. Rick was positive that help would be on this road somewhere. He looked at Melissa and for a brief instant he saw Janice's face superimposed over Melissa's—

(*if it comes down between him and me, take care of him!*)

—for just a brief instant, and then it was gone.

Guess I screwed up on that one, babe. God, I am so sorry.

"You okay, Rick?"

Rick blinked and then it was just Melissa looking at him with concern. A sudden sense of sadness and loss swelled in Rick and for a moment he thought he was going to cry. But he drew a deep breath and reeled it in. There would be a time for mourning later, when they were out of the cold and wet and away from the threat of danger. For now he had to concentrate on getting them off this road and into the hands of rescue workers.

Melissa's eyes still held a sense of fear. He reached out for her, hugging her briefly. "I'm fine. I'm just so glad we're alive."

"So am I, " Melissa said.

Rick broke the embrace and looked down at her. "Let's get out of here."

They turned and began heading south down Route 1.

Two hours later they were picked up by the National Guard and taken to a rescue shelter.

The National Guard's rescue mission sweep hit Phillipsport, Maine at nine thirty a.m. eastern standard time on October 24.

Ten trucks pulled into the town center from the main highway. The high beams of the vehicles picked out the carnage that had occurred. The first truck skirted the carnage easily and pulled over, where the driver promptly threw up. Those following drove farther into the city, fanning out over the town at strategic points. Radio frequencies had become easier to pick up in this part of the state, and within minutes the first message had been relayed by radio of the severity of the situation in Phillipsport. "Center Control, this is unit one thousand, Center Control this is unit one thousand, do you copy? Over."

"Unit one thousand, this is Center Control and we copy. Over."

"Center Control we have a grave situation here. We're in Phillipsport, Maine which is approximately one hundred and fifty miles from Portland in the northeastern corner of the state along Route 1. It looks like everybody here is dead, sir. Over."

"Unit one thousand, did I copy that right? Did you say everybody's dead? Over."

"That's affirmative Center Control. We're rolling through town and I see nothing but dead bodies lining the streets. Over."

"Unit one thousand, assess the situation then report back at ten hundred hours. Over."

"Center Control, that's a ten-four. Over."

"Over and out."

By eleven o'clock, the US Army had set up a command station at the town center at what had once been Phillipsport's sheriff's station. As rescue teams scurried about town, two

Army Commanders and a Corporal occupied the fort at the sheriff's station after trying to locate the local law enforcement. A representative from the Maine State Highway Patrol was flown in and reported back the damage at the station and the town to his superiors in Portland. And for the next three hours the reports came trickling in.

Five hundred people dead by the count of the rescuers.

There didn't seem to be any hope for survivors. During their rescue mission, which went on the rest of the day and through the night, they encountered no living human being.

In addition to the dead, there were what had to be thousands of what could only be described as giant crabs littering the streets. Most of them were crushed, crumpled and appeared partially devoured. Some, however, were whole and quite intact. One rescue worker picked one up by its legs; the creature, in its death spasm, reached a blood red claw out and snapped the man's finger off.

In addition to the dead crab-things and people, it appeared that the citizens of Phillipsport had been involved in a war. Most of the dead were either clutching firearms, or weapons were recovered not far from their bodies. There were shotguns, pistols, hunting rifles and every conceivable form of firearm strewn all over the town. They were found everywhere, from empty living rooms to the stone-dead hands of the people that died brandishing them. One old man was found clutching an antique 1894 Winchester rifle—the old man looked like he'd gone through a paper shredder; the rifle hadn't lost any of its monetary value. Cars were demolished, most parked haphazardly; stores were destroyed, their windows bashed in, their interiors demolished. At the sheriff's station, which was the only seemingly intact place in town, several rifles and pistols were missing from the cache along with several hundred rounds of ammunition. Farther down Main Street, along the pier, the beach was littered with the broken shells of the giant crab-things, along with more human bodies. The rescue workers that were the first on the scene were numbed by the massive carnage.

By midnight, the entire town had been canvassed, including

the shopping center, city hall, the outlying suburbs and the few farms that dotted the surrounding countryside. In every instance, rescue workers encountered the same sight; not a living soul, but plenty of destruction of human life and property damage.

A few hours later a truckload of National Guardsmen pulled up to the GE power plant. Two men waited in the truck while four of them ventured inside the building. A few minutes later, they reported their find via walkie-talkie.

As the night slowly gave way to dawn, one of the things that puzzled rescuers the most was the occasional mass of what appeared to be a frothy liquid substance amid tattered shreds that could only have been clothing. A United States Marine voiced the opinion that it looked like flesh that had been dissolved in acid. Why else would the remnants of blue jeans be intertwined in the puddle of goo?

And so the search continued.

Rick's and Melissa's first stop was the Red Cross emergency station that had been set up in Cherryfield. They were transported there by chopper after the National Guard picked them up and took them to the substation erected about twenty miles south, and thirty minutes later were being treated for their wounds.

The attending physician on duty that treated Melissa and Rick gave them a preliminary examination that resulted in pronouncing them fine, but exhausted. He examined Rick's leg, which had begun bleeding several hours before in their mad flight from the Dark Ones. He patched it up and gave him some painkillers, then directed them to a gym that had been converted to a makeshift recovery area/homeless shelter. Beds lined the floor of the gym, four wide, fifteen deep. Most of them were full, but they found a vacant pair toward the rear of the room that were side by side. The doctor escorted them to the beds, gave them each a tranquilizer and told them to get some rest. They laid down on the cots surrounded by survivors of the wrath of the hurricane.

A lump rose in Rick's throat as he thought of Janice. In his mind, he would see her die every time he thought of her. He heard Bobby scream as he was picked up by the Dark One and Janice's voice floated in his mind again as if to mock him: *Promise me you'll take care of Bobby if anything happens to me.*

Rick laid down on the bed, drew his knees up to his chest and cried. He didn't care that there were other survivors of the storm seeking temporary shelter. He didn't care about anybody else's loss. All he felt was his own. He didn't even notice that Melissa get off her cot and sit at his side to comfort him as he cried himself to sleep.

Rick was slowly coming to consciousness when he felt somebody lightly tapping his shoulder. He was dreaming they were in back of the pickup truck Jack was piloting and the Dark Ones were after them again. Janice was in the truck with Bobby, and this time as the Dark One leaned over and reached out a large taloned claw it wasn't Janice it picked up, it was Rick. He felt its grip around his body as claws sunk into his chest and picked him up. He felt himself being lifted up toward that opening maw lined with sharp teeth—

He came to with a gasp and, for a moment, the figure leaning over him was the Dark One, bending over him to bite his head off. Rick scurried backward, the figure solidifying before him. Then his vision cleared, and he was looking at a uniformed officer, an Army Colonel from the looks of him. Rick's heart fluttered from a heavy beat to a whisper. He took a deep breath. "Jesus, you scared the hell out of me." The Colonel offered no apology. "Are you Richard Timothy Sychek?"

Rick's curiosity was aroused. "Yeah?"

"My name is Colonel Richrath, US Army. Could you come with me, please?" The Colonel stood in front of the cot, waiting for Rick to get up. Behind him, a pair of Army men stood in Army greens awaiting to escort him to wherever it was they wanted him.

Rick glanced over at the cot Melissa had slept in and saw it was empty. The Colonel anticipated it. "Your companion,

Melissa Ann Peterson, has already been escorted by another private to our temporary headquarters. If you'll come with me you can see her."

Rick got up, memories of last night rushing through his sleep encrusted mind. There was a sharp pang in his stomach and he realized he was hungry. When was the last time he'd eaten anything? At least twenty-four hours. He looked around at the shelter which was still filled with people, some sitting on their cots in little groups, others huddled in various corners. Red Cross personnel droned along making sure everything was running smoothly. Rick noticed from the windows set along the walls of the building that it was light and the sun was shining. When they had come in it had been daylight, but cloudy. "How long have I been asleep?"

"You and Ms. Peterson fell asleep at around two p.m. on October 24. It is now ten a.m. October 25." Colonel Richrath's voice was official sounding, brisk, and impersonal. He sounded like a robot. Rick didn't like it one bit.

"I've been asleep almost twenty-four hours?" Rick was alarmed.

For the first time what could have passed as emotion flickered across Colonel Richrath's face in a brief smile, and then was replaced by that flat, detached gaze. "You were obviously both very exhausted. We thought it best that you get your sleep."

Rick's stomach rumbled again. "I'm hungry. Is there a place where we can stop and get something to eat?"

"Lunch is being provided," Colonel Richrath said. "If you'll just come with us."

"Mind if I go to the restroom to brush my teeth and take a pee?"

"By all means," the Colonel said. "Private Donaldson has some toiletries for you to use. Get cleaned up and be ready in fifteen minutes."

Private Donaldson stepped up and handed Rick a small canvas bag. Rick mustered a smile. "Be ready in a second." He headed toward the bathroom.

When he emerged from the bathroom ten minutes later they were waiting for him. Rick stepped out feeling a little refreshed, but more nervous than he'd felt since the arrival of the Clickers three nights before. What the hell did the military want to question him for? With these thoughts in mind, he followed Colonel Richrath and two privates to a waiting car. Private Donaldson held the rear door open for him as he climbed in.

They didn't have to travel for very long. The driver, another private with a somber face, piloted the car down Route 193, then turned down Route 9. They continued on that road for thirty minutes, passing silos, barns, and open, rolling country. They reached the outskirts of a small town—which one, Rick wasn't sure, because he wasn't paying attention to the road signs—and pulled into the driveway of a white building. They drove around to the rear.

The lot was filled with military vehicles; jeeps, trucks designed to carry bunkers of soldiers with machine guns in war, trucks designed to carry missiles. They were at an armory. The private pulled the vehicle into a parking slot and killed the engine. The rear door opened and the private next to him exited the vehicle.

Rick followed him out and they were met by two more privates and another official-looking man in military uniform. This man was middle-aged, distinguished, dark hair graying at the temples. He stood tall and straight. He nodded briskly at Rick and held out his hand. "Richard Sychek, I presume?"

"That's me," Rick said. He shook the man's hand.

"I'm Colonel Livingston, US Army. We'd like to ask you a few questions if you don't mind. It won't take much of your time."

"Sure. Did you bring Melissa here, too?"

They were walking toward the building now. "Melissa Peterson? Yes, she was brought here shortly before you. After we question you, we'll take you out to breakfast and you can both go."

"Fine with me," Rick said. But inside he didn't feel that way. Instead, he felt a sickening sense of dread well over him as they entered the building.

The questioning was in reality more like the third degree.

They seated Rick in a small room that had no windows. The room was right out of a police-procedural suspense film; low lighting, a lone scarred table and a couple of chairs. Rick sat on one side while Colonel Livingston sat on the other flanked by two privates. The questioning started innocently enough; what was he doing in town? Could he clue them in on some background information on why he came to Phillipsport? Rick was wary about giving them such personal information and gave them a simplified version. He filled them in on the basics and then the real questions began. What did he see? What happened? Rick started slowly, beginning with his arrival in Phillipsport and running over the Clicker in the road. He followed that up with meeting Janice Harrelson on the pier the following day, rescuing Bobby from the attacking Clickers, whisking the boy off to Glen Jorgensen's office with Jack Ripley. He related his run-in with Sheriff Conklin, his short stint in the Phillipsport jail. He then went on to explain the arrival of the Dark Ones, and at this the Colonel's features became grave. He remained silent as Rick related how he and Janice watched the creatures maul and destroy the entire town. Then he explained how Janice got him out of the jail cell, how they gathered up whatever weapons they could the following day and ventured out when it appeared the coast was clear. How they made it to the shopping center. How they came upon the others trapped inside the freezer of the supermarket and their attempts at freedom, their various battles with the Dark Ones up until the moment National Guardsmen picked him and Melissa up along Route 1.

Colonel Livingston listened to the story the whole time, nodding politely, stroking his chin occasionally. The privates standing guard remained like statutes, stiff and straight. They didn't react when Rick described the Dark Ones to Colonel Livingston. When Rick was finished he sat back, his throat dry and his stomach empty. He suddenly realized how hungry he was; he was ravenous.

He was about to voice this to Colonel Livingston a second time when the man launched another volley of questions at him, all regarding the Dark Ones. What did they look like, where did he think they came from, what did he think they were? Rick answered as best as he could. He decided to play dumb during the questioning and not even allude to the theories Glen Jorgensen had shared with him in the meat freezer. He had no idea what the Dark Ones were or where they came from. All he knew was that he never wanted to see anything so terrible again.

Colonel Livingston asked him the same questions again, as if to confirm the story, and Rick repeated the same answers. How the hell should he know what the green slimy things were? What did he look like? A scientist? Colonel Livingston nodded, stroking his chin. He looked at Rick, thanked him, then rose and walked to the door. He knocked on it and it was opened. Colonel Richrath was on the other side. Livingston leaned out the door and spoke something in his ear. Livingston nodded. Richrath glanced at Rick briefly before departing, and Livingston waited until the other man left before walking back to the table to resume his questioning.

"We questioned Melissa Peterson along the same lines," he said. "Her story matches perfectly with yours in regards to what happened back there. There's just one small problem Colonel Richrath and I both have."

"And what might that be?" Rick asked. He felt tense.

Colonel Livingston leaned forward. "Where are the bodies? There's not one shred of proof that these … Dark Ones, or whatever it is you call them, existed or did this damage. For all we know it could have been something else—"

"There's a dead one in the freezer of the Lucky Supermarket," Rick said quickly. "Trust me. We killed it when it got in. It should still be there. Go check."

Colonel Livingston regarded Rick for a moment, as if trying to decide whether or not he was telling the truth. Then he got up and went to the door. He spoke in low tones to somebody outside, then came back and sat down again opposite Rick. "I'm having it checked out now."

"Good."

They waited. The twenty-minute wait for confirmation

seemed like an hour, and finally when the word came it was delivered quietly to the Colonel as he stood at the half opened door with another military person. Rick waited with bated breath as he tried to pick up on some of the conversation, but the men were talking too low. Finally, Colonel Livingston closed the door. Rick noted that the Colonel's features had changed; it looked like he had just received bad news but was trying his hardest to keep it to himself. He sat down at the table opposite Rick. "Well, this changes everything."

"Did they find it?" Rick asked, heart racing.

"Yes," Colonel Livingston answered.

"And?"

Colonel Livingston sighed. He looked directly at Rick. "I had Colonel Richrath send a team to the supermarket to check out the freezer. When they got there, two men went inside to check the freezer out. They found the ... creature, you and Melissa described. Their instructions were to verify that ... what you said was in the freezer was still there, then to exit the freezer and secure the building. They're waiting for word from me on what to do next and I don't know what to tell them."

Rick let this sink in. They had the body of the dead Dark One. That was all the proof they needed. "I don't know what they are," Rick said. "But I think this isn't the first time they've made an appearance here." He told Livingston a summarized version of the Lost Village story. Colonel Livingston listened intently, rubbing his jaw with his fingers. "I don't know why they come here once every four hundred years, if indeed that's what happens. All I know is from what Dr. Jorgensen told me about the Lost Village story. That the legend suggests something similar happened to an early British settlement and they were wiped out."

Colonel Livingston rose to his feet and went to the door. "I'll be right back."

Rick waited fifteen minutes, wondering what was going on. He felt both excited and scared by this sudden turn of events. The fact that the body of the dead Dark One was found meant that he and Melissa's story would be believed. What scared him was the uncertain future of what lay ahead. They might not be let back into town for days, weeks, while the clean-up and investigation went on. Worst of all, he still had to face the horror of knowing what happened to Janice Harrelson and Bobby. He had only known them for three days, but their deaths were devastating. He'd felt a connection with Janice that he had never felt with anyone, and it had been severed before it had a chance to take root. He knew that for as long as he lived he would see Janice die over and over again in his nightmares.

He felt the weight of everything that had happened to him come crashing down on him again. He felt like collapsing with the sheer defeat of the situation, and he would have started crying if he hadn't been interrupted by the sound of the door opening and a familiar voice calling his name. "Rick."

Rick looked up. It was Melissa Peterson. She was standing in the doorway with Colonel Livingston behind her. She looked weary, like she had been through hell and back, but she had the look of a survivor. She gave him a smile that said *we made it.*

We made it.

Rick smiled back and got up. He approached Melissa and hugged her. He dimly heard Colonel Livingston: "I've just gotten word that some scientists from Boston University will be arriving this afternoon to have a look at the specimen found in the freezer. I'm having you two driven back to the shelter so you can get some food. Hopefully, later you can go into town to salvage your belongings."

Rick heard Colonel Livingston, but his encouraging words weren't a concern to him now. He closed his eyes against the tears as all the pain and sorrow he felt for Janice and Bobby came to the surface. He hugged Melissa tight to him and she hugged him back just as tight. As long as Melissa was with him he wouldn't have to go through this alone. They would have each other. They would need each other to get through their respective losses if they were to survive this tragedy. Rick felt his stomach rumble. He took a deep breath and looked down at Melissa, who was teary-eyed herself, but smiling. They both laughed, more out of relief that they were alive than anything. "Come on," Rick said, rubbing her shoulder as he threw his arm around her. "Let's get something to eat."

Then they turned and walked down the hall toward Colonel Livingston, who stood waiting for them at the exit.

Epilogue

The Dark Ones had been residing in a cave for the past three days. They'd found it during their initial raid on the shore, and a few of the elders had ventured inside. The cave had quickly become their refuge, and as they sat and huddled within its rocky depths as the storm raged on outside, they slowly grew used to the damp surroundings.

One of the Dark Ones ventured to the mouth of the cave and hesitated as it reached the entrance. They were becoming increasingly more resistant to the light, and now as the sun was dipping in the west it scuttled forward a bit. A large forked tongue flicked out, tasting the air. It breathed through its nostrils, its gills slapping uselessly now along the side of its neck. It could sense more of the people, but they were far enough away for them to be safe. The cave they'd found was farther down the coast from the small town, and it was hidden well from the rocky shore. It cut deep into the rocky shore, and there was a large cavern inside that had a natural lake.

Several of the Dark Ones had already used the lake to bathe in, and several of them liked to rest beside its cool, wet shore. They would be quite safe in this new home for a while. Plus, in time, the people would no longer pose a threat to them. They would serve as a source of nourishment after the long, cold months of winter.

The Dark One scanned the ocean and flicked its tongue out, sensing an arrival of more of its kind. In another moment ripples in the ocean announced the arrival of more Dark Ones coming forth from the watery depths. They emerged from the ocean and crawled up the rocks to the cave, slithering inside as the Dark One moved aside and waited. When they were all safely inside, the Dark One retreated back. Its belly was full and it was warm in the cave, much like it was in a similar cavern that had been their home for so many years. It slithered through to the deepest recesses of their new home where the others were gathered, some curled up together, some alone. They were well satiated, and the feasting they had just partaken in would carry them over well into the spring.

Several of the larger males had planted themselves by the entrance to the large inner cavern, while the older creatures were toward the back. A group of females were curled up in another corner with their eggs, keeping them warm for the long winter ahead. The Dark One looked around and found a spot in the corner by a small female. It settled down next to her. It opened its mouth and yawned, its jaws revealing rows of jagged teeth. The cavern grew quiet as the Dark Ones settled in.

They were asleep in no time.

About the Authors

J. F. Gonzalez (1964-2014) was the author of over a dozen horror and dark suspense titles including *Primitive, The Beloved, Fetish, Survivor,* and is the co-author of *Clickers II: The Next Wave,* and *Clickers III: Dagon Rising* (both with Brian Keene). His short fiction is collected in *Old Ghosts and Other Revenants, Maternal Instinct, When the Darkness Falls,* and *The Summoning and Other Eldritch Tales.* In addition to these, he wrote non-fiction, screenplays, technical manuals and other corporate communications, and the occasional ghostwritten writer-for-hire novel.

Mark Williams (1959-1998) was a multi-talented artist whose work spanned films and comics. As a Special FX Artist, he has worked with James Cameron, David Cronenberg, and was the chief FX artist for Full Moon Productions. In collaboration with Poison drummer Rikki Rockett, he co-created, wrote, and drew several titles for the short-lived No Mercy Comics, including *Sisters of Mercy* and *Nightshade.* He designed album covers for such hard rock bands as Dangerous Toys and Poison, and in the late 1980's and much of the 1990's, was the chief FX artist and coordinator for Alice Cooper's live show. He succumbed to cancer-related pneumonia on May 28, 1998.

Curious about other Crossroad Press books?
Stop by our site:
http://store.crossroadpress.com
We offer quality writing
in digital, audio, and print formats.

Printed in Great Britain
by Amazon

46728512R00182